PLEASE DON'T GO

THE MIDNIGHT STRIKE SERIES
BOOK 1

E. SALVADOR

Copyright © 2025 by E. Salvador/ E. Salvador LLC

All right reserved.

No part of this book may be reproduced or transmitted in any form or by any means, electronic or mechanical, including photocopying, recording, or by any information storage and retrieval system without the author's written permission, except for the use of brief quotations in a book review.

Without in any way limiting the author's exclusive rights under copyright, any use of this publication to "train" generative artificial intelligence (AI) technologies to generate text is expressly prohibited. The author reserves all rights to license uses of this work for generative AI training and development of machine learning language models.

This book is a work of fiction, created without the use of AI technology. Names, characters, places, and incidents either are products of the author's imagination or are used fictitiously. Any resemblance to actual persons, living or dead, events, or locales is entirely coincidental.

ISBN: 979-8-9903219-5-3

Visit my website at www.esalvadorauthor.com

Cover design: Summer Grover

Editing: Erica Russikoff

This book is intended for an 18+ audience.

To anyone who's ever felt they didn't deserve to be seen.
I see you.
I'm so happy you are here!

A LETTER FROM E

Hi reader,
I'm so happy you are here!
Before you proceed, I want to share a little about how and why this story came about, and a warning before you continue. I promise not to make it too long.
I've always struggled with words and feelings (I know it sounds crazy to read considering the size of this book). Along with that struggle, December has always been a weird month for me(no I promise not to trauma dump on you). In December of 2024, after a culmination of events, I felt a heavy weight in my chest, that as hard as I tried, I couldn't shake off.
I knew part of the heaviness was due to holding onto something, hoping in my heart with all my might that things would change but they didn't.
Despite my anxiety, worry, and overthinking, I knew I needed to let go. I just wasn't sure how to do that. Then I realized, if I wasn't sure how to talk about it, I should write about it. And that's when Please Don't Go was born.
The moment Josie and Danny came alive in my head, I had to write them down. And so I did, many words, every inch of my soul, and tears later, their story was written.

Their story, while romantic and at times humorous, is raw, deep, aching, and devastating. It navigates through the tumultuous, turbulent, and harrowing grapples of mental health. How it manifests, and burrows deep in the morrow of the bones of two people who are so different but so much alike.

It's heavy, heartbreaking, and gut wrenching, but I promise, you'll find closure, happiness, and hope like Danny and Josie do at the end.

I know this book will be a tough one to read because it was just as tough to write. But I needed to get these words out, to share them with you.

With that being said, Please Don't Go heavily mentions the themes of suicide and depression. Please before you proceed, read the content warning. Your mental health comes first and is very important!

Thank you so much for taking a chance on this book and these characters. I hope you come to love them as dearly as I love them.

Please protect your mental health and yourself!

Happy reading <3

With Love,
E

CONTENT WARNING

Please Don't Go is a contemporary college sports romance with banter, tender moments, and the right amount of spice. With that being said, it also has some moments that might be triggering to some, and I want to warn you of the content ahead:

- mentions of suicide and on page suicide attempt by a main character
- PTSD flashbacks
- explicit language and sex scenes
- mentions and depictions (on page) of anxiety, depression, and panic attacks
- mentions and depiction of a sibling and parent death
- mention of cancer
- alcohol consumption
- mention of drunk driver and car crash depiction
- mention(flashback) of accidental drowning
- mention of cheating(not by main characters)

Please protect your heart and mind, your mental health is very important! If you have any questions, don't hesitate to DM me @e.salvadorauthor on IG.

PLAYLIST

1-800-273-8255 - Logic, Alessia Cara, Khalid
Weathervane - Hunter Metts
Found - Zach Webb
No One Notices(Extended Spanish) - The Marias
Si Supieras - Kevin Kaarl
After the Storm - Mumford & Sons
White Ferrari - Frank Ocean
To Build A Home - The Cinematic Orchestra, Patrick Watson
listen before i go - Billie Eilish
The Night We Met - Lord Huron
Heavy - The Marias
Myth - Beach House
Nothing's Gonna Hurt You Baby - Cigarettes After Sex
this is me trying - Taylor Swift
Lost at Sea - Lana Del Rey, Rob Grant
DtMF - Bad Bunny
Dead - Madison Beer
The Funeral - Band of Horses
feel something - Bea Miller
United In Grief - Kendrick Lamar
Never Felt So Alone - Labrinth

Luz De Dia - Los Enanitos Verdes
siento tanto aqui - Kevin Kaarl
Yellow - Coldplay
Stay - Rihanna, Mikky Ekko
Anyone - Demi Lovato
Creep - Radiohead
I Saw The Mountains - Noah Cyrus
Never Let Me Go - Florence + The Machine
To Love - Suki Waterhouse
Dark Paradise - Lana Del Rey
Agosto - Bad Bunny
Nettles - Ethel Cain
Mad Sounds - Arctic Monkeys
Call Your Mom - Noah Kahan, Lizzy McAlpine
Last Time(I Seen the Sun) - Alice Smith, Miles Canton

MONTEREY COASTAL UNIVERSITY

THE SIRENS BATTING ORDER

1. Kainoa Kapule- First base (1B)
2. Grayson Devereaux - Center Field (CF)
3. Noah Sosa - Catcher (C)
4. Daniel Garcia - Shortstop (SS)
5. Jamie - Third Base (3B)
6. Lincoln - Right Field (RF)
7. Ryan - Second Base (2B)
8. Logan - Designated Hitter (DH)
9. Bryson - Left Field (LF)

Angel Sanchez - Left Hand Pitcher

Vincenzo D'Angelo - Coach

1
JOSEFINE

I knew one day I'd meet death face to face, but I didn't expect it to be like this. And I certainly didn't expect it to not feel terrifying.

I guess that happens when you come to terms with it. When you stop fighting the current that keeps dragging you under. When you finally cave and let it take you. When you accept taking the grim reaper's hand. Though I've not taken his hand yet, but I will.

I just need a few more seconds to...well, I'm not sure what exactly it is that I'm doing. Feeling something isn't going to happen.

I stopped feeling anything a long time ago.

I tried, maybe not enough, but I did what I could. At least what I thought I should do, but it was futile because I'm here and I'll be gone soon.

Gone and *most definitely* forgotten.

And I have no one to blame but myself.

I inhale deeply; the salty air fills my lungs and a faint taste of salt coats my tongue. I'll be getting more of that soon—and water, a lot of it.

Taking a step closer, I neither falter nor feel my heart ricochet the way it used to when I knew I was in danger or was about to get hurt. No, my body and brain have accepted what's to come. It's why I don't seize with fear as the ground beneath my shoes erodes. The small rocks roll off, tumbling and smacking against the cliffside, but within seconds, the sound gets lost to the harsh noise of the waves crashing violently. They're loud, the impact so strong it reverberates like an endless roar.

One more inhale.

One last glance at the moon.

I close my eyes, meet the grim reaper's wicked smile as he stretches his bony hand for me to take, and step forward.

But I falter, then freeze in my spot, at the sound of a deep masculine voice.

No one should be here. It's close to midnight—I think—and it's Christmas Eve or Day. I'm not sure what time it is exactly because I didn't bring my phone.

I came now because of how dark it'd be and because I knew I'd be completely alone. It's perfect because in the darkness, I easily blend in. Though it really doesn't matter. Even in the daytime, I'm nobody to everyone.

My eyebrows furrow because this is the second thing not going according to plan.

The first is that the moon is full. It's so blindingly bright, I see its reflection on the surface of the dark blue water.

And I hate that because seeing its reflection is like seeing mine. All I see is all my failures and insecurities. They're all bouncing back at me, mocking me, taunting me.

The second is that he, whoever he is, is here.

The third is that I hesitated. I wasn't supposed to do that. I should already be dead.

Goddammit, I can't even do this right.

"Hey." He treads carefully. His footsteps are faint behind me. "What are—"

"I was here first. Go away," I harshly clip.

"Can you take a few steps back?"

"No. Go away."

"Please don't do this," he pleads. His words bounce off my ears and fall down the cliff, sinking or being taken away by the waves, the way the small rocks did.

"Go. Away."

"Please don't do this," he repeats, and again, his words do nothing for me.

"I said go away," I grit, my molars aching from how hard I'm grinding them.

"I know you probably think this is the easy way out, but it's not. I promise you it's not." His voice floods with desperation as I hear him take another step. "Think about the people who are going to miss you."

His words are weighted, pain filled, and desperately aching to be heard.

For the first time in a long time, I laugh. But there's no humor behind it; it's hollow, bitter, almost tastes like bile as it tumbles out of my mouth. "No one is going to miss me."

"Don't say that. They are." He exhales pressingly and urgently.

"I have no one," I voice indifferently...emptily.

I'm not saying that for pity, it's the truth. I pushed everyone away, and the only person who I was the *closest* to by blood, died.

My words must hold some kind of weight because seconds stretch and the silence extends. I don't hear him, so maybe he left.

Making up my mind, once again, I go to take a step, but I stop when I hear the sound of footsteps. Before I can tell him to go away, he's standing right next to me.

I'm taken aback and I have to crane my head up to look at him because he's taller than me. My brows pinch and something stirs in my chest, but I can't distinguish whether it's annoyance, anger, or both.

"What do you think you're doing?" I add some distance between us.

His hand quickly stretches out, but he doesn't grab me. It must've been a knee-jerk reaction because he drops it and stares straight ahead.

"*I* will miss you," he says after a moment of silence. The words roll off his tongue casually, as if we're friends.

A cool breeze sweeps by us, and my skin pebbles, but it's the effect of his words that cause the goose bumps to linger.

I can't remember the last time someone said that to me.

"Don't say that. You don't know me." I stare straight ahead, still keeping distance between us.

I don't know why I'm entertaining this conversation when I'm still going to go through with it. I have no desire or will to live and I'm okay with going out this way.

"My name is Daniel Garcia, but my friends call me Danny." His words are soft, but friendly, laid-back almost as if *he were* talking to a friend. "And now you're my friend, so call me Danny."

My brows hike up and something whirls in my chest, but it's not anger or annoyance. His name sounds familiar, but I'm not sure where I've heard it from. Either way, I don't ruminate on what I'm feeling or his name.

"I'm not your friend," I immediately retort. "I've made up my mind. Go away."

"I will, if you go with me."

Reining in my frustration, I blow out a fatigued breath. "This isn't going to play out the way you're envisioning. You telling me your name means nothing to me. *You* mean nothing to me. *I* mean nothing to you. So do us both a favor and get the fuck away from here before you slip and fall."

He chuckles; it's low but hearty, easygoing. "I mean nothing to you, but you're concerned about my safety?"

"Go away...please." I don't mean to but my voice cracks.

That wasn't supposed to happen.

That must have sobered him up because he quiets down. I think he gets closer, but I don't look.

"I don't like this time of the year." He despondently sighs, like the words were heavy to say out loud. But now that they've been said, they remain in the air, polluting the space between us.

I'm caught off guard by what he just shared with me. Still, I say nothing because I don't know how to respond to that. For all I know, he could be lying.

"A few years ago, I...lost someone." He chuckles but it sounds like mine did a few minutes ago. Real. Raw. And empty. "And this upcoming year, I'm hoping to enter the MLB draft and it feels weird because that was our dream. To do it together."

I still say nothing, and either he knows I have nothing to say or he thinks I'm waiting for him to explain what he means by that.

"I'm a shortstop for MCU," he says.

Monterey Coastal University.

I went there before it all went to shit. I want to voice that out loud, but I can't. My lips feel glued together. The reminder of my first year there and everything that transpired after makes me feel so many things I wish I didn't.

"I don't care." I bristle.

It's a shit thing to say, but I hope it's mean enough he'll get the memo, but somehow Daniel doesn't. Or he does but he doesn't care.

The moon is bright enough, it bathes him with its light, giving me just enough to see him from my periphery. He shrugs, tucking his hands in his pockets.

"No one knows, but friends confide in each other, so I thought I'd share it with you." It's a simple statement, but something so definite.

My brows pull together at his words. They settle on my chest, but they don't feel like stones. More like...feathers...weightless.

As I see him turn his head, I quickly look away. I don't want him to know that his words have somehow penetrated a part of me. Blinking, I quietly sigh, and toss his words out, letting them sink.

"Don't share anything else. I don't care," I adamantly warn.

"Then share something with me."

I say nothing because there's nothing to say.

So, I let my head hang, staring at the roaring water as it collides against the large slab of rock. Every time it does, the air whooshes, blowing against me. A reminder, a glimpse, a tease at what's to come.

"I will miss you." His words penetrate me again, but again, I swat them away.

Words, that's all they are. Meaningless and insignificant; anyone can say them and make you feel special.

"We may not know each other, but I will miss you, and I *won't* forget you," Daniel adds.

I wish it sounded useless and something to fill the space, which feels all too tight and suffocating. Comical considering I'm standing on the edge of a cliff, staring at the ocean that stretches miles beyond.

My head jerks back, and I don't realize what I'm doing until my head is turned, tipped to look up at him. He's already looking down at me, and while I can't see his face well, I know his eyes are on me.

They feel intense, like they've dug deep in my brain, and self-consciously, I fold my arms against my chest.

"You can't miss someone you don't know," I angrily snap.

"Then let me know you," he counters determinedly. "I want to know you."

My skin itches, anxiety crawling all over my body. And my heart races as if I had done laps at the pool.

"No, you want to save me, and you think that's going to happen, but I've come to terms with my decision." I shake my head, feeling my resolve almost crumble before me. The idea of me jumping off is slipping away. Licking my lips, I blow out a committed but weary breath. "I don't know what to...feel." My voice cracks. "And I'm done trying to...understand..."

My heart painfully expands against my rib cage, the beats near deafening, drowning out the noises around me. Giving me the final push to end it all. And so I do. I close my eyes and take purposeful steps toward the very edge of the cliff.

But the fall never comes.

Only arms—strong, thick, and weighted around my torso.

Hauling and holding me back.

Grounding me.

Saving me.

Protecting me.

"Please don't go. Please don't go. Please don't go..." Daniel chants under his breath over and over again. "Please don't go."

I don't know how many times he repeats those three words. I don't know how many times they're uttered in gentle whispers next to my ear. But they sound more like a prayer than a chant now. A plea to whoever is listening.

To you. He's pleading with you! a voice in my head screams.

I blink out of my stupor, feeling oddly conflicted, and something weird cracks in my chest.

"Please don't go," he delivers incessantly, vigorously, but delicately. "Please, please, *please* don't go." He doesn't just hold me; he embraces me. His chest is firmly pressed against my back, and I realize then that the loud drumming isn't coming from the water. It's coming from him. It's his heart that's racing at a dangerous speed, all too rapidly, all too thunderous against me. "Please don't go."

2

DANIEL

I HAVE A MIXED, COMPLICATED RELATIONSHIP WITH this time of the year.

It gets dark sooner, a little chillier at night, drags by excruciatingly slow, and reminds me of my brother.

He loved Christmas. It was his favorite time of the year.

Growing up, our parents didn't let us believe in Santa Claus. It's not because they didn't want us to believe in him, but they couldn't afford to let us believe. At the time, their business wasn't doing well, so money was tight. Instead of letting us wake up disappointed, they were honest and told us why we weren't getting gifts.

It sucked, but somehow despite knowing what my siblings and I knew, my brother Adrian, who was a year younger than me, decided to keep believing he was real. I don't know why, but my parents went with the flow. Eventually, their business grew and money started coming in and so did the presents.

"*I told you Santa wouldn't fail us,*" Adrian would always say.

Even when he was old enough to know he didn't exist, he'd jokingly still say it.

What I'd do to hear it again.

This time of the year is a reminder that he's not here and

Mom and Dad will never get their baby back. It's also a reminder that I'm the reason why.

Dad hardly speaks to me, and Mom thinks I don't see it, but I'll catch her crying when she thinks no one is looking. And Penelope, my sister and Adrian's twin, tries hard to look happy, but I can see right through her.

Which is why I left our family's Christmas party early. I don't belong there. I don't deserve to be there.

I faked a smile, told everyone I was hanging out with friends, left my hometown, Yuba City, and drove almost four hours to Carmel-by-the-Sea.

No one stopped me; they never do.

I didn't want to be at the house, the one I share with my four other teammates. They aren't home, but the house is decorated and it's not something I want to see right now.

That's how I found myself parked at one of the trails and veering off its course. You're not supposed to. They have ropes along the trail for a reason. Stepping away could be deadly, but I'd done it so many times, I wasn't afraid of accidentally falling off the cliff.

I needed to clear my head and stop the dark thoughts consuming me. But they didn't stop and then self-loathing came. They're a destructive and deadly combination. They choked and submerged me under the murky water, until I was practically drowning.

But I stopped drowning once I saw her.

She was standing on the edge of the cliff, head hung low, arms limp by her side, and feet shifting in front of her.

I felt every morsel of my body shrink and run cold. I felt fear for the girl I didn't know, who was ready to end it all.

I try to get the conversation going, but I'm grasping at straws. I'm internally panicking because she's dead set on doing this. Even when I stand next to her on the edge, despite how petrified I am for my own reasons, I have no clue what to do.

I'd never touch a girl without consent, but I'm sure this is the only time anyone would ever approve. Quickly, I wrap my arms around her and step back. I almost trip over my feet and the rocks because of how fast I move us from the edge, but I don't stop until we're far enough away.

She's either zoned out or hasn't acknowledged what's happened because the heels of her shoes scrape against the ground and her body hangs limply against my arms.

The realization at how defeated her body feels, makes my eyes sting.

I hold her, wishing I could take all her pain away. I hold her like my life depends on it. I'll hold her until morning if I have to. I'll keep holding her until I can't any longer because how the fuck am I supposed to let go?

"Please don't go. Please don't go. Please don't go…" I repeatedly beg, hoping, praying, wishing she can hear me, understand me, and not let go.

"*Please* don't go," I punctuate strongly but softly. I plead with everything I've got because my words are all I have. I don't know what else to offer, what else to give to her in hopes she won't go. "Please, please, *please* don't go." My heart is close to imploding. It's so goddamn loud, I can't hear anything but the beating in my ears. "Please don't go."

I lose and stop caring about the concept of time, about how dry my mouth becomes, and how scarily my heart is racing. I stop all together thinking about anything except for the girl in my arms who hasn't moved.

She stays stock-still in my hold, or at least she was because she soon squirms against me. Her movements are slow, unsure at first, but then she jerks and twists forcefully, rapidly, angrily. Her shoulders ram into my chest, her nails dig into my arms, and her voice is flooded with fury.

"Let go!" she yells. I know I should, but I can't.

"Promise me you won't jump," I eventually say because it's all I can muster.

She grunts, still fighting against me. I'm hardly using any of my strength, and the thought sickens me at how easily and quickly the current would've taken her.

It happens all too fast: I let go and she takes two steps back.

My gaze drops down to my arm where she bit me and then at her.

"What did you do?" she shouts with anguish. "I didn't ask you to save me! I didn't want..." Her voice breaks, but she breathes heavy as if she were trying to mask her pain.

"No, you didn't, but I wasn't going to—" I stop mid-sentence as she approaches me.

Her strides eat up the space until she's in front of me. I'm happy she's not attempting to jump, but then I understand why.

She raises her fists and slams them against my chest. Over and over, she hits me, and I could stop her, but I don't. I let her hit me. I let her take out all her anger on me.

"I was ready! I didn't want to be here anymore! What the fuck did you do! What did you do! What did you do!" She delivers each blow with so much vehemence, but it's not the anger I feel; it's pain, so much pain. I feel it in the way her guttural voice becomes high-pitched, the way her fists aren't as heavy as they were, and the way her body sags. "What..." She chokes on a sob, heaving as though her lungs can't gather enough oxygen. "Did you do? Wh...at..."

The despair in her voice incinerates me whole. I go to grab her arms, but she collapses to her knees, burying her face behind her palms.

I drop to mine, reaching for her. Despite knowing I shouldn't touch her, I do anyway. I snake my arms around her, carefully pulling her to me, and hold her.

She sobs uncontrollably into her palms, her body shaking aggressively against me.

I let her sadness encase us because it's the only thing I know I can do. The only way to let her know she's not alone.

"I couldn't let you go." I attempt to swallow past the thick lump in my throat, rubbing small circles on her back.

She attempts to speak, but her words only get drowned out by her violent sobs.

I blink a few times, hugging her as close as I can get her to me.

I hope I'm enough to anchor her, enough she can feel and understand that I'll be her lifeline. I'll be whatever she needs me to be if it means she'll stay and not jump.

I'm not sure how much time passes, but after a little while, her sobs become hiccups and sniffles, and her body on occasion trembles beneath mine. She doesn't move away; she remains in my arms.

"You shouldn't have done that." Her voice is raw and fragile, holding so much sorrow. Not even the water that continuously crashes against the cliffside can scare me this time.

"I couldn't..." I weakly and pathetically offer because it's the only thing I'm able to say. Because my mind is scarily playing her standing on the edge like a film stuck on repeat. I can't shake off the what-if question in my head, wondering what would've happened if I hadn't come here.

A small part of me is angry at her. It wants to ask her—what the hell was she thinking? But the biggest part of me feels so hopeless. I have no idea what to do, what to give, what to say to make sure she stays.

When she pulls back, I hesitantly let go of her. I trace her every move, my eyes vigilant and legs and arms ready to move with her, but she surprises me. She sways to the side, sitting on her ass, legs bent, before she falls back until she's lying down. Then her legs slowly descend until they're flat on the ground along with her arms.

I keep my eyes on her and she must know what I'm thinking because she lifts her head enough to look at me.

"I've lost the courage to do it." She sniffles, her voice vacant. "I promise I'm not going to jump." Then she drops her head, staring up at the dark sky.

I exhale, not realizing I was holding my breath, but still, I can't shake off the weight on my chest. I relax my hands at my sides and decide to do the only thing I can think of: I join her.

Lying next to her, I look up at the sky, and am shocked by how many stars there are.

She must be thinking the same thing because in a hushed whisper, she says, "There're so many."

I turn my head to look at her and find her already staring at me. My mouth parts, but I close it, unable to gather a thought to say out loud.

"I didn't mean to put you through that." She sounds sincere as she shifts, now lying on her side to face me. "I thought...no one would be here."

"Tell me your name." It slips out of my mouth before I can put too much thought into it.

She doesn't immediately reply and as the seconds stretch with heavy silence, I try to think of something else to ask, but all I'm hyper fixating on is her name.

"Josefine."

"Josefine." I mirror her position, lying on my side. "I'm here for you, Josefine."

"You don't know me." A tinge of annoyance coats her words.

"Let me get to know you," I desperately goad.

"There's nothing to know."

"There's always something to know."

"I promise there's not."

"Josefine, please..." I trail off, grasping for something else to ask. "Wh-what's your favorite color?"

She sighs with exhaustion. "Yellow."

Yellow.

"Just yellow, or is there a particular shade of yellow?"

"I'm not a big fan of neon yellow."

No neon yellow.

"I wish you would have let me go."

"I couldn't." I don't know why, but I blindly reach for her

hand and surprisingly when my fingers brush along hers, she lets me hold it. "I'm here for you, Josefine."

I expect her to counter it with something, but she doesn't. She breathes out a weary breath, and shifts to be on her back, but keeps her hand in mine.

Lying on my back, I squeeze her hand a few times, but I don't let go. I stare up at the sky, the thought of her jumping still replaying ceaselessly in my head. Too afraid to spark something that could set her off, I opt for silence.

We stare up at the starry sky, and after a while, when I finally figure out what I want to say, I look at her, but her eyes are closed. She could be pretending or actually be asleep—I don't know, but I don't disturb her. I let her be, but I stay awake and watch over her.

I inwardly groan, lifting an arm to cover my face from the light. God, it's so bright, why is it so bri...fuck.

I push up on my feet, feeling disoriented, and blink rapidly so that my eyes adjust. Once they do, I look around, searching for Josefine, but she's nowhere to be found.

Fuck. Fuck. Fuck. I carefully walk to the edge, but I don't look over.

I think I'm on the verge of hyperventilating, but when I turn, everything comes to a screeching halt when I spot what looks like a yellow Post-it note on the ground where I was lying.

Quickly grabbing it, I feel like I can finally breathe when I read it.

Didn't mean for you to witness that.
I promise I didn't jump.

I don't know how many times I reread it, and even though I

believe she didn't, my chest still feels heavy, and a sense of sadness washes over me.

Why didn't I ask her for her last name? Why didn't I give her my number?

Out of all the questions I could've asked, I asked for her favorite color.

Way to go, dumbass.

3

DANIEL

"The fuck?"

Angel's voice comes from behind me, but I don't move or angle my head in his direction. I keep it straight ahead, afraid if I look away, I'll miss Josefine in case she decides to show up.

"What the fuck, man?" he groans loudly, standing next to me. "I thought you jumped off the goddamn cliff. Scared the shit out of me!"

"Why would you think that?" I absently ask, gaze still on the spot where I first saw her.

"Danny!" Angel punches my shoulder, pulling me out of my internal turmoil.

I jerk my head back, peering up at my best friend. "What was that for?" I rub my shoulder, wincing.

He shoves his phone in my face, the bright light blinding me momentarily before my eyes adjust. I read my name at the top, centering my vision on the blue dot that apparently shows I'm in the middle of the ocean.

"You piece of shit!" He punches me again and snatches the bottle from my hand and takes a long drag from it. "Almost gave me fucking heart attack!" he shouts and chugs the rest of my beer.

"Jesus—"

"Yeah, I thought you were meeting him right now!" Angel exhales a harsh breath, shaking his head as he tosses the empty bottle on my lap. He then aggressively moves his fingers on his screen, probably sending out a message.

"You need a new phone," I state, picking up the bottle and dropping it in the small cooler I brought with me.

He sits on the ground next to me, but he doesn't speak. That shocks me because there is never a time Angel isn't talking, but as the seconds tick by, so does his silence. It draws out, painfully slow.

"Your mom called my mom, asking if we'd seen you because she hadn't seen or heard from you since Christmas Eve," he finally speaks up, bursting the suffocating bubble we were enclosed in. "I saw your location, and I thought…I panicked."

Angel and I've known each other since we were about eleven. Funnily, we didn't like each other when we first met, but once our moms did, they became inseparable.

We had no other choice but to hang out because either his mom was at our house or vice versa. Though it didn't take long to get along because we both came to realize how much we love baseball.

We also came to realize that our dialect is different because he's Puerto Rican and I'm Mexican. Because we were young and hella immature, we taught each other all the bad words. Good times.

I huff a chuckle. "Yeah, I see that. I'm probably going to have a bruise tomorrow."

"I didn't hit you that hard." I can't see him due to how dark it is, but I'm sure he's rolling his eyes. "So, what are you doing here?"

I smile but as quick as it comes, it fades.

It's been seven days since I stumbled upon Josefine.

"I thought you had…" I hear him swallow hard. "Jumped."

Grabbing two bottles from the cooler, I pop the lids off and hand him one and take a swig of my own. The cool liquid bitterly glides down my throat, sitting uncomfortably in my stomach.

I deeply inhale, and flashbacks of that night flicker in my head. Salty air, stars, and the sound of waves will never be the same.

"You're stupid. I'd never kill myself." I force a laugh. "You should seriously invest in a new phone."

"I know. I keep forgetting to." He takes a pull of his beer. "So why are you here on New Year's Eve? You know there's a party at our house, right? Oh, and Amanda was looking for you."

I take a long swig and then another. "I wish she'd move on."

Amanda and I dated for a year and a half. I actually broke up with her exactly a year ago when I found out she was cheating on me. Funny how she always accused me of being unfaithful when it was the other way around.

"I told you not to date, but you just couldn't stop staring at her ass," he snickers, shaking his head.

"She has a great ass, but that's not the reason why I dated her." That's a half lie. Her ass was part of the reason why I dated her, so fucking sue me. She's hot and anyone with eyes would agree.

"Well, why did you?" he asks expectantly.

"Her confidence," I reply as he muffles a snicker. "And fine, okay, her ass. But she was really confident, smart, and great in bed." I roll my eyes at that. Because she wasn't only great in bed with me.

"I told you being single is the way to go. You're young, Danny. Don't tie yourself down to anyone. Let me teach you all the ways, young grasshopper. You have so much to learn from the master."

"You're a dumbass. We're the same age. And I don't need to learn anything from you. Haven't you heard? I'm a slut."

He dramatically gasps as if he hadn't heard that rumor going around campus. "Who slut-shamed you? I'll fight them."

"Unless you're willing to go to jail for hitting a girl, I suggest you not do that."

"These hands aren't rated E for everyone. But I don't think you're a slut, Danny boy. A whore maybe, but not a slut."

A real laugh, the first one in days, rumbles out of my chest.

"Yeah, I saw you sneaking in those two girls in your room the other day." I hear the smirk in his voice.

"That wasn't the other day; that was a few weeks ago."

He shrugs. "Same difference. Didn't know you were into that kind of thing."

There's no judgment in his voice, but rather pride that I did it.

It wasn't planned or something I've ever done, but I'd never been opposed to it. So when a girl approached me and asked if I was down for her friend joining us, I wasn't going to turn that down.

Plus, I wasn't in a relationship, so I wasn't doing anything wrong, but Amanda acted like I did when she found out eleven months after I broke up with her. I don't know what's wrong with that when she'd been doing it when we were dating.

I'm not sure what she thought she was going to achieve, but I couldn't care less. I'm over her and have been for a while, but she can't seem to let go.

"It was hot."

"Told you it would be." He elbows my arm. "But I'm glad you came to your senses. You wasted a year and half on one girl. Glad you're finally enjoying yourself."

It didn't seem like a waste at the time. I genuinely liked Amanda, but I should've known we weren't going to last when I couldn't see a future with her. Because isn't that what you're supposed to feel when you're dating someone?

"Yeah..." I trail off. I guess I'm enjoying myself, but if I'm being honest, afterwards I felt...empty. "I am."

"So again, why are you here?"

Right, I never answered. Taking a swig, I swallow and tell him how I stumbled upon Josefine.

"Damn," he says before he's taking a pull of his beer.

I heave out a breath, staring at the spot she'd been standing at. "It's New Year's Eve and I just thought..."

"That she'd show up since everyone will be busy partying," he finishes off for me.

I struggle to let out the words that cling to the tip of my tongue before I manage to force them out. "Yeah, I'm afraid she'll end it."

"Have you been coming here every night?" he asks but doesn't wait for me to answer before asking another. "Don't you think it's something you should leave to the police?"

"I called and they said they'd keep an eye out, but they didn't sound too worried. Even said it was something that just happens..." I grind my teeth, my hand tightening around the bottle.

"What do you plan to do? Come here every night? Do you not know how many cliffs there are in this city? If she wants to end it, she'll just find another cliff or use another method."

"Don't you think I know that?" I lash out, my voice raising. "I fucking know that, Angel!"

"I'm sorry. I don't mean to sound insensitive, but I..." He sighs. "I'm sorry. I shouldn't have said it like that. I know you and I know you're going to feel guilty, but this isn't your responsibility."

I wish I could think like that. I want to because the thought of her jumping is fucking with my head, but I feel and think too much. So many have called me empathetic, and there's nothing wrong with that, but I've been screwed over by it.

"I know." I wipe my palm down my face. "I just..."

"We'll wait until three."

I turn to look at him even though I really can't see him because of how dark it is. "You don't have to—"

"You're out of your goddamn mind if you think I'm going to leave you alone. I don't understand why you feel the need to be here, but I know it's going to bother you if I make you leave," Angel says. "But if she doesn't show up, you're going to have to let it go because it's not healthy. Call the police as many times as you want, but don't keep coming because it's only going to fuck with your head." There's a poignant sound in his voice but then he clears his throat and says, "Are we clear?"

I don't want to agree, but I know he's not wrong. It's already fucked with my sleep because of the same dream I keep having.

She's always standing on the cliff, and just when I'm about to reach out to grab her, she jumps.

"Yeah." I nod. "Thanks, man. You don't have to be here with me, but I really appreciate it. And—"

He lifts a hand to stop me from talking. "Please don't get sappy. We're bad boys for life, okay? I'm always going to be here for you."

I cringe but laugh. "Please stop saying that, but know I'm always going to be here for you too."

"Okay, enough. We're doing too much." I'm sure he's grimacing and I'm proven right when he pulls his phone out, lighting up his face, and I see the disgust in his expression.

My lips twitch, but I don't smile. However, my jaw does drop when I see a picture of a naked girl on his screen. I look away as another pops up.

"Don't get shy on me now. Don't act like you don't receive them."

"Well, yeah, but I'm not sharing them or showing them to other people."

"She doesn't care if you see." He chuckles as he replies to her.

"Sydney?" I ask because she also sends me pictures even though I've asked her not to. She, in fact, doesn't care who sees.

"Yeah, I didn't ask for them, but I'm not going to deny them. You know, people are paying hundreds for stuff like this on OnlyFans and I'm getting them for free. I'm not going to be ungrateful."

I can't argue with that logic.

We spend the rest of the night talking about stupid shit and the upcoming season. After he replied to Sydney, he never got on his phone again, but we knew the New Year was here because of the fireworks going off in the distance and our phones constantly buzzing in our pockets.

Eventually the bright showers of sparkling lights died and so did my hope of ever seeing Josefine. I had a gut feeling she wouldn't show up, but I held on to hope, and now I realize holding on to it had been pointless.

For all I know, she could be…gone. There's a voice in my head, like the smallest flame of light illuminating the darkest part in my head, that screams to keep the hope alive that she's okay. But as I sit here, it doesn't feel like it. That is until Angel speaks up.

"I'm sure she felt it." I'm confused until he proceeds to explain, "Josefine. I'm sure she felt your care. Whether she's here or…not, at least she knew someone cared enough to stop her. You could have walked away, but you didn't. You stayed, and I'm sure that meant a lot to her."

I want to agree, but this time I can't.

I've never felt so hopeless.

4

JOSEFINE

An endless loop. That's what every day feels like.

The days of the week have all blended together. I can't differentiate what day is what. Night and day are one, and I feel chained to the middle, not being able to experience either but watching them regardless.

It feels like I'm sitting in front of a television, watching my life play out. It's all slow, excruciatingly so, but everyone and everything around me are all moving too fast. I can't keep up.

That's why I wanted to end it all.

I felt no purpose, no energy to continue moving on when I physically and emotionally felt like I was at a standstill. I kept waiting to feel a spark of life, to remind me that I was worth being on this earth, but as I mulled over that thought, I realized whatever spark I was waiting for to happen, wasn't ever going to happen.

I couldn't feel anything, and I realized I was done trying to fight living when I acknowledged that I'd be better off dead. I wallowed in the void of nothingness and walked to the cliff, but then Daniel showed up and pretended to care.

That pissed me off because I hadn't been scared to fall, but he showed up and I felt terror rush through my body. It creeped and spread until I was cloaked in a veil of anxiety, and I knew I wouldn't be able to go through with it. Because I thought about him and how scared he had been for me even though he didn't know me.

I have no desire to jump because now I'm scared, but I'm mad because I don't feel anything and I'm still alone.

Water splashes on my face, recentering my focus on my task and not the metaphorical television in front of me.

"How was that?" the excited, high-pitched voice asks.

Wiping the specks of water from my face, I force a small smile. "You did so good, Sam. I can tell you've been practicing."

The tiny eight-year-old attempts to hold on to the foam kickboard with one hand and with the other raises a thumbs-up in her mom's direction. Her mom, who's sitting on the lounge chair, beams brightly and lifts her own thumb in return.

"I'm doing good, Mommy!" Sam yells.

"I see that." She smiles warmly at her. "I'm proud of you."

I tilt my head, watching the little interaction and wondering what that must be like. Having a mom who genuinely cares.

My mom is dead so I shouldn't wonder. I'll never experience it, and even if she wasn't, I still wouldn't.

"All right, I think that's it for today, but I think next week, we can maybe attempt to swim without the board."

Sam's eyes go round, fingers turning white from how tightly she's clutching the kickboard. Her gaze drops to what's keeping her afloat, then shifts back to me with fear.

"I-I don't think I'm ready." She hugs the board as if she were afraid I'd snatch it out of her hands.

"You want to know a secret?" I stoop down so that our eyes are level. Hesitantly, she nods. "I used to be scared too."

It's a lie because I have no recollection of me learning how to swim. As far as I can remember, I've always known how. But I'm not going to tell her that.

She gasps, staring at me in disbelief. "No way."

"Yes way. I carried my floaties everywhere I went."

"How did you stop using them?"

"I was told I couldn't swim with the mermaid if I used them."

She gasps again, her eyes almost popping out her sockets, but they sparkle nonetheless with excitement. "Mermaid? There's a mermaid?"

"Did you not hear? They have a mermaid at the Carmel Aquarium, and they allow little girls like you to swim with her. Only you can't use the floaties or life jackets because they keep you from going underwater. But if you're not ready to—"

"No, no, I'm ready. I'm so ready!" she voices with determination, but a tiny squeal slips past her lips before she can conceal it.

Her mom chuckles. I brought it up to her before the swim lesson just to make sure it was all right. The last thing I'd want is to get Sam's hopes up.

I didn't know the Carmel Aquarium had a mermaid or that they allowed people to swim with her until a few weeks ago. It's one of their newest attractions and something all the little girls in the city have been going crazy over.

Once the lesson is over and Sam and her mom are out of my house, the smile I'd been wearing from the moment they walked in instantaneously drops.

I thought getting out of bed was tiring, but forcing a smile completely wears me out. I wish it didn't because the rest of the day, I'll feel spent. I already feel it now. The exhaustion is spreading quickly around my body, and now it feels heavy.

I want to lie down, but I don't because my stomach grumbles, reminding me I didn't eat breakfast this morning.

I woke up late, and by the time I was ready, my first client of the day had arrived for their lesson. When it was over, I checked my pantry and immediately noticed it was empty. I could've ordered something, but I booked myself back-to-back.

Why did I do that? Because I hate myself.

I needed a distraction from the emptiness. Because that leads to decisions I can't take back.

Like my decision to almost kill myself over a week ago until Daniel decided to play hero. I could still do it, end my life, and no one would notice but Daniel's incessant—*please don't go*—words, echo in my head.

They occur abruptly and randomly. That's the only reason why I haven't ended it all. Why I'm still here despite how fucking lonely I feel.

My grumbling stomach disrupts my thoughts, drawing me back to reality and the droplets of water falling onto the hardwood floor. I grimace and quickly grab something to wipe them up.

Once I'm done, I throw something on and head out to the grocery store. I didn't expect to still be alive, hence why I have nothing in my house to eat. I've not had it in me to cook, and I still don't. Though I won't be doing much cooking because I don't know how. I never needed to know, so I never made it a goal to learn.

Going to the grocery store feels like a blur and is draining. I don't remember putting my groceries in my car, or placing the cart where it belongs, or driving out of the parking lot.

I feel like I'm working on autopilot. At least I am until a loud pop goes off and my car swerves left and right. It takes me a second to register what has happened. When I finally get a hold of the wheel and manage to pull over to the shoulder, I drop my head on the steering wheel.

Huffing out a loud breath, I absently reach for the hazard lights, and once I hear the soft ticking, indicating they're on, my hands fall to my lap and I close my eyes.

I should move or do something. It's dangerous sitting here, but I don't. I stay in my spot, waiting to feel something. I'd welcome being scared or nervous, but my heart doesn't pound heavily, and my hands don't sweat. Nothing happens.

The sound of a worried voice and light tapping on my window gets me to sit up straight. "Hey, are you okay? I was behind you. That was wild."

Looking to the left and out my window, I see a girl standing on the other side, a concerned look etched on her face.

"Yeah, I'm good." I lift a thumbs-up. Expecting her to leave, I drop my head back on the wheel, but then I hear the tapping again.

"Do you need help changing your tire?"

No. I don't know how to cook eggs, so I definitely don't know a thing about tires, but I don't tell her that. I'm sure I'll be able to figure it out. YouTube always does the trick.

"I got it," I reply, lifting my head.

"Do you have a tire jack?"

Fuck, what is that? "Uh..."

I shouldn't have sounded unsure because she grins like she's figured out I have no clue how to change a tire. "Don't worry, I've got you."

"You really—" I softly groan, lowering my window. "You really don't need to do that. I can call a tow truck. I'm good. You can leave."

She doesn't seem offended at my dismissive words. If anything, she scoffs like my statement is absurd.

"Are you crazy? It's about to be nine p.m., it's dark as shit, and you're a girl. I'm not leaving you alone, and you don't need to call a tow truck. My brother can come help you."

"No, that's really not—"

"I've already texted him. He's on his way." She lifts her phone, showing me the text message exchange between the two.

My lips slightly twitch at the contact name: **Favorite Dumbass**.

"You really didn't have to—"

She stops me mid-sentence. "You don't watch true crime, do you? Or the news?"

"Not really," I admit. My life's tragic enough.

"Mmm," she tsks, shaking her head. "Well even if you don't, you shouldn't be alone. It's dangerous for us girls. We gotta stick together."

27

"Right..." I trail off, unsure of what else to say to that. I know girls should stick together and I know about the dangers. Just never had someone so insistent to stay besides Daniel.

"Do you want to wait in my car? Yours is a lot closer to the road than mine. It's really dangerous for both of us to be here. Someone could hit us."

I hesitate because as thankful as I should be, I don't know her.

She must sense that because she says, "Sorry. Stranger danger. We don't have to wait in my car; we can stand off to the side, but we shouldn't be here. Someone could hit us."

She's right and while I wouldn't mind it, I'd hate for something to happen to her because of me. So, I shut off the ignition, grab my phone, step out of my car, and stand off to the side with her.

When we're far away enough, I take a glance at the busted right back tire. There's no way I would've been able to change that or even have known where to begin.

"Sorry. I never introduced myself." The headlights from her car illuminates her face, showing off a friendly dimpled smile and straight long hair. "My name's Penelope, but some people call me Pen. You can call me whichever, I really don't care. But please don't call me Penny."

"Again, you didn't have to stay, but thanks, Penelope."

"Please don't make me fight you. I know we don't know each other, but stop saying that."

I nod. "Josefine."

"Do you shorten it, or is it just Josefine?"

"I've been called Josie, but if you want, you can just call me Josefine."

"No way, Josie is so freaking cute. I love that name. If you don't mind, I'd love to call you Josie."

"That's fine." I internally wince, hating how awkward I am.

She either doesn't sense it or does and doesn't care. She

proceeds to talk when her gaze coasts to my chest, eyes focused on the MCU Swimming & Diving logo on my shirt.

"You go to MCU too? And you're a swimmer, which explains why your clothes are wet." She lightly laughs to herself, eyes coasting to the damp turquoise cotton material. "I cheer there. Crazy how we both go there and have never run into each other. That's going to have to change, you know, right?"

I uncomfortably shift from one foot and then to the other, folding my arms over my chest. "I was a swimmer."

It's been a year since I swam competitively, and I'll never do it again.

As far as us not ever running into each other, it's for the best. She'll realize I'm a train wreck and run.

"I'm wet because I do swimming lessons and just finished a lesson not too long ago." I cringe because why did I explain all of that?

"We're definitely going to have to grab lunch or something." I can see the gears shifting in her head, probably envisioning us hanging out and whatnot. I don't tell her that's not going to happen; I let her believe it will. "And that's so cool and such a smart way to make money. You know my broth—"

She stops halfway, when a light gray Acura pulls up in front of my car.

"That's him. I promise he'll have your tire changed in no time. He's good at this kind of stuff."

"Not just good, but the best," I hear an arrogant voice say from behind me.

I tense, the hairs on the back of my neck raising. A shudder races down my body at the familiar voice. The very same one that pleaded and begged me to stay a few days ago.

She rolls her eyes at her brother, Daniel. The guy who pulled me back before I ended it all. The guy who held me while I broke down. The guy who watched the stars with me. The same guy who gripped me all night like his life depended on it.

"Thanks for coming so quickly." She smiles at him, but it drops when another guy approaches us.

"Yeah, of course." He and the other guy stand between us. Daniel's gaze is on Penelope before it peers down to me. "You're in the best..." His voice wanes, and when our eyes lock, his brows furrow. "Hands."

Surely, he doesn't recognize me. He will when he hears my voice maybe or my name, but he hardly saw my face. Unless he already forgot about me. I'm pretty forgettable, I've been told.

"Oh God, don't say that to Josefine. Damn, Danny, who raised you?"

"Josefine." He exhales a breath that feels both relieved and frustrated. But the expression on his face is impassive, so I can't really tell what he's thinking. Or whether he's thinking anything at all. "Josefine." This time around, he sounds more relieved than frustrated, hopeful even.

Please don't go. I hear his frantic words echo in my head.

Penelope's eyes bounce between him and me. "Wait, do you two know each other?"

"No," I quickly say, as he counters with, "Yes."

"Oh, oooh..." She slowly nods as though she is piecing everything together.

But she's got it all wrong, and just as I'm about to correct her, Daniel does.

"Not like that, idiot. We met...the other night. Midnight, Christmas Day." It feels like he's saying it more to me than to her.

My tire blowing out didn't cause my heart to race, but his words do?

"I'm assuming you two met on campus?" At Daniel's confused expression, she explains, "She also goes to MCU."

"So happy you're all catching up, but we should really change this tire. It's dark and you all know how shitty the drivers are here, so we need to get started," the guy whose name I don't know says.

I know all about shitty drivers, and maybe it's what I want to happen, but thinking of them getting hurt dissolves the thought.

"Right, yeah, we should." Daniel clears his throat. "We'll need to grab the spare. All we'll need you to do is hold the flashlights."

"Can you do that, or will that be too heavy for you?" The guy directs that question to Penelope, and it sounds a little condescending but also like a tease.

"Angel, the year just started. I thought your New Year's resolution was to be less annoying?"

"Must be confusing yours with mine." Angel smirks, winking at her.

"Don't start," Daniel chides, his gaze straying to mine, but I look away.

The crack in my chest deepens, but oddly enough, there's no ache behind it. I don't ponder over why. Instead, I hold the flashlight just like he instructed.

5

DANIEL

"She's alive," Angel says, slashing the silence in my car.

In return, I only exhale a breath, keeping my eyes glued to Josefine's Mercedes-Benz.

We're following behind her, making sure she gets home safely. She protested against us accompanying her, said she had it all under control, and to some degree I believe that, but she's driving with a spare, so I didn't want to risk it.

I'm also struggling to believe she's really here and not...dead.

I hate thinking that but ever since I left the cliff with Angel on New Year's Day, wondering what she ended up doing has been plaguing my mind.

Even though I'm driving behind her, eyes laser focused on her car, I can't help but feel like this is some kind of dream. I'm afraid to wake up and find out she did jump.

I'm also afraid this might be a nightmare. That she'll drive me to the cliff side, and she'll have me watch her step off the edge, and I won't be able to do anything about it.

"Daniel." Angel softly punches my arm.

I blink, my hands gripping the steering wheel tighter. "Sorry, what?"

"Relax. She's alive," he says lightly, voice humor filled to ease the tension, but it does nothing for me.

"I pulled her back..." My skin flares with goose bumps, and a cold shiver runs down my spine.

"What?"

I didn't tell him that part because I couldn't bring myself to voice it then. Even now, it's hard to get it out because I'm afraid it'll still happen. That I'll speak it into existence.

My hold on the wheel loosens and I grimace at how wet my palms are. "She just...took a step. It was a determined but defeated step like..." I bite the inside of my cheek as the memories of that night resurface. "She was ready to go and had given up on the world."

My stomach painfully sinks, and I find it difficult to breathe. Even swallowing becomes hard. I try but the harder I do, the more intense the pain feels and unfolds throughout. And the place it hurts the most and worst is in my chest.

All the pain resides there, making itself known.

"Are you serious? What would you have done if she would've pulled you with her? What the hell were you thinking? You could've died." He's exasperated and from the corner of my eye, I see him shake his head, his mussed straight black hair swaying on his forehead. "You should've immediately called the police. That wasn't the time to play fucking hero!"

"They wouldn't have made it on time. What was I supposed to do, just stand back and watch her fucking go?" I raise my voice, quickly veering my gaze to his before shifting it back to the road. "Then what? Move on? Pretend I didn't see a human being end their life? Just carry on and pretend it's all goddamn right? Is that what I'm supposed to do?"

"That's exactly what you do because that's life. That's how it fucking works. You can't save everyone. You just fucking can't," he coldly states.

"Fuck you." I sneer.

"Yeah, well I'd rather you be mad than dead." His reply is just as cold as his last statement.

Leave it to Angel to be a dick, but at least he's an honest one. He's not wrong, but I couldn't watch her go.

"If that was you, I would've dragged you back," I say after a beat.

He huffs out a depleted breath. "I'm sorry. I shouldn't have said all of that. I would've done the same thing if I had been in your position. I...I'd hate for something to happen to you."

"It wouldn't have, but I get where you're coming from."

Neither one of us says a thing after. The silence is thick and suffocating, until he opens his mouth and says the most Angel thing.

"She didn't fall in love with you."

"Huh?"

"You saved her and she didn't fall for you. She even said she didn't know you. That must've butchered your ego." Amusement douses his words, along with the tension we were submerging in.

"Shut up. It doesn't bother me. I'm just glad she's okay." At least I hope she is. Physically, she looks like she is, but I don't know about emotionally.

"Damn..." He whistles as we pull into a road that's lined with the most luxurious-looking beach houses. "The Mercedes makes sense now."

I nod in agreement, staring with amazement at her house as we pull into the driveway.

When she steps out of her car, Pen does too. She also decided to come because she was afraid Josefine would feel uncomfortable with us.

I don't climb out, afraid this was all just a dream or a nightmare.

"She's okay," Angel voices, reeling me back in. "She's alive because of you. She's okay," he repeats like he knows it's what I need to hear to feel reassured.

Still the question, *is she really though*, echoes in my head as we get out. As Angel stands next to me, I ask him something I never thought I would.

"Can you distract Pen for me? I need to talk to Josefine alone."

He scrunches his nose, the staring at her like she's already inconveniencing him. "Fine but I can't promise there won't be any arguing."

"It'll just be a few minutes," I say as we walk over to the girls.

They don't hate each other, but they don't care for each other either. I would say their relationship is like a brother and sister, which is great. I'd hate for Angel to get involved with my sister. Considering he's not a relationship kind of person and Pen is.

Not that it matters. Pen got out of a relationship a few months ago and is still reeling from it.

And I trust Angel enough to know he wouldn't touch my sister. I don't care who he messes with, but Pen is off-limits.

"But if she pisses me off, I'm tossing her ass in the ocean," he teases, but I hear the slight seriousness behind it.

"Don't touch her," I warn.

"Can't make any promises." I hear the smile in his voice, but I can't threaten him anymore as we stand in front of the girls.

Pen like always is running her mouth, speaking a million words a minute while Josefine stands there listening to her. She looks like she's absorbing it all, but she also looks like her mind is somewhere else. That's until Angel interrupts Pen.

"I know you took my mini boxing gloves from my rearview mirror," he accuses.

Maybe this wasn't a good idea. He's been saying that for a year and swears it was Pen who took them.

"It wasn't me. Maybe it was one of your many—"

"I'm going to check your car because I don't believe you." His small gold hoop earrings sway as he pivots on his heel, before she can get a word out. She follows after him, leaving Josefine and me alone.

I look at her, but I feel like I'm not really seeing her. She's so fucking close, I could take a step and close the space between us, but at the same time, she feels so far away.

For the first time in my life, I'm speechless.

Since that night, I've been thinking of everything I'd say to Josefine if I ever ran into her, but now that she's standing in front of me, I can't open my mouth.

I find myself soaking her in, feeling a whirl of emotions that leave me feeling perplexed.

"Well, uh, good night," she quietly says, voice low, and I almost don't hear her.

"Wait, please don't go." My fingers twitch at my side, begging to touch her to make sure this is all real, but I fist them and keep them where they're at. "I want to talk to you."

She looks unsure, her gaze flitting to Pen and Angel before meeting mine again. "There's nothing to talk about."

"Please...Josie." I heard my sister call her that. I'd be lying if I said I didn't say it just to test it out on my tongue. It's just as pretty as Josefine.

She raises her hand to her other arm, rubbing it up and down, before she tentatively nods. "Okay, give me a second. I need to get my groceries."

"I'll help you," I offer, but she shakes her head.

"I've got it." She opens the trunk and inside are five paper bags filled to the brim.

I grab them before she can reach the first one. "I know, but I want to help."

I hear her huff frustratedly as she shuts the trunk and pushes the button on the key fob to lock her car. "You have to stop doing that."

"Doing what?"

"Helping me. I'm not helpless," she says as we walk side by side to the entrance of her house.

"Never said you were."

Unlocking her door, she lets me go in first, but my mom raised me right. I don't go in until she does. Once we're in, she flicks the light on, leads me farther inside, and motions for me to set the bags on the kitchen counter.

I realize this is the first time I'm actually seeing her in the light. It's wrong because this isn't the moment to check her out but wow...she's...beautiful.

Raven-black hair, deep brown eyes, and skin a golden tan. Her turquoise shirt is extremely loose and so are her shorts, but they're mid-thigh, so I catch a quick glimpse of her muscular thighs. I fix my gaze back on the logo of her shirt.

"You're a swimmer?" I voice out loud without thinking.

"Was." She tucks a tendril of her hair behind her ear, then crosses her arms as if she's self-conscious. "What did you want to talk about?"

Straight to the point. I wish I could read her, but her face is apathetic. Nothing, not even a flicker of light, shines in her eyes.

My stomach knots at what I'm about to ask, and my heart races the way it did that night. My mind screams to let it go, and move on because she's alive like Angel said, but I know if I don't ask, I won't be able to.

"Can I touch you?"

Josefine stares, surprised, and takes a few steps back. "Why?"

That sounded better in my head. "Because I need to make sure this is real," I pathetically admit. "I need to make sure my mind isn't playing games with me. I—I know this sounds bizarre, but please. I promise I won't make it weird. I just need to touch you. I need to know I'm not dreaming, Josie."

Her eyes drop to my hands, then at my chest, and I wonder if she can hear it. If she can feel how unstable my heart is right now. How it's thundering at a rate that no doctor would consider normal.

The seconds draw out agonizingly slow and I wonder, how badly did I mess up? *That was weird. Why did I ask that? Of course I messed up. Way to make her uncomfortable.*

"I'm sor—"

"Okay." She cuts me off, confliction swimming in her earthy brown eyes. "That's fine. You can touch me."

My brows almost hike up, but I stop myself, keeping a poker face before she changes her mind.

She stands in her spot, but that's okay because I go to her. As I stand next to her, I note how much taller I am than her. She's not short, but I definitely tower over her.

I don't dwell on that as I look at her face. She's staring at my chest, but I hear her breath softly hitch as I raise my hand. She must have her eyes on it, tracking its movement until it's a mere inch away from her cheek.

Please be real, I chant in my head.

I hold my breath as my large palm connects with the skin of her warm cheek and when I finally cup it, I feel all the weight of that night disappear.

You couldn't ask me what time or day or year we're in; it's all nonexistent. I don't realize I'm still holding my breath until my lungs beg for a speck of air. Just one inhale, that's all I take, as I drag the pad of my thumb along the smooth plane of her cheek.

My eyes flutter closed for a second before I open them again and tip her head back. I should let go, but when her eyes collide with mine, I'm struck by how little I see and how much I feel.

"Josie..."

"Hmm?" Her eyes never leave mine.

"I'm so happy you're here."

"You wouldn't let go." Her voice wavers, fragile like that night.

"I couldn't and I wouldn't."

"Did you not get my note?"

I caress her cheek, reveling in how soft it feels and how very much alive she is. "I did."

"Did you have doubts?"

"Nightmares."

"Didn't mean to put you through that."

"I know."

"You don't have to worry anymore. You know I'm here. We can go back to pretending we don't know each other."

"Your favorite color is yellow, but you don't like neon yellow." Aside from the slight twitch of her brow, I see nothing.

"That doesn't mean anything," she hollowly whispers.

"That means everything," I say, filling that empty space.

She stays silent and I want to break her out of it, ask her questions to fill the void, but the moment is shattered. We part, my hand dropping fast, as a knock on the front door fills the quiet house.

"I have a really busy day tomorrow." She crosses her arms against her chest, adding more distance between us, her expression blank. But I know what she's saying without having to say it. *Get out.*

"Yeah, right. I'll see you around?" I shouldn't, but there's a tinge of hopefulness with my question.

"Maybe." *Not really* is what it sounds like, and my hope evaporates.

"Okay, good night, Josefine." I flash her a smile and spin on my heel. I hear her say, "good night," as I make it to the front door. I hesitate, not walking forward, but I have nothing left to do here, so I force myself out.

She's alive, that's what you wanted. You touched her, that's what you needed.

There's nothing left between us.

6
JOSEFINE

I reread the phone number on the Post-it note that was left on my front door. Though I don't need to keep looking at it because after four days, I've memorized it.

I should crumble it and throw it away like I had originally intended to do, but every time I go to do it, I can't bring myself to get rid of it.

Especially because underneath the number, there's a few words that I've also memorized.

> *If you need anything, I'm just a text or call away.*
> *I'm so happy you're here, Jos!*

I've never been called Jos before, but I don't mull over the nickname.

Dragging my fingers behind the Post-it, I feel the indent of the letters on the light-yellow paper. The black ink almost seeps into the back of the paper from the pressure of writing with the ballpoint pen.

Daniel must've left the note after I'd gone to bed, or some time super early because I never heard him pull into my driveway.

While I get the sentiment, I wish he'd stop doing this. He doesn't know me, and knowing my favorite color isn't going to change anything.

We're strangers who ended up stumbling upon each other by accident. Sure, he pulled me back and he did what he thought he needed to do. I'm not dead; that should be enough for him.

At the sound of a door being opened, I fold and shove the Post-it note in my hoodie pocket and stand from the bench across the office.

Monica Jameson, the new Director of Women's Swimming, steps out, a friendly smile greeting me. "Josefine Resendiz, it's so good to finally meet you."

I was genuinely shocked when I received an email from her a few months ago asking if she could meet me.

When Mom first passed, I took bereavement, not because I wanted to but because everyone insisted. So, I did, and as the days meshed into weeks then months, I realized I didn't want to continue swimming.

Everyone was shocked, including myself, because swimming was my life's purpose. But once I stopped, the purpose along with my will to live, died.

I offer a small smile in return and hope to God, she can't see how fake it really is.

"Come on in." She jerks her head for me to step into her office as she retreats.

I follow and take a seat on the chair in front of her desk as she takes her own behind it.

"I'm sorry about your mom," she solemnly says, her smile dimming into something sympathetic. It feels sincere and leaves me feeling stunned. "Claudia was..." She snuffs a laugh, eyes drifting off to the side as if she were remembering something. "Claudia was one of the best swimmers I had the pleasure of competing against. She will greatly be missed."

Aside from the massive achievements Monica has acquired over the years not only as an Olympic swimmer but now as a coach, I don't know much about her. I do know she and Mom were rivals and despised each other, so that's why it's shocking to hear this.

But Mom's been dead long enough for me to know that's what people say out of respect.

My lips tighten in a flat line, and I stiffly nod, unsure of what to say. Not necessarily because of what she just said but I've heard those words, or something along those lines, repeatedly, constantly, endlessly. I wish it would stop.

The condolences, the unwarranted hugs, the letters I refuse to open, and the reminder of how she died. I know how she died. I was the one who had to identify her body at the morgue.

"You didn't like her," I bluntly say.

Her chuckle infuses the room with mirth, no malevolence behind it. "I was young and stupid, listening to whatever the media said. But I didn't *not* like her. I was jealous."

"Oh..."

"Once again, my apologies for not being able to attend the funeral service. I sent a card and flowers. I had..."

I zone out, thinking back to that day. It doesn't bother me that she wasn't there. Matter of fact, I didn't care who was or wasn't there, and I can't remember who was actually present. That day and every day after is a muddled, distant, and blurry memory.

Except not every day, a voice in my head says.

Midnight, Christmas Day, ring a bell? it says after.

"That's fine," I reply, registering how quiet it is. "Why is it that you wanted to see me?"

"Thanks again for coming. I know it's been difficult because of the holidays and everything in between, but I'm glad we're finally able to meet."

Truth is, I'd been avoiding her, and I didn't expect to make it past Christmas.

"Yeah, it's been busy."

"Well, I'm glad you found the time to stop by." She leans forward, lacing her fingers on top of her desk. "I'll get straight to the point. A position in our support staff has opened up for the student assistant coach. With your years of experience, I thought I'd ask you if you wanted to take the position. You'd be a great asset to our team and—"

"No." As rude or abrasive as that single word may come off, I don't need to be anywhere near the sport that almost led me to end it all. "I'm not suited for the position. It'd be best if—"

She stares at me, bemused, but smiles nonetheless. "Maybe I came off too forward, but I saw your films and I'm in awe. You're just as talented and impressive as your mom," she says, her smile sincere.

My heart skeeters all over the place at that statement. I want to correct her, let her know I'm nothing but a disappointment, a fraud. Claudia Resendiz was a beast in the water, I've heard so many people say. I was never going to measure up.

"This is a very coveted position and it comes with a lot of great benefits. I've already sent you the email, and I highly suggest you read it over. You'll be paid for your time, and I promise the pay is great."

Money is the least of my issues. I have a shit ton of it sitting in my bank account.

"I promise I'm not worth the hire and I'm sure you heard a lot of great things about me from Christian Novak," I start because there's no point in holding back.

"He has been dealt with, and that is the reason why I'm here and he's not," Monica gravely states. "I'm sorry for cutting you off there, and please don't be afraid to state your grievances, but I don't want you to worry. Things are running differently now and will continue to."

I want to ask what happened because I was sure they'd never get rid of him. I'd be lying if I said I wasn't shocked when I found out he'd been replaced. The article never said why, and when he was asked, he said it was time he moved on.

It felt like a load of bullshit, but who was I to question the motive?

"Okay." The silence draws out after that because I'm not sure if there's anything else I need to say. "I'm sorry for wasting your time, but I'm not interested in the position."

"Just think about it. We'd love to have you join our team again."

It's not going to happen, but I nod because something tells me she won't let up. She also reminds me of Mom, and I don't want to be around a person who'll remind me of her.

It's crazy how something cataclysmic can make you physically feel like the world has stopped moving, but the reality is that it's only you who stopped.

I wish my brain could pick up the pace, move the way my body has as though nothing changed. I ran an hour straight, and for that one hour alone, I felt like my brain finally got the memo. But once I climbed off the treadmill, I felt the immediate shift in the room. And again, I felt like I had stopped moving while everyone around me hadn't.

I'm back to square one, and the light barely filtering in my head is starting to dim.

"Josie?" My head spins in the direction of the voice as I shut the locker I used to store my stuff while I worked out at the university's gym.

The moment our eyes meet, I instantly recognize the girl standing next to me. "Yeah?"

Her lips widen, a vibrant smile stretching across her deep bronze face, causing her cheekbones to stand out. "Just wanted to stop by and meet the person all the girls keep talking about. I'm Vienna, the mermaid at Carmel Aquarium."

No wonder they hired her; she's gorgeous.

She's also a sophomore, a year younger than me, and a

freestyle swimmer. I found that out in the aquarium's brochure, when they announced she'd be working with them occasionally on the weekends.

"All good, I hope." I attempt a playful tone, but the delivery falls flat.

I'm bad at small talk and just talking in general, so I won't be surprised if she walks away. But a millisecond ticks before she replies, seeming casual and unperturbed.

"Oh, all good. Those girls love you."

I shrug. "I'm just teaching them how to swim. I'm not doing anything special."

She quietly chuckles. "I promise you're doing a lot more than you think."

Throwing my bookbag over my shoulder, I walk around her. "That's great."

"Are you going to grab something to eat?"

It's a little weird that she asked because I am. "Uh, yeah."

"Mind if I tag along?"

I falter in my steps, but she keeps walking, her black braids swishing against her bookbag as she does.

I want to say no because the moment she gets to know me, she'll leave or my nonexistent personality will push her away. Still, I find myself letting her.

"Sure, I'm going to S.S." It's short for Sirenum Scopuli, which is one of the dining halls. Because the university's mascot are the sirens, they decided to name that after an island in Greek mythology. Still, no one uses the full name unless it's transfers or freshmen.

She looks over her shoulder at me, a smile still on her face. "Great, that's where I was heading. What are you getting? I'm usually a parfait and bagel kind of girl, but I've heard they just installed an omelet bar, so I think I might try that out."

I fall into step next to her, still not sure how to feel, but ignoring the voice in my head that's telling me this isn't going to last long.

"I think I might try that out too."

I'm not sure what the hell I was thinking, listening to my advisor about signing up for a hiking class. It's not because I don't have the stamina because I certainly do, or a camera because it's mandatory for the class, but it's about how long it runs for.

The Hiking Seminar: Art Mediums and Nature. Four to six forty-five p.m., my schedule states.

I wanted and needed something easy, and while I didn't explicitly say that to my advisor, it's like she knew and recommended that.

Now I'm running late, hair dripping wet because I didn't pay attention to the clock when I decided to go for a second run.

Stupid idiot, I berate myself, but the words dull when I step in the small classroom. There are only eight rectangular tables, each only fitting two people. I don't have to look very hard, as I spot an empty one in the back.

Thankfully, the professor isn't here yet, but everyone is mostly quiet, scrolling on their phones as I walk past them to take a seat. Minus a table of two girls who seem to know each other.

After hanging my bag on the back of my chair, I grimace as I sit back and feel how soaked my long-sleeve shirt is on the back. If I would've known the professor wasn't going to be here on time, I would've dried my hair.

Ignoring the wet spot, I focus on my planner in front of me. The hardly there light in my head isn't the only thing keeping my life intact. Without this planner, I'm not sure how I'll manage.

Control freak! my mind screams.

I squeeze my eyes, attempting to shove the voice away, but it only gets louder until I hear a very familiar deep masculine voice.

"Jos?"

The harsh words fizzle into nothing as I shift my gaze upward, my eyes locking with a pair of amber ones.

"Daniel."

"Still on a first-name basis, I see." He grins, lifting his backwards cap, and dragging his fingers through his long, dark chestnut strands. When he places it back on his head, I notice how outgrown his hair is. The thick strands curl outward to his ears and rest just beneath the base of his neck. "This is our third encounter. Shouldn't we be past the formal interaction, *Jos*?"

Something weird happens in my stomach, but I ignore it. I must've had a bad omelet. "How is that formal? I was just saying your name."

"Can I take a seat?"

It's not like I can say no. It's the only one available. "Unless you want to sit on the floor."

Pulling the chair back, he settles down next to me, and sets his bag on the floor. He turns to look at me, eyes flashing with glee before they soften. Then he leans closer and whispers, "I'm so happy you're here, Josefine."

My brows knit. "Why do you keep saying that?"

"Because I am." He sounds so earnest, the words feel warm, like sitting in front of a fireplace, wrapped in a thick blanket.

My mind becomes blank, my stomach does that weird thing again, but I don't get a chance to get a word in as Professor Carleson steps in. "So sorry. If I'm being honest, I kind of overslept."

7
DANIEL

I'M VERY GOOD AT PRETENDING.

I've gotten so good at it, the lies easily slide off my tongue like slicing butter. That's how smooth they are, how easy they are for me to come up with on the spot.

That's why as I sit next to Josie, I'm acting like nothing ever happened. I'm smiling and being myself because that's what I need to do. But if I'm being honest, for the first time in a long time, it's killing me having to act like nothing ever happened.

We're in a room full of people, so it's not like I can say much to begin with, but even if it were just Josie and me, I have a feeling she wouldn't say anything. I have a feeling she'd act like she didn't almost end her life.

She's already doing a good job at it. Face expressionless, brown eyes empty, but posture a little too stiff. Despite that, she looks like any other person on the first day of class.

But unlike everyone else, I saw past the wall she now has up. I saw it and I should let it go because it seems she has, but I can't.

If her posture was rigid before, she's now a boulder, body tensing when Professor Carleson announces that he likes to use the buddy system when we go hiking. Whoever we're sitting with will be our partner for the rest of the semester, and we can't switch. He also wants us to do an icebreaker with our partner to get to know one another and to post our questions and responses on Canvas in the discussion board.

Canvas is a website the university uses to manage all classes, and the discussion board is something all professors use to promote engagement. I don't hate it, but it's tedious to use when they make you reply to two other students' posts.

As I grab my laptop, Josie switches her thick planner with her own, but she never looks at me. Even after we've logged in and opened the discussion board, she doesn't glance my way.

I wish it didn't bother me, but it does.

She drums her fingers on her keyboard, lips pinched to the side as if she were considering what she wants to ask.

I decide to break the ice first. Might as well. I have a feeling we'll sit here all day if I wait for her to ask something.

"If you could have any superpower, what would it be?" I ask as I type the question.

Her brows pinch but lips part then close like she doesn't know how to answer that. "I don't know. I've never thought about it."

"What?" My eyes slightly widen, and I turn to look at her, but still doesn't move. "You've never thought about it? That's going to change today. You have to pick one."

Her brows stay pinched, indenting the faintest crease. "What's the point? They're not real, so it's not like it matters."

I grin. "It's called imagination, Jos. Ever heard of it?"

She spins in her seat to face me, pinning me with an unamused expression. She could be shooting me daggers and I'd welcome it. I'd rather have her eyes on me than not. But only because it's hard to get a read on her.

"All right, what would you pick?" she bounces my question back to me.

My grin broadens because it's not something I need to think about. I've known since I was six. "Elemental control."

She stares, perplexed. "What's that?"

"Controlling and manipulating the elements like water, air, fire, and earth."

"That's a thing?"

The severely confused expression on her face is cute. "Of course it's a thing. Just imagine how powerful I'd be if I had it. I'd be unstoppable." And having the ability to control water would mean I wouldn't be afraid of it.

Well, it's not the water itself I'm afraid of, but swimming in the deep.

A memory, one I hadn't thought about in a while, plays in my head as if the moment had just occurred a second ago. The reminder of that day sends my mind spiraling and my heart racing for a moment. That is until my attention shifts to Josie and it all subdues.

She cocks her head to the side, eyes searching mine as if she had noticed I had slipped into a dark place I've been avoiding. But she must've realized I caught on because her back straightens and she draws her eyes to her fingers covered in rings.

There's so many of them, in different shapes and colors.

"So what would your superpower be?" I ask again.

Her knee bounces next to mine, but it's brief, before she moves it away. "Invisibility, I guess. It's probably not a good one, but it works."

There's a twinge of vulnerability that seeps with her words, despite how dry they are. She also sounds embarrassed, like she was trying to make a joke of it.

The thought unfurls annoyance in my head and slithers to my chest. I shouldn't overanalyze, but something tells me someone fucked with her. They must've made fun of her, made her feel small or some kind of way to be like this.

I hope I never find them because I'm not sure I'll be able to hold back if I do.

"You're going to have to pick something else."

She looks up at me again, earthy brown eyes a little angry, a little embarrassed. "Why?"

"Because I don't think it's working. I see you, Jos."

The emotions in her eyes dissolve as she takes in my words and her lips part just a tad, but she doesn't say anything. I know she's reading through the lines, understanding what I said, what I meant.

"I'm just saying, to be invisible, your superpower has to work. So pick something else," I say to fill the void.

She ponders over it, and I can tell she's really thinking it through. Her lips are slightly pursed, fingers twirling the ring on her middle finger on the opposite hand, and her head is tipped to the side.

I smile, not sure if she realizes she's doing it.

"Telekinesis," she settles on with a small lilt in her voice.

"Just imagine how unstoppable we'd be? The duo the world never knew it needed." I type her response. "We need names."

"Names?"

"Yeah, all superheroes have one. We'll need secret identities too. I'm no Clark Kent, but I can pull the hell out of some glasses."

I peek up then look back at my screen but do a double take on her face. I swear I just saw her lips crack a smidge. Did she smile? Holy shit, did I just make Josefine smile?

It was hardly anything, but I know a smile when I see one.

We're only eight days into the year, but I think that's probably going to be the highlight of it.

"You look like you'd be able to pull them off," she absently says, as if she were just pointing out a fact but...

Don't read into it. Don't read into it.

"Are you flirting with me?" I arch a brow, doing everything in my power not to look smug as fuck when the faintest coat of red appears on the apples of her cheeks.

"That's not flirting," she quickly fires back, the red slipping away as if it were never there.

"Kind of sounded like it."

She shoots me a vexed expression. "I was just making a statement. If I was flirting with you, which I'm not, you would know."

Propping my elbow on the table, I rest my chin on the heel of my palm, flashing her a coy smile. "Then you're going to have to show me what you consider flirting because I still believe you were."

She stares at me for a beat like she's contemplating it, but then she shakes her head.

"It's my turn. What's your major?"

"Boo." I point my thumb downward. "That's no fun, but I'm majoring in Studio Art like you." My eyes widen and so do hers. I didn't mean to slip up.

"You read up on me?"

"It's called research," I lamely quip.

"Why would you need to do research on me?"

"Just wanted to know more about Josefine Resendiz." It's the best and only response I can give her. Though I know she knows why, and I don't further explain due to the listening ears around us.

For a moment, neither one of us says a word. Maybe she's found herself at a loss for them like I have.

Though it's not that I don't have the words. I have many of them. I just don't know how to put them together to voice what I want to ask. I don't want to invade her space, make her uncomfortable with my inquisition, but I also want to know about her because the internet only gives you so much.

"There's not much to know." She shrugs.

"There's always something to know."

"We're strangers."

"Friends."

"We can't be friends. We don't know anything about each other."

"At some point, you're going to have to stop using that as an excuse."

She scoffs. "It's not an excuse. And who said I wanted to be your friend?"

"Everyone wants to be my friend," I retort with a grin. When her eyes cast to it, she glowers, but then her face becomes blank.

"They must feel bad for you."

"So, feel bad for me and be my friend."

"You're annoying."

"You mean good looking?"

She softly groans. "We're getting off track."

"Put me back on it then. You're kind of making it hard to focus." My grin deepens.

She drags a deep inhale, like she's trying to muster every ounce of patience she has left. I shouldn't like this, but I do. I *really* do.

"You did that all on your own. Also, that's not called research, that's called stalking."

"Can't be stalking if it's all available on the internet. Though I did find out through Pen that you teach swim lessons. That aside, everything I learned about you is online. Blame whoever put it there."

"You're weird." She aggravatedly punches the keys, typing a few very basic questions.

"And you're no fun. *Are you minoring in anything?*" I read off her question from the screen. "I'm not, but you can ask me anything; I'm an open book. For now, you're going to have to wait your turn because it's mine. If you could watch any show for the rest of your life, which would it be?"

"I don't watch TV."

"You're lying."

"I'm not. It never interested me," she replies. Something tells me she's lying but I don't push. "Well...when I was younger, I watched *Rebelde*."

Good, common grounds. "Which was your favorite character?"

"Roberta."

"She was mine too." I type her response.

Now she cocks a brow.

"I was young and she was hot. Don't look at me like that. I bet you crushed on Miguel, huh?"

"No, it was Diego. I know he was a douche, but he was hot."

"But not as hot as me, right?" I joke because I don't like hearing the sadness in her voice.

"I want to meet the person who over inflated your ego. I need a word or two with them."

And I want to meet the person who fucked her over. I'll have more than words with them.

I chuckle at her grimace. "My mom, but can you blame her? Just look at me." I wave a hand down the side of my face. "I'm devastatingly good looking."

"Mmm...devastatingly annoying."

"Your denial is showing."

"I never said you weren't good looking. I just said...fuck. I'm done talking to you." She furiously moves her fingers along the keys, typing a bullshit-ass response. "I think we've broken the ice."

I smirk, feeling smug. "We've barely scratched the surface."

"Daniel,"

"Yes, Jos?"

"Shut up." She side-eyes me, her face tinged with frustration.

I bite back a laugh, lips twitching as I fight them from parting. "Okay, but I need to ask one more thing."

"What?"

"Did you see my Post-it?" I knew there would be a big possibility she'd throw it away, but I wanted her to know she has someone she can talk to.

She falters as she closes her laptop. "Yeah, I saw it."

"Anytime, don't hesitate. I'm here for you."

I expect silence and nothing in return but then she stuns me when she nods and says, "I'm only keeping it because we're going to be hiking buddies."

So, she's had it for four days. She can't say it's because of this class because I left that before today. *Don't get excited, dumbass. Act cool. Be cool. Play. It. Cool.*

"Cool." *Cool? Why did I say that?*

"Are we done?" she asks and I realize I zoned out.

"Yeah, we're done." I type out a few things on my laptop as she stands, grabs her bookbag, and pushes her chair in.

As she throws it over her shoulder, she goes to walk away but then spins and stands in front of me.

"Miss me already?"

She huffs out a quiet puff of air, like she's uncertain about what she's going to say. "What's your favorite color?"

My smile slips and my heart oddly races. "Green."

"Okay." She walks away and I'm left staring at the spot she was at with my heart racing abnormally fast.

8
DANIEL

"Sparky."

Focus. Quick. Set feet. Transition. Throw.

"Danny."

Focus. Quick. Set feet. Transition. Throw.

"Daniel!"

Focus. Quick. I catch the ball as the machine shoots it at me, but I come to a complete standstill, before I set my feet at Vincenzo D'Angelo's voice. The Head Coach for MCU's baseball team.

Dropping the ball, I raise my shirt to wipe the sweat off my forehead and attempt to control my uneven breathing as I look at Coach D. He's standing next to the machine and I'm assuming he's turned it off since no more balls come my way.

"Sorry, I didn't hear you." I pant. "Have you been here long?" I ask as I bend down to grab my water bottle.

"What the hell are you doing here so late?" He cocks a thick dark brown brow, folding his arms against his chest.

"It's not really that late." I set my bottle down and grab the baseball I had dropped and toss it in the air.

It's very late, close to twelve a.m. on a Sunday, but I felt restless at home. Since I found out four days ago that Josie kept the

Post-it note, I've been on edge, waiting for a text from her. I know I'll never get one, but I keep reaching for my phone more than I ever have.

I'm worried about her. Despite knowing she's alive, I can't get the image of her crumbling in front of me out of my mind. The one that haunts me the most though is her standing on the edge of the cliff.

Then there's my family who text me—well, my mom and sister do; Dad's quiet. He's always quiet.

So, I came to the batting cages at the indoor facility at MCU to work on my footwork because I needed to decompress.

"Daniel." He stares at me listlessly. "Get some fucking rest. I get you're trying to prepare, but the last thing I need is you overworking yourself and getting hurt. We're only a month away from the season starting. I swear to God, I will—"

"That's not going to happen. I promise I'll leave now, I..." I sigh. Dropping the ball again, I stretch my arms over my head until my shoulders pop. Still, the pestering tension resides in my back. "Couldn't sleep, that's all."

Coach D levels me with a disbelieving look and just when I think he's going to call me on my bullshit, he shakes his head. He blows out a weary breath and grumbles something.

"What was that?" I ask.

"Nothing." He fixes his gaze on something else, and that's when I realize he's holding a bat.

But that's not the only thing I notice. He's gripping it hard, knuckles extremely white, face tinged with indignation, and eyes frayed with exhaustion.

"Is everything good?"

He pinches the bridge of his nose, exhaling a harsh breath. "You wouldn't understand. You're young, which means don't be fucking stupid." Now he stands next to me and motions for me to turn on the pitching machine. "Be safe because if you don't, you'll find a baby on your doorstep."

I can't mask the incredulous look on my face fast enough, and at my expression, he rolls his eyes.

Coach D'Angelo may be forty years old, but that hasn't stopped anyone from shooting their shot or making thirst edits of him on social media. But I guess I get it. He's fit, like really fit, always working out and doing things to stay in shape.

"This was years ago. I only have one daughter," I know about his *one* daughter, everyone knows who she is, she's the youngest player to be drafted into the NWSL. "And let me tell you, she's..." he grunts, rolling his eyes again as if he were remembering something. "Just don't be fucking stupid. Now go home before I really make you practice."

I don't call his bluff because I've no doubt he means it. Grabbing my water, I'm rushing out a quick "good night" as I turn on the machine. As I walk out, I hear the loud smack of the ball against the bat and a string of Italian curse words.

I have no idea what that's about, but I'd hate to be on the receiving end of his anger.

"I'm just saying tater tots are way better than hash browns," Grayson states matter-of-factly as we enter S.S. dining hall.

Angel's brows cinch, lip curling upward as he shakes his head in disagreement. "No, they're not. Gray, you're always on some stupid shit. Tater tots aren't—"

"I think they're both good," Kainoa, our Hawaiian teammate, intervenes, lifting a shoulder in a half shrug.

Gray and Angel stare at him judgmentally then fix their gazes on Noah and me, who haven't said anything. We've stayed quiet because they've been going at it since six this morning and it's now three in the afternoon. We're all over it and couldn't care less.

I also don't usually entertain their bullshit because me agreeing with anyone besides Angel is an act of treason according to him. He'll be whining about it for days and Gray will be gloating because he thrives on pissing Angel off.

"They come from potatoes. They all taste the same," Noah boredly says as we stand in line for Chopt. "Now, shut up."

They scoff, pinning him with a look of judgment, then shift their gaze to me.

"Like Kai said..." I glance away for a second, the corner of my eyes catching a black ponytail before I draw my attention back to my roommates and teammates. "They're both..." I trail off, doing a double take on the black ponytail and the person it belongs to.

It's Josie. Her hair is up in a high ponytail, swishing from side to side as she walks to one of the restaurants with a girl next to her, who's a little taller than her.

"They're both what?" I hear someone ask me, but I'm not sure who and I can't bring myself to find out.

Josie is wearing the same stoic expression despite the girl next to her wearing the opposite. The girl is smiling big, talking about who knows what, but even though Josie isn't, she's attentively listening and nodding.

"Sparky?" Angel waves his hand in front of my face, breaking the trance that I'm in.

"What?" My attention is back on them, but I must've been staring for too long. Gray smirks, Noah looks disinterested, Kai stares at the girls, and Angel realizes it's Josefine.

"Why are you staring at Wednesday?" Gray questions, green eyes shining with mischief.

I stare at him quizzically. "Wednesday?"

"Josefine. That's what everyone calls her," Gray explains. "You know, because look at her. Sure, she's hot as fuck, but she's always looking serious and her personality is nonex—"

"Shut the fuck up," I snap.

They stare at me, taken aback. Even Noah looks a little stunned when he finally shifts his eyes back to me.

I don't ever raise my voice or lose my cool. I'm the fun one, always positive and boosting morale when I need to during practice or games, and I'm known to always be smiling. It's actually why I'm called Sparky. Assistant Coach Adam Lewis said I spark energy everywhere I go.

Gray raises his hands in surrender. "Shit, sorry, I didn't know there was something going on between you and Wed—Josefine. Wait, since when are you and Josefine a thing?"

"We're not a thing; we have a class together. Just don't talk about her like that. And Wednesday isn't even all that bad. She'd kill you and not break a sweat." I grin, hoping it'll ease the tension coiling my body.

Just when I think it's gone, it appears like it never left.

We're not friends. I've extended my hand and have kept it extended for her, but I doubt she'll ever take it.

Kai narrows his eyes in suspicion. "So, there's really nothing going on between you two? You're not using her to get back at Bryson?"

Now I'm taken aback, feeling more annoyed than shocked. "Why would you say that?"

"Because Josefine is Bryson's ex," Gray supplies like it's something I should know.

That shocks me and I realize now why they were staring at me skeptically and bemused. Bryson isn't only my teammate, but the guy Amanda cheated on me with. It feels like I've solved a puzzle I wasn't aware I was piecing together.

Bryson mentioned a *Josie* once, but it was in passing. You wouldn't have known they were dating because he was constantly flirting around. I didn't think much of it or really care because while we're teammates, we've never been close. Still, I talked to him during practice and games and if we ran into each other somewhere, I made small talk.

But since I found out he was the guy Amanda was cheating on me with, I don't talk to him unless necessary. And I'm nowhere near his vicinity unless we have to because we're teammates.

If I don't, I'm afraid I'll lose my shit. I didn't when I found out he was fucking my girlfriend, and I haven't despite his taunts. No matter what he says, I told myself I'd keep my cool.

I remind myself of that as I feel something spark inside me. It slowly spreads like lava, and I feel dangerously hot inside.

Was he part of the reason why Josie wanted to end it? The thought triggers something, but I force the raging thoughts racing in my head to calm down.

"I had no idea they were a thing." I cast my glance toward Angel who shrugs as if he were saying the same thing. "How do you know?"

"I may have attempted to ask her out," Gray says all too fast, embarrassed more than annoyed.

Kai snickers, cocking a brow. "May have? Please. He tried but she knocked him off his massive-ass ego and turned him down. He also—"

"Shut up." He shoots him a glare, but Kai only grins wider.

"He also tried to sign up for one of her swimming lessons, but she never replied to his email." His snickers become bubbles of laughter.

"Smart girl," Noah quips.

Gray deadpans but then perks up, smiling, unbothered. "It was for the best. After all, I know how to swim and *some* people don't." He looks directly at me when he says that, humor lacing his words. "I'd hate to take the spot from someone who really needs it."

I don't take offense because I know he's not being a dick. He sometimes comes off that way. He also comes off as a snob and a condescending asshole, but Grayson isn't that bad once you get to know him.

He knows, like everyone else, that I don't know how to swim. The guys have wanted to teach me, but the deep terrifies me, so I've never let them.

"Maybe you should sign up for those lessons," Kai suggests jokingly.

Angel grins. "You know, that wouldn't be such a bad idea."

"But good luck trying to get her to reply to you," Gray patronizingly adds.

"I'm not going to do that," I say just as it's our turn to order.

Doing that would require me putting my fear aside. But why would I sign up for those swim lessons when it's obvious she wants nothing to do with me? She probably wouldn't reply to my email anyway.

I shake the thought away, but as she walks past me, our gazes collide and something weird happens in my chest. When she looks away, the weird feeling stops but the thought comes flying back.

I'm not going to do it.

"You're thinking about it, aren't you?" Angel quietly says to me as the guys place their orders.

"I'm not."

"Right," he drawls.

"I'm not." I shouldn't but I sound defensive as hell.

"Sure, Danny."

I can't reply because it's his turn to order. But it doesn't matter, I'm not going to do it.

9
JOSEFINE

I'M NOT SURE WHAT I'VE DONE TO MAKE VIENNA WANT to stick around, but she's been meeting me for lunch since last Wednesday. It wasn't something we planned, but we ran into each other again on Thursday and by the end of it, she was saying she'd see me the next day. Sure enough, Friday at the same time, we met and had lunch together.

I don't know what to make of this. I thought by now she'd be put off by me. I have a track record of not keeping friends.

It's so bad, people call me Wednesday. Though I'm not sure if they still do; I haven't been around anyone enough to know.

Vienna—Vi, she insists I call her that, wipes her mouth and her gaze shifts all over S.S. Though it doesn't look like she's looking for someone, she almost looks like she's a little nervous.

"You okay?" I hope to God she says yes because I'm shit at comforting people.

As her eyes settle on me, she huffs out a quiet laugh. "Yeah. I don't want to be that person." *Oh no, here we go. I knew this was too good to be true.* "And I'm not going to be, I promise." *Wait, what is she on?* "I want to welcome you to the dead mom's club. I didn't want to make things awkward and express my condolences because it's weird. I mean because I get it. The suffocating hugs, the overwhelming need people have to be all up in your space when all you want is to be alone, and the inclination people have to constantly remind you that she died when *you* know. Like what do I know? She was only my mom for seventeen years."

A knot of ambivalence twists in my stomach, my mind blank because I actually don't know how to respond to that.

Vi blanches, seemingly embarrassed. "That was weird. I shouldn't have said it like that. I just wanted you to know that I get it. I'm so sorry. I've been told to stop using humor to...I'm going to shut up."

My lips involuntarily jerk, but only briefly.

I thought she was going to ask for tips and tricks about swimming because most people do. Once they get what they want I'm forgotten about.

"Don't apologize. I don't mind it. I've been told I have a dry sense of humor, so it's nothing to me." The reminder of how much Bryson hated my sense of humor rushes in my head. "I'll welcome your humor over hugs any day. So please don't hug me."

She giggles as she picks up her sub. "No hugging you. Got it."

Daniel is the exception because I wasn't thinking when he hugged me on Christmas Day. But I'll never let him or anyone hug me again. Hugs feel too personal and make me uncomfortably itchy.

Somehow as I think that, Daniel's eyes clash with mine. I don't know what's going on, why the universe is so intent on me running into him. But everywhere I turn, he's there.

He's sitting with his friends a few tables away from us. I swear I wasn't looking for him, and I doubt he was looking for me. Somehow, like magnets, we found each other, forced to connect by an odd electrical pull, and now that we've connected, it feels hard to look away.

He flashes me a lopsided smile, sweet and flirty, and that feels strangely dangerous.

Thankfully, Penelope stands in front of me, splitting the pull our eyes seem to have on each other.

"Josie, hey," she perkily greets. "I thought I'd never run into you. I guess it's my fault for not getting your number that day."

"Hey, Penelope." I smile but realize it might look forced so I drop it.

"Please call me Pen," she playfully scolds then directs her focus to Vi. "Hey, you're Vienna, right?"

She grins, sitting up straighter. "Yeah, how did you—"

"You're on the aquarium's brochure and I've seen your pictures around campus," she explains. "Speaking of the aquarium, I need your ab and makeup routine because you just look..." She kisses the tips of her fingers and tosses them in the air. "Chef's kiss."

"Please, have you seen yourself, Pen? Can I call you Pen?" Vi asks and pulls the empty chair next to her and pats it for Pen to sit. "You can call me Vi."

She happily takes the seat. "Yes, of course. So tell me all your secrets. Don't get me wrong—I love the way I do my makeup, but I could definitely improve."

I eat my sub as they get immersed in their conversation. I make myself invisible and watch them so casually and easily talk to each other as though they've been friends for a while. That's how effortless their conversation is.

Maybe I should say something, but a wave of apprehension unwinds in my stomach and uneasiness prickles my body.

"What about you? What's your secret because your skin is so glassy," Penelope asks me.

My brows hike up. "Oh, me? No, I don't—"

"Don't be humble now," Vi cuts me off. "Your skin is flawless."

"It is." Pen nods earnestly. "Thanks to Accutane my skin looks so much better, but I still have a few acne scars and don't get me started on my pores," she says but not in a way like she's fishing for compliments but something she's just pointing out. "I'd kill to have your skin."

"I know this is hard to believe, but I don't usually break out."

I have no idea who my father is, so I don't know what his skin looks like. But I know Mom's skin was impeccably flawless, so I guess I should thank her for that.

"No, I believe it. Danny's dumbass best friend, Angel, never breaks out." Pen scrunches her nose. Disdain flickers in her eyes. "Lucky asshole."

My lips slightly jerk up again.

The few minutes we have left, they talk about makeup and what works for them. Even though I can't contribute much because I haven't worn makeup since Mom passed, they still include me.

It's weird but kind of nice.

Before we part ways, Vi creates a group chat and insists lunch together is a must. I agree only because I wasn't really given much of a vote. I know I'm being pessimistic, but I can't help but wait for the shoe to drop.

It's happened before. I'll make friends, group chats will be created, and then I'm being excluded and not told everyone is going to be wearing matching pajamas. Or finding out through Instagram that everyone went out for dinner and a separate group chat had been made.

I blink the memory away and trudge down the brick way to my hiking seminar class.

"You never came up with your superhero name or secret identity."

I gasp, head snapping up to my right at the idiot next to me. Daniel leisurely walks next to me, the same smile from earlier still displayed on his face. He's wearing a hat, but it's not backwards this time, and annoyingly, it looks good. And right as I turn, I catch gold from the corner of my eye and realize he's wearing a chain with a safety pin on it.

"We need names and secret identities, Jos."

"Have you been behind me all this time?"

"No, but I caught up to you. You're kind of a slow walker," he says, amused.

I scoff. "I'm not a slow walker."

"No, of course not," he sarcastically draws out. "So, names and secret identities."

"Why are you still on that? The discussion board is over; we got a hundred."

"I'll let you think about it."

I cast him a deadpan look and stop in my tracks. He quickly catches on and stops too. We step to the side as a few students pass, and I wait until they're gone to say what I need to get off my chest.

"What's wrong?" Worry and confusion flicker in his gaze as they sweep over me.

My chest clenches, but I push past the discomfort at his expression. "I'm not dead and I'm not going to kill myself. So, for the love of God, stop acting like I am. Stop following me. Stop looking at me. Just fucking stop. Because before the cliff, you didn't know who I was, even though I knew who you were."

I was going to pretend like our past interaction didn't happen, but it did. He was the one who drove me to my house when Bryson was too drunk to do so.

"Josie, I—"

"You're free from obligation. You can stop pretending like you care."

I leave it at that and stalk off.

He obviously pities me. Why else would he be this persistent?

I think I've read the first sentence in the email Monica sent me like twenty times. Every time I restart, my mind wanders to Daniel.

After I walked away, he showed up to class a few minutes later after I did. He didn't talk to me, and I didn't care to attempt to make conversation with him. Though we really couldn't because Professor Carleson spoke the entire time. And Daniel ended up leaving forty-five minutes early too.

Twirling the ring on my middle finger, I shake the memory of him away and attempt to read the email again. But the moment I reach the second word, my laptop dings, announcing I've got a new email.

I blink a few times, dumbfounded at the name that appears on the top right corner for a few seconds before it disappears. I find it hard to believe until I go back to my inbox and see an email from Daniel Garcia, but it's the subject line that severely throws me off.

Swimming Lessons

I stare at it for a long beat, my vision blurring in the process until I blink to clear it. Tentatively, I click on it and don't feel any less shocked when I read his email.

From: Daniel Garcia <danny6garcia@gmail.com>
To: Josefine Resendiz <josefineresendiz@gmail.com>
Subject: Swimming Lessons
Date: Monday, January 13 11:11 PM

Don't laugh but I don't know how to swim. I hear you're the person who makes it possible. How'd you like to make that possible for me?
I'm so happy you're here, Josefine! And I mean that.

10
DANIEL

"Ball!" Coach Lewis, the assistant for hitting, infielders, and catchers, shouts from home base as he tosses the ball up in the air and swings the bat, striking it hard in my direction.

Staying low to the ground, I quickly shift on my feet, watching the speed and direction of the ball. Once I get in front of it, I turn my glove over, sweeping it forward and catching it backhanded. Then I rapidly shift on my feet, aligning them, and throw it to the pitching net on the first base.

I catch my breath, easing from my position when he waves his hand, signaling that practice is over.

During the offseason, practice is brutal. We're on the field six to seven hours a day, in the batting cages for an hour to an hour and a half, weightlifting to build mass, then on the weekends we have scrimmage.

It's exhausting, but I welcome being busy. It helps me from staying in my head, especially now more than ever.

I can't stop thinking about Josie and the hurt look on her face. Her eyes glazed with sadness, and became distant and heavy.

Because before the cliff, you didn't know who I was, even though I knew who you were.

I feel so clueless because I don't know what she meant by that. And she thinks I pity her—fuck, that's not what I wanted her to feel.

They lower the music as we all gather around Coach D now that practice is over.

Angel stands next to me and bobs his head to the beat of "Moscow Mule" by Bad Bunny. Bryson subtly curls his lip, contempt flashing across his face at the music. That only causes Angel's smile to deepen and quietly mouth the words to him.

Bryson rolls his eyes and directs his attention to Coach D.

He can't stand that it's in Spanish. He's thrown fits, saying it's unfair he has to listen to something he can't understand. No one has ever had an issue with the music and all, minus Bryson, vibe with it.

Not sure when it happens, but I zone out staring at Bryson. When his eyes meet mine, his brows furrow but then they soften and he smirks.

I know the intention behind it. It's the *I fucked your girlfriend and she loved it* smirk.

Usually, those smirks piss me off and I have to repeatedly tell myself not to punch him. But I surprisingly don't feel anything but annoyed.

What did Josie see in him? Why him? Was she devastated when she found out Bryson cheated on her? Is that one of the reasons she wanted to end it?

"Stop looking at him," Angel whispers.

I look away, forcing the irritation and anger away. It hadn't been there before, but now I'm really fucking angry and have the desire to do more than just punch him.

"All right everyone, get a partner. Sparky, get us going," Coach announces.

That manages to diffuse the resentment fueling me.

After every practice, Coach D has us stand at the line in front of one of the guys and bump chests or high-five each other.

I stand in front of Angel, smiling as he continues to bob his head and now shimmy his shoulders. But it somewhat dips as I think about Adrian and what life would've been like if he was here with me.

I shake out of it, knowing the guys are waiting for me. "All right, boys, you know what to do. Go big or go home!" I shout as some of us take a few steps back and when we're far away enough, run toward our partner who is doing the same, jump in the air, and bump our chests against theirs. We do it a few more times, me giving them words of affirmation and enthusiasm. After all, I'm their captain.

We circle around Coach again. The atmosphere is lighter now. Even Bryson seems to be in a decent mood.

"I'm proud of all the hard work you've all been putting in this offseason. From my pitchers and my outfielders to my infielders, you guys are doing an absolute great job. I can see you've all been working hard, and it'll pay off this coming season." Coach D pauses, a miniscule smile tipping on his face before it fades. "Don't get cocky; keep working hard and don't slack off in or off the field. Now let's have a good lift and then we'll call it a day. Nice work, gentlemen."

"Bring it up," I say as he takes a few steps back and I step in the middle, raising my hand and the guys follow suit. "*Family* on three."

"One. Two. Three. *Family*!" we raise our voices in unison.

We all disperse, grabbing our stuff, and head out of the field to the weight room.

"You know that saying if looks could kill..." Angel trails off as he throws the strap of his bag over his shoulder. I nod, not sure where he's going with that. "You've never looked at Bryson that way, and today you did. Look, I know Amanda was your girlfriend and I hate that that happened to you but—"

"This isn't about Amanda," I interrupt but regret it. "I mean this isn't about either one of them. I zoned out and didn't realize I was staring at him."

"You could detonate the whole goddamn world with the way you were staring at him."

"That's dramatic. I can't help the way I look. Can I not make faces anymore?"

"You can. You can make all the faces you want, but that face was something else."

"I was just thinking of something I did."

"What did you do?" He smiles, sounding entertained.

I swallow hard. "I emailed Josie about swimming lessons."

He comes to a complete stop, but I only slow my steps.

"You did what?" he asks, dumbfounded. "When?"

Angel catches up to me, his gaze laser focused on me, but I still don't look at him.

"Last night," I replied coyly. I have no desire to learn how to swim. I don't mind getting in the water, but I refuse getting in the deep end. I didn't message Josie with the intention of actually learning; I just wanted to know why she was upset at me. I wanted to know what I did wrong because I want to fix it. "But I was being funny. Since I don't have her number and needed to ask her something about the class, I figured she'd reply, but she hasn't."

That's what I get for listening to Gray. Last time I do something like that.

At his silence I say, "Also, don't tell Gray about it. I don't need him gloating."

Still, his silence extends, making me feel uncomfortably warm until he finally talks.

"But you're—is everything good?" Angel sounds genuinely concerned. It throws me off.

"Yeah, why?"

He stares at me skeptically. "You're weird about the water. How are you going to—"

"I told you I was just being funny. I'm not going in the water, especially with her of all people."

"But what would you do if she were to answer?"

I think about it for a moment but shake my head. "I highly doubt she will."

The next day, I pull into the parking lot of the trail we'll be walking today. Because it's the first, Professor Carleson said we'd start with something light, nothing too exerting. But said as the semester progressed, the trails would be longer and steeper.

Josie is already here. She's standing by her car, camera in hand, staring at the ground. She must be deep in thought because she doesn't look up when I approach her.

"Hey, Jos." I dip my head, smiling down at her.

She doesn't acknowledge me and pushes away from her car when Carleson makes us all gather around him. He goes over a few rules, the same ones he went over in the classroom, and then he's guiding us into the trail.

We all walk side by side with our partners. Most of them are talking amongst each other or listening to Carleson as he explains the history behind the trail and marvels at the beauty of it.

I'm doing neither. It's hard to focus on a thing he's saying because all my attention and energy is generated towards the girl next to me.

She's staring straight ahead, still hasn't talked to me, and I believe she'll spend the rest of the trail ignoring me until she looks up at me thirty minutes later.

Aggravation mars her face. Her eyes are hardened, mixed with anger and irritation.

"What are you playing at?" she accuses.

My brows draw in confusion. "What are you—"

"Swimming lessons? Are you serious?" she scoffs patronizingly. "Is this some joke? Who put you up to it? Was it Bryson?"

"What, no. Bryson didn't put me up to anything." I detest him, but I don't tell her that.

"Isn't it funny how he and his dumbass friends have said the exact same thing on the subject line of the email." Fury springs in her voice. Her jaw is ticking, and her lips are set in a tight line.

Dammit. I knew I should've gone with something different.

"It's not like that. Matter of fact, I don't really talk to Bryson, and he didn't put me up to anything. I—" I pause, my heart hammering fast. "I don't know how to swim," I voice quietly.

"Right," she drawls. "Are you going to tell me your member also needs help floating?"

"Member? What are you—"

Her gaze draws down below my waist. I grind my teeth, swallowing down my frustration, not at her but at Bryson.

I grab Josie's arm and pull her to the side. Thankfully, we're all the way in the back, so no one notices we're not following along.

She jerks her hand back, fury brimming in those pretty brown eyes. "What the hell do you think you're doing? I don't give a damn that you're six foot five, I'll beat your ass if you touch me again."

I need to focus but I'm still stuck on the fact she knows exactly how tall I am.

"You stalking me?" I smirk at the realization in her eyes.

"Wh-what?" she stammers. "Seriously, what's wrong with you? You don't touch a girl without her permission, ever, Garcia."

And now I'm stuck on the way she said my last name. Why did that sound hot?

Focus.

"I know, I'm sorry. I just want you to know I have no part in whatever that piece of shit has done or said. But if he or any of this friends try that again let me know and I'll—"

She folds her arms defensively. "I'm not helpless. I don't need your help."

"I never said you were, but you don't have to handle it alone. And I want you to know, I'm not pretending to care or doing this out of obligation. I want you to know that I'm here for you." I smile at her.

Her gaze locks in on my lips and for a moment she softens but it's only brief. She goes quiet then sighs. "I didn't mean for you to witness that moment at the cliff, but you need to let it go. I'm not dead, and we're not friends. Colors and names don't mean shit. So do us both a favor and move on."

"Why? What's so bad about me, we can't be friends?" I challenge.

She must've not expected that because she looks surprised. "Because...because..." she groans exasperatedly. "Why are you so insistent? If you're trying to save me because you think I'm some broken—"

"Because if I'm not, who will be? I just want to be here for you. That's all."

Her brows hike up, stupefaction written all over her face. She glances down, drops her arms, and twirls the ring around her finger. She grows quiet, and I almost break the silence until she looks up at me.

"You're so fucking..."

"I'm so *fucking* what?" My lips tempt to curl upward.

"Fucking frustrating. You and your goddamn insistence." She quietly groans.

Now I can't stop them from lifting all the way up. She glares at me, and I only smile wider. "Would it make you feel better if I told you—"

"No, no it wouldn't." She sulks.

I laugh. "You didn't let me get it out."

"I don't need to hear what you have to say." She huffs. "Do you really not know how to swim, or are you messing around?" She stares at me intently, inquisitively.

I mask the shock at her question. "I really don't know how."

"I don't work with adults or men because I teach the lessons at my house."

Thank God. I didn't want to go through with this. "I get it. You really don't—"

"If you pull anything weird, I'll break your arm. And don't test me, Garcia, because I will," she threatens.

It's harder this time, but still, I manage to somehow conceal my shock. Holy shit, it's happening. Wait no. This is a bad idea. A really bad idea. I'm a mess in the water.

"You really don't have to—"

"You're not getting this offer again."

I don't want to do this, but spending more time with her wouldn't hurt.

"I'll just be wasting your time. I don't think I'll learn and—"

She raises her hand for me to stop talking when she pulls her phone out of her black belt bag. She types something and then I feel my phone vibrate in the pocket of my shorts.

"I texted you my address."

She didn't have to do that. I memorized it the moment I left her house. Just in case she ever needed me. It was a reach, and I know she never would, but it's good to be prepared.

"You don't have to worry about it." I plaster on a playful smile, hoping she can't read between the lines and see and feel my trepidation. "It's really not a big deal."

"It is a big deal. Knowing how to swim is important. I'm going to teach you and then we'll go on about our lives."

I know what she means by that. We'll never interact with each other once it's over. And I realize this is probably her way of returning the favor.

Except I don't want anything in return but for her to be happy, safe, and okay.

11
JOSEFINE

I SUCK IN A SHARP BREATH, AND THEN ANOTHER ONE, doing my best to tether the frustration bubbling inside me.

I don't know what I was thinking, agreeing to teach Daniel how to swim. I saw the discomfort that crossed his eyes, his pulse ricochet against his neck, and how his lips strained into a smile.

It's obvious he didn't want to do it, and the moment I noticed his hesitation, I shouldn't have pushed. But I did and now I'm angry at myself, not at him.

Angry because I told myself not to overanalyze his unmistakable trepidation. I should've listened to the voice in my head to drop it, but I didn't. All because I kept replaying his stupid boyish grin in my head and his words.

Something about them just made me feel…a little warm.

It was an odd feeling, something I hadn't felt before, but the warmth didn't last long because a few hours ago he texted me.

> Daniel: I'm sorry but I have too much going on and won't be able to commit. I don't want to waste your time

There's nothing wrong about what he said. I'm glad he told me. I'm just annoyed at myself for agreeing to begin with. I don't change my rules, but for him I did. How stupid. Who would willingly want to spend time with me? Why did I think Daniel of all people would want to? I should've known better but no, I had to learn the hard way, again.

At least now, I don't have to be with him more than I need to.

Walking down the cobblestone walkway, I shift my focus on the quaint fairy-tale town. This coastal town looks like it came out of a book. With its cottages, the beach right next to you, and the incredible views.

But as pretty and calm as it is, I don't know if I'll keep living here. This place holds too many memories that I wish I could forget. Once I get my degree and sell Mom's house, I'm leaving. I'm not sure where I'll go, but it doesn't matter as long as I'm far away from here.

I wouldn't even be here, but since that night Daniel intervened, I haven't been able to bring myself to end it.

Maybe it's a punishment from Mom. If she were here right now, I know she'd reprimand me for attempting to take the easy way out. She'd tell me her exit from this world wasn't easy, so why should mine be?

My chest constricts painfully, but the tightness dissolves once I stand in front of Coastal Swim and Surf. Shaking the thoughts of her away, I enter and stand in front of the register.

"Hey, how can I help you?" The employee greets me with a professional smile.

"I need to return these items." I set the foam kickboard and goggles on the counter.

I didn't have a board big enough for Daniel. All the kids I teach are between the ages of three and ten, and they're all half the size of Daniel. So I knew I needed to get him something bigger and I always get all my new clients goggles.

"Was something wrong with them?" the lady asks.

"No, I just won't need them anymore."

She nods and once she's done, I walk out of the store and head back the way I came.

I contemplate grabbing something to eat since I'm in town, but I decide against it. I think I still have a frozen meal in my freezer.

I don't make it very far before I hear familiar voices behind me. "Josie!"

Spinning, I find Pen and Vi beaming at me, bags hanging from their hands.

"Where the hell have you been?" Pen is the first to say.

I stare at her, puzzled. "Here?"

"We know that. She means, why haven't you answered your phone?" Vi questions. "We're going to a party tonight. You need to come with us."

I grab my phone from my back pocket and realize I forgot to charge it again. "It's dead and I don't do parties."

I'm awkward as hell. I get too hot, too claustrophobic, and I've been ditched too many times to ever want to go again.

"You have to come, please," Pen begs, lacing her fingers together, placing them under her chin and pouting. "I promise you'll have a lot of fun and there's a pool. I swear it's clean-*ish*."

"Heavy on the *ish* but you don't have to get in the pool if you don't want to. Just come with us," Vi insists.

"No, I really don't—"

Vi scoffs, pinning me with a look that holds me in place. "It's Friday night. Unless you're going to another party or hooking up with someone we don't know about, you're coming with us."

It's been a few months since I last hooked up with someone. It was mediocre at best or maybe it's my fault because everything in me has died. After that night, I swore I was done. It was pointless when I couldn't feel anything.

"I'm not, but I really don't do parties." I shrug.

"What are your plans for tonight?" Vi cocks a brow, folding her arms against her chest.

"A frozen meal and cleaning my house." My homework is already done.

They both blow raspberries.

"You're coming with us and that's final," Vi adamantly states, leaving no room for discussion.

I'd be lying if I said it didn't feel nice that someone actually wants me around.

"Okay, I'll need to go home and change."

"Yay!" They perk up, their smiles lifting again.

"We'll send you the outfits we're wearing and we'll pick you up in forty minutes or so," Pen lists, already pulling her phone out and typing away. "Oh, and Danny will be there. I hear you guys have a class together and are hiking buddies?"

"Yeah, but not by choice." I want to ask her what all he said to her or anyone else, but I don't. I'm sure if he had told her about the cliff, she would've said something, right?

Pen softly chuckles. "I promise he's not that bad. He's sweet and very single." She wiggles her brows, giving me a knowing grin.

"Not interested," I quickly supply.

Her grin only grows, but she doesn't comment on it.

Once they're done, we go our separate ways. A voice in my head tells me I'm not ready to leave the house and be around other people, but another is fighting against it, screaming that it's time I live.

I just wish I could figure out how to do that.

The streets are packed and the house is overflowing with people. The music is blaring loud enough you can hear it a block down. I'm surprised the cops haven't been called, and for a moment, I worry about it. The last thing I want is to get arrested.

"The houses had been vacant, but someone bought them and now they rent them out to students," Vi explains as if she could read my thoughts. "Trust, I wouldn't be here if that were the case. The last thing I need is to lose my scholarship."

I nod, folding my arms across my chest, regretting not wearing anything other than a green bikini top, linen mini skirt, and my white high-tops. Despite living in California, the weather gets cooler around here at night. Though I know wearing a sweater or something thicker would've been pointless; it's a pool party, after all. I've been to a few parties, so I know how hot the houses get.

"I love that green on you." Pen runs her eyes down the length of my body and lingers on my chest. The mesh bikini top has different shades of green—some dark, light, and bright. "Vi, you did a fantastic job on the makeup."

The girls insisted I do a little more than just mascara and lip gloss. I have nothing against it. I used to wear it, but all my makeup expired, and I never cared to replace it.

But Pen came prepared. She brought her makeup bag just in case I needed something. And because we're the same skin tone, it worked out. Vi told me to sit, and I didn't argue. In no time, she was done and when I looked in the mirror, a thick shard of glass lodged itself in the middle of my throat.

It wasn't only because I felt pretty, which I hadn't felt in a while, but it reminded me of a picture of Mom when she was my age.

I swallow hard, pushing past the discomfort.

"I feel like Edward," I joke but it comes off so dry, I wince realizing that may have come off rude, but Vi snorts and hums the beginning of "Eyes on Fire" by Blue Foundation.

The girls burst out into fits of giggles, and my lips twitch.

I'm flooded with relief, the nerves that had quickly built up disappearing.

In Vi's defense, she was going for *Euphoria* vibes and she nailed that. Our skins are sparkly from the body spray Pen brought, and our eyelids are shinier than a disco ball.

"Hey, I'm all for it. Who knows, I might have a biting kink." Vi winks at me, voice louder as we enter the house. "Let's go to the kitchen for drinks!" she shouts, interlocking hands with Pen, and Pen interlocks her hand with mine.

She does it so casually, as if it's something we've always done, it catches me off guard. I almost tug my hand away at the instinctual reaction that I have about people touching me.

I know I'm thinking too much into something so simple but it really...threw me off.

We squeeze past the crowd, taking every inch of space in the living room. I don't make it a few feet in before I get hot, I'm elbowed, and I'm hit in the head with a beach ball.

Pen peers over her shoulder, smiling at me, and squeezes my hand before she looks forward again.

"Ladies!" We're greeted by a guy with a slight deep Southern twang, sparkling green eyes, unruly light brown hair, and a well-maintained mustache. His lips stretch into a wide smile, gracing us with the whitest and straightest pair of teeth I've ever seen. He and a few girls stand behind a table, two large glass dispensers filled to the top with some kind of punch. One is filled with blue liquid and the other with red liquid. There are also tons of alcoholic beverages and chasers that litter the table. "Well, if it isn't my favorite Garcia."

"I better be." Pen beams teasingly. "Grayson, these are my friends, Vienna and Josie. Girls, this is Gray. Don't let his pretty face and abs fool you. He has a thing for being *nice* and forgetting your name."

Grayson dramatically gasps, staring at her like she stabbed him in the back. "Now baby G, why are you doing me like that? I'm very good at remembering names. I just get a little distrac..." He trails off, his gaze landing on the chest of a girl who leans over the table to grab a bottle of Pink Whitney.

When she leaves, Pen cocks a brow as if saying *told you so*.

"I didn't forget your names," he defends himself. "That's Vienna and that's Josie."

"No, you forgot we were here," she counters.

"I—" His lips part before they close then part again. "So, Vienna and Josie, what would y'all like to drink?"

"And me," Pen states.

"Yeah right. You're underage and your brother will kill me."

She rolls her eyes. "We're the same age, dumbass. I do what I want." She grabs a cup from the table and fills it up with the blue liquid.

"If Danny asks, I said no." He raises his hands in surrender. "Ladies?"

"How strong are we talking?" Vi questions, gaze bouncing between each glass dispenser and not so subtly tracking down his torso.

"You'll get fucked up on both, black out even. But I can guarantee you'll remember the next day with the blue. Now as for the red, you might end up in another state," he tentatively answers, eyes narrowing on the red liquid. "Actually, that one is still pretty questionable but it's good."

He offers her the friendliest smile, but I feel the subtle hints of flirtiness behind it, and I don't miss the way his eyes rake over her body. It's quick and smooth but leaves a lasting impression as I note the tinge of red that creeps on her deep bronze cheeks.

"Blue," she says.

"Great choice, Vienna," he replies and fills a cup then hands it to her, winking. I don't find anything appealing about it, but Vi eats it up. "What about you, Josie? Feeling adventurous, or do you want to play it safe?"

"I'll get fucked up either way, so there's no playing it safe."

"Yeah, you're right, but hey, one isn't questionable and the other is." He chuckles and shrugs.

"I guess red."

He stares, impressed, and pours my drink into a cup. As he hands it to me, he says, "Danny should be outside."

I stare, perplexed. "Why does that matter to me?"

He shrugs again but smirks. "Just thought you'd want to know."

"I don't," I deadpan, but I can't help the way my stomach flips at the sound of his name.

Gray doesn't say anything else as a few other girls approach the table. We move out of the way and somehow end up back in the living room. We stand in the corner but not for long before "Safaera" by Bad Bunny plays loudly from a speaker.

"Danny's probably DJing," Pen yells over the loud music. "We're about to get a variety of music, thank God. Listen, I'm all for the new stuff, but a little mix never hurt anyone. We have to go dance! Do you dance, Josie?"

I shake my head. I know how, I just don't. "No, but please go. I'm good right now."

"Come on, please?" Vi grabs my arms and attempts to draw me close to the people grinding and shaking ass, but I stay rooted in my spot.

"Maybe the next one." It's not going to happen, but I know they'll persist. It's my first party in a while, and everything already feels a little too much. I shouldn't but I feel a little anxious. My heart is racing and I feel out of body. "Go. I promise I'll be here."

It takes them a moment to go, but when I give them both a gentle shove, they promise to be back and make their way through the crowd until they blend in.

I take a small sip of drink, in hopes it'll ease the way my heart swiftly palpitates. I grimace, squeezing my eyes tight as the strong, burning liquid settles in my stomach. "Fuck." I shudder.

"Let me guess. You got the red."

I don't have to turn to know who's speaking to me. My grimace deepens and I shudder again, but this time it has nothing to do with the drink.

I ignore him, hoping he'll go away, but unfortunately, like a pestering mosquito, he annoyingly invades my space until he's in front of me.

Bryson lazily grins, taking another step closer as I take another back. "I thought I was seeing things, that there was no way. But I'd recognize those tits anywhere." He brazenly drops his gaze to my chest. It stalls there before he idly lifts it back up to me.

Why did I ever date him? Right, because I hate myself.

"Bryson, fuck off."

"Don't be like that. I was just messing around, but you look really hot. I'd almost forgotten how..." He drunkenly chuckles, gaze dipping to my chest again. "That color is doing you wonders. It's a nice change from all the dark colors. You know people were calling you Wednesday," he innocently says but I don't miss the taunt that undertones it.

My chest constricts again and a bead of sweat rolls down my spine. I take another sip and fight the shudder. "By people, do you mean you?"

"Not me, I was always defending you, Josie, but you made it so hard. It doesn't hurt to fucking smile once in a while or do things with your boyfriend." That's a dig at me for not always having sex whenever he asked for it.

I swallow but the glass seems to have returned, making it hard to do so. "Ex."

"We were good for each other, Josie. We could've made things work. We still can."

"Were you good for me when you fucked that girl multiple times? Or told your friends I liked to get passed around because your ego couldn't handle that I broke up with you?" The hurt doesn't reside anymore, only disgust. Someone thought it'd be great to send me a video of Bryson fucking some girl.

He rolls his eyes, huffing out harshly. "For fuck's sake, I fucked up and I was drunk when I said and did that. Why do you always have to bring that up? I made a mistake. I told you I was sorry. She didn't mean anything. I swear I was thinking of you the entire time. What more do you want me to do for you to believe I'm really sorry?"

Right, because that's every girl's dream, to hear their boyfriend's thinking of them while their dick is in someone else.

And he never apologized, but he likes to believe he did.

I stare at him, bored. "To evaporate. That's a great start."

"Jesus fucking Christ, I swear ever since your mom died, you've become a bigger bitch." He closes his eyes, lips flattening in a tight line. "Shit, Josie. I didn't mean—"

My chest painfully squeezes and maybe it's the air that feels too thin, making it hard to inhale. I don't think as I throw my drink at his face.

"Fuck you," I spit out and stalk off. I'm not sure where I'm going, but I walk and pick up the pace until I'm in the backyard.

People pass by me in a blur. I distinctly hear someone calling my name, but I keep walking until I'm standing in front of a fence.

I fan my blistering face, attempting to breathe, but it feels difficult.

Why did I come? I knew I wasn't ready. I don't belong here. I can't breathe.

"Josefine." I feel a warm hand on my bare shoulder, spiking my already accelerated heartbeat, but when I turn, it slowly wanes as I look up at Daniel.

Concern veils his face, his body shielding the world behind him, but still leaving space between us.

"What's wrong? Are you okay?" His eyes search mine, and when he notices that my gaze is drawn to his hand, he drops it.

I don't know how to tell him I wish he hadn't done that. I don't know how to tell him to put it back because it did something to me. Something I can't explain and now my brain is spasming out on the simple gesture that I'm pretty sure was and is insignificant to him.

My mouth opens, but it feels dry, and the words I want to pour out get caught behind the shard of glass in my throat.

"I didn't mean to touch you. I'm sorry," he sincerely says.

"It's okay." I drop my gaze, feeling embarrassed. I just want to stay in the dark and be forgotten. I should've stayed home. "I'm fine. You can leave."

"Are you sure?"

I hesitate before I reply, "Yeah, I'm okay."

"What if...I stay but keep my distance?"

I lift my head. "Why are you always so insistent?"

"Because if I'm not, who will be?" His lips quirk into a small smile.

My stomach somersaults.

Whoa.

"Don't feel obligated. I'm okay."

"It's no obligation. I want to be here."

"Uh, okay then." I tuck my hair behind my ear, finding it a little harder to breathe but for different reasons now.

What the hell is going on?

"I'm so happy you're here, Josefine."

Those words are all it takes to confiscate the little bit of air left in my lungs. I know he's not saying that because I'm here at the party; he's saying that because *I'm here. I'm alive.*

And for a moment, his back to the world, his figure shielding me from it all, his smile that does weird things to my stomach, I feel a bit...fine.

12

DANIEL

MAYBE SHE WANTS TO PURPOSELY STAY IN THE shadows because she thinks that's where she belongs, but that would never work for her because I see her.

I can't point out one singular thing that stands out because there isn't just one—it's her whole. She is light, a blinding color that's hard to ignore. Like a lighthouse guiding you home.

She's complex in her own way, but that doesn't make her any less deserving. She doesn't smile, but that doesn't mean she never has. Her eyes don't spark with life, but I'm sure they once did.

Maybe she thinks she's broken and not worth fixing, or maybe I'm just projecting because that's how I feel.

Broken...lost...empty.

I hide behind smiles and being the life of a party, but I'm nothing but a big fucking fraud.

I wish I would've died that night. Or all the other times.

No you don't, a voice in my head counters.

"You're quiet." Her soft voice pulls me out of my head, shocking me.

I let the smile easily slip on my face. "Miss my voice already?"

The light behind me helps cast a glow around her face and

body, allowing me to see the tiny furrow of her brows. "No, you're just...unnaturally quiet. That normally doesn't happen."

"Aren't you observant," I tease or at least I attempt to, but I think I do a shit job because her brows soften like she's figured something out, but then her face becomes impassive. Clearing my throat, I draw the focus to something else. Something that's actually important. "Can I ask you something?"

"Sure."

"What did you mean by, before the cliff I didn't know who you were but you knew me?"

Ever since she told me, it's been eating at me.

"It's really not a big deal. Just forget about it. It happened a while ago anyway." She tucks a tendril of her wavy hair behind her ear.

"It is to me because I've been trying to figure out what I did to piss you off more than I already do." This time, I genuinely smile and when I see the faintest jerk of her lips, I can't help but feel like I won something. "Come on, Jos, tell me."

"You drove me home one night."

I try to recall that moment, but I'm drawing a blank and she must realize that because she sighs.

"It was about a year and two months ago." She leans against the fence, her gaze focused on the people jumping in the pool. "I'd been drinking that night and Bryson was drunk, so you offered to take me home. You said something about being the DD that night. You spent the entire ride talking about cassette tapes, vinyls, and your favorite artists."

I'm instantly teleported to that night and how I assigned myself the DD. It was Gray's job since he was a freshman. We usually have freshmen or transfers as DDs. But even though I was a sophomore and it wasn't my responsibility, I needed to get out of the house.

"It's really stupid to have gotten mad. The interaction was small. I didn't even speak to you."

"It's not stupid." I also lean against the fence, still making sure

I maintain my distance. "And if it makes you feel better, I wasn't supposed to be the DD. I just needed to get out of the house. My girl—*ex*-girlfriend," I quickly correct myself. I don't know why I emphasize *ex*, but I do. "She had once again accused me of cheating and we got into an argument. It got bad and I knew if I didn't leave, she'd continue arguing with me."

And now thinking about it, I wonder if she knows my ex slept with her ex? I want to ask but I don't, afraid I'll ruin the mood.

"Well, did you?" Her question isn't accusatory but curious.

I can't help my chuckle because something tells me she doesn't know. God, how fucked up is this?

"No. I'll have you know, I'm very and I mean *very* loyal despite what anyone says. I don't remember that night or you because I couldn't stop thinking about the argument and how it spiraled out of control. I couldn't stop thinking about how I felt guilty and relieved that I didn't have to deal with her anymore. I couldn't stop thinking about how shitty of a boyfriend I was because I chose to drive a girl I didn't know, over a girl who'd been my girlfriend for a year. I know you probably think I'm stupid for—"

"I don't," she talks over me. "I don't think anything at all. Actually, I'm not in the place to make assumptions. My last and only relationship had been a total shitshow all because I had bad judgment, so who am I to judge you for what you did?"

"Last and only?" I cringe, wishing I could take that back because I hadn't intended to say that out loud. I shouldn't have drunk tonight.

She sardonically laughs, slouches down to the ground, and glances up at me. "You really don't need to be here. I'm good alone."

"You know." I drop down, sitting next to her. "You really have to stop trying to push me away. The harder the push, the more you make me want to stay."

"In that case, please stay. I could really use the company," she sarcastically says, but I don't miss the smidge of sadness that tones her words.

"See, I thought you'd never ask." I happily say.

Her mouth drops and for a second, I get lost in the shape of her lips and how full they are. I clench my jaw, shifting my gaze away, but then I get lost on how her face shines from the array of colored lights hanging all over the backyard. There's this effervescent gleam about her. Like a moth to a flame, I can't stop looking at her.

"Did you just use reverse psychology on me, Garcia?"

I inhale a deep, quiet breath, my lungs filling with the faintest hint of lavender and vanilla. I'm tempted to do it again, but I snap out of it, realizing I still haven't answered.

"Some people call it that, others would call it getting played."

"What can I do so you'll leave me alone?" She stretches her legs out, crossing one ankle over the other.

I mirror her position. "I really like all those shades of green."

"Don't change the subject," she chastises. "Answer the question."

With Josefine, I feel like I'm standing on a fine line. She's on one side while I'm on the other. It'd be easy to step back, stay safe, and keep my distance.

But I really don't want to do that.

"Did you wear it for me?" That's bold and too forward of a question, but I can't help myself.

She scoffs and side-eyes me, brows drawn in and eyes filled with unfiltered judgment. "Self-centered much?"

I attentively observe the bright green that glimmers on her eyelids and the rhinestones that are scattered around her eyes. "You didn't answer the question."

"I didn't know you were going to be here." She pries her gaze away and stares straight ahead. "Weird to assume I'd wear anything for you when I don't know you."

"You know I'm a shortstop. You know how tall I am. You know my friends call my Danny, which you have yet to do.

Annnnd you know my favorite color is green. I would say you know me." I knock my knee against hers, watching her keenly.

She twists the ring on her middle finger, dropping her gaze to where my knee touched hers, then stares up at me. The mask she wears is impenetrable, so it's hard to decipher what could be going on in her head.

I wonder what I need to do to see behind the mask. I've no doubt this is the real Josefine, but I know there's more, and I want to find out all the things that make her who she is.

"I don't know the specific shade," she softly says.

"I don't have a specific shade," I answer just as softly as if we were sharing a secret.

I truly don't but that changes today because my favorite shade is whatever Josie wears. And today happens to be a combination of all the green hues on her bikini top.

Lime green. Yellow green. Dark green.

"We shouldn't be friends," she wistfully says.

"Why not?" I inch a little closer, but still leave enough distance so I don't hover.

The light she was just exuding, dims. Even though I'm not touching her, I feel her tense and shift uncomfortably.

I stiffen, my heart twisting painfully at the thought she still might want to end it all.

"You don't want to waste your time hearing this."

"Nothing about this is a waste of time. Talk to me. Are you having those thoughts again?" I fiddle with the tiny safety pin on my chain.

"Am I suicidal? Is that what you want to know?" Her words sound so hollow, but ingesting them feels deep; they're hard to absorb.

"Yes." I hold my breath.

"No, I'm not suicidal. I'm just..."

"Just what? Talk to me, Jos," I plead.

"Empty." She tips her head up, and I watch as the column of her throat bobs. "I'm not saying that because I want you to feel bad for me and I certainly don't need you to stick around to make me feel better. I just don't know how to not feel, but it is what it is. You should probably leave now. Trust me, you'll end up hating yourself if you don't."

Given the circumstances, I don't know how to tell her that ever since I saw her again, it feels like a switch has been flipped up. I don't know how to express that or how to begin to explain to her what that even means because I don't understand it.

"Give me until the end of the semester."

She looks up at me, cocking her head to the side, staring at me, confused. "What?"

"Give me until the end of the semester to help you fill that emptiness. If it doesn't work, I'll leave you alone if you want to be alone that badly, but until then, let me help you."

She laughs humorlessly. "You don't know how to give up, do you?"

"What can I say? My middle name is *Jesus*." I chuckle, hoping it masks the hollowness behind it. "Let me try."

"You'll regret it," she announces, already defeated.

Did she somehow get closer, or did I? I only scooted an inch, or was it more?

Why am I even focusing on that?

"That's not going to happen. I promise." And I mean that.

"We'll see..."

I don't know who gave up on her, but I know I won't.

13

JOSEFINE

"I really don't want to hear that." Pen scrunches her nose, lips curling in disgust.

"I'm sorry but I'm just stating facts. Your brother is fine." Vi looks at me from the mirror as she washes her hands as if she were asking me to back her up.

Pen also looks at me from the toilet, where she's currently sitting. I had no idea we were at that level of comfort, but they're also very tipsy, borderline drunk, so I don't think they really care.

I'm leaned against the wall, attempting to maintain my balance. When I was with Daniel, I lost track of time and forgot the girls were still inside. They found me and dragged me back inside. They grilled me with questions on why I left, how I ended up with Daniel, and gave me a new cup that they kept refilling.

I didn't really tell them anything because the last thing I want is for them to pity me. I'm the idiot who decided to give Bryson a shot despite the million warnings in my head and gut not to do so.

I just told them I got hot and bumped into Daniel as I was going outside.

Shrugging, I glance down and blink a few times as my vision doubles. "I mean…Vi isn't wrong."

I leave it at that because I don't want to tell Pen what I really think about her brother. And I'm certain I'm bordering on drunk. If I open my mouth, I'm afraid I'll say something like it took everything in me not to glance at his abs when I was with him, or that he has a nice smile, or that he has hair I'd like to run my hands through.

As quick as the thoughts come, I squash them down. My inhibitions are limited and I really don't want to do something stupid like admit out loud that Daniel is hot.

The flush of the toilet and Pen's loud groan has me lifting my head, and I notice that they're both looking at me. *Did I say that out loud?*

Vienna lazily smirks, her glazed eyes idly shifting from Pen back to me. "You think Daniel's hot? Do you like him?" she drunkenly singsongs as she stands next to me.

I shake my head, but regret it as everything spins. "No, he's just...ugh, it doesn't matter. Stop looking at me like that. I promise I'm not into your brother," I say to Pen. "He's nice and overly insistent but we're...I don't know...getting along. We have a class together and we're paired together because of that class and—"

Pen giggles as she washes her hands. "You don't need to explain yourself to me. I really don't care if you like him or if you..." She shudders dramatically. "Mess around with him. I just don't want to know the details. So please, please, please, spare me from them because the girls on the cheer team have no filter and I constantly hear their feral thoughts about him."

"I have no intention of sleeping with him." But why am I thinking about it now?

She stifles a laugh, the expression on her face saying, *I've heard that before.* "Whatever happens between you and my brother, stays between—"

"Please don't spare me any of the details. I'm here for it. So don't be afraid to share anything with me," Vi interjects, her dopey smile stretching from ear to ear.

"As long as I'm not there," Pen quickly adds. The terrorized look on her face almost makes me laugh, but I don't. Though Vi doesn't hold back, she tosses her head back and laughs. "I'm serious. That includes your filthy dreams and fantasies about him."

"Nothing is going to happen. I promise, I'm not into and never will be into Daniel." I twist the knob and pull the door open. The last words get lost by the intensity of the volume of those who are singing "Knife Talk" by Drake as it plays downstairs.

I amble toward the stairs but stop when I don't feel the girls behind me. When I peer over my shoulder, they're looking at each other like they're sharing a secret. Knowing smiles then are directed at me, and something mischievous shines in their eyes.

I want to ask them what that's about but when the song switches to "Mo Bamba" by Sheck Wes, the girls are rushing down the stairs and hauling me with them.

"No more Danny talk! We need shots!" Pen announces.

"Don't worry, you can talk about Danny all you want to me." Vi winks, laughing as Pen shoots her a glare. "Details included."

It takes us longer to get past the crowd in the living room as there's more people. I can't even hear the girls as everyone sings—well, more like screams—the song at the top of their lungs.

Once we make it to the kitchen, Vi grabs three mini Solo cups and manages to find a bottle of tequila on the counter. She fills each cup to the brim and before I can question her about how we'll be feeling the next day, she shoots me this *don't think about it, just drink* look. And then she pours another and another.

As the third shot hits the bottom of my stomach, the entire house becomes louder than before, singing the four words that gets everyone going. More alcohol is brought up from another room and keg stands are placed in the middle of the kitchen.

The fourth shot has my vision tripling. I have to set my cup on the counter, shaking my head that I'll be black-out drunk in the next few seconds if I drink any more.

The girls giggle uncontrollably and drag me back to the living room as the next song comes on.

Everything's happening too fast and before I can tell them that I really don't want to dance and pull back, someone bumps into me and almost knocks me down.

A hand grabs my wrist, stabilizing me, before my face meets the ground.

"Shit, I'm sor—" Daniel looks apologetic at first, but when he realizes it's me, his face lights up. "Sorry, it's tight in here."

"That's what he said," I snort but cover my mouth a few seconds later. Not sure if he heard what I said, but at the knowing grin, I know he did.

Daniel's eyebrows hike up, his lips shifting into a cunning smirk. There was hardly any space between us, but when he tugs my wrist, pulling me forward, I can't help but let myself close the remaining distance. His bare chest is almost pressed to mine, and if I wasn't already intoxicated, the scent of his cologne finishes the job because I feel extremely delirious right now.

He leans down, until I feel his warm breath at the shell of my ear, his thumb gently grazing the curve from my wrist down to my thumb. "I wouldn't know anything about that but..."

He might be just as drunk as I am because I don't think sober Daniel would say that, at least to me. The hint of beer on his breath tells me just as much.

If it was someone else, I'd feel repulsed, but I oddly find myself standing straighter until my chest is pressed against him. "But what? Do you want to find out?" The words spill out slow and slurred. My head becomes a jumbled, fuzzy mess, my face numbs, and my entire body tingles with anticipation.

My eyes widen as a pulse settles between my legs and my heart stutters out of control.

"You're drunk," he points out and thank God because it sobers me momentarily. Like a bucket of water, the heat is doused. "But I want you to dance with me."

"As long as you behave." I wince internally, feeling embarrassed. What the hell was that? That didn't sound flirty, but why am I trying to flirt with him?

"That won't be a problem, Josefine." His voice deepens, sending a shiver to scatter down my spine. "Unless..."

"Unless?" I say, almost breathless.

"Can I touch you?"

My breath hitches and my nipples harden. "Where?"

"I want to put my arm around your back. Can I?"

"Yeah."

I feel a zap shoot throughout my body as his finger brushes over the skin above the waistband of my skirt. I swallow hard as he in the most torturous way, drags his fingers across the small of my back until his palm finds the other side of my waist. He holds a firm grip on it, fingers gently but securely holding me.

Our bodies are pressed against each other, and there's no space left between us.

Breathe. "Are you not going to tell me?"

"Tell you what?" I hear the smug smile in his voice.

I roll my eyes. "Unless what?"

"Desperate?" His fingers dig into my skin, searing me.

"Insufferable and cocky," I grunt, doing my best not to let the shudder that's built up expel from my body. "You're really starting to get on my nerves."

"Was I not already?" He lets go of my wrist and snakes the other behind my back.

I clamp my mouth shut. This should be the moment I bolt, but I don't. And it has nothing to do with the physical hold he has on me, but the weird mental hold my brain has on him. I feel linked to him and it's fucking with my mind.

"I say stupid shit when I'm drunk. You're not missing out," he says after a beat.

"Just when you're drunk? Tell me something I don't know," I quip.

Daniel looks down at me, a self-assured look on his face. "Dance with me, Josie," he demands before he's spinning me around, my back flushed against his chest, his large hands splayed in front of my stomach.

My heart slams against my rib cage at the sudden movement, but my body burns when I meet the girls' stares. Pen smiles at me but grimaces at her brother. Vi is giving me a thumbs-up and this *fuck him* look.

That's not going to happen, but I swear whoever's in charge of the music must be really horny because they're all the kind of songs you grind and shake your ass to.

I'm going along to the beat of music, relishing the feel of Daniel's calloused hand grazing my stomach, his hot breath next to my ear, and occasional *stupid* words that leave his mouth. Though they're far from that, and now I'm burning up and it has nothing to do with the way we're dancing or how crowded it is.

"I need a drink," I announce, separating myself from him, and the moment I do, something feels off, but I try not to dwell on it. I don't wait or watch to see if he follows me. I'm off before I can put thought into the weird feeling.

I search for a clean cup in the kitchen, but I can't find any, but then Daniel hands me a cold-water bottle.

"Thanks." I take it and uncap it, chugging almost half of it. A stray drop glides down my chin and clings to my jaw, almost falling, but he catches it with his thumb.

"Sorry." He rubs his thumb and pointer finger together, smearing the liquid between his fingers. "I should've asked."

"It's okay." I tuck my hair behind my ear and hate that I've picked up on that nervous habit again. "I think I'm going to go home now."

"Let me take you home."

"I came with Pen and Vi."

"They get nicknames, but I don't?" he asks jokingly.

"They kind of insisted." I nonchalantly shrug.

"So did I," he counters. "Do I need to beg on my knees to make it happen?"

The corners of my lips uncontrollably twitch and his eyes

track the flicker before it's gone. That makes his smile widen and my heart flutter.

I take another sip, not sure how to respond to that.

"I can make it happen. Just say the word or snap your finger. That works too."

Breathe. "I—"

"Danny, hey. I've been looking for you." A girl stands next to him, a girl I remember all too well. The very same one who appeared in the video with Bryson.

She wraps her arms around his waist and stares up at him, smiling sweetly at him.

Wow, she was pretty in the video, but it didn't do her any justice because she's even prettier in person.

The flutters freeze and disintegrate. My chest expands until it aches and when it deflates, the cycle repeats.

He removes his hand and takes a few steps back, but the hurt look on her face tells me everything I need to know. She likes him, that much is clear.

She smothers the look and offers me a friendly smile, but something about it feels fake. "Sorry, I hope I'm not interrupting."

"Not at all. I'm actually leaving."

"I'm going to take her home," Daniel rapidly says, standing by my side, looking irritated.

"No need. I'm leaving with the girls. Thanks for the water." I quickly exit the kitchen and in no time, I find the girls. Thankfully, we're all on the same page about leaving and all head out together until we're stopped by Angel.

"I'm taking you all home and I don't want to hear it, Penelope."

She folds her arms against her chest. "I'm going to get a Lyft. You don't need to—"

"I'm taking you all home. Don't argue with me," he sternly says.

"I'm not arguing."

"Good. Let's go."

"Whatever. You're going to get us something to eat."

"The fuck I look like?"

"Like a dumbass," she snarkily tosses over her shoulder at him as she grabs my hand and Vi's and drags us out the door. "Hurry up, we're hungry."

There's a small part of me that wants to look back, but there's a voice in my head telling me he's not back there. And because the voice has never been wrong, I don't look back.

Looking back would've only instigated the disappointment that resides in the corner of my head.

14

JOSIE

I don't usually fall victim to being easily influenced, but tonight, I didn't fall, I willingly took the drinks and shots. Now I'm paying the price.

My head is still spinning, my body feels heavy and sluggish, and my balance has long left me. I'm swaying and tripping over my own feet as I stumble into my dark house.

I don't bother with the lights or attempting to take my shoes off.

Why did I wear high-tops again?

Ambling into the living room, I throw my phone and keys onto the table and drop onto the couch, face down, reveling in how cool it is.

Exhaling a heavy sigh, I close my eyes and attempt not to think about Daniel, his persistence to be around, and the girl that had her arm around him. Unfortunately, I do a shit job. The last thing on my mind before I fall asleep are those soft amber eyes and her arm.

The long chime of the doorbell pierces the dead-silent house. The sound echoes throughout, waking and frightening me.

I quickly scurry up to sit, searching for my phone until it

dawns on me that I threw it on the coffee table. I reach for it in the darkness and squint when the bright light blinds me.

With bleary eyes, I read the time on my phone: **2:36 a.m.**

Though that isn't what has me blinking repeatedly until my vision focuses, has my heart slamming against my rib cage, or is scattering my thoughts all over the place.

It's the four messages from Daniel.

> Daniel: Are you awake?

> Daniel: I found something that belongs to you. I can wait until Monday to give it to you, but if you want it now, I can take it to you

> Daniel: I feel like this might be very important, so I'm going to take it now

> Daniel: I'm here

That last message was sent two minutes ago.

My fingers hover over the keys as I contemplate whether I want to reply to him. As far as I know, I didn't drop or leave anything. I only took my phone and my house key, and I have those with me.

I almost type to leave whatever he found on the doorstep, but my fingers work of their own accord, typing what they please.

> Me: I think you got the wrong person

> Daniel: No, it belongs to you

> Me: I'm pretty sure it doesn't

The thought of him accidentally bringing me something that belongs to another girl does weird things to my chest. But more than that, I feel a flash of anger coursing through me. It makes me wonder if he confused me with her, if he was with her after I left and mixed us up. Because Bryson did that.

My phone buzzes in my palm, interrupting my thoughts and horrid memories.

> Daniel: I promise it's yours
>
> Daniel: Let me give it to you and I promise I'll leave

Huffing out a harsh breath, I stalk to the door, unlock it, and pull it open. The light fixture that's pinned to the wall helps slightly illuminate Daniel's figure. He stands on the other side, now wearing a backwards cap, still shirtless, wearing swim shorts, socks that reach his midcalf, and sneakers. The gold chain with the safety pin somewhat glints in the darkness.

"What is it?" I ask, getting straight to the point. The sooner he leaves, the sooner I can go back to sleep and pretend like I didn't enjoy having his hands around me earlier.

He digs into his pocket and opens his palm. I scoff a laugh because I see nothing until a small glint catches the corner of my eye. I turn my phone light on and stare, dumbfounded, at the tiny round rhinestone sitting in the middle of his palm.

"You drove all the way over here to bring me that? How do you even know it's mine? The girl who had her arm around you had some on too." I stare at him, irked and bemused.

"I didn't drive, I, uh, ran here." He scratches the nape of his neck. I peer around him and only spot my car in the driveway, which shocks and somehow melts the frustration away. "And I know it's yours and not hers because you have ten of these on each eye. You're missing one right"—he lifts a finger and points beneath my right eye, faintly touching the skin—"there."

I don't want to stand here and act oblivious, but I'm having a hard time grasping the fact that Daniel counted the rhinestones on my face. I don't know when he had the time to do that. And he *ran* here. That explains the little beads of sweat clinging to his temple.

"Oh." I bite the inside of my cheek, hating the way it warms.

"You didn't—you shouldn't have bothered. I was just going to throw them away."

"Oh," he chuckles sheepishly, slips the rhinestone back in his pocket, lifts his cap, and runs his fingers through his hair. "I guess I should've waited until Monday."

I fidget with my ring. "You should probably get back to—"

He laughs this time, but it holds no humor, just bitterness. It shocks me because I've never heard him sound like that before. Granted, I've not known him for long, but he's always so happy.

He sighs deeply and exhaustedly, and again he removes his cap and runs his fingers through his hair. God, why does he keep doing that? And why do I so badly want to touch his hair?

"I didn't want to say anything because it wasn't the time and I figured maybe it wasn't something you wanted to know. But the girl who stood next to me is my *ex-girlfriend*, Amanda."

My jaw goes slack. It physically drops and it takes me a few seconds to recover, and Daniel must know that much because he doesn't speak—probably letting me absorb the information or connect the dots. Though I don't need to. I recognized her the moment I laid eyes on her.

"The one who—"

"Slept with Bryson," he says.

"Wow..."

"Yup..."

"Did you get—"

"The video?" He sardonically laughs. "Yeah. I got it."

"Oh..."

"Yeah..." He tucks his hands in his pockets, shrugging and chuckling. I also find it comical, but I don't outwardly show it.

"So...not that I care, but she was very comfortable around you."

He rolls his eyes irately. "She likes to believe we're going to fix things and get back together. She likes to pretend she didn't cheat on me with my teammate. And she likes to pretend she *didn't* know he had a girlfriend."

Now I understand why she was staring up at him like she was in love with him and why he was quick to remove her arm and stand next to me.

"Wait, so she knew—" I stop mid-sentence, remembering how Bryson insisted she didn't know about me because he didn't tell her. "I can't believe I believed that fucking piece of shit. God, I'm so stupid."

"Don't say that. You're not stupid. He—"

"No, I am because he said she didn't know. He was very insistent about it and because I was over it, I believed him. I didn't want to be that person. I didn't want to be the girl who blamed another girl because her boyfriend is a fucking—fuck!"

I inhale a breath and blow it out harshly as I stalk back into my house. I faintly hear Daniel ask what I'm doing. When I march back out with a knife and my car keys, his eyes go round.

After I shut and lock my door, I turn and see the shock on his face swiftly shift and become grave, but that doesn't stop me from walking past him.

"So, we need to have alibis and shovels, and we need to make it quick. Also, we need to keep the blood to a minimum because you know that's hard to get rid of, or at least it's what I've seen in the shows."

I halt in my tracks and spin around. He almost crashes into me, but he manages to stop in time. "What are you talking about?"

"Are we not murdering Bryson?" he asks casually, but I hear the hint of amusement and confusion in his voice.

I cock a brow. "We?"

"I got your back, Jos," he states, no amusement or confusion in his voice this time.

My heart does that weird thing again. I'm almost tempted to stab myself in the chest to make the rapid beats stop, but I don't want to traumatize him again.

"I'm not murdering anyone. If I'm going to keep existing, I'm not going to do it behind bars."

It's meant to come off as a joke, but I deliver it too dryly. I internally wince, but Daniel smiles, decreasing my desire to slip into the corner of darkness.

"*We* would be behind bars. Bryson's not much taller than you, but, and I hate to admit this, he's pretty strong. I'll knock his ass out for you and you can do all the stabbing. Not a big fan of blood." He scrunches his nose.

The corner of my lip jerks upward and before it disappears, his gaze lands on it and it stalls there briefly before his eyes lift again to meet mine.

Surely there must be heart condition problems running in my family I don't know about because the way my heart is racing is terrifying.

"I don't want to kill him. I'm going to slash his tires. It won't hurt him physically, but it'll hurt nonetheless. And that's good enough for me. I'm sure you know how much he loves his Audi."

Aside from how much Bryson loves himself, that car comes in second.

He nods, grinning. "Remind me to never piss you off."

"I'm still a little drunk if I'm being honest with you. I'm not sure I'd do this sober and I might regret it in the morning, but he didn't give a fuck, so why should I?" I lift both shoulders apathetically as I start walking backward.

"I'm going with you," he adamantly states.

"Uh, no, you're not."

"Uh, yes, I am."

"Daniel."

"Josefine."

I drop my head back, groaning. "No. The last thing I need is for you to get in trouble. It'll be quick anyway."

His grin broadens. "You care about me?"

"You and your assumptions. You're an athlete and I assume you're on a scholarship. If you get arrested, you'll lose it. So go home. I'll see you on Monday." I go to walk away but stop in my tracks, peering over my shoulder. "If you want to send me her address, I'm more than happy to also pay her car a little visit." I wave the knife and then pretend to slash the imaginary tire.

He throws his head back and laughs. It's hearty and the deep timbre feels like it's touching me, the vibration shocking every nerve in my body. I shouldn't like how his laugh sounds, but I do, a lot.

"We should start with one and maybe do hers another day. They'll know it was us if it happens on the same night."

Hmm, I hadn't thought of that. "Okay, well, I'll see you—"

"I'm going with you. This isn't up for debate. Plus you said you're still kind of drunk. I'll drive. I burned off all the alcohol on the run anyway."

"Daniel." I suck in a breath. "I don't need you to come—"

"Do I need to speak in Spanish to you to get you to understand?"

"How do you know I understand Spanish?"

"For"—he clears his throat—"research purposes, I saw one of your interviews." He smiles sweetly at me, melting my hesitation for a second.

What's wrong with me? Am I that big of a loser that a smidge of attention from someone doing *research* on me makes me feel strangely acknowledged?

"Well?" I impatiently tap my foot.

He takes one step forward. "*Voy a ir contigo, aunque quieras o no. Y no discutas conmigo porque está conversión ya ha terminado. Sí me entendiste esta vez?*"

Wow. "*¿Estás seguro?*"

"*Contigo, siempre.*"

My lips involuntary part open. My brain quickly attempts to scramble for something to say. It even sends signals to brush it off, walk away, to do something other than stand here and look stupid as I stare at him with stupefaction.

Two words, that's all they are, but they feel like more than that. They make my heart light up, as though a wick has been lit.

The tiny flame warms and illuminates the middle of my cold, black heart.

I shouldn't put too much thought into words that could be trivial, but something about them makes me feel...something. I don't know if it's because they genuinely sound so sincere, but I'm having a hard time finding a flaw.

Words. They're just words. Snap out of it.

"If you get in trouble, that's on you." I don't mean it because I'd hate myself more than I do now if he did.

"The consequences will be worth it," he says. "I need you to grab another knife. Preferably a box cutter or something you wouldn't find in your kitchen."

I stare at him quizzically. "Why?"

"Because..." His smile turns devilish. "We're going to slash the last tire with the box cutter and leave it there. So when he calls the insurance, they'll think he did it himself. It might or might not be considered insurance fraud. I guess we'll find out..."

"How do you know that?"

"Angel happens to be a little petty."

"A little?"

He shrugs innocently. "Don't ask questions. Just go get it."

I could ask more questions, but something tells me he's just going to be vague. So, I do as he says.

"Give me your keys," he asks once I'm back out.

"I may be slightly drunk, but I'm not stupid. I wasn't going to drive there. There'd be nowhere to park and if there are cameras, they'll catch my car."

"So what were you planning..." His voice drifts off as I point to my bicycle. "No problem, you can stand on the pegs."

"No way. You can stand on the—"

"Jos, I'm over two hundred pounds," he states matter-of-factly. I know that but I don't say it out loud because he'll know, I too did *research* on him. "So we're done arguing about this. Let's go."

I shouldn't like how deep and affirmative his voice sounds, but I do.

He doesn't waste time to grab my bicycle and get on it, while I still stand in my same spot. "I know you probably want revenge because he slept with your girlfriend—"

"*Ex*," he emphasizes like he did earlier.

"Right, *ex*," I emphasize just the same. "But you can find another way to get back at him for sleeping with her."

"I'm not doing this because he slept with Amanda. Don't get me wrong, I was pissed at first, but I genuinely don't care anymore. I'm doing this because he fucked with you and *that*, I'm not okay with," he gravely says.

I think the flame is burning a little hotter. I need to find a way to put it out.

"*Oh*." I amble toward him. "Okay."

I set the knives in the basket that hangs on the handlebars then stand behind him. I know how to climb on, but it's the thought of touching and being so close to him that makes me hesitate.

When he peers over his shoulder, I wave off the hesitation and stand on the pegs, my hands on his firm, broad shoulders and my front almost pressed to his back.

In silence, we make our way to his house, but after a few minutes, I break through it.

"If it makes you feel better, she was faking those moans. Though I'm sure you knew that..." I trail off, realizing what I said and not liking the visual that plays in my head. It's not Bryson and Amanda I'm picturing but Daniel and her. I squeeze my eyes tight, blocking the image. "And I'm certain he was jealous of you now that I think of it."

"How would you know that?"

"He'd always make a comment in passing about you but I never—"

"No, not that. I mean her faking the moans. Did you have to fake them too?"

My eyebrows skyrocket at his bold question. "Yeah, I did."

"Wait." He comes to a complete stop, and looks over his shoulder and up at me. Our faces are just an inch apart from each other; we're so close I can feel the warmth of his breath on my chin. "Are you serious?"

Breathe. You've been close to a lot of guys before. None like him though.

I nod. "And his dick isn't as big as she shouted in the video. She really put on a show for him because I promise he's not that great. I bet you're better—" I clamp my mouth shut, wincing. "Forget I said that. Let's go."

Thankfully, he doesn't comment and continues pedaling until we arrive at his street. I tell him to leave the bike a few feet away before I climb off.

"I am, by the way," he quietly says, not looking down at me as we walk side by side.

My brows draw together in confusion. "You are what?"

"Better," he confidently and arrogantly states.

I scoff, rolling my eyes. "Tone the cockiness down. I didn't mean to say that. I just meant—"

"I know what you meant, and I know my abilities."

"Right," I drawl.

"I'm more than welcome to show you."

I almost falter in my step. "Th-that's not necessary."

For some weird reason I do believe that he'd be better, but I'm not going to say that out loud. And I don't want to keep engaging in this conversation, not because it's making me uncomfortable, but because I'm afraid of what I'll say.

The alcohol is still buzzing in my system, and my inhibitions are at an all-time low. The words, *well show me* could easily slip out of my mouth.

"I'm kidding." He softly elbows my arm, amusement dripping from his tone. "Don't take me seriously."

Of course he is. He's Daniel Garcia, the guy who's got his life together. Why would he want to sleep with me? I'm a fucking train wreck.

15

JOSIE

"Are you okay?" Daniel asks as he pulls into my driveway and parks my bike.

Once I can, I step off the pegs and grab my knife and keys from the basket. "Yeah, I'm fine. It's just a tiny cut."

I didn't think as I stabbed into his first tire angrily, but that was a stupid move. Once the knife punctured the rubber, air blasted out rapidly and I nicked my finger. The cut was tiny and drew a little blood, but you would've thought I was massively bleeding by the way Daniel reacted. I'd be lying if I said it wasn't a little endearing.

It didn't take long for me to figure out the best way to slash his tires and not cut myself. I was done in less than ten minutes while Daniel stood there and watched over me like a bodyguard. He also said encouraging, affirmative words that oddly stirred something in me. The effect was extremely rewarding. I felt invigorated and validated. Sure, slashing tires isn't the mature thing to do. I could've handled my anger differently, but I didn't, and Daniel didn't stop me either.

"The movies make it look easy." He stands in front of me and carefully grabs my hand so casually, I don't move. He raises my hand, inspecting my fingers, and I hold my breath. I don't know why but I do. "Do you want the good or bad news first?"

I muffle my chuckle, confused by his question. "The bad?"

He delicately turns my hand every which way, inspecting my finger from every possible angle. "The bad news is that you won't be able to cut limes or lemons for a little bit. And I hope you have Band-Aids because you'll have to wear one. For a day or two, give or take."

The corner of my mouth jerks up and in a flash his eyes gravitate to my lips, but he still keeps my hand in the air.

"And the good?"

"Um..." His eyes lift back up to mine and they stay there. "You get to keep all your fingers."

An avalanche of butterflies breaks loose. Maybe it's the flutters, the hold he has on my eyes and hand, or the link I have with him, but for the first time in a long time, both corners of my lips lift.

I'm not sure I can categorize it as a smile. I'm sure most people wouldn't call it that, but I'm going with it.

His gaze immediately locks in on my lips and either he pulls me forward or I shift, I'm not sure which, but I'm closer to him than I was. I should pull away, break the trance that I seem to be in, but I can't.

"That's good to hear. I don't know what or who I'd be without my finger."

"You'd still be you and that's all that matters," he softly says.

Don't stab yourself. Don't stab yourself, I repeat because my heart is racing crazily fast.

I'm thankful for the cool breeze that sweeps by us because I shiver. It had nothing to do with the air, but everything to do with the guy who's set my heart aflame.

I remove my hand and take a few steps back, folding my arms against my chest, as if I were cold and not actually burning up.

"I'm sorry. It's probably fifty degrees and you're still wearing...

that." The tension in his voice is resounding. Like he struggled to get that single word out.

I don't know what that was about and I don't want to find out. I'm getting carried away with words.

"I should get going." He walks me to my door.

Looking at my door then at him, I make the decision before I think it through. "Do you want to spend the night?"

Shock mars his face. "You want me to stay?"

"I have a few spare bedrooms and it's late and you were drinking." I unlock and open my door.

He goes quiet, eyes darting to the inside of my dark house then back to me. "Are you sure? I really don't mind running back to my house. It's not that far."

"Do you really want to do that?"

"I will if I have to, but I'll do whatever you want me to do."

"I just want you to be safe."

A smile so fucking warm and sweet blooms on his face, inciting the flame to grow. "Then I'll stay."

I motion for him to go in, but he refuses until I go in first.

"Your room is this way." I lead him up the stairs then down the hall where my room is also located. "I don't have a change of clothes, but there's a robe in the bathroom and a toothbrush underneath the sink and a few other toiletries. You can use whatever you want. Mom...always stocked up for guests. You're also welcome to shower if you'd like." I show him around the bed and bathroom and almost bump into him when I turn around, but he manages to grab me before that happens.

"I got you." He smiles down at me before he releases me.

I take a few steps back. "My room is actually across the hall. If you want anything from the kitchen, you're more than welcome to grab it, but I should warn you, I don't have much."

He stares at me strangely. "Didn't you just buy a bunch of groceries?" He raises his hands in surrender. "I promise I'm not judging."

"I actually bought already made meals. I don't know how to

cook, and sometimes finding the time or energy is...well...it's just faster, and my life is busy so I buy them."

Daniel nods understandingly and doesn't ask about my lack of cooking skills. Thankfully, he doesn't read between the lines of me not finding the energy. Because the reality is that some days I feel so overwhelmed with the emptiness I feel inside, I don't have it in me to do anything.

"No worries." He smiles like he always does. "I'm not hungry anyway. It's probably three or four in the morning?"

"Something like that." I blow out a breath and take a few more steps back. "Well, I'm going to get ready for bed. Good night."

I walk away as I hear him say, "Good night, Jos."

I'm not sure if it was the shower, the fact that someone since Mom passed away is sleeping here, or that it's Daniel just a few feet away from me, but I can't sleep. And because I'm tired of tossing and turning, I put on a one-piece, grab a towel, and head out of my room.

But I don't make it very far because when I swing my door open, so does Daniel.

I gasp and he curses under his breath.

"Sorry, did I wake you?" he asks.

"No, I can't sleep. Are you..." I trail off, squinting since it's so dark and drag my gaze down to his bare feet. He doesn't have his shoes on, so I guess he's not leaving. "Can't sleep?" I ask instead.

"No and I got thirsty." It may be dark, but I swear it felt like he raked his gaze over me. "Is that a towel?"

"Yeah, I'm going for a swim. Figured since I can't sleep, I might as well do something than just lie around. Do you want to come?" I shift from one foot to the other, feeling like I'm on edge.

It's not a bad thing, but inviting him to do something I usually do alone is not something I do. Especially when it happens to be him of all people. My body and mind react differently to him, and I'm not sure if I like it or not.

Silence envelops us and I figure he's trying to decide how to say no until he speaks up. "I'll watch you instead."

"Don't feel obligated to come. I might be up for a while."

"Then it's a good thing I have no plans this weekend. And it's not an obligation because I want to be there with you."

My heart patters. "Okay."

We walk side by side in a comfortable silence. There's something nice about being with him. There's no pressure to fill the void, and he doesn't add mindless conversation for the sake of getting me to talk.

I don't feel worried, and I'm not overthinking whether my silence is making him uncomfortable. Mom, Bryson, Christian Novak, and many others made comments about my lack of smiles and small talk. One thing they all agreed on was that my *resting bitch face* made others wary of wanting to be around me.

Once he grabs his water and we're outside, Daniel sits on the edge of the pool, sinking his feet on the side that's shallow. Despite the lights that surround the inside of the pool, I can't really see his face, but I didn't miss his hesitation as we stepped out. Or the vigilance in his voice for me to be careful as I set my stuff next to him.

Swimming is second nature to me, but I'm useless to anything outside of it.

I could make a list of all the things I'm shit at, but it would never end. But one thing that has always been on top of said list is people. I never know what to say or how to say what I want to say to them.

I still don't understand how Vi and Pen still talk to me, but that's a question for another day.

So why I'm sitting next to Daniel, even though this could end horribly wrong, is beyond me. I know something is wrong. I can feel his tension, and from my periphery I see how he wrings his towel with his fingers. He's also looking down at the water, and hasn't said a word.

I want to ask what's wrong, but what if he tells me, and I

don't know how to respond to that? Most people never tell me what's wrong with them, but Daniel isn't most people.

"If you want to help me, you're going to have to let me help you" is what I settle on after a few minutes.

"Huh?"

"If you're going to help me with my issue, I might as well help you with yours. And don't give me that bullshit excuse that you're too busy and can't commit because if you are, you might as well not help me at all."

Was that too abrasive? Shit, I'm already failing.

"My issue?" I hear the humor in his voice.

I sigh with relief. "Not knowing how to swim."

"You don't need to waste your time on me, and it's not necessary. I don't usually get in the water, so it's not like I'll ever... drown." His voice sounds so dry despite how amused he's trying to make it sound.

"Then I don't want your help."

He slightly turns his body to face me. "Don't be like that. I promise I'm not worth the time or trouble."

"I'm not your problem to fix, yet here you are for whatever reason trying to fix something that isn't fixable."

He reaches out, covering his large palm over mine. "I'm here because despite what you believe, you're not a problem and you're not broken. I'm not trying to fix you. I just want you to know that I'm here for you. As a friend, as a person, as whatever you want me to be. I'm here for you, Josefine. Whoever or whatever made you believe that is wrong."

I feel a pang in my chest, the strike so fierce it knocks the air out of me.

"Believe me," he desperately adds.

I look away from him because he doesn't see or understand that I'm really a lost cause. In a few weeks, he'll give up and decide I'm not worth it. I know I'm not.

"You have to let me help you. It doesn't matter if you get in the water or not. It's important to know how to swim."

"I don't have time to—"

"But you have time for me?" My own question shocks me because I never thought I'd hear those words coming out of my mouth.

"Yes." He doesn't miss a beat.

My breath hitches and I swear my heart collapses.

"Daniel..." I draw my hand away, letting his palm rest on top of my thigh, and place it on top of his. "Please let me teach you."

His gaze drops to our hands and his throat bobs, before he shifts his attention back on me. "Okay, I'm all yours."

He gently squeezes my thigh, eliciting goose bumps. Before I act upon my strange thoughts, I pull back and let go of his hand. I'm not going to mistake his kindness for anything more.

After all, he almost witnessed my death, so I know he's just being nice.

"Well, I'm going to swim a bit." I add some distance between us and walk over to the deep end.

"I'll be right here, watching you, Jos." I hear the smile in his voice before I dive in.

The next morning, I find his room empty. I know the bed was slept on despite it being made but everything is how I showed it to him last night. The only thing that stands out, that wasn't here last night is a Post-it note lying in the middle of the bed.

When I pick it up and read it, my heart jolts.

I'm so happy you're here, Jos!

16

DANIEL

> La Patrona 🩶: Hola mijo como estás? Sé que estás bien ocupado, pero nomás quería saber cómo estás? Te extraño mucho y espero que estés bien

THE KNOT IN MY THROAT GROWS AS I REREAD THE message from Mom a few times as I contemplate what I want to say.

I haven't seen or spoken to her or Dad since Christmas. Ignoring them is a shit thing to do, but I can't bear to think of what's going through their minds when they speak or see me. Not that I have to worry much about Dad because he hardly speaks to me, but when he does, we always end up butting heads and our small conversation blows up.

The reminder makes the knot feel like it somehow slipped out of my throat and is now snaking around it like a noose.

A slap on my shoulder startles me. Huffing out a quiet breath, I type out a brief message and set my phone inside my locker.

Angel stands next to me, already dressed for lift this morning. "Don't think you're going to get away with not talking about Friday."

"There's nothing to talk about." I change into my workout clothes, ignoring his probing stare.

He scoffs with disbelief, crossing his arms against his chest, and leans the side of his body against the locker next to mine. "Nothing to talk about? Does Josie ring a bell?"

"We're just friends."

A friend who happens to make me feel a little like my old self anytime I'm around her.

He laughs patronizingly. "You guys were dancing for almost an hour, and don't act like you didn't run to her house because she *forgot* something. What was it that she forgot again?"

In my defense, I thought it was really important to her. I've seen Pen freak about little things like that, but now I know Josie didn't care for it. At least now I know for next time.

My lips lift into a small smile. "Were you keeping track of how long we were dancing?"

"I wasn't keeping track, but you were both *super* close." He wiggles his eyebrows suggestively. "Hey, I'm not judging; you do you and all of that, but didn't she try to...you know..."

My smile slips, and my molars grind against each other. "Don't bring that up here, but what does that have to do with anything?"

"Sorry." He raises his hands in surrender. "I'm not trying to sound like a dick—"

"You're tipping close to being one."

He sharply exhales. "I'm not trying to upset or offend you, but I don't want you to get hurt. Sometimes you have this savior complex thing and—"

"Angel," I clip. "This isn't that. I'm just trying to be a friend."

"I know and you're a good one. No, the best one, and as my best friend, I'm looking out for you. Being with Amanda fucked you up, and I don't want that to happen to you again."

I shouldn't be annoyed. I know his intentions are good, but I feel this surge of protectiveness over Josie. I don't like the assumptions or what he's insinuating about her.

"This isn't an Amanda situation because I'm not dating Josie, nor do I like her like that." Frustrated, I drag my fingers through my hair before I put my hat on. "Can't two people just be friends?"

"They can but you guys only became friends because of that situation. You don't want things to get messy." His face softens. "And look, I get it, Josie's hot. Her tits are distracting, but—"

A pinch of annoyance grabs ahold of me, but soon it's not just that but something else. They collide, becoming green and ugly.

"Don't say that again. This has nothing to do with her chest. I'm—"

The door to the locker room slams open, and loud footsteps and a harsh voice take over the already loud room. "Where the fuck is Daniel?"

"What?" I snap, pivot, and look down at Bryson.

"It was you, wasn't it?" he seethes, pointing his fingers at my chest.

Right, I forgot about that. Josie didn't hold back and I sure as fuck wasn't going to stop her. He deserves that and more.

"What are you talking about?" I innocently ask.

"Don't fucking act like you don't know. You fucking slashed my tires, didn't you?" His jaw tics, his eyes are dark, and his body vibrates with rage.

I fight back not to smile or laugh. "I have no idea what you're talking about. I have better things to do than to—"

"Don't fucking play stupid with me." He jabs his finger at my chest. "You're still pissed because Amanda cheated on you with me, but it's not my fault you couldn't keep her happy. Couldn't fuck her right. Get over it. I get you're upset because she texted me and sent me nudes but..." He smirks, spewing the words with so much venom.

I'm sure he expects me to go off. Probably thought that was going to set me off, but unfortunately for him, it does nothing. I'm so unaffected, I half zone out, wondering if Josie knows just how pissed off he is. I wish she could see this. I wonder if she'd laugh because I know I sure as hell want to.

"Bry, *chill out*." Angel speaks over him, smiling and talking to him the same way he did to me when I found out he slept with Amanda. He used those two exact words in that same nonchalant tone. "Danny was drunk as shit Friday night. Puked his brains out all over his room."

"Yeah and I had to clean that shit up," Gray says from the other side of the locker room, scowling and shuddering as if he were remembering it.

Kai rolls his eyes. "You had to clean it up? You mean I had to after you gagged and complained you had a weak stomach."

"And because of that, I couldn't sleep because you were all being loud as shit," Noah grumbles.

I almost lose it at Noah jumping in, but I shouldn't be surprised. He may be quiet, but he's the kind of guy you know will always have your back. Though I'm kind of shocked at how quick and easy my roommates came up with that lie.

I'm going to owe them big time, but seeing Bryson all riled up is worth it.

Bryson's nostrils flare and he grunts, but then realization flashes across his face. "Of course it wasn't you, fucking Josefine. That bitch," he mutters under his breath.

"Don't call her that." All my humor disappears in an instant.

He stifles a pathetic laugh and cocks his head to the side, studying me. "I saw you dancing with her. I know what you're trying to do so don't act like you care about her. You're trying to get back at me, but I don't care about that bitch. Fuck her for all I care."

I clench my jaw, fury twisting around my insides until all I see is red. "I'm not playing, Bryson. Don't talk about her like—"

"She's. A. Fucking. Bitch." With his eyes locked on mine, he slowly punctuates each word, taunting me. "A. Fucking—"

I've never blacked out before because I was so consumed with anger I couldn't think.

Black takes over every inch of my vision, which is why I don't think when I fist my hand, pull it back, and collide it with the side of his face.

His head jerks and he stumbles back. He tries to gain control of his balance, but he loses it and falls on his ass.

His eyes go round with shock, his hand cradling the side of his face. Then his gaze jumps to my hand, still fisted to my side with a smidge of blood on my knuckle. Seeing that, I stare at the large gash on his lip and the blood that seeps from it onto his white shirt.

I'm tempted to hit him again at the reminder of Josie standing on the cliff, but whoever is standing next to me must've heard my thoughts because they bring me back.

Their hands on my shoulders pull, fanning the black fog away, and that's when I realize how silent the entire locker room is and how all of their eyes are on me.

Loosening my fist, I stare down at Bryson who stills on the ground, staring with caution like I'm going to punch him again. I want to but I don't.

"I don't care what you say or what you do but don't talk about Josie like that again. I'm not fucking around." I forcefully slip my shoes back on, slam my locker door shut, and stalk out of the room straight to the weight room.

Grayson: So...

Noah: Shut up

Grayson: I didn't say anything

Kainoa: So we're going to ignore the elephant in the room?

Angel: Leave him alone. I got you papi 😉

I grin at Angel's message in the group chat. No one bothered me in the weight room, during study hall, or when we were in the film room. I'm pretty sure everyone knew and could feel how angry I still was or maybe they were shocked they'd never seen that side of me.

I don't regret punching Bryson, but I do regret doing that in front of everyone. I'm the captain; I'm supposed to set the example, be the leader, but instead I lost my shit.

Thankfully, Bryson didn't snitch on me because if Coach would have found out, he would've punished everyone. He did that when I sort of got into it with Bryson.

But I'm not letting my guard down because Bryson is petty and knowing him, he'll find a way to get back at me.

> Me: Sorry you all had to witness that. That won't happen again

> Grayson: Now why the fuck are you apologizing??? That motherfucker not only deserved it, but that had been a long time coming! If I was you, I would have punched him again

> Grayson: Also did you slash his tires?

> Kainoa: Did you see the look on his face? He looked so scared. It took everything in me not to laugh. And I promise we won't judge if you did

> Me: No that wasn't me

> Angel: Do you know who did it?

> Me: No comment

> Grayson: It was Josie? Wasn't it?

> Me: No comment

> Grayson: Hot and savage? I think I'm in love with her. Please don't punch me
>
> Grayson: Also, it took everything in me not to take a picture
>
> Angel: Same because the look on his face was priceless
>
> Noah: It was
>
> Grayson: So I'm curious...does this mean that you and Josie are F.U.C.K.I.N.G?????
>
> Kainoa: Jealous, Gray??
>
> Grayson: If I say yes, will you punch me too?
>
> Angel: You've just signed your death sentence
>
> Me: Stop being stupid. We're just friends
>
> Grayson: You were dating Amanda and you didn't once lay a hand on Bryson. If that was my girlfriend, you better believe I would have thrown hands. All you did was have a little spat with him and called it a day
>
> Kainoa: He's not wrong
>
> Angel: Are you all forgetting what he called Josie?
>
> Grayson: Please. Let's not act like people weren't calling Amanda names. I didn't see Danny boy doing anything about it
>
> Kainoa: Oop??!?!! Explain yourself, Danny!

I glance out the window to see if Josie has arrived, but she hasn't yet.

I did check up on Amanda after I heard what people were saying about her. Despite what she did, I wasn't a dick, but things changed when I found out she willingly recorded herself having sex with Bryson. And it wasn't just a one-time thing. She'd been hooking up with him for a while, sending him pictures, sexting him while we were in the same room.

> Me: I have nothing to explain. She didn't care so why should I? And I just don't want anyone fucking with Josie. Are we clear?

> Grayson: Yes sir 🫡

> Kainoa: Aye aye captain 🫡

> Angel: Anything for you papi 😘

> Noah: So how much are we betting? I give it three months.

My jaw falls slack, but I don't have time to read the rest of the messages as Josie parks next to me. When she climbs out, I follow suit, grabbing my camera, the envelope, and my hiking bag.

I slip the strap over my head, letting my camera dangle from my neck as I stand next to her. "Hi, Jos."

"Hey, Garcia," she says as we all gather in front of Professor Carleson.

I try to focus on what he's saying but her being this close to me numbs all my senses, even dulls the ache in my middle knuckle. Something about that makes me smile wider because standing next to her, as I inhale her lavender and vanilla perfume, I feel better about punching Bryson. Now my only regret is not having punched him a second time.

Once Carleson stops talking and gets a head count, he makes way into the trail, with everyone following behind him. Like last time, Josie and I are all the way in the back.

"So guess who was very pissed off this morning?"

She peers up at me, a twitch in her cheek, and like all the times she's done that or remotely smiles, I document it and store it in a filing cabinet dedicated to her in my head.

"Did he accuse you?" She winces.

"Yeah but no worries, my roommates backed me up so he doesn't suspect it was me."

"That's good because you didn't do anything. It was all m—"

I shake my head, shushing her up. "No, we don't know who did it. I was home black-out drunk and you stayed with Pen that night." I give her this look and she slowly nods, pressing her lips together.

"Right, right. I was with Pen and you were black-out drunk. Right." She gives me an okay sign, her eyes shining with mirth.

Dios, no tengo suficientes palabras para explicar qué tan hermosa es. "How's your finger?"

"It's all right." She lifts it and twists it, showing me the small cut.

"You're not cutting limes or lemons, are you?"

She huffs a laugh, dropping her finger. "I'm not a cook. So no."

I meant to cook breakfast for her, a *thank you for letting me stay the night* but Grayson called me freaking out because he lost his Audemars Piguet watch. I had to go help him find it.

I'm about to bring it up but then I notice her gaze drop to the envelope in my hand.

"This is for you." I hand it to her.

She stares quizzically at the black envelope with my sloppy handwriting. I practiced writing her name on something else before I wrote it, but it still looks like shit. I'll definitely do better next time. "What's the special occasion?"

You being alive. You being here. You letting me in. You.

I want to say all of this, but I don't know how without making her feel uncomfortable.

"The new year," I supply instead, tucking my hands in my pockets because what they really want to do is reach out and hold her.

The confusion deepens on her face, but when she opens the envelope and pulls out the card, her lips faintly quirk up and I feel fireworks go off.

I did that.

I want to capture it with my camera, but I don't want to make it weird.

I made her a card. On the front of it, there's a yellow duck with a black top hat, black shades, gold leis around its neck, and a gold fringed noisemaker hanging from its beak. Next to it, it says, *Have a Quacking New Year!* On the inside, the duck looks like it's passed out drunk, feet up in the air, and on the other side it reads, *Here's to making more bad quacking decisions! Happy New Year!* Underneath that I wrote, *And to making new friends. You can call me Danny now.*

She softly chuckles. Holy shit, I made her chuckle.

Breathe. Calm down. She just chuckled. No big deal. No. Big. De—fuck, she chuckled.

I did that.

"You drew and colored this?" Her voice is in awe, fingers tracing over the duck's webbed feet.

"Yeah, sorry about the handwriting. I know it's shit."

"You think this is sloppy? This is probably the prettiest handwriting I've ever seen."

My face heats.

"Why a duck?" Her gaze casts down, fingers now tracing over the letters.

"You said you like yellow and the duck is yellow and well...you know the card is a given." I'm speaking too fast. I need to calm down.

"I do like yellow, and the card is something else. Thank you, Garcia." She doesn't smile, but she doesn't have to because I feel the warmth in her eyes. They're not hardened or vacant. They're just brown, the prettiest brown I've ever seen.

I click my tongue, sighing in feigned disappointment. "So, we're still not on a nickname basis?"

"It's not a bad thing, it's..." Her words are cut short when she spots the little Post-it note I stuck in the envelope. Her breathing hikes and she falters in her step before she resumes walking after she's done reading the little note. She folds it in half before she tucks it in her black belt bag instead of the envelope. "We should talk about what day or days will work best for you."

I don't hold it against her for not saying anything about the note. I know how hard it is for her to open up, to feel safe, to surrender her will to not doing it all alone. I know and I understand but I don't voice that, I just smile at her and nod.

I'll be here whenever she's ready.

But if she's not, at least she knows I'm here because that's what I wrote.

I'm here for you. I see you. You're not alone.
I'm so happy you're here, Jos!

17

JOSEFINE

"You're back." The employee at Coastal Swim and Surf says as I set the foam kickboard and goggles on the counter. I'm pretty certain they're the same ones I returned. "Change your mind?"

"Yeah."

I'm not sure how this is going to work out. Not me teaching Daniel; that isn't an issue. I could do that in my sleep, that's how confident I am, but where I'm confident in the water, I know he isn't.

But I know it's more than lack of confidence. He's terrified.

I still don't know or understand why, and while he didn't vocalize it, I could feel his fear. It's been exactly a week, but I still remember feeling his vigilant eyes tracking my every movement in the pool as I swam. That isn't me assuming; it's me knowing because somehow my body has become aware when I have his attention. It's odd, my stomach flutters and my heart, well...I'm still not sure what's going on with it, but the point is, it wasn't that kind of situation.

This is different and even though I would have preferred to stay longer in the water, I didn't. Once I sat next to him, I could feel his tension ooze off, his stiff posture laxed and his pretty, easy-going smile plastered back on his lips.

After paying, I grab the bag and step out of the store.

Every few seconds, my gaze flickers to the bag as I walk back home. I'm second-guessing myself and my abilities to help Daniel. I've taught many people to learn how to swim, but they've all been kids.

Daniel isn't a kid. He's an adult who's two hundred pounds of pure muscle. It's very evident in the way he felt when we danced. And if that wasn't a given, his abs and thick, toned arms and thighs were.

It'll be okay. I'm sure I'll find a way to—

My thoughts get disrupted when someone calls my name. The moment I detect who it came from, I regret acknowledging it.

"Josie," Bryson calls my name again, but I pretend to not have heard him. But he's dead set on getting my attention because he says it a little louder and then is walking next to me. "Josie, hey."

I keep walking and unfortunately, he still follows. "Yeah?"

He exhales a resigned breath. "I know you're mad about Friday. I shouldn't have said that. I'd been drinking and you know me. I wasn't thinking."

"Do you ever?" I shoot back.

He sucks in a deep breath. "What do you want from me?"

"To leave me alone. I'm not sure how much clearer I need to be," I grumble. I really should've brought my bicycle.

"Josefine." He grabs my arm and ushers me to the side.

"What's wrong with you?" I jerk my arm away from his hold and take a few steps back to add distance between us. "Don't ever touch me again."

I walk away, but his next words freeze me.

"I know it was you. I know you slashed my tires."

"I don't know what you're talking about," I toss over my shoulder. I'm not worried or scared of him finding out it was me but I'm also not going to admit it.

He stands in front of me and that's when I notice a purple

bruise on his cheek and a gash on his lip. They're both swollen, but his lip is more.

I'm not sure what happened and I genuinely couldn't care less, but he must mistake my silence for concern. He was always good at interpreting things the way he wanted to see them and not for how they were.

"I promise I'm okay. It's really not as bad as it looks." He softly rubs his cheek, smirking like he's all right, but I don't miss the slight wince or the way his eye twitches as if he were in pain. "It was a fly ball."

"What'd you do, catch the ball with your face?" I can't fathom how he managed to get hit that bad when he's playing D1 baseball.

He looks sheepish, like he's thinking about that day. Something about it feels off, but I don't ask. I'm done with this conversation.

"Something like that," he replies as he removes his hat and drags his fingers through his dirty blond hair.

Makes me think of Daniel and how thick and long his brown hair is. Never cared for guys in hats, but somehow, he's made himself the exception.

"Okay, well, bye."

"Josie, wait." He follows my step, blocking my path. "I don't care that you slashed my tires. I don't care about the drink you threw at me. I just want you back."

I stiffen, shocked by his solemn declaration. By no means am I shocked in a good way, rejoiced by the fact that my piece of shit, cheating ex-boyfriend wants me back. It's the fact that he's really making himself look devastated. Or that he really wants me back. That's hard to believe.

"I didn't slash your tires, and you deserve the drink for being a dick," I unapologetically say. "And get the idea of us out of your head because we're done."

I attempt to sidestep him, but again he blocks my path.

"Bry—"

"I'll do anything, babe," he desperately says.

I frown. "Don't call me that, and get out of my way."

"I don't understand why you're so quick to give up on us. I still love you and want us to work."

I try to gather all the patience that's rapidly slipping. "Let's not do this. I'm tired and have a busy day tomorrow."

"Busy day doing what? Teaching?" He rolls his eyes and stares at me with discontent. "I don't understand why you gave up swimming. If your mom was here, she would be disappointed in you for giving up so easily. You're the fucking best. Did you forget that at sixteen you won your first gold medal in the fucking Olympics? And look what you've done since then. Teaching kids isn't going to get you anywhere."

My patience maxes out and my frustration morphs into anger as it flows like raging lava through my system. "Don't you dare speak about her. And lucky for me, I don't give a fuck about what you think will benefit my life or career."

"I'm just saying how it is. Don't get mad. If your mom was here right now, she would be disappointed and you know it."

I ball my fists so tight, my nails dig into the heels of my palm. The shard of glass returns, sitting in the middle of my throat, making it hard to swallow.

I can't disagree with him because he's not wrong. If she was here right now, she would have me back on the roster or would have disowned me.

Swimming was our only connection and without it, I was nothing to her.

I retreat into the darkness of my head, balling myself up and hiding behind my insecurities and loneliness. I want to detach myself from this conversation, but he insists on pushing, probably knowing he's hit a nerve and has me where he wants me.

I want to move, to say something, but I feel stuck in the pitch-black corner of my brain.

"I know I shouldn't have brought it up, but you need to think about your future. Think about us. We can still make this work.

We're good for each other. I know we've had issues, but we can move past them. If you want, we can pretend like they never happened. I know I have." He takes a step forward, forcing himself into my space. "Just imagine what our futures together could look like. Me in the majors and you being a professional swimmer. You're already established. I don't understand why you're willing to throw it all away."

The blatant disregard to him cheating on me manages to help me step back. There are so many reasons why I'll never take him back and I could point them out, but there's no use. Not only do I not see a future with him, but I don't see a future at all. But despite what happens tomorrow and every other day, I'd rather spend every ticking second alone than to be with him.

Looking at him dead in the eye, I ask, "What's my favorite color?"

He laughs. "Blue, why?"

"It's yellow."

He wryly grins. "Is that why you won't give me a chance?"

A string of Spanish curse words come to mind, but I decide to save my breath. "On top of you not knowing that, don't act like you didn't look at the camera when Amanda had your dick between her breasts."

His grin slightly falls at the mention of her name. I guess he thought I'd never find out who she was. Probably thought I didn't know about the intentional way he fucked her.

"Not only did you cheat on me, but you slept with your teammate's girlfriend."

Now his lips instantaneously fall. "What did Daniel tell you? It's not—"

"I'm bored and over this conversation." This time I don't let him block my path or cage me in, but at his words, I falter in my step.

"Are you fucking Daniel?"

"No, and even if I was, that—"

"He still loves her. I lied about the ball. He punched me

because of her on Monday. He saw us talking Friday night and it bothered him."

Now that sounds reasonable, but it makes my stomach plummet. "I don't care."

"I'm just trying to look out for you. He's most likely talking to you to get back at me. Don't let him use you, Josie."

"Are you done?" My heart races but for different reasons I can't begin to explain.

"He likes to fuck around *a lot*. If you don't believe me, just ask around."

This time it's him who walks away, while I stand here, my thoughts conflicted and heart heavy.

18

JOSEFINE

"Sorry I'm late." Vi says out of breath, taking a seat across from me and next to Pen. "Let me tell you, getting out of a mermaid tail is not as easy as you would think it would be."

Dinner was planned last minute by Pen. She said she needed to vent and so here we all are at SeaSide Tacos. I wasn't going to come because once again, I didn't think and booked myself back-to-back. In retrospect, if I don't overbook myself, I'll get lost in my head, and that's currently a dangerous place to be. There's hardly any light filtering through, and I know the moment it gets pitch black, I won't be able to shut down the ugly thoughts still lurking in the back of my head.

I'm currently struggling as it is and being alone on a Saturday night or really any night does nothing for my cause. I also didn't want to be alone tonight because I'd probably mull over what Bryson said yesterday.

It's been nagging at me, and it shouldn't. Even if Daniel is potentially using me to get back at Bryson, I can't say it necessarily bothers me. I'm fucked up, I know, but I sort of relish the idea of it bothering Bryson.

What's been incessantly on my mind though is Daniel

punching Bryson because of Amanda. I shouldn't care, but apparently I do because it's all I've been thinking about.

You don't punch someone that bad for someone else unless you really care about them. Maybe he feels more than he made me believe. Maybe Daniel still cares for her but feels guilty for doing so. After all, she cheated on him but even so, she cares for him. It was very obvious in the way she stared at him.

"It's seriously awesome that you get to do that. Is it as fun as I'm thinking it is?" Pen asks.

"Yes." Her dark brown eyes glitter. "The staff is amazing. I get to switch tails and bras. The kids' faces when they see me is priceless. Though putting on the tail is work all on its own, and staying underwater for so long gets exhausting, but it's honestly worth it."

"Maybe if things don't work out for me, I'll become a mermaid," Pen muses jokingly.

Vi and I glance at each other, hearing uncertainty and frustration seep from her voice.

Because I'm afraid to fuck it up and say something that could sound insensitive, I let Vi do all the talking.

"You want to tell us what's bothering you? We're here for you," she sympathetically questions.

Before Pen replies, the waitress takes our orders and once she's gone, Pen doesn't waste a second to tell us what happened.

She sighs. "How do you go from dating and telling someone you love them to them breaking up with you because they need to focus on themselves to then dating your best friend?"

Vi and I lock eyes, but still, I say nothing. I don't want to be the person who attempts to make Pen feel better by telling her my shitty experience with my first boyfriend. That won't help her cause, and I don't want her to pity me. Plus, this also involves her brother, and he's not someone I should be talking about.

Again, Vi does the talking. "Wait, hold up, so your ex-boyfriend is dating your best friend? Please tell me you're not still friends with her?"

She puffs out an aggravated breath and slouches in her chair. "Yes, and well...I...I'm not...she's not...we're...it's complicated. She's on the cheer team and because I'm captain, I can't...I need to keep it...amicable," she flounders and drops her face to the table. Still keeping her forehead glued to the table, she says, "And we live together."

I scoff incredulously. "You don't need to do shit. You don't owe her anything. She was your best friend and is now dating your ex? Absolutely fucking not."

Vienna nods in agreement, showing solidarity for what I just said. "And she lives with you? Yeah, fuck that, her, and him."

"I know. I know, but I..." She softly groans as she lifts her head. "I just need to get over it. He broke up with me months ago. It's not like he cheated on me or anything. She said she didn't mean to fall for him, but..." She trails off like it pains her to say it. "They have a class together, they're partners, and one thing led to another."

"Oh Pen," Vi empathically says.

"It's fine, I guess. I want to get over him, I really do, but every time I see them together, I see us. Everything he does for her, he did for me." She smiles but it doesn't reach her eyes. "Actually, he does more for her than he did for me." She sighs and shakes her head like she's trying to forget the memories. "I'm sorry for sounding so dramatic. I just needed to get that off my chest."

"Shut up. You don't sound dramatic," I chide.

"She's right, you don't. You're venting and there's nothing wrong with that," Vi remarks. "Honestly, you're taking it better than I would. I would have crashed out."

Penelope's face brightens and she giggles.

I wish I had the ability to make that happen. To ease someone's pain or discomfort instead of adding more to it. I wonder if my mom would have loved me if I had been different.

I take a sip of my water, then drop my hands to my lap to stop myself from fidgeting with my rings.

"This is going to sound very cliché, but you know how that

saying goes. To get over someone you have to get under somebody else," Vienna suggests mischievously.

"I've tried that and it hasn't worked. All the guys make me think of him and then I miss him and I cycle back to the what-ifs and what could I have done to make us work."

"This might not work but have you tried messing around with someone that doesn't look like him? I just ask because I know from experience, and if you're trying to rebound with someone that looks like him or acts like him, you'll never be able to let go."

Granted, it didn't take much for me to get over Bryson, but I can tell it's really weighing hard on Pen.

"It might not work, but maybe don't listen to me because I've only ever had one boyfriend and that didn't end well. And—"

"No, you're right. I didn't even think about it like that, but I realize now I have been trying to replace him with someone like him." She meekly smiles, cheeks staining a light pink. "I'm pathetic, aren't I?"

"No, you're not," I sternly say. "If anyone's pathetic, it's them. Not you."

She stares at me like a weight has been lifted off her shoulders. "Thanks for listening to me. I was going crazy with this."

"Don't thank us. We're here for you. Now..." Vienna folds her arms on the table, staring at her with a look of determination. "Who's your ex and what does he look like so we can definitely stay away from anyone looking like him."

Pen pulls out her phone and shows us the picture of her ex.

Luke Rodriguez, junior, point guard for MCU's basketball team.

Vi nods repeatedly and slowly to herself, staring long and hard at the small screen like she's computing and analyzing data. Then she sits up, smiling from ear to ear as if a lightbulb went off in her head.

"You and Angel have great chemistry." She wiggles her brows.

I might've been slightly drunk last week, but I definitely felt it too.

Pen's face pinches with aversion. "Now that sounds cliché and so wrong. He's Danny's best friend and I practically grew up with him. I know everything about Angel, and nothing about it is good. Next."

"So, you've really never thought about it? Not to instigate anything but Angel's hot."

"No, I've never thought about it because I don't see him like that."

"You didn't answer me." Vienna smirks.

"Okay...yeah, he's hot but like I said we grew up together and he's Danny's best friend. And we're kind of friends. I don't want to make anything weird between us. And even if I wanted to, which I don't, he wouldn't be on board. Plus, do you know about his reputation? Yeah, no thanks. Next."

Vienna blows a raspberry. "You have any suggestions, Josie?"

"My judgment is poor at best so you don't want to listen to me."

"I highly doubt that," Pen says as the waitress brings our food. "But I trust your judgment either way."

"Oh." I tuck my hair behind my ear.

"I have swim practice and will be working at the aquarium for a little tomorrow, but I'm free after six. We could meet up and—"

"I can't. I have a lesson tomorrow."

"I thought you only did those on Saturday?" Pen asks as she squeezes lime juice on her shrimp tacos.

"It's still only on Saturdays, but I've managed to convince Daniel to let me teach him," I answer, pouring the green salsa on my carne asada taco.

When I raise my taco, it stays suspended in the air. Penelope stares at me wide-eyed, her immaculate eyebrows pinched together and lips slightly parted. Then a disbelieving laugh slips past her lips.

"Daniel? Daniel Garcia, my brother? That Daniel?"

I nod, side-eyeing Vi because I don't know what's going on or why she sounds like she's crashing out.

"Yeah, he actually reached out to me first then changed his mind, but we managed to work things out," I explain.

"Daniel did that?" she questions inconceivably.

"Yeah..." I hate prying but I set my taco down and contemplate how to ask my question without sounding invasive. "I noticed he's very hesitant about the water. Is there a reason why? I just want to know what I'm getting into and figure out how I can best help him."

For a long moment she doesn't say anything as she stares down at her plate of tacos. My chest fills with apprehension.

Did I overstep? How do I backtrack? What did I do?

"You don't have to—"

"Our brother Adrian, my twin, drowned, and Danny watched it happen." She bites her bottom lip. "Since then, he's had a rocky relationship with water. He...well...he actually agreed?"

"Yeah, but I didn't know." God, I'm horrible. I pressured him into agreeing. "He didn't tell me. I didn't—"

"This is great. He's never allowed anyone to teach him. My parents paid people and did all these things to help him, but he'd always shut down. He actually agreed?" she asks again, staring at me, bewildered.

"Yeah, but I might've pressured him. I'll talk to him and—"

"No, don't do that." Pen cuts me off mid-sentence, her eyes filled with hope and something I can't pinpoint. "You're the first person he's ever willingly allowed to help. You have to help him, please."

"I may not be the right person. I'm not good with people and what if—"

"But you're good with him, and that's all that matters. He trusts you. Please help him." She begs like I'm her only hope, but I highly doubt that. There are experts who are trained for these kinds of things.

A war of emotions whirl in my chest, all battling against what I should and shouldn't feel and do. I could fuck it all up before it even really begins, but I concede anyway.

"Okay, I'll help him."

19

DANIEL

"Come on, Adrian. Wake up. Please don't go. Please don't go," I chant under my breath as I watch the lifeguard do CPR on him. "Come on, Adrian. Wake up. Please. Please. Please don't go. Wake up."

"Danny!"

I flit my gaze to the bedroom door where Angel stands, watching me with worry.

"What?" I stuff my towel in my bag and zip it closed.

"You good? You look a little pale." He steps into my room and drops down in my desk chair.

"I'm good." I smile even though my stomach churns. It makes me so nauseous; I feel bile rising up my throat, but I swallow it down.

His skeptical eyes jump to my bag on my bed. "Where are you going?"

"To swim with Josie."

He sits up fast, almost falling off the chair, and stares at me, stupefied. "Swimming? With Josie?"

"Yup. She's going to teach me how to swim."

Angel's eyes go round, and his jaw drops. "She agreed, and you're actually going to do this? Are you doing this because you want to learn, or are you doing this to get laid, because if you are, you're fucking stupid. I've seen you in the water."

"Neither. I'm doing this because it's the only way she'll let me help her."

"What's that supposed to mean?"

I grab my duffle bag and drape it on my shoulder. "Nothing. And would you stop assuming I'm into her or want to fuck her or whatever you have in your head? We're just friends."

He snickers but it turns into a laugh as he stands. Before he walks out of my room, he looks over his shoulder at me and laughs again.

"What? Why are you—"

"If I would've known you'd be this desperate, I would've bet more. Dammit." He groans, leaning against my doorframe.

"You guys were being serious?" I walk past him and make my way down the stairs.

All the guys are gathered in the living room. Kai and Noah are playing COD and Gray is talking to someone on the phone.

"I'm telling you, Saint—"

"Hang up," I demand and stand in front of the TV, blocking the guys from being able to see.

"Fuck out of the way!" Noah shoots me daggers.

"What the fuck?" Kai stands, hands raised. "You got us kill—"

"The bet is off," I adamantly say once Angel has joined us in the living room. "I don't know why you are all—"

"You got me killed over the bet?" Noah questions, his face stoic, but I hear the agitation in his voice. "You dumb motherfucker. Get out of the way."

"There is nothing going on between Josie and me. So, stop the bet. I'm sick and tired of you guys—"

"I'll talk to you later. Yeah...Danny is losing his shit...wait, really?" Gray laughs into the phone. "How long was it before TJ... couldn't be me...I can hardly take care of myself...I couldn't make my bed...you get it...we should—"

Snatching the phone, I place it on my ear. "He'll talk to you later. Bye, Saint." And I hang up before I toss it back to him.

"Okay, rude." His eyes slightly narrow, and his brows furrow. "What's wrong with you?"

"No more bets. Got it?" I sternly look at each one of them.

Kai scoffs. "Is this about Josie? Because we're just playing around."

"No, we're not," Noah disagrees. "You want to fuck or like Josie. Whatever it is, we're—"

"It's not like that."

"Then what's it like?" Gray tilts his head to the side, eyeing me with curiosity. "Because you punched Bryson for her. Or did we all not see the same thing? Do you know how many times he's antagonized you over Amanda, but the minute he calls Josie a bitch, you swung."

Truth is, I don't know what it's like. I don't think about fucking Josie, but I also won't lie and act like I haven't checked her out. Still, I don't want to disrespect her. She's gone through a lot. But if she hadn't—what am I saying?

"We're friends."

"I've fucked many of my friends. Just saying." Angel noncommittally shrugs.

I narrow my eyes at him, letting him know he's not helping, to which he shrugs again.

"The real question is who haven't you fucked?" Kai snorts.

"This isn't about me, dumbass, and you have no room to talk," Angel retorts.

"Don't be lame Danny. I mean if you fall for her or fuck her what's the problem? Why are you against it?" Gray asks.

It's not that I'm against the bet because I've thought about Josie more than a time or two. But things are different, and our relationship isn't the kind of relationship I've had with other girls or even with Amanda.

Though I'm not sure I can even call it a relationship. She

hardly lets me in, and the only reason I'm making any progress is because I agreed to let her teach me how to swim.

I'm not even sure Josie really likes me.

Somedays I feel like I'm getting a read on her and other days, I can't read her at all. She only tolerates me because we have a class together and we're hiking buddies, but if it wasn't because of that, I'm sure we wouldn't be on speaking terms.

"Just stop the bet. It's stupid and nothing is going to happen between us," I exhaustedly say, securing the bag on my shoulder.

"Where are you going?" Kai asks.

Before I get the chance to dodge the question and look at Angel to keep his mouth shut, he's speaking.

"Swim lessons."

"You got her to agree?" Gray looks severely offended.

"You gave me the idea. I guess it's time I learn." My hand tightens on the strap as another wave of nausea crashes against me. "I'll see you guys later."

I ring the doorbell, breathing in slowly and then out. I do this a few more times in hopes the nausea will vanish, but it continues to persist.

But it and my headache only worsen when Josie swings the door open. The realization of what I'm going to do sets my body in a panic.

"Hey, Gar—" She studies me, eyes sweeping over my face then down to my full hands. "What's with the bags?" she asks, although I feel that's not what she wanted to say and I'm thankful for it.

She motions for me to come inside and I follow behind her, telling her, "I'm going to make you dinner."

There are instances where reading her is difficult, but then there are some moments her vulnerability seeps through, and reading her is as easy as breathing.

The conversation we had about her groceries stuck out to me. I knew without her having to go into detail why she lacks the energy to cook. I want to tell her that I've been there, but it's not about me.

As we step in the kitchen, she staggers and spins to face me. "You don't have to—"

"I am and I will. Plus, I'm a great cook, and if baseball ends up not working out, I'm considering becoming a private chef." I smile at her as I set the bags down on the island. "Okay, maybe I don't have what it takes to become a private chef, but let me tell you my rice is private-chef-level quality. You just wait until you try my *tinga*, and don't worry, I'll make it extra spicy for you."

My anxiety has lessened but now I feel...nervous but for different reasons. Am I overstepping? I want to make her happy, I want to help her fill the emptiness, I want to do whatever I can to make her feel good, but I don't want to push.

She comes a little closer, standing on the other side of the island. "You know how spicy I like my food?"

"You said it's hard for you to enjoy most foods if they're not spicy. I also feel the same way."

We were hiking when she said that. I was trying to get to know her as much as I could, asking her random questions here and there.

"I don't remember telling you that." She looks into the bag, but I don't miss the faint jerk of her lips.

Fireworks. Every single time she does that.

"I'm very good at paying attention. Not to brag or anything, but it's what landed me captain and how I became shortstop."

Her lips jerk again and so does my heart.

"I'm pretty sure it was your—" She stops mid-sentence when she pulls out two containers. One has slices of limes and the other slices of lemons, but when she pulls out the lemon squeezer, a laugh slips past her lips. "I..." She trails off, her lips slowly curling upward into a small smile.

Wow...whoa...*whoa*.

I don't blink or breathe, afraid it'll disappear or this is all a dream, but when she locks eyes with me, her small smile just barely deepens, and I swear my brain short-circuits.

Why was I anxious again?

"I figured you could use them. I know it's been a week, but sometimes the smallest cuts take the longest to heal." My gaze drops to her plush lips. "And I wasn't sure if you had a lemon squeezer, but if you do, now you have another so the other doesn't feel lonely."

"As a matter of fact, I don't have one, so this one will come in handy. And you know..." she says, her eyes distant and reminiscent. It makes me wonder if she's thinking about her mom. She never talks about her, and I don't want to ask questions because it's hard for me when people ask about Adrian. "It's been a while since I put limes and lemons in my water, but I think I'll be doing that again. Thanks, Garcia."

I don't mean to, but I puff out my chest, feeling immensely proud. "You know, you can call me Danny since we're friends, or are we not..."

It's not a question, but at the same time it is. Maybe it's desperate, but I just want to hear it come out of her mouth.

"I thought that was already established? Don't friends call each other by their last names?" She seems genuinely confused, and I feel like a dumbass.

"Right, that was already established. I'm sorry. I didn't—"

"You don't have to apologize. That's actually on me. I..." She becomes quiet as she takes out the stuff from the bags. When she opens the fridge, my heart sinks at how empty it is. With her back still to me, she says, "I'm sorry if I was...*am* a bitch. I know I come off abrasive and I'm not the most...bubbly. I mean, people call me Wednesday and—"

"Josefine, look at me."

She still doesn't turn, so I go to her. Once I'm standing in front of her, she cranes her head back to stare up at me.

My fingers itch to brush them along her cheek. There isn't a day I don't think about how her skin felt on my fingers the night I helped change her tire.

"I don't know who made you feel that way, but I don't see you like that. I just see Josefine." I take one step closer; my arms hang limply at my sides, but they feel anything but that. They feel heavy, and I'm desperate to reach out and hold her. "I still don't know you as much as I'd like, but like I told you that night on the cliff, I want to get to know you. I want you to let me in and when you're ready, I'll be here. And if there's ever anything you want to talk about, like your mom, I'll be here too."

Her nose flares and those beautiful brown eyes soften before she casts them down. She tucks her hair behind her ear and nods.

That nod tells me everything I need to know, and for the first time since I met her, I feel like she's really allowing me in.

I don't push or prod and together we stock up her fridge and then head out to her pool.

Anxiety flares in my stomach and I start sweating despite how cool the weather is today. Just as I'm about to tell Josie that this is a bad idea and walk back inside, she slips her hand in mine, keeping her gaze on the pool.

"Your sister told me about your brother, Adrian," she solemnly says, looking up at me. My heart painfully aches, but as she begins to rub soft circles with her thumb, I feel it less. "I'm not going to force you to do something you're not ready to do. But I want you to know that if you want this, I will help you."

I'm a little at a loss for words because where I'm usually riddled with so much anxiety, the fear paralyzes me, I don't necessarily feel that right now.

Maybe it's my sweaty palm that she feels or how tightly I'm gripping hers, but she squeezes my hand and stares at me so deeply, her eyes become engraved in my brain.

"I got you," she softly and earnestly says, but more than anything, it sounds like a promise and I believe her.

20

JOSIE

I watch him closely, still with my hand in his. I spot the haphazard pulse on his tanned neck, the way it bounces madly like it's caged and trying to be let out. And I feel his sweaty hand tightly clutching mine.

I don't point out or wince at how firmly he's holding my hand. I only continue to rub soft circles and repeat the same words he said to me the other day.

"I got you," I gently say, keeping my gaze on his apprehensive one. "I promise, Danny."

His dark brown brows quirk up, his breath quietly hitches, and his hand loosens.

After I left the girls yesterday, I came straight home and did as much research as I could. I may professionally know how to swim, have been taught by some of the best there is, and be certified to be able to teach swim lessons, but that doesn't mean I know exactly how to help him.

I can't begin to imagine what Daniel went through. His sister didn't go into detail about what happened, but the little she shared is enough for me to understand how he's feeling. A combination of survivor's guilt and a persisting trauma.

I could've looked into what happened because he's popular

enough an internet search would've been sufficient, but I don't want to invade his privacy. I'm sure if it's something he wanted to talk about, he would've already told me. Or maybe he's trying to not think about what happened because like me, I don't like thinking about what happened to Mom.

Whatever it is, I did research. I spent hours trying to find the best way to help him. I might not be able to help him get over his fear, but it doesn't hurt to try.

And as shitty as this might sound considering the circumstances, I've found a little purpose in my life.

He was and has been there for me. The least I can do is return the favor.

"Did you just call me Danny?"

"Yes, but I think I like Garcia better."

A smile grows on his face. Bright and sweet like he is. "I think I prefer that too. You're the only one who calls me Garcia, anyway. So it can be our thing."

My heart stutters. "No one else calls you that?"

"No, I'm either Danny boy, Danny, Sparky, and occasionally when I get in trouble, *Daniel Jesus Garcia*." He says those last three names in Spanish.

My lips twitch. "Occasionally?"

"I got drunk freshman year and found myself laying on my parents' lawn. I guess I gave the Lyft driver their address instead of mine. Angel was there with me, so he also got chewed out." He chuckles as if he were remembering the moment. "But that's the last time in a while I've been called that."

"And Sparky?"

He waves his hand in the air. "I spark energy everywhere I go."

Yeah...that seems pretty accurate.

I can't help but smile a little at that and I don't miss the way his eyes drop to my lips. "Cute."

"You called me cute; you can't take it back."

"Are you always misinterpreting things? Because I can help you in the water, but I fear I won't be able to help—"

"I know exactly what you meant. Don't deny it, Jos, you think I'm cute." His eyes twinkle with mischief.

"No, I think you're hot, but if you prefer cute then..."

A splash of pink colors his cheeks and his smile drops before he picks it back up. "No, no. I like hot. So, you think I'm hot?"

"And shallow." He's far from it. In fact, sometimes, no most of the time, he feels too good to be true. He grins, not believing I actually mean it. "Okay, we need to stop wasting time; it'll get dark soon. Do you still want to do this? Don't feel pressured or obligated. I'll do whatever you're comfortable with."

He goes silent, eyes shifting to the pool and back up at me. "Are you sure I won't be bothering you?"

"I have no life, so I promise you're not."

"You understand I'm going to consume your life? It's going to get so bad, you're going to get sick of me."

It's only been a month since he stopped me from ending it all, but since then, my days have revolved around trying to keep moving, and thinking of him.

I wish I could make my brain cut the wire that seems dead set on being attached to him. I didn't even think of Bryson this much when I was dating him.

"That's not going to happen." I slip my hand away from his and note the way his palm remains in the same position as if he were still holding my hand.

He follows my line of vision and tucks his hands in his shorts' pockets. They're shorter than most shorts guys wear, exposing his thick, muscular quads. And he has the right amount of hair on his legs.

Why is everything about that...attractive? *Jesus, get a grip.*

"Don't say I didn't warn you." He shrugs blithely.

I refrain from rolling my eyes and smiling. "I got you something." I pad over to the chaise lounge chair and pick up the foam board and goggles. When I turn, I find him already behind me, just a few feet away. "It's something I get for all my clients."

He takes them from my hands and drags his finger around the lenses before feeling the dark green silicone strap. He smiles, but it doesn't reach his eyes. "I hope you don't regret this."

I pull my shirt off and toss it on the chaise. "My only regret will be not being able to help you."

There's a clench to his jaw, his eyes hardened, and it makes me wonder if I'm doing too much. Am I pushing too hard, too fast?

"I really want to help you, but if you don't want to do this, we don't have to. I actually found a few people online who are trained and certified specialists. I wrote their information down; I can go get—" I throw my thumb over my shoulder in the direction of my house.

"That's not necessary. I..." He scratches the back of his neck, cheeks a rosy pink. "I'm...I don't know how to say this without coming off as a..." He coyly looks down. "Pervert..." He draws that word out, eyes meeting mine now.

"Okay?"

"You're just..." He waves a hand down my chest. "God, I swear I'm never this awkward. Matter of fact, I'm—"

"Spit it out, Garcia." I tap my foot impatiently.

"*Hot.*" He clenches his jaw again. "You're hot and you're wearing that, Jos. I just needed to get that off my chest. I'm not trying to make it weird, but you've got nice—"

"Please shut up." My cheeks flame. No. Scratch that. My body is an inferno. But I play it off. Act like I'm not affected at all by him whatsoever. Act like he wasn't going to say that I have nice tits.

"Right, yeah." He presses his lips together, eyes flitting to my chest swiftly before shifting back up to mine. "I don't know why I said that, but disregard it. I promise I'm not going to be weird or creepy."

I glance down at my bikini top. I didn't wear my usual swimsuit because I wanted to make him comfortable. I didn't want to make this too formal, but maybe I made a mistake. Not that him staring at me makes me uncomfortable. It's actually the opposite. But right now is not the time for me or my libido to act up.

"It's a good thing I didn't wear the bottoms that came with this." I pull my shorts off and toss them with my shirt.

He smiles, grabbing the neck of his shirt, and tugs it off. "Why's that?"

Abs. Beautiful, tanned, sculpted, firm, and whatever other positive adjective can be used to describe his abdomen is that.

"It's a thong. If you're flustered over breasts, I'd hate to see what my ass would do to you," I absently throw out, but cringe a second later because why am I trying to flirt and why did that sound...ehhh.

"Do you want the truth or the lie?"

Our eyes lock. My heart goes berserk. And my body burns so intensely, I feel like I'm lying on top of lava.

"Pool. We should get in the pool," I say instead because I can't be trusted. This is going from G to PG-13. "You won't need the goggles or board right now. You can just set those down."

"Right behind you." I hear the taunt in his voice. *Who's flustered now?* I'm sure he's thinking.

He follows behind me and once we're waist deep in, his entire demeanor shifts. All the playfulness feels like it was sucked out of him and he's a different version of the Daniel I know.

"Hey, look at me." I stand in front of him, leaving a few inches of space between us. "I got you. I promise." I place my hand over my heart and he follows it. His distressed eyes soften before he nods.

"Sorry, I'm...nervous."

"Don't apologize. I promise I'm not going to do anything you're not comfortable with," I gently reiterate. "Just follow my lead."

I stretch my arms at my side, my palms hovering above the surface. Slowly, I wave them back and forth, sink them underneath, and repeat the motion. He follows, his eyes trained on me.

"I'm going to ask you a few questions."

He nods.

"How do you feel about going under shallow water?"

Daniel falters before he picks up where he left off until we're in sync again. "I don't mind it, but I can't keep my head underwater for long."

"How long do you think you can keep it for?"

"Ten seconds...something like that."

"How do you feel about showers?"

"That doesn't bother me because I can breathe, but when I'm underwater, I just..." He stops moving and swallows hard. "I don't like it."

"How do you feel about Marco Polo?"

That causes his lips to curl into a small smile. "We're playing a game?"

"Don't tell me you're too good for Marco Polo?" I feel good knowing I made him smile.

"No, of course not. I'm just competitive as fuck so..." He drifts off before his smile falls again. "You're not going to have me close my eyes and then push me deeper in the pool because—"

"Did someone do that to you?" I cut him off, and my blood boils when he nods.

"It happened years ago, but they didn't know. I was too... embarrassed to say anything."

My heart aches for him, but I wonder if I'm getting too in over my head. He needs professional help. *What if I fuck this up? What if I*—he must have heard my thoughts because he speaks up.

"I did try the whole therapy thing, but it didn't work out. So don't feel discouraged if things don't pan out. Like I said, I don't get in the water much, so you won't ever have to worry about me drowning or something," he quietly says.

"My expectations are hellishly low. So..." Was that too dry? *Dammit, Josephine, get your shit—*

He chuckles, face brightening and the tension in his body rolling off. "Are you doing that reverse psychology thing on me?"

As discreetly as I can, I begin to turn and he follows. I'm not sure if he realizes he's doing it, but he follows my lead.

"Uh...if that's what you want to call my horrible lack of sense of humor, sure."

That made no sense and I was definitely not trying to be funny, but Daniel laughs. He tips his head back, eyes closed for a mere second before they're on me again. But all my brain seems to register is how deep and hearty his laugh sounds. I'm momentarily distracted by the glint of his gold chain from the sun.

I want to ask the story behind the safety pin, but I withhold.

"Noah has an excellent dry sense of humor, and I happen to excel in reading it." He grins, still following my lead as we go in a slow circle.

"Noah? Noah Sosa?"

"The one and only."

"Tell me about Noah."

"Why? Are you interested?" He lifts a brow, lips pulling into a teasing smile, but his eyes don't match it.

He's attractive. Olive-toned skin, a face structure that seems like it was carved by the gods, tall along with all the other guys on the team, but he carries himself differently. I don't know why but he does.

But am I attracted to him? No. The only guy who seems to have my head and heart in disarray happens to be the guy right in front of me.

"No, I'm not interested in him or anyone." Because I'm a hot-ass mess and while I don't outwardly show it, inwardly I'm crumbling into nothing. Guys don't like messy girls or girls who...are like me.

All to show, nothing to give.

Bryson said that a few times while drunk and sober. I was stupid for staying, but sometimes you get a taste of something you've never had and every time it's fed to you, it makes you want it a little more. It's not the real thing, but it's enough to get you hooked.

I was hooked on what I couldn't have and he gave me enough; it made me stay. It made me stupid. It made me hate myself.

All to show, nothing to give.

A moment of silence stretches between us. It unnerves me because he's thinking something, I just don't know what.

"He's my roommate and will make you think he hates living with me and the guys, but I know he secretly loves it. Don't tell him I said that." He winks at me. "He's our catcher, six three, doesn't smile too much, but he likes to fuck around. Has a nice face—also don't tell him I said that. I'll deny it. Fun fact, he's Coach's foster-ish son. He didn't foster or adopt him, but he sort of raised him. So, Coach has a soft spot for him, although he doesn't show it."

Relaxed and playful like he always is. Good.

"You and the guys? How many of you live together?"

"Five of us. Noah, Angel, Kai, Gray, and me," he replies. "Gray wasn't supposed to move in with us but there was a mix-up. He's a pompous, obnoxious pain in the ass, but he's not that bad."

"So, which is it—pompous, obnoxious, or not that bad?" We keep moving in circles, still staying in the shallow end but moving around.

His lip twitches. "Honestly, still thinking about it."

My lips mirror his. "Do you like living with all the guys?"

I wonder what having a roommate must be like. But then again, I shouldn't because I lived with Mom and we might as well have been roommates because family is far from what we felt.

"Yeah, except on the occasion when I'm tired and want to sleep but can't because of the parties or someone acting like they're shooting a porno."

I understand what he means by that, and it makes me think of what Bryson said: *He likes to fuck around a lot.* I didn't have to ask around because I heard the stories. Since he and Amanda broke up, he's been making up for everything he missed out on when he was in a relationship.

I've done an embarrassingly amount of *research* on him.

"Can't say I relate."

"Never had roommates?"

"Unless you want to count my mom. That is until she..." I swallow past the knot that came out of nowhere. "I've been living alone since."

It gets lonely and depressing, but it is what it is.

He stares at me longingly and a streak of empathy flashes in his eyes. "If you're looking for a roommate, I'm more than willing to move in," he jokingly says. But like he's really trying to sell himself, he adds, "I'm a great cook. I'm clean. I'll keep the noise to a minimum. And the season will be picking up this coming month, so you'll hardly see me around."

I shouldn't but I play into it. "I tend to be a little bit of a control freak."

He hums. "I like people telling me what to do."

"No, I mean it. I like things a particular way." That's not a joke. I need structure and organization. Without my planner, I'm nothing.

"I'm a fast learner and I'm good about following the rules."

"I don't cook."

"You won't have to."

I can't help the way my lips just barely stretch. "Parties aren't allowed."

The house is in my name, but it still doesn't feel like mine.

"Thank God. Maybe now I'll be able to get some sleep."

"I take my sleep seriously. So, if you were to..." The knot grows, and my stomach plummets. "Bring *someone* over, you'd have to keep the noise low."

"Why would I invite anyone over when you're here?" He stares, perplexed, but then his eyes widen like he realized what he said. "I didn't...I wasn't trying to insinuate that we'd fuck. Jesus Christ. I'm..." He shakes his head, but an amused expression mars his face. "I promise I'm never like this, but you just..."

"I just what?" I hold my breath.

"My brain short-circuits when I'm around you," he honestly replies.

I'm not sure what to say or how to feel about that. "Should I be offended or—"

"No, God no. It's hard to think when I'm looking at you."

"I—" A rumble and a strike of lightning in the distance disrupts me.

"This sucks. I didn't mean to waste your time. I'm sorry."

"Don't be sorry. You didn't waste my time."

"We didn't play Marco Polo and—"

"We did twenty circles."

He drops his hands when I do. "What do you mean?"

"Twenty circles and we moved around a bit." I flick my gaze to the spot we had originally been in and then to the one we're now in.

"Oh." He looks genuinely surprised. "I hadn't realized we moved. Wow. You...you did that."

"I didn't do anything. That was all you," I proudly say.

"But you helped." He approaches me, his hand grazing mine under the water. Holding my breath, I stay still. "And—" Blinding streaks of light spread across the sky and the rumble is louder than before.

"We should really get out," I urge and climb out, making a mental note to stop letting myself be so close to him. I'm not only struggling to think but to breathe.

21

JOSIE

As I enter the kitchen, I freeze at the sight before me. So much is going on, I'm not sure what to focus on first: Daniel singing along to a song in another language. The glass containers on the island. More bags of groceries that I know I didn't see when he showed up. The pots and pans he has on all four burners.

"What are you doing?" I scan the counters and see fruits, vegetables, meat, shrimp, salmon, a variety of sauces, and seasonings. "And what's with all the food?"

After we came back inside, I got a call from a potential new client. I guess the call ran longer than I anticipated because there's so much going on, this definitely didn't happen in the span of a few minutes.

Daniel lowers the music as he turns to look at me. "I should've asked you, but I figured you would've said no."

"Said no to what?" I walk farther into the kitchen, eyeing everything and surprisingly, I don't feel overwhelmed. It's not messy; it's organized despite how much space everything takes.

"I'm meal prepping for you." He grabs a wooden spoon and one of the pots and fills three glass containers. "I hope I'm not overstepping. I know you said you didn't have the energy and life gets busy. I know it's easier getting takeout or buying already made meals, but sometimes there's nothing like a home-cooked meal. I hope this is okay. I promise to clean all of this up."

I'm at a loss for words. I attempt to speak up, but nothing comes to mind.

"Um..." Still nothing. "Ah..." I'm blanking here but the bridge of my nose stings and my heartbeat gets scarily fast. "How much do I owe you?"

He sets the pot in the sink and turns the one burner off. "I don't want you to pay me. This is the least I can do since you won't let me pay for the lessons."

"Because that's the least *I* can do..." It's an open statement that I don't have to explain. I know he's reading between the lines. "You really didn't have to do this. The already cooked meals are fine."

"I wanted to. Pen says it's my love language or whatever that's called."

I make a mental note to get referred to a cardiologist. The excessive beats are getting out of control, which can't be normal.

"Did she now?"

"She made me take a test." He grins. "Don't be surprised if she sends you one. They'll be random and have no purpose but to make you question if you got the correct answer. She once sent me one that said, 'Can we guess which type of dog you are based on the way you eat your food?'"

"Which one did you get?" I step a little closer to him.

"It's not right."

"Which dog did you get?"

"Don't laugh."

"Tell me."

"Chihuahua." He sulks, and it's adorable. "But I think it's bullshit and they stereotyped me because I'm Mexican. I should definitely sue for emotional distress."

I bite the inside of my cheek, but he looks so serious, I can't help but laugh. "You're an idiot."

That makes him smile. "I hope this is okay."

"I...don't know what to say. This really isn't necessary." I don't tell him that I could hire a private chef if I wanted to, and that before Mom passed, we had one. "This is a lot. How much did you spend on all of this? I really need to pay you."

"Please don't." He pauses like he's considering what he wants to say. "Not to brag but I have NIL deals and they pay well."

"It doesn't matter. I—"

"Grief is funny," he blurts out. He scratches his head, like he's embarrassed he said that. "I...don't know about you but after my..." He rubs the bridge of his nose and doesn't meet my stare. "Brother passed away...I felt small and everything felt so...big." He sucks in a heavy breath, like he's struggling for words and oxygen. "Finding the energy to...brush my teeth felt like such a big task. Even after all these years, that feeling is still there. Grief...never gets easier. It keeps evolving and all you can do is adapt to it because it's always going to be there."

My heart leaps before it comes to a standstill. He didn't just perfectly explain how I've been feeling but he opened up. He's not being funny, he's not attempting to get me to smile, or saying something for the sake of trying to make me feel better. He's sharing a little bit of himself to me—the raw, vulnerable side he probably doesn't let anyone see.

But guilt bleeds from his words, like he feels wrong for feeling that way.

"Grief is...funny," I murmur, dropping my gaze.

He tucks a finger underneath my chin, forcing me to look into his soft, cloud-like eyes. "Very." He smiles tenderly and something about it feels like a caress to my soul. It ignites the light in my heart again. "You're not alone."

I feel like we're in this bubble and it freaks me out because bubbles can easily pop.

But this also feels different, like the bubble isn't as self-destructive as it usually is. Maybe I'm getting ahead of myself, but I know that Daniel needs someone.

I've never been someone's person and I doubt I'm what he needs. I'm probably the last person who should be comforting him. But at this moment, it can't hurt, right?

My smile is far from what might be considered one but his eyes, like they always do, are drawn to my lips. It feels like an automatic response or like two magnets. Whatever it may be, his eyes are there, and his face glows, and my heart does the only thing it can do: it goes mad.

I don't dwell on the condition of my heart, though, because I notice something I never have. His eyes. Light, gentle, and kind. I've always seen them, but now that I'm really looking at them, all I see is a heavy sadness. His eyes have always been so bright; I never noticed the shadow hiding behind them.

It feels like a stage lighting tech, who makes sure the spotlight is on everyone, making sure they're getting enough of it while he stands in the background. The shadows.

I try to garner words, something to help me help him know *I see him.*

All to show, nothing to give. The thought hammers in my head, like an incessant woodpecker, drilling and reminding me that I'm not good enough to help. Not good enough to be someone's something.

But I don't let myself pull back and hide in my corner of darkness. Instead, I cup his cheek, rubbing slow, gentle circles. "You're not alone, Daniel." And I've never felt more seen. But does he feel seen? "I'm here," I opt for saying instead of asking.

Nerves are bubbling in my chest. I'm afraid I'll say something wrong and ruin this moment.

I've never had a frozen-in-time moment, but this sort of feels like it. I want to encapsulate it and not let go. Store it in a safe place. But the moment gets disrupted by whatever's boiling in the pot. The lid clinks and the boiling water attempts to spill out.

"Shit." He scurries over and moves the pot onto the empty burner. "I promise I know what I'm doing."

"I hope so because I don't." I eye the food on the counter,

especially the raw chicken. I wouldn't even know where to begin. "How long have you known how to cook?"

"Eight...no nine, I think it was. Mom didn't play around. Our age didn't matter in the Garcia household. She'd always tell us, *'Tienen que ponerse las pilas, porque si me muero, que van hacer?'* There's never a day she isn't saying that. And she's also a firm believer in equality and hates all the *machismo* bullshit. So unfortunately, she didn't play favorites, but I like to make Pen believe I'm the favorite to make her mad."

The glee in his voice makes me smile. "What's having siblings like?" The words tumble out of my mouth before I can stop myself. "I—"

"You can ask me anything, I don't mind." He pours the water into the sink, making sure the potatoes don't fall. "It's...annoying. I'm the oldest so anything that ever happens falls on me." My stomach painfully knots at the melancholic sound in his voice. "But uh, they're great when they're not annoying the fuck out of me. Pen, God, she knows how to make a situation go from zero to one hundred in seconds. Don't ever put her down as your emergency contact. And Adrian, he would..." He chuckles emptily but mournfully. "Whine and lie about everything. He'd smile, popping those dimples—that I didn't inherit—to get away with anything. And it always worked."

He grabs milk, butter, and a few condiments, and that's when I realize he's making mashed potatoes, my favorite.

"I don't have an emergency contact but—"

"Put me down," he casually supplies and grabs the masher just as casually. Actually, everything he's doing seems like something he regularly does.

This feels so domestic.

"No, I don't want to—that's not necessary."

He mashes the potatoes, hardly adding pressure, but it's enough to make his biceps flex. I bite the inside of my cheek and force myself to look away.

"You don't want to what?" he presses, insistent as always.

Be a bother. Annoy you more than I already have. Inconvenience you. "It's not necessary."

"Mmm, I disagree. I think it's very necessary. Put me in your phone."

"No, stop being so insistent or I'm going to kick you out." I'm not. As much as I like being alone, I like having him here more.

He flashes me a cute, boyish grin and before I know it, he's grabbing my phone off the island, holding it up to my face, and unlocking it. I quickly go to him and try to grab it, but despite me being five ten, he's still taller than me.

"Daniel, no." I'm practically climbing him, but he's not budging. I'm breathing harshly, trying to get it out of his grasp, but he only spins as he continues to put his information in my phone. "That's not—"

"All—" He looks down at me, and it doesn't dawn on me until his eyes descend between our chests that I realize how close I am to him. Or that when he spun, I followed him, and now I'm pinned between the counter and him. "Done."

"You didn't need to do that." I track his tongue as it pokes out and drags along his top and bottom lip.

"I did and I wanted to." He pushes the wayward strands of hair away from my face and behind my ear. His finger stalls at my hair before it drops down to my shoulder. He slides the blunt tip of his nail in a circle, sending a chill down my spine. "You're O positive and an organ donor. I'll need to know more about you."

His eyes darken, smoldering but freezing me in place.

"There's not much to know," I quietly reply, fisting my palms and clenching my thighs.

"I didn't believe it before, and I don't believe it now."

My breath staggers when his finger bumps the strap of my tank top.

His eyes dilate and mine flutter.

Disappointedly, my phone buzzes in his palm, breaking the trance we found ourselves stuck in.

"Sorry. Here." He steps back while handing me my phone.

When I look at the caller ID, I know I could call them back later because it's one of my clients' parents, but I answer it anyway because I don't know what to say. I can't wrap my head around what we did even though we didn't do anything. He just...lightly touched me and I...liked it.

"I have to take this."

He gives me a thumbs-up and resumes cooking while I do everything in my power to cool down as I step into my bedroom again.

A few minutes later and he's cooking more things. My kitchen smells ridiculously good, and he's singing that song that's not in English or Spanish.

"What language is that?"

"Italian. This doesn't bother you, does it? I can put something else—"

This is so endearing, I can't begin to explain why.

"No, it's okay. I really don't mind it. I feel like I've heard this before but in English? And I didn't know you spoke another language."

"This is 'Con Te Partirò' by Andrea Bocelli. You've heard 'Time To Say Goodbye' that he also sang but in English." He switches the song and instantly the dots connect. "I don't know if you were obligated to at your high school, but we had to take two foreign languages. I picked Italian and for our final, we had to pick a song and sing a few lyrics. We got extra credit if we sang the entire song."

"Aren't you an overachiever?" I tease. "So, you can speak it then?"

"What can I say? I like getting good grades, and my dad would have also beat my ass," he sheepishly admits. "Can't say I blame him. He and Mom came to this country and worked their asses off to give us a better future. Getting good grades was the least I could do for them. I still struggle with a few words, but overall, I can speak and understand it."

I nod because I know. Mom might've been one of the highest paid professional swimmers, but her life wasn't easy before it. Then she accidentally had me and it fucked up her plans.

"I was homeschooled, but foreign language was still in my curriculum. I'm basic; I took Spanish." I shuffle on my feet, twisting my ring.

When he notices, I stop. Nothing horrible or traumatic happened to me, but I hate talking about those years. The loneliness. The long hours of constantly working at my desk with my teacher on the other side of the monitor. Mom reminding me how useless I was anytime my grades weren't where they needed to be.

"Say something to me," I say before he gets the chance to get a word out.

He thinks about it for a second and exhales.

"Sto facendo di tutto per non baciarti in questo momento."

I lift a brow, holding back a smile. "Well? You know I have no idea what that means."

He stares at me for a long beat, his amber eyes holding me in place and burning me up. "I said, I hope you're ready to eat."

22

DANIEL

Angel hits me with a curveball that just misses the outside corner, making the count 2-2.

We're hitting live at-bat, and while we consistently do this throughout the preseason, we've been ramping up more on it. Spending more hours in and outdoors, so the coaches can calculate our batting averages and we can work on anything we need to improve on.

From the corner of my eye, I see Noah positioning back into a squat as Angel readies himself.

"Stay ready," Noah lowly says from behind his mitt.

With the slight tip of my head, I position my feet, tightening my hands around the bat. He pitches but I mistakenly swing and miss because it's a fastball dot on the black, and it's a strike.

Now that makes the count 2-3. I'm out.

"I told you to stay ready." Noah stands, removing his face guard.

"*Perdon papi!*" Angel shouts from the mound, the corner of his mouth just barely quirking upward into a small smile. It's meant to come off as *I'm sorry, better luck next time, I'm a team player* kind of smile, but I know him enough to know he's full of shit.

That's his *I'm better than you, you suck ass* smile.

I grin, not letting his secret taunt get to me. Not that it ever does, and either way I'm in too good of a mood to give a damn.

"Bring it in," Coach D announces, waving his hand in for us all to gather around. "Good job out there." He praises us once we're all circled around him and spends the next few minutes going over things we need to tweak to improve before he releases us until we have to show up back tonight for our second practice of the day.

"Sanchez, Garcia, once you're done showering, in my office," Coach says as he walks out of the field.

Angel and I look at each other and while he furtively smiles, my mood isn't as positive as it was a second ago. I know what it's about; it's something we talked about a few months ago, something I knew was bound to come.

I should be ecstatic, but my stomach only knots, twists, and churns when Angel and I are both sitting in his office.

"I want to start off by saying that I'm immensely proud of you both." He bears a small smile, but I feel it exude with pride. He's not always a man of many words, but the faintest smile is enough to express exactly what he's feeling and is struggling to say. "I don't want to prolong this more than I need to, but I'm honored to have been able to coach you both."

"Aw, Vincenzo D'Angelo." Angel places a hand on his chest, brows drawn together and lips pursed in a pout. "You love us."

On a normal day, Coach D would not let that slide, but I know this is a special occasion, so he'll let it pass.

"Coach, I'm so touched," I force a smile.

I fold my hands on my laps, hating how they're slick with sweat. They haven't stopped sweating and my heart hasn't been able to beat the same. It's slow, dead almost, and maybe it'd be better off that way.

I pinch my chain and pull on it and away from my neck before I let it fall. The safety pin softly taps my chest, reminding me of my promise.

"I won't draw this out or leave you in suspense. You will or should have already received your MLB Draft Prospect Link email." His lips tip up a little higher, eyes shining with pride. In other words, that link is an invitation and a step closer to entering the MLB draft, so it's a big deal.

You did it!

I mimic or at least aim to mimic Angel's *excited but trying to keep it cool* posture. Because this is a big deal; it's something we've been busting our asses for since we realized we could potentially make a career out of baseball.

So I should be over the goddamn moon because I'm a step closer to finally making the dream a reality. But as happy as I want to be, I can't. It feels wrong.

My stomach bottoms out and the protein shake I had before we came into his office threatens to rise. Between the nausea and the guilt-consuming thoughts, I zone out. I hear him go over what's to come, but I don't feel like I'm really here.

Everything has gone on autopilot. I smile, shake his hand, and deliver a *thank you* and *I couldn't have done this without you*. There are many more words we exchange and then I watch him do the same with Angel.

I don't feel like myself but it's not until Coach asks me to stay back and shut the door that I feel like I'm somewhat back to reality.

"What's going on?" he asks, eyes assessing keenly over me.

You did it!

I smile wider, hoping I'm masking how disoriented I feel. "Nothing, why?"

He tilts his head, crossing his arms against his chest, like he's not believing me. "You look a little pale. Don't let this all overwhelm you. If you have any questions, don't hesitate to ask for help, Danny. I know it's a lot of information, but you've got me and everyone here ready to help you. We're all rooting for you and want to see you succeed."

My chest constricts, but I brush away the discomfort. "Yeah, it's a lot but I promise I'm good. I think the protein shake isn't sitting right in my stomach," I lie.

"Please don't puke in my office because if you do, I will make you clean it up." He grimaces, backing away like he's afraid I'll throw up any second.

I quietly laugh, still not feeling better, but at least now it's easier to pretend like I'm fine. "Don't worry, I'm leaving now."

Join MLB Draft Prospect Link

I reread the subject line too many times.

You did it! my subconscious voices, reminding me this is what I've worked for, what I've wanted, what I've dreamed of.

My finger glides along the touchpad, and I'm hesitant and anxious about clicking the email.

Making up my mind, I close my laptop instead and shove it back in my bag.

You did it! it reminds me again. *Call Mom and Dad. Tell Pen. Answer the guys' messages they left in the group chat.* Angel told them so they've been blowing up my phone.

You did it!

I shouldn't be alone. I should be doing something, right? I shouldn't be holed up in a room in the university's library.

You did it!

With each reminder, the air becomes more shallow, the weight on my chest heavier and unyielding, and the guilt all-consuming.

You did it!

I should be happy...

Before my hollow thoughts can extinguish whatever air is left, I toss my bag over my shoulder and slip out of the study room.

Still, I struggle to breathe and to keep up the fragile mask threatening to disintegrate off my face. It doesn't help that as I walk out of the library and head to the university's parking deck where my car is, I feel like I'm fighting against gravity.

"Danny!" Pen calls my name, halting me before I make it inside the parking deck.

I hope to God Angel didn't tell her because I told him not to.

I turn, masking a smile. "Hey."

"Where's your phone? I've texted you like twenty million times." She stands in front of me, panting and slightly sweaty.

I should tell her. She's right here. She deserves to know, but so did Adrian and he's not here.

The bridge of my nose and the back of my eyes burn.

"Did you run here?" I blink the feeling away, but that distorts the color making everything one blur of black and white.

Smile harder.

"Yeah, I wouldn't have if you would have answered your phone." She aggravatedly blows out a weary breath.

"Sorry, I was busy." I fish my phone out and sure enough find ten messages from her. All of them are her asking if I have cash on me. "Really, Pen? You know there are ATMs everywhere."

"I know but they tax you like five dollars, and in this economy, I refuse to lose that." She wipes the sweat off her forehead. "So can I borrow twenty dollars?"

"Borrow?" I cock a brow, knowing damn well she has no intention of ever paying me back. "You owe me like a thousand dollars."

She gasps, pretending to look offended. "That's not true. I've never borrowed that much."

I pull my wallet out. "Do I want to know what it's for?"

"Nope." She sweetly smiles at me when I take out forty dollars. As she goes to take the money from my hand, her eyes do a double take on my wallet. "What's that?"

"What's what?" I quickly shut it and tuck it in my pocket.

Her eyes narrow in suspicion. "What are you hiding?"

"What are you talking about?" I take a step back when she takes a step forward.

Her gaze burns a hole in my jean pocket, and she takes another step. "What's in your wallet?"

I stretch my hand out, my palm on her face to stop her from taking another step. "Do you have no sense of personal space? You're worse than Angel."

She slaps my hand away. "I don't think your boyfriend would appreciate you talking about him like that. And I'm your sister; personal space doesn't exist between us."

"Is that right?"

"Don't do that thing where you mix my words and use them against me," she says and again, she tries to get closer. Somehow, she manages to achieve it because she's right in front of me. I try to push her off, and if it weren't because we're on campus, I'd put her in a headlock. We play around a lot and have playfully fought, but not everyone sees it that way and I don't want them to think I'm attacking her. Which is why she finds a way to take my wallet out and opens it. Her eyes excitedly shine until she sees what's inside. Her entire face morphs into confusion. "Why do you have this?"

"*No seas pinche metiche.*" I snatch it away and tuck it deeper in my pocket.

"Is that the—"

"It's not. I gotta go to my hiking seminar. Do you need anything else?" I step back, adding enough distance between us, but something tells me she's not going to get in my space again.

She saw it and knows exactly what it is. But I deny it regardless.

Her lips stretch wide into a knowing grin, eyes sparkling with hope. "Oh Danny."

"Shut up. It's not like that. I meant to take it out."

"Mm-hmm, sure, right," she drawls sarcastically. "So is it what I think it is? Because I'd recognize that anywhere."

I inhale a patient breath. "I gotta go. You need anything else?"

Pen's face softens. "I'm proud of you."

My heart accelerates. "For what?"

"Josie told me about the swimming lessons. I've been meaning to text you, but I felt like that wasn't a text message conversation." Her voice is poignant, despite the small smile on her face. "Mom and Dad are going to be proud too."

I feel too much and then nothing at all. "I highly doubt that. Well, Mom maybe, but Dad—"

"Don't say that. He—"

"You didn't tell them, did you?"

"No, but you should. I know it'll—"

"There's a big chance this isn't going to work. I tried to talk Jos out of it, but...I'm doing it because we agreed on something. Don't tell them because I don't need them getting their hopes up over something that isn't going to help." By the end of that, I feel annoyed and more tired than I already was. If it wasn't because I know I'll be seeing Josie, I'd skip class.

"You called her Jos." She stifles a laugh and flattens her lips when I give her an unimpressed look. She's my sister so she's unaffected by my slight lash out, but still, I feel bad.

"We're friends." I shrug.

There's a beat of silence, only a second long, before she's beaming. "What did you guys agree on?"

"You're so nosy. I'm leaving." I wave goodbye and hear her say she'll text me later and that I better answer or she'll kill me.

I just hope I don't do it before she does.

By the time I arrive at the new trail, I'm surprised to spot Josie already there.

She's leaning against the driver's door, camera in her hand, and eyes trained on the small screen. When I pull in next to her, she lets it hang from her neck, and it's not until I'm out that she's standing next to me.

I'm scrambling to get my thoughts together, hoping my heart

won't explode from how fast it's beating, and attempt to look and sound as nonchalant as she does.

Everything I was feeling earlier leaves, like it always does when I'm around her. I don't know what it is about Josefine that makes my thoughts run mad but also makes everything in me feel calm.

I wanted to explain that to her yesterday in her pool, but my nerves coupled with the fact that I was so close to her made it hard to explain.

"Hey, Josie." I smile down at her.

She looks up, lips lifting slightly. "Hey, Garcia."

Fireworks, a million of them, go off in my chest.

Like usual, we gather around Professor Carleson, and he explains the do's and don'ts of hiking and then we're walking.

"Have you decided what you're going to do for your final exam?" she asks and surprises me because usually I'm the one talking first and asking all the questions.

It'll be a while before the semester is over and we need to submit our final exams, but Carleson has already assigned it because of everything it entails.

Along with a ten-page paper and twenty pictures we take while on our hikes, we have to pick one color and create something with it. We can use any art medium form with that one color, but the catch is mixing it with nature.

"I have an idea but I'm still thinking about it. You?"

From my periphery, I see her shrug. "I'm still thinking about it too. Have you picked a color?"

"Brown."

"Brown? You know there are so many colors you could've picked from?"

"I know but I have a thing for brown."

Her eyes meet mine and the sun hits them just right; they look like two pools of incandescent amber. Mesmerizing and magnetic, making it hard to look away from.

"A thing for brown?" She sounds amused. "I thought your favorite color was green?"

"Yeah, a thing. I happen to really like that color." I reply. "And it is but it's a bit too obvious and brown is different. Brown is...I just have a deep thing for it."

She stares, a little dumbfounded, like she can't fathom why I would pick that color out of all the colors. "I'm intrigued."

So am I.

"What about you?"

"Still thinking about it," she answers as she fiddles with the zipper of her bag strapped to her chest. It's almost like she's anxious, and I wouldn't have picked up on it except I see her twist her ring and tuck her hair behind her ear. "I have something for you."

She unzips her bag and hands me a small square envelope.

"Can I open it now?" My mind is running wild and my heart is racing again.

"If you want, or you can wait." She busies herself, taking pictures of the trees and things we pass by while I open the envelope and pull out the small handmade card.

"You made this for me?" I hold back my smile at the piece of toast with the words, *Here's A Toast*, above it.

"Yeah, I'm not super creative or funny like you, but I tried," she quickly says like she's embarrassed.

"I think you're funny."

She rolls her eyes, but I spot a small tilt to her lips and that makes me smile.

When I direct my attention back to the card and open it, my breath hitches at the silver key taped on one side. On the other side, it says, *To Your New Toaster*. The bottom has two different toasters drawn inside that look like little homes. One is old with two slots for bread, while the other is new with four slots.

"Josie."

"You don't have to stay, but if you ever feel like you need to um...get some rest, you can. Don't feel obligated to spend the night or come over. But if you ever need space from your roommates, you're more than welcome to stay."

For the first time in a while my thoughts aren't running manic because I have none. I'm genuinely shocked. I don't know what to say until I snap out of it.

"Thanks, Josie." I take it off the card and immediately attach it to my key ring.

"Yeah." And then she goes quiet again for the rest of the trail.

And so am I because I'm struggling to accept that she trusts me so much, she gave me a key to her house.

23

JOSEFINE

I'T'S WEIRD HOW SILENCE CAN FEEL SO LOUD, SO suffocating, so isolating.

It's my fault for craving it back then. I wished for it, prayed everything would just for a moment be quiet.

And now that I have it, I hate it.

Whoever said be careful what you wish for wasn't lying.

I wanted to stop hearing Coach Novak constantly remind me how I wasn't as good as everyone thought I was. And that was just a grain of what he said to me. He patronizingly laughed and said it was tough love, that he meant nothing by it.

I wanted to stop hearing Bryson whine about me not wanting to have sex with him. Or when I would, it wasn't enough.

I wanted to stop hearing Mom agree with Coach Novak. I wanted her to stop making excuses for how everyone treated me. I wanted her to stop blaming me for being so withdrawn.

I just wanted silence for one fucking second, but I got more than one.

Was it worth it?

I pull my hand away from the door handle that leads to her office. I need to go in there because I need to clean, but like every other time, I can't bring myself to do it. If she was here, she'd be annoyed. Mad even because I can't scrounge up the courage to just go in and dust everything off.

For as long as we've lived in this house, I've never set foot in there. She never allowed me, but now that I have nothing to stop me from going in, I can't.

Sighing, I turn around and put all the cleaning supplies away. I almost contemplate not eating because I'm lacking the desire to do so, lacking the energy to move, but the reminder that Daniel spent all evening yesterday meal prepping stops me from doing so.

Maybe he knew that'd be the motivation I needed to eat something. It works because I'm grabbing one of the glass containers and popping it in the microwave. Just like I did this morning and during lunchtime.

He made breakfast, lunch, and dinner meals for the entire week. They're all different things too, but for dinner they all consist of salmon, mashed potatoes, and brussels sprouts.

I don't know how he knew but this just happens to be one of my favorite meals—something I could live off and never get tired of.

Why was I going to skip dinner again? I find myself asking as I pull the drawer where I have the forks and spoons, but the thought leaves me when I spot a pale yellow Post-it note inside.

I hope you enjoy, and I'm so happy you're here!
With love, Garcia

I was rushing out the door this morning because I struggled to fall asleep last night. So, when I grabbed my breakfast and lunch, I didn't take a spoon or fork, thinking I'd get one when I got to campus.

Picking up the note, I reread it and even though the microwave is beeping every few seconds, letting me know it's finished, I don't move from my spot.

I don't understand why he continues to do nice things for me, but he does and it makes me feel like shit because *I see him too* and the only nice thing I could think of doing is giving him my house key. As if that'll make a difference or change his life.

The last thing he needs is to spend more time with me. I'll probably make him regret it or drain all of his energy.

When I gave him the key earlier today, he didn't say much. I shouldn't have ignored his silence. I should've known it was weird to give that to him. Why would he want to spend more time with me when he has his friends, his own house, and—

The front door opening freezes my thoughts.

I turn at the sound of heavy footsteps and the familiar deep voice that has been consuming my thoughts.

"Honey, I'm home!" Daniel greets and I'm met with the same playful smile when he enters the kitchen. "I've always wanted to do that."

I take him in, trying to absorb the fact that he's not only here but he has a large duffle bag that looks heavy and full.

"What are you doing here?"

His eyes bulge. "Please don't tell me that I just made a fool out of myself. Were you kidding about the key because I can leave. I—I'm sorry, I didn't—"

"No, wait. The key wasn't a joke." My thoughts are everywhere and my heart is leaping nervously but...happily. "I just didn't think you'd come today" or ever.

"Well..." He approaches me but stands on the other side of the island. "I did and unless you don't want me here, you should get used to seeing my *hot* face."

My lips twitch. "Hot face?"

"Hot face. Hot body. Hot everything." He raises his hands in surrender but stares at me unapologetically with a shit-eating grin on his face. "This really pretty girl said I'm hot and she's not wrong."

I roll my lips together to stop myself from smiling. "That girl might've been lying to you."

He shakes his head, his damp hair moving with the movement. "I highly doubt that *really pretty* girl was lying."

My heart rampantly flutters. "You don't get compliments often, do you? Is that why it went straight to your head?"

"I do but not from her." His soft eyes level with mine, steadying me as if they knew I felt a little off balance from his words.

"You should take her words with a grain of salt. Her words tend to be fickle."

"Unpredictability happens to be my middle name. So, I guess that makes the two of us fickle."

"I'm not sure that's how it works, and I thought it was *Jesus*?"

"That too." He grins.

I smile a little. His eyes flicker down to my mouth and stay there a little longer.

It feels like we're encased in a bubble again, but before we can get carried away by it, the microwave beeps again, reminding me I haven't eaten.

"Are you about to have dinner?" he asks, looking at the time on his phone.

"I am." I reheat my food knowing it likely got cold. "Have you eaten?"

"I haven't. I just got out of practice. I came over really quick to let you know I am going to stay before I grab something—"

"I have a lot of food. Do you want some?" I'm asking but already taking out one of the containers from the fridge and placing it in the microwave when mine is done heating up.

"I don't want to take your food. I made that for you," he says, and not a second later, his stomach is grumbling loud.

I give him a pointed look, letting him know I'm not going to argue with him.

"Thanks, Jos." He tenderly smiles at me. "I should probably go put this away." He pats his duffle. "Same room?"

I nod. "Same room."

"Be back, roomie." He winks at me before he's casually

walking away as if he's been here plenty of times before. As if this is an everyday occurrence, something he's used to.

When he's back, I tuck the Post-it note in the waistband of my shorts, and grab the silverware.

"How do you feel about eating outside?" He grabs his food and mine, stacking one on his forearm like a waiter, and grabs the glasses of water with the other.

"I guess it's going to happen whether I like it or not." I go to help him, but he doesn't allow me. "I can grab that."

"I know but I've got it." I open the door and guide us to where the table is.

"What are you trying to do? Show off?" Once he's set our food down, I take a seat, and he takes one next to me.

"Why? Are you impressed?"

"Maybe a little." I act nonchalant as I stuff a brussels sprout into my mouth. I softly moan, savoring how sweet and spicy it is. "I should send your mom a thank-you card. She did a great job with you. I can't believe how good this is."

He chuckles. "They're just brussels sprouts."

"Amazing brussels sprouts. These are my—"

"Favorite."

My eyebrows furrow. "How'd you know."

A simpering smile curls on his face. "Uh, in your interview you said your favorite meal after training was this. That you could live off this so..." He clears his throat. "If you do that, just be prepared." He cuts into his salmon and I shouldn't but I raptly watch him place the fork between his lips, reveling in the soft hum of his satisfaction.

I'd joke about his stalker tendencies but I can't. I've never had—no one has ever—I can't believe—I don't know what to think. But I do feel...overwhelmingly emotional.

"Why's that?" Looking away, I drink water, and shift my thoughts from his lips and his hum to the sound of the ocean not too far from us and how warm it feels tonight.

"Because she'll send you a Facebook friend request. Show you all my baby pictures. Then she'll not so discreetly ask you questions while she's actually plotting our marriage and making fake scenarios in her head about our future with our nonexistent kids and yeah, she's a lot. If you think I'm annoying, just wait until you meet my mom."

"I don't think you're annoying. Relentless until you get your way and cocky but not annoying."

"You forgot hot," he adds.

I scoff. "You don't have to worry about that because if your mom ever met me, she'd tell you to run."

He studies me, taking in my words, then his eyes sweep over me.

My brows scrunch together. "Why are you looking at me like that?"

"Because my mom would love you," he says so matter-of-factly it sends a shiver down my spine.

"Oh yeah?" I stuff my mouth because I don't know what else to say and instead look down at my steaming food. Jesus, this salmon is good.

"Yeah." I feel his eyes on me and eventually when I finally cave and look up, he's still looking at me. "She'd really love you. If you ever meet her, just be warned."

I nod, letting the silence settle between us.

"I hope I don't sound—you know what, let me shut up." He scoops up another forkful and my eyes betray me as they follow it slipping in and out of his mouth.

"Tell me." I softly kick him under the table.

He swallows. "It's not my business and I don't know why I thought of asking but—"

"Daniel, just ask me."

"Do you want to get married and have kids?"

My heart stutters and my hand tightens around my fork. Something is wrong with me for letting my mind run wild with that question. He's not asking me. He's just asking.

"I've never thought about it. Mom always said men were

useless and served no purpose other than to get you pregnant and leave you," I answer, eyes drifting to the pool. "Mom told me that's what happened to her when I was eight. I made the mistake of asking about my father and...anyway, it made me never want it or to think about it."

"I'm sorry," he empathetically says.

"It's okay." I shrug. "Mom wasn't in my life as much either because she was always busy with swimming and stuff."

"You know, if you ever want to talk about her, I'm here."

From the corner of my eye, I see him stretch his hand close to mine. His fingers flex before he fists his hand and leaves it resting next to mine.

"I know," is all I can bring myself to say because despite not having either in my life like I would have wanted, my life wasn't shit. I may have grown up with nannies, but they took care of me well. And I spent most of my life in swim meets and practices anyway.

But did I notice their absence? All the time.

"Do you want to get married and have kids?" I now ask.

"I never thought you'd ask." He flashes me a haughty smile. "But listen, I'm all for women taking the lead. I'm a supporter and all, but if anyone is going to propose, it'll be me."

"You're really willing to spend the rest of your life with me?" I don't know why I play along but I do.

"Yes." His knuckles brush against mine.

My cheeks flame. "Are you sure you want that?"

"I'm sure it's what I *need*," he instantly replies, not missing a beat.

I should call 9-1-1. Surely, I'm hallucinating. "And the kids?"

"As many as you want to have," he replies just as quickly.

"I was an only child and I didn't really like it so..." I pretend to think, but pretending becomes easy as images play in my head. "Two or four. I really don't like odd numbers."

He drums his fingers on the table, head tilted to the side as if he were pondering it. "Four sounds nice. What are we talking, back-to-back or a little age gap in between?"

I can't help but giggle. Did I really just giggle? I'm losing it. "It depends...have you heard about the terrible twos? Imagine a newborn, a one-year-old, a two-year-old, and a three-year-old. I'm sure that can't be safe anyway. Maybe a little age gap? We're also going to need the break to catch up on sleep."

"I'm not sure we'll be getting much sleep." I hear the innuendo loud and clear. I know I shouldn't but I do imagine it—him and me.

"As long as you promise to help me with the kids."

"You won't have to worry about anything. I promise to be the best DILF." He wiggles his brows.

"Oh God." I roll my eyes, ignoring the way I'm burning. "So, you want to get married and have kids?"

"With you, yeah. Just tell me when and where and I'm yours forever." Something sounds different now, but I'm sure I'm reading into it.

"Be careful what you wish for."

"I know. That's why I'm wishing for it." His smile and eyes seem different. Even his voice sounds different.

I bet he'll make it to the MLB. He'll have babies with a woman who isn't emotionally stunted and compared to Wednesday. A woman who has her shit together and didn't want to kill herself because she forgot how to feel.

Yeah, he'll find a pretty awesome woman to spend the rest of his life with, someone who isn't me.

24

DANIEL

I know I'm screwing myself over by drinking coffee past eleven p.m., but it gave me an excuse to spend more time with Josie.

I didn't want to say good night and maybe I'm hoping she didn't want to either. Because after I washed the dishes, I saw her fancy coffee maker, and made a comment about it. I said, "I bet the coffee tastes as fancy as it looks."

It was a lame comment, but the faintest smile curled on her lips, and she offered me a cup. I couldn't say no even though coffee's the last thing I need because I need to be up at five thirty a.m. for morning lift.

In hindsight, it really doesn't matter because morning lift could've been at two in the morning and I still wouldn't have said no. Though she could ask me to do just about anything. I'm not sure I'd ever have the ability to say no to her.

"You know, you really could've just put the dishes in the dishwasher." She hands me a steaming mug then settles down on the couch next to me with her own.

We would've stayed outside longer but it got a little chilly, and while I don't mind it, Josie is wearing a tank top and these tiny shorts. I hadn't noticed them at first, but then I did. I wasn't trying to stare, but when we came inside, she accidentally dropped something and bent over. It happened so fast, I didn't get the chance to turn around or shift my gaze away. I got a view of her ass cheeks. They were just there, hanging out, and I was there, staring like I'd never seen a girl's ass before.

"Growing up, we always washed all of our dishes by hand." Not only did we not have a dishwasher, but even if we did, Mom would've refused to use it. She said it'd make us lazier.

"Just letting you know, dishwashers save more water." She raises her mug, blowing into it to cool it down.

"Don't laugh."

"Why would I?"

"I don't know how to use a dishwasher," I admit and point an accusatory finger at her when I spot the slight twitch of her lips. "You said you wouldn't laugh."

"I'm not laughing." She raises a hand in surrender but still I hear the humor shining in her tone. "You know there's YouTube and the internet and—"

"I know. I guess I could've looked it up." I stifle my chuckle. "But I've just always washed them by hand, and the dishwasher at the baseball house is broken. We actually use it to store extra dishes and whatnot. When you go over...maybe don't look in there."

She takes a small sip, but I think that's to hide her smile. *Fireworks*. "So what you're saying is that I need to teach you how to use one?"

"You don't have to do that. I really don't mind washing them by hand." I blow into my cup before I take a small, careful sip. Yeah, just as good as I envisioned it.

"I'm going to show you." Her voice is firm and nonnegotiable.

"Okay," I concede, not that it would've taken much to get me to agree. "Show me, but washing dishes is the least I can do. You won't let me pay rent, clean, or do anything but be here."

We talked about it after we got done talking about our

pretend future. Though that got me thinking. Before, during, and after Amanda, it never crossed my mind. I have too much on my plate right now to have considered or wanted it.

But now I wonder about it and about hers too.

"Because the house has already been paid for and I clean, so you don't have to worry about it," she absently replies, eyes lost and detached.

"Hey." I reach for her hand but again, I curl my fingers into a fist and I don't touch her. I do keep my hand next to hers though. "We can compromise. I'll start buying groceries and cooking." Her lips part, and I don't doubt she'll argue against me doing that. "Take it or take it. I'm not going to argue with you, Josefine."

"You mean take it or leave it?"

My heart stutters at the graze of her hand against mine. "Usually but this isn't negotiable. I'm going to be here and I really want to be useful to you."

She turns her body to face me, raising her leg on the couch, but that causes my hand to brush against her shin. I jerk my hand back, resisting the sudden urge to *really* touch her. But that doesn't stop me from dropping my eyes to her parted legs. Or notice the way the seam of her shorts is wedged between her pussy.

Fuck me, maybe staying isn't a good idea.

I look away and notice something flash across her face, but it's gone before I can take it in.

"Daniel, I didn't give you a key to my house because I wanted you to work or *be useful*." She breathes a heavy sigh. "If I wanted a maid or chef, I would hire one." She shifts in her seat, like she's not sure if she wants to voice what she's thinking out loud or if she's comfortable enough. "I have enough money and—I'm going to leave it at that, but I want you to know that I see you too."

I'm uncertain what she means at first, but it dawns on me a second later. My chest constricts, and a knot the size of an entire continent lodges in the middle of my throat, making it hard to breathe.

I want to speak but I can't find the right words. I scope through my brain and try to find the appropriate thing to say.

Her throat bobs and she sits up straighter. "I may be the last person you want to talk to or even confide in. I'm not good at giving advice or being the most affectionate. I may be overstepping and you can tell me to never bring this up and I won't, but I just want you to know that I see you. *I see you,* Daniel," she reaffirms, like she needs me to understand that she knows what I'm feeling, that she can see it and isn't going to pretend it's not there. "I don't want you to feel like you need to make yourself cheerful or useful in order to be around me. I just want you to be you. And if you need someone to talk to, vent to, someone who will just listen, I'm here." Her brown eyes level with mine as she says that. "But if you don't, that's okay, too."

All the air I was struggling to breathe in, whooshes in so rapidly. I'm inhaling so much, my lungs burn and my chest hurts. I want to make it stop, I want to stop breathing, to stop thinking, but I can't.

I blink to not give myself away but as I do, images that haunt me play in my head. So many of them and all at once.

You have to help him! Help him!

"Garcia?" Her gentle voice stops the memory from playing on repeat. "Do you want to talk about it?"

I take a small sip of my coffee, letting the hot liquid burn my throat. I smile at her and hate myself because I should be helping her and not the other way around.

"Don't worry about me. I'm fine." I force my lips to lift higher, feeling angry that she looks genuinely concerned. "I promise."

I'm the guy who has his shit together. I don't worry people or make them sad. I'm the guy who people go to whenever something's wrong.

I should be that for Josefine, not the other way around.

The air whooshes in again, fast and heavy. My lungs burn and my head spins. I drink more coffee, not bothering to drink it slowly or carefully so I don't burn myself. At first, I wince as it goes down my throat, but then the pain subdues until I feel nothing.

Her lips pinch in a flat line. "Okay. I just wanted to let you know that I see you and I'm here for you."

"Thanks, Jos. I'm here for you, too." Again, I'm tempted to grab her hand, to hold her, to touch her, but I stop myself.

She stiffly nods, not really looking at me. Now I really hate myself. We were good, and now I ruined it.

"I—"

My phone vibrating in my pocket halts me from saying anything else. I don't know who could be calling me since it's late, and while the guys don't know where I am, they think I'm with a girl. It's not a lie; they just don't know the girl is Josie.

When I pull it out, I don't mean to, but I groan.

The guys told me to block Amanda's number, but I didn't want to be a dick. Which is really funny considering what she did. Now I'm not only regretting not blocking it but also not setting boundaries.

"Booty call?" Josie questions.

"No," I show her my screen. "Just an ex-girlfriend who won't get the hint."

Something sparks in her eyes and her lips twist in a small grimace. But then her entire expression morphs into something wicked. She sets her mug on the coffee table and stands in front of me.

I crane my head back, staring up at her, and clench my jaw. She's so close and smells so good. All I want to do is touch her.

"You helped me with Bryson. I want to help you. Do you trust me?" She holds her hand out, palm up, and I realize she's asking for my phone.

It stops vibrating and without giving it a thought, I unlock it and hand it to her.

"Can I sit on you?"

My heart careens and my body thrums with need. "Yeah, sure, go ahead."

She takes the mug from my hand, sets it next to hers, then makes herself comfortable on my lap. I think I hold my breath. I'm not sure because her ass is nestled right above my dick, so it's hard to focus on anything else.

"What do you want me to do?" My voice is gruff. Fuck.

"Nothing. Just stay still and breathe. You'll pass out if you don't." The tease in her voice doesn't help me. She's nonchalant and I'm struggling.

"I'm breathing just fine." My voice, fuck, why does it sound like that? It sounds breathless, husky.

"Mm-hmm." She lays my phone on her lap and pulls the thin straps of her tank top down and under her arms. Everything still remains as it is but her shoulders are bare and I'm still here struggling to breathe like a fish out of water. "Kiss my shoulder."

"What?" I croak but then clear my throat. Jesus Christ. "What?"

"Put your lips on my shoulder. I'm going to take a picture and send it to her."

I'm so dizzy, drowning in the scent of her lavender perfume, I can't think. I do as she instructs, placing my lips on her shoulder. *God, she's soft.* I don't move them as she shifts the camera so that it faces us. The screen only captures half of my face, from my nose down to my lips on her shoulder.

"Keep doing that, I really like that," she says, her voice a soft rasp but when a breathy moan escapes her lips, my cock throbs.

My hands flex at my sides, urging me to touch her but I don't.

"I got it," she says.

I pull back and don't say a word, not trusting my voice won't betray me.

"I left the picture on Live," she explains, pointing at the top right corner where it says LIVE. "I know she'll hold the picture down and look. That's why I said that. Sorry, I should've warned you, but it just came to mind."

Yeah, she should be apologizing because now I want to hear her say it over and over again.

I'm so out of it, I'm hardly able to listen or focus because she's still sitting on me. I'm in a stupor, stuck in a daze as she goes to my messages and finds her name. I'm glad I changed her name right after I found out she cheated on me. She clicks on it, sending her the picture and a message.

> Me: He's busy.

And then proceeds to put it on **Do Not Disturb**.

"I hope this is okay?" she asks, still staring at the screen, watching those three dots appear and disappear.

But me, I'm a piece of shit because my gaze trails from her shoulders down to her ass. I'm stuck on her sitting on me like this, and I picture things I shouldn't, like her bouncing on my cock and screaming my name.

What the fuck is wrong with me?

"Thanks, Josie, but I should go to bed. I gotta be up really early." My voice is hoarse and every part of me is sweating.

"Oh, yeah." She quickly gets up and hands me back my phone. "I got your cup." She eyes my empty mug, and I'd clean up after myself, but this is the one time I won't.

"Thanks." I'm up and turning around, making sure she can't see how hard I am. With my back to her, I say, "Good night, Josie," and rush up the stairs.

25
DANIEL

Slowly, I sink into the cold tub, my muscles tense, and I hold my breath until the frigid water sits right below my chest. Exhaling a breath, my body goes slack, my eyes flutter closed, and my head lolls back.

"I know that's right," Kai softly groans as he sinks into the tub next to me followed by Angel, Gray, and Noah. "Jesus Christ," he sighs, body sagging.

Practices are already brutal, but because we're about two weeks away from Opening Day, they have intensified times ten.

"They must hate us because what the hell? My arms." Gray tips his head back and shifts in the water, trying to get comfortable.

"Stop moving," Noah grumbles, muttering something in Portuguese under his breath.

Our Brazilian friend likes to do that to spite us because he can occasionally be a dick, and it brings him great joy knowing we have no idea what he's saying. He didn't voice that or smile about it, but I can see the elation in his eyes when he sees the frustration on Kai's and Gray's faces.

For Angel and me, our dialect may be different, but we can semi-ish pick up a word or two.

"Don't act like you're not sore, Sosa." Kai muffles his groan, his voice and body drained from today's demanding schedule.

He doesn't reply because he knows he'd be lying. We're all tired and no amount of lying can hide how spent our bodies are.

"That's what I thought," Kai loftily retorts before his gaze skids in my direction. "So...Danny..." His lips stretch into a sly grin.

I should've gone home. I've been able to avoid their inquisition all week, but I know it was inevitable and their questions were bound to be asked. But that doesn't mean I have to answer, and I'm not. I have six minutes in the tub. Just six more.

"Yeah...so Danny boy. Where have you been, *papi*?" Angel cocks his head to the side, observantly watching me just like the other guys are. Even Noah is staring at me, waiting for an answer. "You've not slept over since Monday. That's four days now. Today's Friday. Are we going to five?"

I abstain from laughing because they're all staring at me curiously.

"Why are you guys keeping tabs on me?" I avoid the question, asking my own.

"Who is she?" Gray all too eagerly asks.

"I've been staying over to work on my swing."

I'm not lying. I've been staying over and working on a few things. But then again, I guess the reason I've been spending extra time in the batting cages is because of Josie.

After she sat on me on Monday, I realized that I may be a little sexually frustrated. Maybe *a little* is an understatement because every day this week, I may have...ugh...even admitting this to myself is pathetic, but I've been fucking my own hand.

It's not Josie's fault my dick can't seem to calm down every time I'm alone and thinking of her.

I hate myself because it's wrong. She's allowing me to stay in her house and I'm taking advantage by thinking of her when I come. I've also overstayed my welcome because she didn't say I could move in. Only said I could go over whenever I needed space from the guys. She hasn't said anything, not that I've seen her much this week. We've been so busy, I didn't get to see her Wednesday because I had a meeting with my coaches.

Still, I want to stay despite the slight awkwardness on my end Monday night. I actually plan to bring it up tonight, that is, if she's awake. I know she has swimming lessons tomorrow, so she might be asleep but if she's not, I'm going to talk to her about me potentially making it official and moving in.

Maybe it's too fast, too soon, but I hate that she's alone and maybe she prefers that and I'll respect her decision if she does, but it doesn't hurt to ask.

"But you're not coming home," Kai pointedly inserts.

"Okay and?" I lift a shoulder in an indifferent shrug and unlock my phone. I peruse Instagram, blatantly ignoring all their questions until a message at the top shuts them out.

> Josie: Hey. I need to talk to you

Despite the freezing water, I find myself sweating. I probably —no I *definitely* overstepped and invaded her space and boundaries.

I made sure to keep the house as it is. Josie wasn't lying when she said she likes to keep things a particular way.

I try to recall if I left anything out of place or if I did anything that would upset her, but nothing comes to mind.

> Me: Be there in 30 mins. Is that alright?
> Josie: Yeah. Please drive carefully Garcia!
> Me: I will. I promise

"I'll see you guys later." I climb out of the tub.

More questions get thrown my way, but I can't focus on a single one.

"It's Josie, isn't it?" is what Gray asks. I don't mean to give myself away, but I tense. "I fucking knew it." I hear the smirk in his voice as I walk away.

I could've been at her house in less than twenty, but I needed to make a stop at my house first. But as I pulled into the driveway, I regretted it as I spotted a white Toyota parked in the driveway and Amanda perched on the first step of the front door.

Sucking a breath to muster up every ounce of patience, I climb out of my car and walk over to her.

"Hey, Danny," she softly greets, her voice melancholy and full of longing.

"Hey." I keep it short because the last thing I need is for her to get the wrong idea.

She must sense that because she gives me a tight-lipped smile. "Can we talk?"

"I really can't right now." I walk around her to open the front door.

"Please, I just need you to hear me out," she pleads and even though my back is to her, I feel how close she is. "I promise I'll leave once I say what I need to say."

I close my eyes, garnering the strength to say fuck it and tell her to leave. But I'm not that person. As much as I want to be a dick, I can't.

"Okay but make it quick. I need to be somewhere." I open the door and let her walk in first, before I do.

She stands by the staircase, no doubt waiting for me to give her the green light to go up to my room, but I jerk my head in the direction of the living room.

"I'd like for us to speak in private." A pinch of annoyance crosses her face when I shake my head.

"We shouldn't be interrupted. The guys won't be here for another twenty minutes and we need to make this quick," I supply.

She stares at me, offended, and scoffs but she sighs and takes a seat on the sectional. I swallow back my grumble and take a seat on the recliner.

"I know nothing I say or do will change what I did but if I could go back and change it, I would."

I stand because we've had this conversation several times and it never ends well.

"We can't keep doing this. I told you I'm done and—"

"I understood that loud and clear when you sent me that picture Monday night." She stands, anger flooding her blue eyes. "If you want that to make us even, then we're good. I promise." Her eyes soften. "I'm over it and I can look past it."

I incredulously scoff. "Look—"

"I miss you." Her voice cracks and eyes fill with unshed tears. "I know I fucked up and I hate myself for it."

She steps closer but I take two back. Shaking my head, I heave a deep sigh. "Please don't do this. Please don't."

"Danny, I'm sorry. I'm so sorry." Her bottom lip trembles and a tear streaks down her face. There's a pang in my chest but it hits harder at her next words. "Have you forgotten everything we did together? What about karaoke? And all those pictures you took of me, of us? All the promises we made to each other and how much fun we had. Remember when we fell asleep at the beach? Or when we got locked out of my car and it rained? Please don't let my fuckup taint the good memories. We have so many, remember?"

Amanda steps closer, but this time, I don't move. She approaches me and snakes her arms around my torso. She peers up at me, those blue eyes glistening red and a trail of tears staining her cheeks.

"I love you," she feebly implores.

"I..." I hesitate but she weakly smiles nonetheless, standing straighter against me. "I don't love you."

I didn't hesitate because I'm not sure what I feel for her. I hesitated because despite what she did to me, I don't want to hurt her, but I guess I did anyway because the look on her face morphs in pain.

"What—but—I—" she blubbers, and more tears cascade down her face. "You really don't miss me?"

"Amanda." I grab her shoulders, staring down at her and as I do, I think of brown eyes. "I don't. I don't miss you and I don't have any more feelings for you." I gently push her away from me until her arms fall at her sides. "I think it's best if we stop talking to each other."

Her brows pull, lips thin, and bloodshot eyes hollow. "You really don't want to give us a second chance? You really can't forgive me?"

"No," I firmly say. "I don't want a second chance and I've moved on."

Her face grows taut and those saddened eyes turn ice cold. "Moved on with Bryson's ex? Is that who you're going to see now?"

"I don't need to explain myself to you."

She ruefully laughs and folds her arms over her chest. "I saw you both at the party. I saw the way you were dancing with her. Is this your way of getting back at both of us? If this is your way of making me jealous, congratulations. It worked. I'm jealous. Really fucking jealous, Danny."

"I'm not doing this to get back at you. We're friends and we were just dancing." I grind my teeth, doing my best to hold it together.

"Just friends? She had her ass all over you. That's not a friend!" She drops her hands at her sides then points an accusatory finger at me. "Wait, that was her in the picture, wasn't it?" She sullenly laughs when I don't answer. "You had your fun, petty moment. I get it, I deserved it. If there's videos too, send them my way. I deserve that too. But I'm willing to overlook it all. I don't care what you've done. I just want you back."

"No!" My voice raises more than I intended it to. "I can't keep doing this. I'm trying so hard to keep the peace but you just—"

"I just what?" Her voice raises. "I'm just trying to get my boyfriend back. I'm just trying to apologize because I know I fucked up. I know what I did was wrong. I know! I'm so sorry!"

"You fucked *my teammate* on my birthday!" She flinches but I can't bring myself to care anymore. I've been too nice, and she has the audacity to act like she's in pain as if she didn't cause me my own. "You sexted *my teammate* on our anniversary! You looked at the camera when *my teammate's* dick was between your breasts and smiled. You fucking smiled, Amanda! You're not sorry, you're just sorry you got caught. We have *so many* memories, but in all of those, he was there too. So don't make yourself the victim."

The worst of it is that it wasn't just Bryson. She may not have slept with the other guys, but she flirted with anyone who'd give her attention. She loves that and that's why she fucked around with Bryson because he gave it to her.

"I didn't know he was going to send it to you," she meekly says.

I laugh, because she's got to be kidding me. "Not only did you fuck him but you knew he had a girlfriend. You knew he was dating Josefine. You knew and neither one of you cared. So whatever I do with Josefine is none of your goddamn business."

She's shaking with rage, fisting her hands at her sides, blowing a ragged, brittle breath.

"Fine, whatever." She stalks past me, but before she's out the door, she looks over her shoulder. "He wants her back, you know. Bryson." She says his name as though I need the clarification, and then she storms out and slams the door.

A second later, the guys walk in, pretending like they didn't hear that, but I know they heard everything.

"See, now this is why I don't do girlfriends," Angel announces and I know it's more to lessen the tension but I'm so mad, I go to my room, grab what I need, and leave.

I'm speeding into Josie's driveway forty minutes later. I'm only ten minutes late but she could have already gone to bed. I'm hoping that's not the case and my hope is kindled when I see her outside, her driver's door opened.

All the anger coursing in my system instantly vanishes at the sight of her. My thoughts of Amanda, Bryson, and the email I have yet to open shift to the back of my head. Incandescent brown eyes take over my field of vision when I put my car in park and hop out with the gift in my hand.

"Hey, what are you—"

"What the fuck is wrong with you?" Josie lashes out, voice cracking with fury and eyes burning with a lethal rage. I stagger in my step.

"What's wrong?" I walk towards her, but she steps backwards and away from me.

"What's wrong?" she repeats in disbelief. Her sharp, seething voice pierces me, her body vibrating so fiercely it stuns me. "What's wrong? You said thirty minutes! You said..." She stalks towards me and jabs her finger at my chest. "Thirty minutes, Daniel! You said you would be..." Her voice goes hoarse and then it cracks. "Here in thirty minutes. You promised!"

"Josefine, hey, I'm here now, I'm sorry. I didn't—"

"No!" she shouts, backing away, raising a hand for me to stay away from her. "I don't want you here. I want you to leave. This was a mistake. Grab you stuff and get the fuck out!"

She blows out a heavy, pain-filled breath and storms into her house, leaving me alone outside.

26

JOSIE

> Mother: Be there in thirty minutes. I hope everything is as I left it.

I DON'T UNDERSTAND THE POINT OF HER COMING HOME when we're not going to spend Christmas together.

I sit in the living room, deciding I'm not going to reply to her message. I stare at the Christmas tree she put up without me. Not that we've ever put it up together, or really do anything together. Unless it has to do with swimming. That's the only thing she wants to be involved in.

After an hour of waiting, I decide to put my irritation aside and text her. She should've already been here.

> Me: Everything is as you left it.

One hour and a half later.
I'm pacing and bouncing between texting, calling, or doing nothing at all. She'll get annoyed with me if I text her too much. But this is so unlike her. If she was going to do something else, she would've told me so I wouldn't wait up for her.
Two hours later.

Fuck it.

"This is Claudia Resendiz, leave a message after the tone."

"Mom, hey, I'm sorry for bothering you, but I just wanted to make sure everything's okay. Just text me back."

Four hours, ten voicemails, and twenty text messages later and the doorbell chimes.

Scurrying to the door, I don't think as I open it. Two police officers stand outside, their hardened expressions softening when they look at me.

All the blood rushes to my head, making me dizzy, but I firmly hold the doorknob, doing my best to stay balanced.

"Hey, I'm Sergeant Grant Hanson and this is my partner, Jorge Chavez. Are you Josefine Resendiz?" I nod. "Do you mind if we come in?"

I absently shake my head, pulling the door back to let them both in. Then he asks if we can take a seat, but I stay standing because I'm not sure I can physically move anymore.

He sighs. It's so quiet but I catch the heaviness of it, feel it deep in my bones and the faintest, most empathetic smile on Jorge's face has me seeing black dots.

"Are you the daughter of Claudia Resendiz?" Grant asks and all I can do is nod. "Your mom was in a serious car crash and she was rushed to Monterey Regional Medical Center, but she did not survive."

"No," I laugh, shaking my head in disbelief. "She said she was going to be here in thirty minutes. She texted me." I pull up the message and show him. "See? That couldn't be her. That's not her. That couldn't...no."

He speaks for what feels like an eternity, but even though he's standing right in front of me, I can't hear a word he's saying. I try to call her again, but she doesn't answer.

I hear "I'm sorry" a multitude of times. From both Grant and Jorge. But it doesn't settle until Grant asks, "Is there a friend or relative who could come over and drive you to the hospital?"

"No, I have no one else."

Sinking down to the floor next to my bed, I bring my legs to my chest, circling my arms around them. My heart is racing and I'm profusely sweating. My hair sticks to my neck.

I shut my eyes, doing my best to control my shallow breathing and to stop myself from hyperventilating. *He's alive, I know he's okay, I saw him.* It's what I tell myself, over and over again, but even though I saw him, I'm struggling to breathe. I can't stop sweating.

"Josie."

I lift my head, turning it to my right where it came from. Daniel's in my bedroom, standing before he's sitting next to me.

"I thought I told you to leave." I look away, biting the inside of my cheek to stop myself from going off on him again. My face burns and my vision blurs, eyes welling with tears I refuse to let spill.

"Jos, look at me," he gently says, his voice pleading.

I don't want to, but I can't shut him out.

"What?" I sniffle and hate myself as a lone tear streaks down my cheek, but staring at him only forces more out. A lump grows in my throat, making it hard to speak but that doesn't stop the stupid choked sob to get past my mouth.

"It's okay, Josie. I'm right here."

I don't fight him when he wraps an arm around my shoulder and the other around my front, hauling me to him. He holds me firmly, letting me break down in his arms. He doesn't ask me what's wrong or badger me with questions. He only rubs my arm until I'm sniffling.

I'm not sure how I manage to speak, but once I do, I can't stop. "You can't promise you're going to be here at a certain time and then not show up. You can't make those kinds of promises. You shouldn't make them if you can't keep them."

"I'm sorry, Josie." He hooks a finger under my wet chin and makes me look at him. His eyes bore into mine, then sweep over my face, before he wipes away the remaining tears. "I had every intention of being here on time. I'm sorry for worrying you. I promise I didn't mean to."

Words get caught in my throat. Ugly, vivid images play in my head.

"I'm here," he says and grabs my hand, making me cup his cheek. He keeps his large palm over my hand, the other still around my shoulder. "Do you feel me?"

I sniffle again and nod.

"I'm right here," he fervently says. "I'm not going anywhere."

"You can't make those promises," I croak.

"I know, I'm sorry. I didn't mean to put you through that," he sincerely says. "Do you still feel me?"

I nod again and when he drops his palm, I brush my finger on his cheek. It's not until I do that, that I realize I'm holding my breath and when I release it, everything in me eases. It's then I realize something I hadn't before: I'm sitting on his lap.

He doesn't look uncomfortable or weird like he had Monday night, but I know I should move. I'm okay now and I'm sure he knows that, but as if he were reading my mind, he says, "I'm here as long as you need me to be. You do what you need to do."

I should get up, but I don't. With my hand still on his cheek, I rest my head on his shoulder, close my eyes, and exhale a shaky breath.

"Mom texted me and said she was going to be home in thirty minutes."

He holds me tighter. I know he knows, like everyone in town knows, how she died. A man had been on something, was speeding, and hit her head-on. He lived because of course they always do, but she died on impact.

"Please..." I whimper. The thought of something happening to him painfully grips me. "Don't do that again."

"I promise I won't," he says against my head, and I feel him place a chaste kiss there.

My face warms, but I don't put too much thought into it. "I'm sorry for yelling at you."

"Don't apologize. I'm sorry for worrying you."

I drag my fingers down his jawline. There's more I should probably say and do. I should get off him, stop touching him, stop whatever it is I'm doing, but I can't bring myself to do anything that my brain is shouting at me to do.

When my fingers are at his chin, I lift them but hesitate when they're beneath his bottom lip. But then he tips his head down just a little and my fingers slip.

I brush them along his lips and feel his warm breath. My heart rate spikes when he kisses them or at least that's what it felt like to me. But when I feel it again, I know it wasn't my imagination.

I want to look up at him. I want it to be my lips instead. I want a lot of things, but those things aren't meant for me.

Daniel is perfect and I'm far from okay. I should think it through, but I also don't want to.

So I tilt my head back, looking up at him and find him already staring down at me. His eyes burn me and hold me in place, then they dip to my lips.

He doesn't make a move, he doesn't do anything but smile at me, and says something that feels like a slap to reality.

"I just want to remind you that as your friend, you can confide in me, Josie. Talk to me about whatever you want. I'm here for you."

Friend. Right.

He's just a big flirt, too friendly by default. He'd never like me like that.

"Thanks." I go to climb off him but feel him tighten around me. I'm sure it's my brain messing with me because when I do it again, his arms fall to his side. As if him running away Monday wasn't an indication that he's not at all remotely interested in me. He's being nice; I shouldn't mistake that for anything else.

For a moment neither one of us says anything. We sit next to each other until I finally break the silence.

"The reason I texted you was because I wanted to talk about our living arrangement."

He tenses next to me and winces. "Yeah, I know, I'm sorry. I didn't mean to overstay my welcome. I promise to get all my stuff and—"

"No, that's not it." I twist my ring, feeling anxious about what I'm going to say. Maybe I should think it through some more but that would do nothing because I know what I want.

"No?"

"No. I wanted to ask—and you don't have to and don't feel obligated—if you wanted to move in?" I know it's too soon, he's only been here for a week, but he's slept over since Monday. "I know you have your house and bills and you'd have to find someone to take over and whatnot, but if you want to, you can move in."

For a long moment, he's silent. Did I rush this? It's only been a week? What the hell was I thinking?

It just feels nice having someone here. Sure, when he's not, it's quiet, but it's not the same silence as before. It's a different kind of silence, like the kind you know is temporary. I can't believe I'm saying this, but I look forward to hearing his alarm in the morning. It's not any different than mine, but it's nice knowing it's someone else's. That someone else is here, filling the silence I've been struggling to fill.

"Forget I said anything." I go to stand, but his words stop me.

"I was actually thinking about asking you the same thing."

"Really?"

"Yeah, I've been thinking about it all week. I almost chickened out because I thought maybe it's too quick and maybe you want your space back. But I see I was wrong because you like having me here as much as I like seeing you, even if it's not much."

I almost smile but force my lips to remain still until my cheeks betray me, and I know he notices.

"It's not that I like having you here, but you cook. So don't get it twisted. That's the only reason why I want you here."

"Mm-hmm, right. I'm going to pretend you don't enjoy my presence as much as I enjoy yours." He grins.

"You enjoy my presence?" I make it sound playful but really, I'm a little desperate to hear him say yes. Because as stupid as it's going to sound, I want to hear someone say it again. Someone to say how much they like being around me.

"Yes." He doesn't miss a beat when he answers. "I love being around you and doing things with you. I wouldn't be here if I didn't."

This time, I smile and his eyes don't miss it. They never do. "So...you really want to move in?"

"How much would you judge me if I told you my car is sort of packed?"

My lips part in surprise. "You have stuff in your car?"

"Just a few necessary things."

I tuck my hair behind my ear. *Dammit. Don't do that.* He's *not* into me. "Oh, I'm judging you, but also, do you need help getting your stuff out?"

He offers me a crooked grin, his gaze coasting down to my lips. I'm not smiling but now I want to. They stay there, then he blinks and looks away.

"No, Josie, I don't need your help but thank you." His gaze dips to my lips again. *I need him to stop doing that.* I watch his Adam's apple bob, but his grumbling stomach makes the hot atmosphere cool.

"Hungry?" I tease, pretending like I don't want to kiss him again.

He's not into me.

"Can you tell?" He stands and holds his hand out. "You want to grab something to eat?"

I take his hand, and he pulls me to stand. "What do you have in mind?"

27

DANIEL

"Are you sure you didn't elope?" Kai questions.

"We promise we won't judge you," Gray adds.

"Are you dying of jealousy, Gray?" Angel taunts him, smirking when he rolls his eyes.

Gray flips him off. "Shut up."

"So did you elope?" Kai asks for what seems like the millionth time.

"Is she pregnant?" Gray asks.

That makes me stop packing and look up at my roommates who have decided to take every inch of space in my room.

After practice today, I told them I'm moving out and where I'm moving to. The moment I said Josie's name, they started throwing questions left and right and haven't stopped. And they all happen to be the same questions. Except the pregnancy one; that one is new.

"We'd have to have sex for that, and we haven't and we're not." Because we're friends and I'm not going to ruin that even though I've been dreaming of it.

"That didn't stop Mary from getting pregnant." Gray shrugs,

and for a moment, we all look at him and instead of saying anything, we all shake our heads.

"It's true!" Our heads whip to the voice coming from the door. Pen is grinning from ear to ear, her eyes wide and glittery. "You are moving."

I glance at Angel, but he shakes his head. "Don't look at me. I didn't say anything."

Gray looks every which way except for my direction.

"You couldn't have waited until I was out?"

"Hey! Why couldn't I know?" she snaps, coming further into my room.

I continue packing, ignoring her and all their probing eyes.

"So...is she pregnant?" Pen throws out as she tries to find space on the floor to sit.

"Jesus Christ, what is it with you guys and that question? We're friends. Can't friends live together?"

They all laugh like I've said the funniest thing in the world. I don't usually glare, but I find myself doing that. Particularly at my sister who has no business being here.

JOSEFINE

"We're just friends," I tell Vi.

She texted me and asked me to come over to her place. Pen would've come but she said she had things to take care of and that she'd come later. Which works out because I'm not sure I'd be able to talk about her brother in front of her.

"Just friends..." She sets the platter of sushi in the middle of the table, along with the other things she ordered. "With benefits?"

I wasn't going to tell her about Daniel moving in, but she started pleading and asking for crumbs. I've never had friends, at least stable ones, and Vi feels stable. I don't usually like to open up to anyone, not that I do it to begin with, but I figured it couldn't hurt to talk to her.

Now I'm regretting it.

I balk at her. "No, where do you get benefits from *just friends*?"

She gives me a cunning smile. "Come on, fess up. It's just us. You can talk about Daniel all you want. Pen isn't here to gag or beg us not to."

Using my chopsticks, I grab a roll and dip it in the soy sauce. "There's nothing to fess up. We're just friends."

She huffs an exasperated breath and gives me a thumbs down. "You gotta give me something, Josie. Something, anything. You guys are going to live together for the rest of the semester. He's literally moving in with you. Like how does one do that?"

"You pack your things and get out."

"You know what I mean. He has bills and stuff to pay."

"I'm not making him pay because it's not necessary, but he is going to cook. And Gray, do you remember him?"

She hums with pleasure. "Yeah, there's no forgetting him… that mustache and his little Southern accent."

"He's going to pay whatever Daniel was paying. Apparently, he has the money or whatever, I don't know. I didn't ask."

He texted me earlier today after his practice. He said he talked to the guys and just as expected, they took it well. We haven't talked any more because he's busy packing and I want to give him space.

Last night was a lot. My emotions were all over the place and they still are. I'm not sure if I'm doing the right thing by letting him move in. It's not because I don't want him to, but after I went off on him yesterday, I realized how much I care about him and that scares me.

Vi tucks her legs under her butt after she's done filling up her plate. She squares her shoulders like she's getting ready for business. "Just answer this: do you want to fuck him?"

"Uh, no."

"Ah! You hesitated."

"I didn't hesitate. I was chewing."

"Bullshit."

DANIEL

"Bullshit," Kai calls out.

"I suggest you all get help because your way of thinking is so unhealthy." I finish placing the last of my vinyls in a box then tape it up.

"You want to talk about unhealthy? You're moving in with a girl you've only known for a month, yet your ex-girlfriend asked you to move in with her and you said no," Angel counters, dead set on making a point just like everyone else has.

Except for Noah—he's been quiet, and I really appreciate that.

"That's not unhealthy," Noah says. I'm pleasantly surprised that he's sticking up for me.

"Thanks No—"

"It's delusional. I'm adding more money. No way they don't end up together before the end of the semester."

I spoke too soon. "Noah, shut up. Matter of fact, everyone shut up and get out. If you're not going to help, you have no use for me here." I set the box on the floor and grab another empty one. "Wait, are you guys still on with the bet? I told you to stop that."

"Bet?" Pen's gaze bounces over the guys. "What bet? I want to be part of it."

I grumble. "Pen, why are you even here?"

"So how much are we talking?" She ignores me.

"I'm moving in with her because you're all getting on my nerves."

"You know, if I were you, I'd also be living with her. You guys should see her house. It's so fucking nice," Angel says.

"Wait, how do you know what it looks like?" Kai looks between Angel and me.

"We helped change her tire and we followed her back home," he supplies.

"If you're not going to be useful, get out," I repeat.

"Are you just going to pretend like you didn't hear Angel's question?" Kai instigates, smiling innocently at me. "You guys eloped, didn't you?"

"*Váyanse a la verga.*" I wave my middle finger at all of them and continue packing my cassette tapes.

Kai places a palm on his chest, shocked and appalled written all over his face. "Do you kiss your mother with that mouth?"

"Danny, I'm going to tell Mom." I roll my eyes and ignore her but she's like a fly, dead set on being annoying. "Anyway, if she's your friend, why do you have—"

"Shut. Up," I grit.

"Have what?" Gray asks and that makes them all look a little too excited.

"Nothing," I mutter.

JOSEFINE

"I think he's hot, but that's it."

We've been going on about Daniel for forty minutes now. She won't drop it and I'm on the verge of leaving.

"Okay, let's play a scenario."

"No."

"Just hear me out, okay?" She doesn't wait for me to reply before she's giving me a play-by-play of her scenario.

"I have for the past forty minutes, Vienna," I grumble.

"You're so cute. My little ray of sunshine," she coos, grazing her index finger under my chin.

I blankly stare at her. "I'm not little. You're literally a year younger than me."

"I'm taller than you," she smugly states.

She's not wrong; she's six feet tall to be exact.

"Your AC stops working and the only working fan in your

house happens to be in his room. It's an inferno in your house because the temperatures have spiked and—"

"That would never happen."

"It's just a hypothetical."

"You didn't say that before."

"Well now I am. *Hypothetically* speaking, let's say that your AC stops working—"

"Vi, what is it with you and sex? Can't two people of the opposite sex live together platonically?" I take a sip of my drink, hoping I'm not giving away how warm my cheeks feel.

"It can happen, but you guys have known each other for what? A month? And now he's moving in? Yeah, I don't buy the *we're just friends* platonic bullshit."

DANIEL

"You know, friends with benefits *is* a thing," Gray starts.

JOSEFINE

"It was made for people like you and Danny," Vi supplies, mischief thick in her voice.

DANIEL

"I swear if you guys don't stop talking about it, I'm going no contact," I warn because they have been talking about this for almost two hours. This is getting ridiculous.

JOSEFINE

"I'm going to walk out if you don't stop because this is getting ridiculous," I threaten because she keeps going on and on about the hypotheticals. "He'd have to be remotely interested in me for any of your scenarios to happen and he's not."

She sits up, the glass of wine in her hand close to sloshing out. "What do you mean he's not interested? I find that hard to believe. Have you seen yourself? You're gorgeous, Josie."

I almost smile at that but take a sip of my own glass as last night's events play in my head. I don't like sharing about myself, but the alcohol forces the words out. I tell her about our exes, the video that was *accidentally* sent to us, about him punching Bryson, about Monday night and how I sat on him and took a picture to send to his ex. How he practically ran to his room and wouldn't look at me. I don't tell her about why things played out the way they did last night, but I do tell her about him calling me a friend.

"Wait." She takes a long drink before she speaks. "Why would he punch Bryson in the face that bad and then let you send her a picture of you on his lap? That doesn't scream he's still in love with her."

"I don't know and I didn't ask because I was returning the favor. What he does is none of my business."

"What do you mean you were returning the favor?" Her Cheshire grin freaks me out.

"He might have helped me slash Bryson's tires."

"Stop." She coos, softly swats my arm. "That's so freaking cute. You can't tell me he's not—"

"No," I immediately cut in. "I know you believe in..." I try to find the word, but I struggle to think of the correct one to describe what I want to say.

"Love?" she giggles.

"Right, that. Love...I know you believe in it, but I don't."

She dramatically gasps, but I think it's genuine because she looks completely devastated by my admission. "What? You don't believe in love? But you and Bryson dated for like a year or something. Did you not love him?"

"No." I convinced myself enough that I liked him because I was so lonely, but in the end, I still felt so lonely while I was with him. "I didn't."

"That's valid. He was and is a piece of shit." She muses for a moment. "So you don't believe that someone out there is made for you?"

There's a pang in my chest at the question. "No and I'm okay with it. I've seen what love does and it's definitely not something I think I'm cut out for. I mean look at Daniel and Amanda: she hurt him, but he still wants her or at least still has feelings for her. Bryson did what he did, and I can't help but feel repulsed by him."

"I don't know. Pen made it sound like he was definitely over her."

"Maybe he wasn't honest with her. Who knows? All I know is he doesn't see me that way and that's okay with me." *Is it really?* "We're going to live together now and I don't want things to be weird anyway." *And why would he want someone fucked up like me?*

"Okay, so here's another hypothetical."

"Vienna, I swear." I groan, chugging the rest of my wine, but she doesn't waste a second to grab the bottle and pour more into my glass.

"He doesn't have to love you and you don't have to love him but that doesn't mean you guys can't fuck. Hypothetically speaking, what if you guys—"

"I'm so done with you." I go to stand but she throws her long leg over my legs.

"Okay, I'm kidding. Don't leave." She chuckles. "I do have one more question and then I'll shut up."

"What?"

"All jokes aside, would you sleep with him?"

"Vi, why are you—"

"Yes or no?"

"Vi, stop ask—"

"It's just a yes or no question."

"Why does it matter?"

"It just does. Yes or no?"

"Are you always this pushy?"

"I can be. Yes or no?"

"I don't think I want to be your friend anymore."

"Babe, that ship sailed a long time ago. You're stuck with me for life. Remember we're in the dead mom's club. I don't make the rules, so get used to me."

I can't help but smile this time.

"Wow, look at that. So she does smile."

My smile fades but that doesn't stop her from smiling at me.

"Yes or no?"

"You're so weird with your fixation on me and Daniel fucking." I clench my thighs.

"It's just a question. Yes or no, Josie?"

Yes.

"No."

DANIEL

When I return to my almost empty room, the guys and my sister are still standing there, all staring at me expectantly. They keep throwing out questions that I refuse to answer.

So what if Amanda asked me to move in and I said no? I don't see how that's something to focus on. She had other girl roommates who she knew had attempted to flirt with me before. That didn't stop her from begging, and I'd always say no.

Josie, on the other hand, is alone and I hate that. I'll miss living with the guys and how much closer the house is to campus, but the drive from Josie's house isn't too bad.

"Okay, I have another question for you." Pen's eyes drift around the room. "Who's going to stay here now?"

The guys and I shrug. It was all last minute, but I don't think they'll offer it to anyone. I'm pretty certain I heard Gray say he's going to convert it into an extra closet or something. Since he so graciously decided to pick up my part of the bills. I told him he didn't need to since Josie won't let me pay, but he said not to worry about it.

"How do you guys feel about having a girl roommate?"

"No," Angel and I say simultaneously.

"Why not?" She frowns.

"Because you'd be living with a bunch of guys," I reply, though I shouldn't because it's obvious.

I trust them, but I also know Pen wouldn't last living here. The guys love to bring girls over, and Kai and Angel are a little too comfortable. They've walked around naked a time or two. Then there's Noah, who can be an asshole, and while he's never been mean to Pen, I could see her doing something that would annoy him. And I've seen Gray check her out so many times. Pen is a relationship kind of girl and he's not. He'd only break her heart, and that's the last thing I want or need.

"Wow. I hadn't realized that. You're telling me..." She sardonically muses and points at her chest. "That you all have penises?" Then waves that finger around the room, gawking at us in disbelief.

I stare at her, unamused, but Kai and Gray snort.

"I'm more than welcome to show—"

"Don't you dare finish that, Grayson," I threaten, scowling at him.

He raises his hands in surrender. This is why I can't let that happen.

"What's wrong with your place?" Angel questions, feeling as unamused as I feel.

"You guys are closer to campus and this space is bigger." She shrugs, not meeting our stare. "I'll pay the bills."

"Is this because of your ex, because if it is—"

"No." Pen cuts Angel off with a glare. "This has nothing to do with him. I just need more space, and you guys have a lot of it." She looks at the guys for support, but at my stare, they shake their heads.

She scoffs. "You guys are dicks."

"Sorry, sweetheart. Maybe next time." Gray winks at her.

She flips him off.

"Anyway, you and Josie..." Kai starts again.

"Drop it. We're friends." I shut him down, but Gray only encourages it.

"Should we remind you how you punched Bryson because he called Josie a bitch."

Pen looks just as angry as I felt that day. "He did what?"

I thought my sister loved drama, but the guys seem to love it just as much because they share all the details about how Amanda, Bryson, Josie, and I are connected. Then tell her about the punch in the locker room and Josie slashing his tires and everything else. They're all so engrossed in it, even Noah looks entertained. Fucking hell.

"You never punched Bryson when you found out about Amanda, but Josie—"

"Don't," I grumble. "Just—"

"*Friends*," she flippantly remarks and uses air quotes around it. "Yeah, sure whatever but 'just friends' don't keep a single rhinestone in their wallet. Just saying."

"Penelope, shut the fuck up." I sigh as all their eyes dart to me.

"What do you mean?" Gray sounds a little too eager when he asks.

"I'm over all of you. I'm leaving." I grab the last two boxes, but I stop at Kai's question.

"What if Josie wanted you? What then?"

"What do you mean, what then?" I ask, a little more annoyed than I mean to be.

"What if...Josie wanted you and let's say you wanted her too... what then?"

"Kai, just say it how it is. Would you fuck Josie if she asked you to?" Gray cocks a brow.

Yes.

"No. Good night."

28

JOSEFINE

"Are you okay?"

"Yup, I'm good." Daniel gives me a shaky thumbs-up then places his goggles on his forehead and climbs down the steps to get in the water.

I wade through water once he's standing inside the pool. It stops right below his waist line but with the blanched look on his face, you'd think he was in the deep end.

"Hey, you have to be honest with me. I promise I won't judge." I grab his hands. "For this to work, you have to trust me. Otherwise, I won't be able to help you, and I really want to."

An apprehensive, uneasy smile curls on his face. "Sorry, I... yeah, I'm a little nervous." His eyes dart to our connected hands and stay there until his hands have stopped trembling. When they lift, his smile looks and feels more relaxed. "I *was* nervous, but I'm okay now," he corrects himself.

"I promise I won't make you do anything crazy. But you still have to communicate when something I'm doing is making you uncomfortable. I'm able to adjust and rearrange, but you have to talk to me, okay?"

He nods and I note how less tense his broad shoulders are. "Okay, Jos, I will. I promise."

Today will be our second swim session and hopefully will go without any interruptions. I did check the weather channel and app multiple times to make sure there weren't going to be any storms.

With his hands still clutched to mine, I slowly tug him away from the stairs. "I'm not taking you to the deep end, but I do need the water to be at least below your chest. I'm going to have you blow bubbles under the water."

His hands tighten on mine, but he doesn't pull away. He easily moves with me.

"You're doing good, Garcia," I praise once the water sits at his chest. Because he's so tall, we couldn't stand by the stairs. "Really good."

His face brightens, his smile invigorated. "I haven't done anything."

"You're trusting me, and that's the most important part of this entire process." Gratification rolls down my body and back up, but then it evolves into something else. I don't let myself mull it over before I'm shifting my attention back to him.

"You're easy to trust." His thumb skims over my fingers under the water. "It makes this feel less daunting."

I stop myself from smiling proudly at his compliment. "Let's see if you still feel this way after the lesson."

For the next thirty minutes I have him blow bubbles underwater for five seconds. I also have him float while holding on to the edge of the pool. He looked relaxed but I couldn't risk having him float on his own or using the board yet. Still, he's doing really good.

"I hope I'm not wasting your time," he says after he's dropped his feet back on the floor. He pushes the goggles back up to his forehead and wipes the water away from his face.

I'm trying to maintain professionalism, but he's making it hard not to look. He's already got an attractive face as it is, now add the abs and how firm and muscular everything is, and I'm straining my eyes to keep them on his.

If I had HR, I'm sure they'd write me up or fire me.

Snapping out of it, I pinch my brows together at his statement. "Why would you think that?"

"Because we've been going at this for thirty minutes or so and all I've done is blow bubbles and float." He rubs the nape of his neck. His cheeks are flushed pink. "That's thirty minutes of your life you're never going to get back."

"I love doing this." I grab his bicep to—I swear I didn't do that to feel him, but he does feel really nice—reassure him. He leans into my hold, his gaze burning mine. "Knowing that you'll learn how to swim someday feels really rewarding. So no, you haven't wasted my time. Like everything else, we have to start slow and that means blowing bubbles and floating like this until you feel comfortable enough to use the board then float on your own. So far, this has been one of the best thirty-minute sessions of my life."

The sun does a wonderful job of hitting his face just right because it glows. His cheeks burn a darker shade of pink, and his eyes look like two rich pools of honey. Sweet and thick, consuming and blazing.

"You sure know how to make a guy feel special." He drags his fingers through his damp locks, causing his bicep to flex and the water to ripple down his arm.

"Were my compliments not already doing that?" I cock a brow.

His cheek twitches but his eyes smolder, growing dark. "They were, but hearing you say that was the cherry on top. So keep them coming. I really like hearing how well you think I'm doing, Josefine."

"You gotta earn it, Daniel." I shouldn't have said it like that, slow and seductive, but it just left my mouth that way.

A crooked grin grows on his face and something about the unevenness in his smile makes my body feel...coiled. Everything feels tight, like I'm in a box, confined, and the oxygen is thick and hot, making it hard to inhale.

I breathe in the salty air, hoping it'll give me some semblance that I'm not struggling with my thoughts right now. But in his next words, the box only gets smaller.

"I'm willing to do anything to earn it." He casually drops his comment as though it didn't hold an innuendo that we both know did.

For the next thirty minutes in the pool, we pretend like it didn't because we're living together now. We're not only roommates but friends.

Besides teaching him how to swim, it's been a while since I felt like this. Although I'm not sure if I can really say *a while* because I can't remember the last time I actually felt human. Like I'm in my body and not outside of it, watching life happen around me.

The void in my chest is nowhere near or even halfway full, but I feel something enough that I don't dread waking up in the mornings. I don't know what to call that, but I feel...okay.

And okay is the most I've ever felt.

"So how did I do?" he asks, dropping on the chaise lounge chair after our hour session is over.

I wring the water out of my hair, keeping my gaze trained on his face and not let it coast down the way it wants to. I don't know why I'm struggling. He's just a guy...a guy who happens to be firm in all the right places, with abs that look unreal, light brown skin that glows beneath the sun, and a smile that makes me feel things.

"Is this another way to get me to praise you?" I tease and take my towel that he holds out for me.

"Why? Is it working?" He brushes the damp hair that falls over his forehead back, but it only falls forward. A drop clings to one of the ends and temptation screams for me to touch it, but I don't.

"You got a praise kink I don't know about?"

"I don't know, but I'm willing to find out." He smirks.

I'm not sure how much he's joking right now, but my brain

still accepts it as an invitation. My body goes taut, and a pulse grows between my thighs, but I don't shuffle on my feet or squeeze them the way they desperately want to.

"I think I'm good. You're a little needy for my taste," I apathetically reply.

He gasps, placing his palm on his chest. "Needy? Josefine Resendiz, I'm anything but needy."

A small chuckle claws out from the back of my throat. "Yeah, okay, Daniel Garcia."

"Don't mistake my willingness for neediness because I'm more than welcome to show you just how *needy* I can make *you*." The muscle on his jaw tics and his gaze sweeps over me in a slow, longing motion. This time I can't stop myself from shifting from one foot to the other and clenching my thighs.

I tried not to make it obvious, but I know he notices because his jaw clenches and I hear his breath hitch.

Thankfully we're saved by his vibrating phone on the table. While he answers, I grab his goggles and place them in the small shed I bought to store all my swimming gear.

When I'm out of the shed, the atmosphere doesn't feel as charged as it did a few minutes ago. He approaches me with a smile on his face and pretends he hadn't implied what he did.

"Go get changed or you can go like that too." His eyes this time don't graze over me, and I should be glad, but instead there's this dip in my stomach. I shouldn't want him to look at me, but I do.

We're friends.

"What's with the demand? Where are we going?"

He grins, grabbing the ends of the towel he has draped around his neck. "We're going to the beach to play volleyball with the guys, have dinner, and then they go for a swim."

I take a step back, everything good I was feeling rushing out. "Thanks for the invite, but I'd rather not go. I really don't want to run into Bryson or—"

"It'll just be the guys I was roommates with. We do this

roughly two weeks before the bonfire and the season begins. It's a little tradition we started my freshman year. It's just us, though sometimes Pen comes and brings her friends. She was going to ask you, but I told her I'd tell you. I meant to do that yesterday but with me moving in, it slipped my mind."

"I think I'm going to stay and—"

"And what are you going to do?"

Stare at the email from Monica Jameson and contemplate my life. I haven't answered her and have been avoiding her on campus. I know I should turn her offer down, but for some reason, I can't bring myself to do that.

"Tomorrow is Monday and I have classes and—"

"And I do too, but you're still going to come with me. Okay?"

"But—"

"*Pero nada. Vas a venir conmigo. Ve agarrar tus cosas y apúrate.*" It's a nonnegotiable demand.

I should tell him that he can't boss me around because I hate nothing more than a man telling me what to do but...this is Daniel, and I find it hot.

29
JOSEFINE

I SET THE BALL FOR DANIEL, AND HE JUMPS AND SPIKES it hard. No one on the other side is fast enough to get to the ball before it's landing on the sand.

Behind us, Vi and Kainoa loudly celebrate our second win as the music from Daniel's Bose speaker plays "Pa'Que Retozen" by Tego Calderón.

"This can't be." Grayson stares, bewildered, raking his fingers through his disheveled hair.

"Oh, it be," Daniel returns with a smirk and holds out a sand-covered fisted hand in my direction.

I don't gloat about it the way the others do, though I do bump my fist against his and press my lips together to stop myself from laughing at the other team—Pen, Angel, Grayson, and Noah—who are arguing about their failed strategies.

Well, it's Pen and Angel arguing. Grayson looks like he was blindsided by their loss, and Noah is staring at the pair with a bored expression on his face.

"H-how? Have you played volleyball before?" He stares at Vi and me with narrowed eyes, suspicion lacing his words.

Vienna laughs, brushing the sand off her stomach. "I told you I haven't, but the game is pretty easy when you're not playing by the rules." She has, but they don't need to know that.

"I don't like to lose, so I don't," I add.

He scoffs. "Are y'all saying I suck?"

"Yes," Kainoa and Daniel fill in for us.

"You're just not that good, Gray. Face it, you suck ass." Kainoa clicks his tongue, trying to look serious but his lips crack into a furtive smile.

While Grayson tries to defend himself to the guys, Vi and I step aside to drink water.

We've been at the beach for almost an hour and I surprisingly feel okay. Usually, I'd feel awkward, but everyone's been nice. Though Noah's been quiet, but Daniel says he usually is. Not that I have room to talk because I've been quiet too.

"You seriously can't tell me you don't feel that?" Vi says once we're out of earshot.

I grab my water bottle and hand her hers. "Feel what?"

She softly groans, eyes widening as if she were asking *are you for real?* "The insane chemistry between you and Danny. Like please just *fuck*," she exasperatedly whispers that word. "Already."

I pretend I didn't hear that and drink my water.

But she's not giving up because she continues to speak.

"I know I'm being annoying, but I'm telling you I feel it and I'm not even involved. No, I'm pretty certain everyone feels it. Hell, the fishes probably feel it too."

"I think you're reading too much into things."

"Point one: He stares at you a lot. I bet you if we turn around right now, we'll find him staring at you." I don't turn but she does. A muffled squeal gets trapped in her mouth as she presses her lips together when she looks forward again. "He's looking over here."

"His stuff is over here. Maybe he's looking at his water."

"Point two: He calls you Jos."

"Wow, a nickname. You all call me Josie."

"Point three: You call him Garcia."

"Again, it's just a nickname."

"No one else calls him that."

"Because they call him Danny."

"Gray tried to call you Jos and Danny told him not to."

"I'm sure he was just messing around. They seem to do that a lot."

"He may have looked like he was joking, but we both know damn well it didn't sound like it."

"Again, you're reading too much into it."

A tight-lipped smile graces her face and she blinks slowly like she's about to lose it. "Point four: He touches you and you don't like being touched."

I close my bottle and throw it on top of my bag. "Mild shoulder squeezes. That means nothing. And are you forgetting I'm teaching him how to swim? We touch each other a lot."

"You're killing me, Josie." She tips her head back and grumbles, "Killing. Me."

"You're delusional, Vienna. Delusional. Daniel's a flirt. Trust me, he's not into me. He wouldn't ever be."

Life would be grand if I was the delusional one. Because then I could picture scenarios of Daniel and me together, and I could let myself be a hopeless romantic. Pretend like he wants to touch, hold, and kiss me. I wish I could put myself in a bubble and live in ignorant bliss.

I really wish I could because maybe then I'd believe that someone decided to look past my flaws and like me anyway because I was enough it didn't matter.

But things don't work that way. No one *just* looks past the flaws and decides they like you that much to stay. Maybe it works for other people but not for me.

I don't mean that in a *please want me, like me, need me* pity way. That's the reality of my life, and accepting things for how they are is easier than pretending it'll happen eventually because the world is filled with nothing but disappointment.

I already have enough of it; I don't want any more. It is why after we arrived at the beach, I decided to annihilate the light he had set in my heart.

It was painful to do but necessary. Either way, we wouldn't work out. Relationships and I are complicated. We don't align. And it has nothing to do with my failed relationship with Bryson but rather with my mom.

How can I manage to be with someone when I couldn't manage to figure it out with someone who was family?

I must've zoned out or my face must've given something away because she stares at me with remorse.

"I'm sorry. I promise I'll shut up. I was excited and got carried away." She pauses, chugs half her water, then says with all seriousness, "I've no doubt you two would be mates in—"

I hold my palm out. "Stop, just—" A snicker tickles my throat. "Mates? Vienna, no. Please don't finish that."

Vienna's a romantic. Anything and everything is a little love story waiting to happen. I don't get her fascination with falling in love, but she's a firm believer of that word. Also, she's a huge fan of paranormal romance.

We walk back to everyone as she explains what knotting is and why wolves do it.

"Wait." Grayson's head snaps in our direction. "What did you just say about penises?"

I shake my head, but it's already too late. Vienna's eyes glitter with excitement.

"*Werewolf* penises," she says and like she did with me, proceeds to explain how knotting works to everyone.

Surprisingly they raptly pay attention, a little too intrigued.

"That sounds insane," Daniel says to me. I hadn't realized he was standing next to me or when he moved, but he's close, too close. I can feel the hair of his arm brushing against mine. "Mates. That's kind of cool. Insane but cool."

"Cool?" I lift a brow and look up to find him already staring at me. "That just sounds insane to me."

"I don't know. The thought of someone out there being made just for you sounds nice." He stares at me deeply, like he's studying me for long enough that my heart beats a little harder. When he looks away, the beats wane. "Don't you think?"

"No."

"No?" He doesn't look shocked, just curious.

"No." I add some distance between us because friends shouldn't be this close to each other. His eyes flicker between the gap, pausing there momentarily before shifting back to me.

Thankfully, everyone seems to have moved on from mates and knots because they grab the volleyball and we start our third game.

At our fourth game and the other team's third loss, Grayson requests a change of teams.

"These two are doing nothing for me." He points at Angel and Pen who stare at him, annoyed. "And I'm sorry, buddy..." Now he's talking to Noah. "But you also suck."

"Are you high? Or where the hell is your mind because you sucked worse than all three of us combined," Pen shoots back.

"I wish I was. That way I could pretend you guys weren't shit." He darts his attention to us. "Can I have Josie and Vi on my team now?"

"No," both Kainoa and Daniel instantly reply.

A devilish smirk curls on Grayson's face, and something glints in his eyes, almost like mischief or something knowing. I'm not too sure but he directs that look only toward Daniel.

"Don't be like that, Danny." It feels like there's more to that sentence, but he doesn't add to it. There's something about his smile and the way Pen smiles, inserting herself in the unspoken conversation, that makes me feel weird.

I don't have the time or energy to try to figure out what the hell is going on, so I turn to Vi. "Pen, you, and I with Grayson? What do you think?"

"Yeah, this game was getting boring. Maybe this will make things a little more interesting."

"Hey! I thought we were having a good time together." Kainoa sounds offended and follows Vi as she goes under the net.

"You're abandoning me?" Daniel playfully asks.

"Just for a little. I'm kind of curious."

"About?"

"How many wins it'll take before you call it quits."

There he goes, flashing me his crooked grin. *Fuck, my heart.* "Cute," he patronizingly drawls. "So, this is what the game has done to you?"

"The game? No, I'm just a confident person who never loses."

"Loser drives back home?" He arcs a brow. I can't help the way one corner of my lips just merely curls. His eyes clock the movement and his own smile widens. "Deal?"

"As long as you promise not to be a sore loser?" I go under the net.

"Wow, okay. Let's get the game started," he orders and hands me the ball. "But just so we're on the same page, once you lose, we'll still be good, right? You won't hold any grudges?"

I scoff and stand in front of him with the net between us. "Daniel?"

"Yes, Josefine?" His voice is light and teasing but haughty.

"Disrespectfully, fuck off." Mine, not so much.

He throws his head back and laughs. "I like it when you're mean to me."

"I thought you were into being praised?" I say, a little quiet and playful.

"I'm into anything you do," he murmurs just as quietly and playfully. Then he winks at me and we part.

We all gather just a few feet away from the ocean after three more rounds of volleyball.

The games were the most intense but fun I've had in, well,

forever. I swam competitively all my life and that was intense, at times fun, but never left me feeling the way I do now. Even though we did lose the second round, we won the first and third.

And Gray—he insists I call him that just like Kainoa insists I call him Kai—hasn't once stopped bragging about our win. Though Angel and Kai keep saying he's lucky the girls and I were on his team because he was pretty much useless. But I know that's a lie; they're just messing to annoy him because the truth is he's really good. I think it pains them to admit that.

"So, the base of the dick just..." Angel demonstrates with his hands—one has his fingers in a half circle to indicate the vagina and the other hand is supposed to be the penis. He inserts his fingers through the hole then creates a fist.

"And it's supposed to stop the cum from getting out then?" Gray asks, disgusted, perplexed, and intrigued.

I don't know why but the guys seem really invested or maybe they're confused. I'm not sure, but either way, they're still talking about knotting.

"Here." Daniel holds a water bottle for me. "With lemon juice. Just the way you like it."

I see the pulp floating about as I take it. Recently he's been doing more than is deemed necessary like having lemon water ready for me. I know he's doing it out of gratitude for letting me live with me. I told him it's not necessary, but he doesn't listen, so I've given up reminding him. I realized it's easier if I just let him be because he's going to do something whether I want him to or not.

"Thanks," I say appreciatively and take two sips of it just as he pushes his sister, who's sitting next to me, out of the way.

He literally squeezes himself between us and she grumbles and pushes him back. That only ensues a pushing war, but she's not a match for Daniel because he hardly budges.

"You know, there's space right over there." She points at the space between Noah and Angel.

"Well, go sit over there."

She rolls her eyes. "I can't stand you."

"Love you too," he returns, voice arrogant, and I can't help but smile a little at that. I don't know how he does it, but he must've sensed my lips moving because he's staring at me, those rich amber eyes locked on my mouth.

I look away, watching Kai and Noah pull out stuff covered in aluminum foil from the large blue cooler they brought with them.

"Vi, Josie, have you guys ever eaten spam musubi?" Vienna nods merrily but I shake my head. "You're in luck because you're about to." He hands me and everyone a small rectangular thing covered in the foil and Noah hands out something larger, also covered in the foil. "Prepare to fall in love."

I unwrap the small rectangular one and assume it's the musubi because it's covered in dry seaweed and inside there's rice and spam.

Everyone is already eating theirs, but Kai and Daniel are staring at me expectantly.

"Stop looking at me."

"I made it with lots of love, so I need to see you fall in love with it," Kai explains.

"He's weird like that," Angel says through a mouthful.

"What's your excuse?" I question Daniel.

"Seeing you try something new." He grabs his phone and holds it up.

My cheeks burn. This can't be happening. "What are you doing?"

"I'm going to record your first spam musubi experience." I hear the smile in his voice, but now I'm self-conscious because everyone is staring at me.

"He's very dad-like. Does this all the time. Pretty sure he has pictures of all of us trying different things. So just let him be." Angel takes one last bite of his musubi. Wow, he scarfed that down.

"*Right.*" Gray snorts. "Pictures of all—" He grunts and I only catch a glimpse of Kai digging his elbow in his rib cage.

"Come on, Jos, try it." Daniel absently places his hand on my thigh. Any other time I wouldn't have cared, but everyone's eyes follow the movement. They're fixated on it and us because they're staring hard, but it only lasts a second before they're looking away and getting lost in their own conversation. As if they knew I really wanted them to stop looking.

I take a bite and hum in delight. "Whoa, okay. This is good." I swallow and take another bite. Kai looks pleased with himself then gets immersed in a conversation with Vi.

Daniel puts his phone down and removes his palm. "Right?"

I nod, eating mine slowly to savor it and Daniel catches me doing that.

"Have mine." He sets it on my lap and grabs the bigger thing wrapped in foil.

"No, I don't want to—"

"I've eaten a lot of these. Plus, we have *tortas*." He removes the foil and sure enough there's a *torta* underneath it.

"Thank—this is really good," I say instead because he gives me this look that warns me not to thank him.

"Yeah, you're welcome by the way," Pen deadpans at her brother.

He sighs exhaustedly. "I told you I was going to be busy. Did you forget about the swimming lessons?"

"I'm sure Josie would've understood."

"Understood what?" I ask.

"That you would've been okay to cancel the lesson. Our parents own a *panadería* and met me halfway to deliver the *bolillos* for the *tortas*. Danny was supposed to come but didn't." She stares at her brother under her thick lashes, irritated when he shrugs indifferently.

I mask the shock because I had no idea his parents owned a bakery and now to think of it, I don't think I *really* know him.

Though it's my fault because I've never gone out of my way to ask about him. It's always the other way around.

"I'll go next time, I promise, Pen." He sweetly smiles at her, but his lips look a little too forced, like he's fighting between looking happy or not.

That satisfies Pen because she lets it go, not noticing the tension behind his eyes or shoulders. While everyone is busy eating and talking, I gently jab his side to get him to look at me. When he does, I smile at him and instantly notice the tension from him subside.

I communicate with my facial expression if he's okay. I'm not sure if I did a good job, but when he smiles at me, small and soft, neither nodding nor shrugging, I know he understood what I'm asking.

I shouldn't but I take his hand in mine when no one is looking and squeeze it. I attempt to let it go, but he holds on to it. He squeezes in return before he lets it go. Then we proceed to scoot closer to each other.

Not very confident I won't fuck this up, but he definitely needs a person or friend or someone to confide in.

Whatever it is, I'll be.

30

JOSEFINE

"Almost done." Vienna grunts a little, struggling to get the right leg in her turquoise and silver mermaid tail.

I marvel at the way she finally gets it in then applies conditioner to the other leg and stuffs it in the tail. "I can't believe you have to do all of that just to get it on."

She huffs out a fatigued breath. "The first time I put it on, it took me a good thirty...forty-five minutes-ish. The silicone makes it really hard to put on; that's why I have to lather myself with lots of conditioner."

Once both legs are in, she lays on her back and has me help her roll the rest of the silicone over her stomach.

"Thanks so much," she pants, wiping the dots of sweat on her forehead away with the back of her hand. "And thanks for coming. It would've been so much harder to do this on my own."

"How could I say no? You texted me over twenty times." I hand Vi her mirror.

Vi scoffs and takes it. She inspects her face and hair again before giving it back to me. "Don't exaggerate. It was like fifteen and how else would I have convinced you to leave your house?"

I set it back on the white table that's supposed to be a

makeshift vanity made for her. "I didn't want to come because I don't really care about these things."

MCU is having their annual bonfire. It's a tradition that's been going on for years, to commence the start of baseball season. The parking lot and beach get decked out with the university's name and colors: turquoise, black, and white. They have all sorts of games on the beach, food, and a fair in the parking lot. Once the sun starts to set, they start a large bonfire and announce all the players and talk about the upcoming season and other things regarding baseball.

The whole town and every student at the university comes.

I came once with Bryson freshman year and regretted it. It had nothing to do with the number of times he forgot I was there. But when we were together, he'd make little snide comments about how I wasn't smiling enough or doing enough to make it known that I was enjoying being there with *him*. Then he'd throw little passive comments saying he's "thankful I'm hot otherwise it would've been a problem."

If I could go back in time, I would slap the shit out of myself.

Vi scoffs dramatically. "What? That's not very school spirit of you."

I stare at her, unamused. "I am showing my school spirit."

Her gaze drops to my chest and I follow, making sure I didn't accidentally pop a tit, but everything is intact. I'm wearing an oversized, white long-sleeve linen button-down, a dark turquoise bikini set, and denim shorts.

"You look good." She grins, eyes still on my chest before they scan down the rest of my body. "So…"

"No, don't go there."

"I'm not going anywhere. I just said *so*."

"You're going to ask something about Daniel."

She smacks her lips, staring at me, taken aback. "No, I wasn't, but since you brought him up… Are you going to go see him?"

"No." I twirl my middle ring finger. "He's going to be busy all day and night."

That's not a lie. He told me on Wednesday that all the players will be doing meet and greets, participating in games, and doing other activities. He did ask me to come, but knowing he was going to be around Bryson put me off. Plus, like I told Vi, I don't care for these things because a lot of people in town and the university know Mom and might want to talk to me.

The university literally changed their aquatics building name to Claudia Resendiz Natatorium in her memory. I also heard they're working on a scholarship named after her, but I've not kept myself in the loop. The aquarium has a plaque with her name somewhere. One of her favorite restaurants, Agua Clara, has a drink named after her.

Her name is everywhere and even though I shouldn't, I hate it because it's a reminder to everyone that she was one of the best swimmers in the world. The girl who came from Mexico with nothing but a dream and made something of herself.

While it's a reminder to me that I'll never be like her. That I'm nothing but a failure and a disappointment. I'm sure from the grave she's fuming that I gave up.

I hate myself.

"Someone there?" she asks, derailing my train of thought.

"I'm right here. I'm just not listening. Why don't we talk about what's going on with you and Kai."

She laughs like the thought of them together is ludicrous. "He's funny, smart, and really hot."

"But?"

"He messed around with Mary Novak, and she's still not over it. I wouldn't be surprised if she was with him right now."

Mary Novak, Christian Novak's daughter, is a bitch. We got into it a few times. She assumed I'd cower because her father was the coach, but she was mistaken. She's also a junior so I can see why Vienna is not wanting to go there.

Fortunately, her father is gone, but unfortunately, she's not.

"Oh…" I don't mean to but my lips twist wryly.

"Yeah, I'm too hot to fight over a guy. If I ever do, please take me out." She scowls. "Look at me, I'm gorgeous. I shouldn't have to vie for any man's attention. Fuck that." She pretends to gag.

The severity in her voice makes me laugh and like her more. "I promise."

"Vienna, are you ready?" a masculine voice asks from outside the tent.

Since MCU's mascot are the sirens, they hired the aquarium to bring Vienna out since she's their mermaid and knows how to swim in the tail. They also somehow managed to find a pool/tank thing to give her space to swim and filled it with stuff you'd find in the ocean.

"I'm ready, Carson!" she shouts. "So are you planning on being with me all day or are you going to—"

"I will punch you if you say his name."

She snickers. "I'm messing with you. But at any point if you want to leave, don't feel obligated to be with me. I've got Carson."

He waltzes in, bends down, and picks her up. He's a student, swimmer, and also works at the aquarium. One of his jobs today is helping Vienna in and out of the water. He's also helped her get undressed a few times after hours.

The next few hours I stick by Vienna. I'd hang out with Pen but because she's a cheerleader, she's busy. They may not cheer for the baseball team, but the school still wanted them to dress up and do what cheerleaders do.

Vi stays busy taking pictures, swimming, and blowing bubbles underwater. She also does other things I admit are insanely cool.

I definitely don't from time to time look for Daniel and hope to see him. No, because that would be stupid. I'm definitely not semi-disappointed that the sun has set and I've yet to see him.

"Josefine?" The familiar voice makes my body stiff. It takes every cell in my body not to hide. It's too late anyway because I know she saw me and is coming my way.

"Hey." I force a smile and glance down at the two kids I'm

assuming are Monica's and the man who stands beside her who I assume is her husband.

"It's so good to see you again. I've been trying to find you on campus."

"I'm not there much unless I have class." I do use their gym, but I don't tell her that.

"I figured. It's so good to see you again." She smiles warmly at me. "This is Jack, my husband. And my kids, Iris and Avery."

She points at the girls, but they're not paying attention to me. Their attention is on Vienna.

"It's so good to finally meet you. I've heard a lot of great things about you." Jack offers the same friendly smile as his wife. "I—"

"Can we take pictures with the mermaid?" Iris asks but both girls are grabbing his hand and pulling him toward the pool.

"Sorry about that. My girls are impatient." She looks around me, staring at her little family.

Something pricks at my chest, but I push the foreign feeling away.

"Well, I won't hold you up."

"No, that's all right. Jack's got them. I'm actually glad to have run into you. I wanted to ask if you've looked over the email?"

The dreaded email. "Not yet. I've been busy, and you know life is well...life," I awkwardly supply.

"No, I get it. No rush. Either way, the season is almost over, so I don't need your answer now. Let's say by the end of the semester?"

I should say no, but I can't bring myself to voice the single word. "Sure," I find myself saying instead. "End of the semester you'll get your answer."

She nods and her eyes flick up to her family again before they land on me. "You know, if you ever want to talk about swimming, your mom, or anything, I'm here. I know we don't know each other, but—"

"I'm good." I cut her off. "'There's not much I need to talk about."

"Well, you know where my office is."

I nod and settle on silence because I'm not sure what else to say.

"I'll let you go now." Her smile is still as friendly as ever. Vienna says she's a hard-ass during practice, but after, she's everything but. She said the atmosphere is better, livelier because of her. "My daughters are going to want a thousand pictures and no doubt want me to buy them a stuffed mermaid."

I nod again and watch her walk to them.

"Can I...please have this one?"

Mom merely glances at the stuffed animal in my hand. "What are you going to do with that, Josefine?"

My hands get clammy, nervous flutters spreading in my stomach. "Play with it."

"You have a lot going on to be playing with toys. Put that back."

Monica and her family walk away once they're satisfied with pictures and buy the girls stuffed mermaids.

The memory, like bitter coffee, clings to my tongue, leaving a nasty taste. I attempt to focus on what's going on around me but all that's swimming in my mind is how happy they all looked.

For a while I think my night will consist of that memory, but one of the guys on the team walks past me. He's decked out in his uniform; Daniel said they had to wear them.

"Go find him." Vienna clings to the end of the pool, her tail flowing back and forth. God, she's so natural at this, she almost looks like the real thing. No wonder kids eat this up. I am.

"Who?"

She gives me this *I'm not stupid* look. "You've been here for hours helping me. I promise I'll be okay. I've got Carson anyway. So go." She flicks water at me.

"I'm not going to look for him. I'm sure he's busy, so—"

She waves more water with the back of her hand. It almost lands on me before I move out of the way.

"Go," she orders.

"You know I'm older than you, right?"

"I'm not sure what that has to do with anything, but don't make me cuss you out. I'm a mermaid and we don't do that." She smiles primly.

I roll my eyes. "I'm just going to see what he's doing, but I'll be back."

"Please don't." She sounds too excited as I walk away.

There're too many people and so many things, I don't think I'll ever spot him. I don't even know why I'm bothering. I should go home, and I almost turn the other way until I hear his voice.

He's standing a little farther away from everything and when I pivot my head a little more, I see he's not alone. He's with two people, an older man and woman.

Whatever they're talking about is none of my business and just as I'm about to look away, Daniel's eyes connect with mine. I must be hallucinating because he looks relieved to see me.

You need to leave! You need to walk away! a voice screams in my head.

But my legs do the opposite.

31

DANIEL

"I got busy but it's not a big deal. Nothing is for certain anyway." My chest constricts, making it hard to inhale or think.

"*Muy ocupado para contestar nuestras llamadas también?*" Dad's thick brow quirks up, and he folds his arms over his chest.

My tight smile almost wavers. "*Sus llamadas? La única que me llama es mamá.* Unless your phone stopped working and you've been using Mom's?"

He hates when I do that, switching languages. I didn't mean to, but it happened and I'm sure he'll find a way to make it seem like I'm starting something. Though I did give him a smart-ass reply, so I guess I did start something.

I try to breathe in again, but I can't and now my hands are trembling at my sides. I feel dizzy. My head is spinning and I feel like I'm both drowning while simultaneously feeling like I have a ton of bricks on my chest.

He takes a step forward, dropping his arms to his side, but Mom places a hand on his chest, stopping him from getting any closer.

"You better watch how you're speaking to me," he threatens, voice dropping an octave.

I want to speak, but my lips feel glued together and...fuck...I can't breathe. I inhale again, desperately, urgently, begging my lungs to work.

"Julio, that's enough." She pierces him with a discontented look and then pins me with the same look. "Both of you. Why didn't you tell us about the email?"

White dots dance in my vision, my heart and lungs slowly shutting down from the lack of oxygen until I lock eyes with my favorite pair.

Breathing becomes a little easier, but still the rest of my body is trying to catch up and work together. Some days it takes me longer to feel somewhat decent, but right now everything is working as is. Still, something looms in the corner. My hands are still shaky and sweaty, my heart is racing, and I still feel a little dizzy.

But for the most part, I feel steady, grounded, and I'm able to breathe.

Then she approaches us and once again I'm struggling. There's never a day that goes by without thinking about being around her, but right now is not one of those days.

I don't want Josie to see me like this or to think that I'm broken because I'm not.

"Hey." She stands next to me, offering the faintest smile, and for a moment I forget it all as the fireworks go off. I need to stop staring at her lips, but I can't bring myself to. Not until she turns to my parents. "Sorry for interrupting. I—"

"Not at all," Mom interjects, her face softening and lips lifting in a curious smile. Oh God, I know that smile all too well. "We're Danny's parents. I'm Esmeralda." She extends her hand for Josie to shake it.

She does then dad extends his. "I'm Julio."

"I'm Josefine. It's so good to meet you both."

It may be dark out, but there are enough lights that I see the spark of realization in Mom's eyes before it sweeps over her face. "You're Josie? Danny's new roommate?"

Dammit, Penelope.

"Uh, yeah." Josie casts me a glance before it drifts back to my parents.

"It's so good to finally meet you. I've heard so many good things about you."

Josie's eyebrow's furrow before they smooth out. "That's good to hear."

I mentally facepalm myself and intervene before Mom starts to pop out questions. "Can you both give me one second? I need talk to Josie really quickly."

Dad tersely nods, but Mom only smiles wider. Josie doesn't know what's going on, but I see the wheels spinning in Mom's head. I don't want to get her hopes up because nothing is going on between us even though I've—no, I'm not going there.

They climb back into their food truck and once I know they're busy selling their bread, I draw my focus to Josie.

"I didn't mean to ambush you. You looked a little in distress and thought maybe you'd—"

I force a chuckle. "Why would you think that?"

She tucks a wisp of her hair behind her ear. "You looked anxious."

"Me, anxious?" Blood roars in my ears and my hands become clammy again. "I don't know why you'd think that but I'm good. My parents just like to ask a million questions."

"You know you can be honest with me. I won't judge."

I slip my hands in my pockets as my fingers twitch with tremors. "Honest about what? We've talked, remember? I'm good. I'm sorry you assumed I was anxious but I'm not. They're just a little annoyed because I didn't tell them about the MLB email and they—"

She stares up at me, astonished. "You got *the* email? That's—"

"It's really not a big deal. I'm not sure what I'm going to do yet."

Her brows pull together and her inquisitive eyes study my face. "Is everything okay?"

The muscles on my face strain to keep my smile from falling. "Everything's good. It's just been a busy and long day. I'm tired and my parents — they like pestering me with questions. And I'm sure they're going to bombard me with many more. I didn't tell them about you, by the way. That was all Pen."

"Right." Her expression becomes impassive, and she adds distance between us. "Well...I won't hold you up."

Please don't go. I want to yell and hold her, but my mind is static and my body isn't responding the way it should. Sweat rolls down my back, and my hands are trembling worse than they had before.

"Josefine, here." Mom climbs down the little steps and holds a brown paper bag with the name of the bakery stamped on it. "I hope you like *pan dulce*. I added some of Danny's favorites and a few other ones. You have Facebook, don't you?"

"Mom, please," I warn but she doesn't look at me.

"I put my card in the bag. When you've tried them, message me on Facebook and let me know which ones you liked and I'll send you more."

"Thank you." Her lips lift. It's hardly a smile, and I hate myself for it. "I'm going to get going. It was so good to meet you."

"You don't need to leave. Julio and I need to keep working. We'll call Danny later. You kids go have fun and—"

"I just came to say hello. I'm actually helping the mermaid so I should be going now. Thanks for the bread again." She doesn't meet my stare anymore and walks away before letting Mom get a word out.

Mom's eyes narrow in suspicion. She places her hands at her hips. *"¿Qué le hiciste?"*

I don't have the energy to pretend, but I also don't have it in me to tell her either.

"Daniel," she says in a stern Spanish voice. *"Qué pasó?"*

I pinch the bridge of my nose, exhaling a breath through my nose. *"Nada, nomás que soy un idiota."*

She slaps my shoulder hard. "Don't call yourself that. What happened?"

I could tell her but then we'd have to talk about Adrian, and I don't want to do that. She'll get worried, Dad will hear, and we'll end up in the same bullshit cycle. I can't deal with either one of them and their looks of disappointment and grief. I just can't.

I side-eye the spot Josie was just at, and guilt unwinds in my stomach. It rises to my head, making it hurt. I deserve that.

"¿*Te gusta ella?*"

My head jerks and my heart stops. "What? I—we're friends and I live with her."

She cocks her head to the side, expression impatient. "We're still going to talk about that by the way. I can't believe I had to hear it from your sister. But that's not what I asked you."

"Please don't do that." I groan. "Stop romanticizing things."

"You can lie to whoever you want but I'm your mom. I know you better." She pinches my chin and tugs my head downward to her eye level. "*Te gusta?*"

"*Mamá, por Dios es mi—*"

"Tell me the truth," she incessantly demands.

"I've only known her for six weeks."

"Your father knew me for a week and knew I was the one."

"Yeah, well this is different," I retort and attempt to pull my head back, but she has a strong grip on my chin.

"She's really pretty."

She is, she really fucking is. "Mom, please stop. We're friends and roommates."

"You didn't deny it." She lets go and places her hands back on her hips. "I don't know what you did to her, but you better go make things right." She flicks her hand as if saying that I need to leave now.

But I don't walk away. I stay in my spot and cave a little. "How did Dad know?"

Her eyes widen in disbelief before she recovers. She knows what I mean by that. "Why don't you ask him."

My gaze jumps to the food truck and linger for a moment, but I snap out of it and shake my head. "No, you know it's not going to end well. I should go find her."

She wraps her arms around me and releases a debilitated sigh. "You know, he loves you very much. He's just having a hard time."

I hug her back, feeling the knot in my throat. "Don't lie, and we've all had a hard time."

"He does. He's just—"

"Please stop making excuses." I let go, feeling angry. "I lost him too," I grit, aggravated. "I was there and I'm paying for it every day. He knows that and doesn't care and you keep making excuses for him."

"Daniel—"

I step back, hating the grief-stricken look on her face and the way her eyes glass over. Dammit, I should've kept my mouth shut. "I'm sorry, I-I'm really sorry. I should go."

She offers me a small smile. "I love you. Don't forget that, okay?"

"I love you too." I walk away before I make a bigger ass out of myself.

I don't know what I'm going to say to Josie, but I need to find her. I make my way to the tank, but when I get there, she's not around.

"Hey, Danny." Vienna smiles at me from inside the tank.

I blink, flabbergasted by how she looks like a real mermaid. "Hey, have you seen Josie?"

"She was supposed to go find you."

She didn't come back. Way to go, idiot.

"Danny, hey." Amanda approaches.

I hear Vienna mumble something under her breath, but she moves away to the other side of the tank. I want to explain myself to her, but Amanda is already in front of me.

"Not right now." I sidestep her but she follows behind me

and calls my name. "What?" I spin to face her. "What now, Amanda?"

"I just wanted to congratulate you." She crosses her arms against her chest. "Sheesh, what the hell is wrong with you?"

I lift my hat, running my fingers through my hair before I place it back. "I'm sorry. It's been a long day."

"It's okay, I get it." She sympathetically smiles at me. "Can I hug you, or are you going to bite my head off?"

She unfolds her arms and raises them, but I don't embrace her.

"It's just a hug. I'm not asking you to have sex with me." She deviously grins. "I mean unless..." She trails off as if she were letting me fill in the blank.

"Don't—" My peripheral vision catches something white, and despite there being hordes of people today wearing that, black, or turquoise, I know it's Josie. I'm right when I spot her but see she's not alone.

"Danny, what are you..." Amanda's voice dwindles I think, I'm not sure, as my gaze stays locked on Josie and Bryson.

She looks a little irritated, but Bryson has a shit-eating grin. I don't have the slightest clue what they could be talking about, but she doesn't move away when he takes a step closer. Something creeps up in my chest and takes a hold of my heart.

Josie must've felt me looking because our eyes collide, but she only holds my stare for a moment before they flick to Amanda.

"Danny." Amanda grabs my arm, urging me to look at her.

I shrug her hand away. "I can't keep doing this with you. We're done and I don't want you back. Just leave me the fuck alone."

Her jaw drops and hurt flashes on her face, but I can't bring myself to care.

I go to search for Josie, but she and Bryson are nowhere in sight.

32

JOSEFINE

> Bryson: Please just think about it
>
> Bryson: I miss you Josie
>
> Bryson: I want you back

AND BLOCKED.

I don't know why I didn't do that sooner. *Maybe because he stopped texting me for a while and I thought I'd be dead, so I didn't see a point in blocking his number.*

Tossing my phone on my nightstand, I let myself fall back on my bed.

I don't understand why he all of a sudden has found me interesting again, but I wish he didn't.

Bryson found me as I was making my way back to Vienna after talking to Daniel. Apparently and unfortunately, he was looking for me. I attempted to walk away, but he wouldn't take no for an answer. Even my silence wasn't enough to get him to leave me alone.

I relented only because he said he would if I listened. That was a mistake because what he said to me in the text messages is what he told me in person. Along with unnecessary comments that aren't worth thinking about.

Though it's easy to forget about him, not only because he's that forgettable, but because I can't stop thinking about Daniel and how dismissive he was towards me.

Next time my brain screams at me no, I'll listen to her because why did I think he'd care to see me? I can't believe for a moment I thought he looked relieved.

Squeezing my eyes shut, I roll onto my stomach and sink my face into the duvet, until I can't breathe.

I'm in the middle of self-loathing when I hear heavy footsteps climbing up the stairs. I twist onto my back, hating the eager way my heart wallops. It's pathetic, really, my body buzzing knowing that he's home. Especially after what he said. It wasn't bad, but it stung nonetheless.

His footsteps grow closer and just when I think I'll hear his door shut, I hear a knock on mine. "Josie."

I don't make a sound or a move. It's childish to ignore him, but I really don't want to talk to him right now.

"I know you're awake."

Not sure how he would know that, but I still ignore him and stay silent.

"Your light," he explains as if he could hear my thoughts.

Right, dammit. "Good night."

"I'm sorry." I hear a thump against my door followed by a heaved sigh. "I didn't mean to be short with you. I was…I'm sorry. Can we talk?"

"It's late. I have a lesson in the morning and I still have to shower."

"I'll make it quick. I promise," he begs.

His mournful voice almost gets me to concede, but I shake my head and sharply say, "Don't want to talk to you."

I hear his footsteps recede into his room along with faint shuffling. I figure he's going to leave me alone until I hear a rustle beneath my door. My attempt to ignore whatever that is is abysmal as the corner of my eye catches onto pale yellow on the floor, making me do a double take.

A Post-it note lays on the floor with black ink on it. As quietly as I can, I grab it and read what it says.

I'm sorry Josefine!

"Daniel," I grumble but my lips appallingly tilt up. "I told you—"

Another Post-it note is slipped underneath my door.

I'm not talking. I'm communicating with you. They don't mean the same thing

"I still don't—"
And another.

I'm sorry for being an asshole!

"How many of these do you have?"

Tons! I can do this all night

"I thought it was a long and busy day? Aren't you tired?" I repeat what he said to me earlier.

Never for you. I'm sorry about earlier. I promise I was on my way to find you, but my parents found me. Then I almost got into it with my dad. I'm sorry for being an asshole.

He was looking for me? I want to ask just to make sure I heard that right, but I don't.

"Yeah, you were an asshole," I mutter, dropping to the floor and sitting next to the door. I hear noise on the other side and I'm certain he's doing the same thing followed by a chuckle.

You're not supposed to agree with me

"Just repeating what you said."

Can I talk now?

I can't stop myself from smiling. "No, I like you like this." He chuckles again.

Does this mean I'm forgiven?

"Let me think about it..." My voice carries a slight tease until I think about the email and his parents. "Do you want to talk about the email and your parents?"

No.

He quickly slips the Post-it under the door and then another.

I really don't want to talk about either

I rest my head against the door. "You know, I see you. You can act like whatever you feel doesn't matter, but it does." I have no idea where that came from, but it only encourages me to keep going.

For a long moment I don't hear anything or get a note from him.

"Garcia, you there?" I sit on my knees, my hand reaching for the doorknob until another Post-it is slipped underneath.

I really need you.

My breath catches.

I've never been someone who anyone needs and I almost wonder if this is a ploy to get me to come outside. But his handwriting is rushed, the ink seeps into the back of the paper, and the lines are indented from how heavy he was holding the pen. The other Post-its don't look and feel like this.

He needs *me*.

Daniel's going to regret this. I know he is, but regardless of my conflicting feelings and the voice in my head saying I'm going to fuck this up, I open the door.

He's sitting on the other side, his gaze lost, but when his eyes find mine, I swear I see every morsel of sadness and tension on his face and body dissolve. He looks...genuinely happy and relieved to see me.

A small, devastating, crooked smile curls on his face as he scribbles something. I quickly rake my gaze over him, taking in his uniform, chain with the safety pin, and hat. He looks good... really, *really* good.

This isn't the time to gawk!

He holds the note up for me to read.

I'm so happy you're here!

On my knees, I scoot closer to him and before I can talk myself out of it, I circle my arms around his shoulders. I think I caught him by surprise because he momentarily tenses but then his body goes slack against mine and he wraps his arms around my waist.

I feel his heart race against my chest, or is it mine? I'm not sure, I can't tell, and I don't want to let myself think because this is already too much. Surely, he'll realize this is a mistake or at least I keep thinking he will but seconds tick by and he continues to hold me like I'm his lifeline.

"I needed this. *I needed you*," he murmurs against my chest, the deep rasp of his voice vibrating against me.

The wick in my heart lights back up, easily and instantaneously, almost as if it had never been out. I hate that I let it happen and most of all hate how the single flame warms my entire body.

It sends ripples of heat throughout, slowly spreading like a wildfire but not hot enough to incinerate me, just warm enough I feel a little...alive.

My throat dries, making it hard to swallow, but that's the least of my worries because my heart pounds against my chest, the blood rushing too loud in my ears, making it challenging to listen to the other murmured words leaving his lips.

"It's just a hug," I heedlessly reply.

"A hug that came from you. This is all I wanted."

I wish I could stop my body from reacting.

"Maybe what you need is to talk about it," I say in hopes it'll distract my racing thoughts and heart.

"I really don't—"

"I don't get you." I cut him off and pull back, letting my arms dangle around his shoulders.

He tips his head back to stare up at me and keeps his arms firmly around me. "What don't you get?"

A warning flashes in my head to draw away, far away because we're too close. My lips are just an inch away from his, and our bodies are tangled in a position that isn't deemed appropriate for people who are just *friends*.

"How you think it's okay to prioritize my feelings but disregard your own."

His brows pinch together, lips parted, but nothing leaves his mouth. He stares like he's speechless, shocked, and anxious all at once.

"They matter too, you know." I cradle his cheek, gently caressing it with the pad of my thumb. "*You* matter, Daniel."

A haunted look takes over his eyes before they get washed away with sadness. It lingers like it's letting itself be seen. Like it's asking for help and doesn't know how.

I feel his chest expand against me and he thickly swallows. His fingers dig into my sides, like he's holding on to me, and I let him. I shift closer to him, letting him use me as an anchor.

"Don't hide," I softly say, letting those two words seep in our bubble and hoping he's absorbing them, hearing them, feeling them. "I'm right here."

A muscle in his jaw works before his eyes cast down as if he were embarrassed. Or maybe I've said something wrong.

"I'm sorry if that came off brash. I'm not good at this kind of thing. Maybe you should look up a therapist. I hear they're good at this kind of thing."

That gets him to lift his head and smile. I even get a soft snicker to squeeze past his lips. "That wasn't—who made you think this way?"

I shrug. "It doesn't matter. I tend to come off cold, so if—"

"You've never come off cold, and you said nothing wrong. I'm the one with issues. I struggle to talk about myself."

I scoff, dropping my hand from his cheek and placing it back around his shoulder. "You're the one with issues? Have you met me? I'm *a* walking issue. And that makes two of us because I hate talking about myself."

"You're not a walking issue." He brightens. "You know, I really like it when you talk about yourself. I want you to do more of it."

"Not until you do."

"I talk a lot about myself," he weakly defends.

"Calling yourself hot doesn't count."

"But you can agree I am, right?" He bats his eyelashes with hopefulness.

I almost laugh, but I swallow it down. "I'm not going to stroke your ego, Garcia."

"But I want you to stroke it," he utters throatily then tenses like he's realized what he said but doesn't correct himself. "Just once. That's all I want. *Please*," he gruffly says. The last word leaving his lips is an impatient and eager plea; it's far too enthusiastic but also heated with urgency. *"Josefine, please."*

I drag my palm up his spine until my fingers reach the back of his jersey. I should stop because I have no idea what I'm doing, but he's not stopping me. He's only staring at me like I'm everything he's prayed for.

His eyes dilate, breath puffing out shakily as I skate my fingers up the nape of his neck and weave them through his hair. It's far softer than I imagined. It feels good and again I tell myself to stop but I don't.

I'm enthralled with how firm and large his hands feel on my waist, and his rock-hard chest is pressed against mine.

I click my tongue, sighing like I'm disappointed. "That wasn't good enough."

"Please, Josefine, just say it once. Only once, that's all I want. Please say it," he pleads incessantly and then switches to Spanish. My weakness. *"Por favor dímelo. Nomás una vez. Hago lo que tú quieras."*

His hands squeeze tightly. I can feel my pulse against each finger and the one between my thighs.

I inhale as steadily as I can, hoping my voice won't betray me. I fist his hair, forcing his head back as I bring my face close to his, my lips just a mere centimeter from his. "You're hot. Ego stroked?"

"Barely." His fingers slide down the curve of my waist. Forget dilated, his eyes are blown, shot with heat. They drift until he's staring at my lips as I stare at his.

The bubble we're trapped in fills with electricity until it becomes unbearably hot and bursts. Static shock sprawls through every cell in my body, causing my brain to combust and stop working.

"Josie..." His hands continue to descend until they're right above my ass.

"Yeah?" I absently move until I'm straddling him, but I still hover over him, granting him with my position to do what he's thinking.

He cups my ass, forcing me to sit on him completely. He stifles a groan and I swallow back a moan as I feel his erection press against me.

We shouldn't do this. I shouldn't be okay with this, but I can't think coherently.

"Just once?" he roughly asks, letting him use me to rub him. My bikini bottoms and the seam of my denim shorts dig into my pussy, eliciting the best kind of pressure on my clit.

To get it out of our systems.

My rational thoughts are clouded. I'm dizzy and the pit of my stomach coils as the pressure of me grinding against him grows.

"Just once."

We need this. It'll be a one-time thing.

He closes the small gap between us, sealing our lips and stealing all the oxygen. My lips become pliable against his, letting him take control and do as he pleases. I follow along, savoring the way his lips and teeth suck, bite, and nip my lower lip.

I moan into his mouth, encouraging him to deepen the kiss. He slips his tongue into my mouth and fervently kisses me, obliterating whatever oxygen I have left until I'm panting not for air, but for more of him.

I'm humping myself faster on him, my fingers getting lost and tangled in his hair. I pull it back and he groans, squeezing my ass punishingly.

But our kiss is short-lived and we wrench back, panting breathlessly as his phone vibrates against the floor. A picture of him and his mom appears on the screen. She's calling him, but he goes to ignore it.

"Answer it." I lick my swollen lips, feeling lightheaded and in need to get off but his phone continues to vibrate.

"I can—"

"Answer it. We got it out of our system, right?"

My body is screaming at me to finish what we started, but I'd feel like shit if he didn't answer.

His molten eyes burn me, and I almost stop myself from getting off him, but I force myself to stand.

"Right," he supplies tentatively as he stands.

He looks just as disheveled as I feel. Locks of his hair are sticking out, and his hat is on the floor. I don't remember that coming off.

Neither one of us moves but when his phone vibrates again, we part, neither one of us saying good night. But a few moments later, he slips a note under my door.

Is it really out of your system?
It's not out of mine.

33

DANIEL

"This is insane." Adrian subtly and slowly scans the field and stadium, his voice low, almost in a whisper as we take our seats in the home plate grandstand.

Like me, he's playing it cool, not showing how inside we're eagerly buzzing.

We're at Opening Day for Monterey Coastal University. Dad surprised us; he didn't tell us anything this morning but to pack because we were going on a mini trip. Which is unusual because he never lets us skip school, but he said it'd be an exception because today is Friday.

"I know." My gaze shifts down to the dugout. The players aren't there yet, but it won't be long before they're piling out.

"One day we're going to play here," Adrian confidently and arrogantly states.

"I don't know. You're kind of shit."

"Pinche pendejo. I was being nice." He scowls before his expression morphs into an easygoing one. "When I get recruited and you don't, don't get butt hurt over it, okay? I promise to put in a good word."

I burst out laughing, but I don't counter it. Instead, I say, "One day, it'll be you and me down there."

He looks up at me, smiling wide, those dimples on display. "One day."

"You good, brah?" Kai asks as he slips his belt through the loops of his pants.

My chest burns at the memory, but I shake it away and smile at him. "Yeah, why?"

"I was talking to you, but you zoned out."

"You weren't talking to me, but I also zoned out. I mean have you heard yourself talk?" Angel snorts. "It's nonstop. Blah blah blah."

"You really want to talk?" Kai shoots back. "No one cares about—"

"Happy Valentine's Day, bitches!" Gray springs into the locker room, voice elated and eyes vibrantly shining. "Who wants a kiss from—"

"Pass!" almost everyone in the room shouts.

He stands in front of Noah, lifting and stretching his arms wide, but Noah pins him with a blank expression.

"Don't touch me," Noah warns before he finishes getting ready.

That doesn't stop Gray from smiling and moving onto his next victim: me.

I'm not in the mood, but I need to find a way to be in it because it's Opening Day. First game of the season and I need to be at my best mentally to play.

"Sparky, bring it in." He grins. I spread my arms, letting him pull me in for a hug. "Love you, baby." He plants a loud kiss on my cheek.

My chest painfully aches. I have to do everything in my power not to exhale the air in my lungs that feels like heavy acid.

He reminds me so much of Adrian. So lively, so full of energy, a smile so big and bright it blinds you of all the bad.

"Love you too, bro," I chuckle, telling myself not to hold on to him because he's not Adrian; hugging him isn't going to change anything.

"I'm so fucking hyped, man." He pulls away and moseys on over to his next victim, Kai.

"You okay?" Angel stands next to me as I finish buttoning my shirt.

"Yeah, it's Opening Day," I reply, my fingers grazing the safety pin attached to my chain.

He tracks the movement but doesn't make a comment about it. Still, he scrutinizes me as if he can sense something is wrong.

"Actually," I quietly say and discreetly sweep my gaze over the room, finding Bryson on the other end. Our eyes lock on each other briefly, but it's long enough for him to glare at me before he looks away. "I kissed Josie."

I don't want to talk about this either, but it's Josie or Adrian, and she's easier to talk about than my brother.

Angel gawks at me in disbelief before he masks it away and bears a smug smile. He leans against the locker, folding his arms over his chest, eyes drifting over to where Bryson's standing and then back to me.

"So much for just friends and roommates?" he faintly spurs, lifting a brow. "When was this? Are you guys..."

He doesn't finish, but I know what he's asking.

I shake my head, although I wish I was nodding it instead. She and that kiss is all that I've been thinking about, dreaming about, wishing about. God, it's all I fucking want, but I know it's not what she wants. No, it's obvious she's over it, probably long forgotten like it never happened because that's how she's been acting for a week.

No different then when we hardly knew each other. She hasn't even said anything about my note.

"Last Friday after the bonfire. I was a dick and...I'm not going into details. It doesn't matter anyway." I lift my hat, raking my fingers through my hair frustratedly, then place it back.

His brows pull together and he stares at me in a way that makes me feel uncomfortable. Then his arms slip, falling limply at his side, lips part in a muted O, and eyes slowly go round in what looks like realization.

"Holy shit. You like her." It's rhetorical but he wants an answer because he prods. "Danny, do you like her?"

My gaze swings back over to Bryson. "I doubt she likes me like that."

"Okay and? That's not what I asked. Do you like her?"

I rub the nape of my neck, dropping my gaze to the floor. My heart rockets, taking off, and fireworks explode. She doesn't need to be in front of me anymore. I don't need to see her smile for them to appear. Just the mere thought of her makes me feel...me.

I exhale a breath, my stomach intensely fluttering. "Yeah... I do."

Angel smiles, clicking his tongue. "You're so fucking cute. You're going to make me throw up."

I roll my eyes. "Shut up and don't say anything. Nothing is going to happen."

"Why not?"

"It was one and done."

My walk-out song, "Pursuit of Happiness" by Kid Cudi blasts through the speaker. It was the last song Adrian listened to.

For the longest time, I couldn't hear it without breaking out into tears and at times panic attacks. I still don't listen to it fully, only when I'm at bat. I only brought myself to listen to it because a therapist told me it was good exposure therapy and I feel like I'm with Adrian, even if it's for a few seconds.

Puffing out a breath, I step up to the plate. The bases are loaded, and this is the reason why I'm the fourth in the lineup. I'm the cleanup hitter, the cleanup spot. I bring the home runs. Just last year I led the NCAA in batting. I'm a damn—exceptionally brilliant, as a few have said—good hitter.

My accolades and achievements are all thanks to my father,

the man who I know is somewhere up in the stands, who will probably utter a measly, *"síguele echando ganas"* or *"podrías mejorar"* after the game. That is, if he decides to stay afterwards.

I hope he doesn't. It's always awkward. Mom and Pen try to fill the silence with supportive words of affirmation, but in the end, it never helps. Whenever we're standing in front of each other, it feels like I'm in front of a distant relative, a stranger even.

It's been that way from the moment...

I blink away the memory that attempts to play in my head and take a practice swing. My hands tighten around the bat and I side-eye Noah who stands next to first base, knees slightly bent as he shuffles back and forth, ready to steal a base if he'll need to. He's third in our lineup and is exceptional at stealing.

My gloves crinkle as I grip the bat, squeezing it as I take my stance. My left foot is planted on the ground, but my right, I use the tip of my cleat to dig into the dirt as I lift my heel and bring my knee inward. My stance is something that always has the sports analysts, sports reporters, and everyone and their grandpa talking about.

I hear a mingled laugh and scoff come from the catcher. I agree, it's an odd stance but it helps me and he knows that too; that's why I have kids copying and tagging me in their videos.

"Don't be jealous, Petey," I mumble and make sure not to move my lips.

He scoffs again but doesn't make a comment.

Wyatt, freshman and pitcher from Cal Poly, is feeling the pressure. He doesn't show it, but the chants from the crowd are boisterously loud. We're playing home and baseball season has commenced. It's expected, but Wyatt isn't playing like he saw it coming; he's nervous as hell. It's why the first three in the lineup have walked, and why I know I'll be bringing my team home.

He exhales, pitching a fastball, but it's too far out, nowhere near the box.

The umpire calls, "Ball."

He pitches another, still using a fastball, but couples it with a slider. The ball moves in a way to trick you, pulling downward as it spins quickly my way. They're tricky but all you have to do is... swing...just...right.

The contact is loud, the crack of the ball against my bat resonating throughout the stadium. Despite how loud the fans are, the slam still beautifully echoes in my ear. I don't watch it fly out of the field, but I do glance up at the sky briefly before the knot forms in the middle of my throat.

Noah, Kai, and Gray wait for me at home plate. We remove our helmets and bump them against each other. My teammates are all out of the dugout, gathered around, creating a tunnel. They slap my shoulder, butt, and back as I jog down it, and they shout enthusiastically at me as I make my way into the dugout.

The knot only grows, my eyes mist, and my chest squeezes painfully. I barely manage to pull myself together and hand my helmet to one of the student athletic trainers.

I stand next to Angel on the padded railing, watching Jamie, our third baseman, walk up to the bat. He goes on about something, but it's hard to pay attention to him.

First games are always the hardest for me and I know it's only a matter of time before the feeling wanes. In the meantime, I scan the stadium, trying to distract my mind from my dark, destructive thoughts. I don't search for my parents—I know they're here, but Pen isn't. She's in North Carolina at an away game with the basketball team.

I know Josie's not here either. I asked if she was going to come, but she said she was meeting up with a potential new client. I know it's her job, but I wish she was here instead.

34

JOSEFINE

I SWORE I WAS NEVER GOING TO WATCH A BASEBALL game, but here I am, at Salty Rims Bar & Grill, along with many other MCU students. There are a handful of TVs playing different sports, but the only one that has my attention is baseball.

Anything revolving Bryson repulsed me and that included baseball. Or it did until a certain six-foot-five guy with a golden smile changed my mind.

All my attention gravitates to Daniel, and Bryson's existence is forgotten. The only time I remember he's playing or part of the team is when the camera pans to him, but even then, it hardly does because the cameraman knows he's not what the people want.

It's Daniel Garcia, with his quirky stance and the finesse that exudes him.

I shouldn't call it quirky, but it's the only way to describe the way he stands on the point of his cleat, pulling his right knee inward. He stands almost awkwardly, at an angle that doesn't look comfortable, at least to anyone watching it. But Daniel doesn't look uneasy; he looks placid, blithe, confident, and hot.

I never really paid attention to the sport, only tolerated it because of Bryson. After him, it was the last thing on my mind, and I made sure to stay away from it.

But now it's different. Watching Daniel, seeing him in his uniform, how it sinfully molds to his body, especially his thick thighs, watching him dive to the base and adeptly rise, cockily flashing a crooked grin, dusting his pants off as if that'll do anything to clean off the orange dirt staining them—it does things to me. Things that I can't explain, but I swear I've never found anything hotter or more interesting until now.

I semi understand the stats and half of what the commentators are saying, but I wholly comprehend that Daniel is wickedly talented. I understand why they fawn over him, praise him, boast about him like he's already in the majors.

I get it, I really do.

The girls crowding the bar next to me feel the same way.

I should've gone home after my meeting, but the game had started shortly after I got done. So I stumbled into Salty Rims because I didn't want to miss a second of watching him play.

They're at the bottom of the eighth inning. I should go home now—they're at the advantage and winning 9-3—but the conversation the girls are having next to me stops me from moving from my stool.

"Daniel and I had fun last time. Of course he's going to reply to me," the brunette brags.

"I know because I was there," her blonde friend adds, drunkenly giggling. "But that was months ago. We haven't talked to him in a while."

"I still can't believe you two and Daniel..." Their other friend trails off. "What was he like?"

I shouldn't be eavesdropping or discreetly side-eyeing to find Daniel's Instagram popped up on her screen or see her go to messages. She's so close and the screen's brightness is high, I can make out their conversation and see a nude picture she sent him.

His response makes me look away and green colors my vision. My stomach twists and dips painfully fast.

"I messaged him. You wanna tag along, Brenda?" the brunette asks the blonde who joined them.

"He hasn't even replied. How do you know he's not already going to be busy?" the blonde questions.

"Because I just know," she haughtily answers.

I don't care who he's messed with. I don't care how many girls he's fucked at the same time. I don't care. After all, it's done.

His note meant nothing. I'm convenient; I was the closest thing around.

When I step into the house, I freeze by the entryway. It feels like I've been doused in floral perfume, but it doesn't smell artificial, just organic.

After I left the bar, I went to the beach to clear my head. I wanted to stop thinking about Daniel, the threesome, and knowing he was going to see her message and reply to it.

The game ended about two hours ago. It's only six, but I didn't think he'd bring them here or at least not now.

He said he wouldn't invite women over, but he did; they're in my house.

I can't move. I want to, but I can't.

Taking one step back, I'm halfway in the house and halfway out. I don't want to leave, but I don't want to go in either. I don't want to hear them, but I shouldn't leave because this is my house.

Making up my mind, I step inside and slam the front door. Each step I take feels heavier than the last, but I somehow find the will to keep going. I wait for the inevitable moan or groan, but I hear nothing.

At least he has the decency to be quiet.

I bite the inside of my cheek, hating myself for letting this get to me. Who cares what he does, who cares that he brought them here, who cares that I—

Everything comes to an abrupt halt. My thoughts, my legs, the ugly whirl of emotions just stops.

An explosion of yellow.

A variety of yellow flowers with the exception of a few whites scattered here and there litter my kitchen and living room. The last time I saw this many flowers was when Mom passed, but these aren't those kinds of flowers.

Wait. How did they get here? There must've been a mistake.

"Daniel?" I shout. I know he's here; his car is parked outside. I search around for a little note or card because there must be one; isn't there usually one? "Daniel! Did you see the..."

My voice dwindles as I finally spot the envelope. The front says, *Happy Valentine's Day*. Carefully I take out the card, and my breath catches in my throat.

The front of the card has one smiling piece of toast and it says, *I Knead You To Know...*

And the inside of the card has two pieces of toast, holding hands. One has what looks like strawberry jelly and the other I think has grape jelly and it reads, *You're the best toast mate ever!* On the bottom, he wrote, *I'm happy you're here, Jos!*

It's corny but I'm such a dork because I'm smiling so big, my cheeks start to ache. I'm not sure how long I stand here looking at the card I know he made for me.

He did this for me. He got me flowers. Tons of them. This is insane? Wait—

Everything comes to an abrupt halt again. Why did he buy me flowers? This is a lot of them. Does he want something? Did he do something? I've only ever been given something to make up for something. Mom and Bryson did that a lot—well, Bryson did; Mom just liked to pretend it never happened.

"Daniel?!" I shout again and take the stairs two at a time. It's safe to say those girls aren't here. Still, I knock on his bedroom door, but I don't get an answer. "Daniel, I swear if you don't open up, I'm going in."

Still nothing.

"Fine, I'm going in!" I make a show of twisting the knob to give him some time to cover up in case he's naked or something, and after a few seconds, I open the door.

There's no indication that anyone but him has been here. The room looks more lived in than the whole house ever has. His stuff takes over every inch of the room—vinyls, cassette tapes, and CDs in one corner, and other random stuff scattered about.

I snap out of it, knowing I'm being nosy and need to find him. I check his bathroom and don't find him in there either. Then I check every other room, except Mom's office, and still nothing. He wouldn't go in there because I told him not to and he promised he wouldn't. Still, I take a quick peek and see nothing.

I'm back in the living room, about to call him, but stop when I spot someone outside from the corner of my eye. I'm quickly moving in that direction but slow when I hear him sniffle.

"Daniel?"

He's sitting on the grass, legs pressed to his chest, arms circled around them, forehead pressed to his knees.

"Oh." He quickly sits up, looking away, and gingerly uses the sleeve of his hoodie to wipe his face. "Hey, Josie."

"Hey," I cautiously say, standing behind him. "Are you okay?"

"Yeah." His voice is hoarse, but he clears it and nods. "Yeah, I'm good. Just came out here to get fresh air. The wind picked up a bit, and I got something in my eye. Pretty sure it was sand," he explains, wiping his face again, still not looking up at me. "Yup, it was sand. Maybe you shouldn't be out here; you might get it in your eye too."

"I'll take my chances." I settle down beside him, but I don't look at him.

"You sure? The wind is kind of aggressive." He rubs his eyes and sniffles. "Trust me, you don't want to get sand in your eyes. It's a bitch to get out."

"I bet it is, especially when it gets in your hair."

"Yeah, so why don't you go inside. I'd hate for you to get it in your hair."

"If I get it in my hair, you can help me get it out."

He goes quiet for a moment, then I hear him swallow.

"Thank you for the flowers." I try to bite back my smile, but it slips, making it hard to hide how giddy they made me feel.

I hear him wince and feel him go taut. He stifles a laugh, dragging his fingers through his hair. "I made a mistake." My lips fall, *oh*... "I didn't mean to order that many. I mean I wanted to order all the flowers that are in there, but not two dozen of each. I hope you don't have any allergies; I didn't think to ask. I'm sorry."

"It's okay." I'm smiling again. Why am I like this? "Wait, so you're telling me you were probably charged a ridiculous amount of money and you didn't think of disputing it or asking questions? You just let it be?" Who does that?

"It was for you. The price didn't matter. I figured they'd be worth it." He pauses and this time I feel his eyes on me. "I hope they were. Were they worth it?"

I look up at him and my fingers twitch to touch him, to embrace him, to ask him what's wrong and who I need to fight because his eyes are bloodshot and rimmed with unshed tears. The tip of his nose is red, and his hands are shaky.

As much as I want to do that, I don't because I don't want to push and make him uncomfortable. So, I focus on his question.

I nod, not bothering to hide my smile from him. "Yeah, they're worth it. I've never been given anything just because. I'm sorry I didn't get you anything."

His lips stretch as his gaze darts to mine, but then his brows knit together as if he's registered what I said. "I didn't do this because I expect something from you. I did this because I wanted to. It's Valentine's Day and well, what can I say, I love a good holiday."

"Did you accidentally get everyone dozens of flowers too?"

"Just my toast mate."

My heart stutters.

"Wait, are you telling me Bryson never—" At the shake of my head, he scowls. "Fucking piece of shit."

"I know. My standards were low," I embarrassingly admit even though he knows that. "I was stupid and—"

"You weren't stupid."

"Trust me, I was. He treated me like shit and yet there I was." I shrug. "Stupid."

"Then I was stupid too. My ex-girlfriend didn't treat me like shit, but she did shitty things." He scrunches his nose.

"Look at us, bonding over shitty exes." I bump my shoulder into his.

"Exes that will..." He pauses, gaze flicking away, fingers drumming along this thigh. "Stay exes, right?"

"You don't want Amanda back?" I don't know why I asked; it's obvious he doesn't.

"Fuck no." He doesn't miss a beat and winces. "Was that too harsh?"

"No. I don't think you sounded mean enough. Fuck Amanda. Fuck Bryson. Fuck them both."

"Yeah, fuck them." He nods, a smirk on his face. "So, I can assume you don't want Bryson back, right?"

"No. I blocked his number and everywhere on social media," I admit.

His brows lift and I swear for a moment he looks like he's relishing this news. "Really?"

"Yeah, he's doing too much. Never thought something like that would make me cringe, but it does."

Daniel presses his lips together to muffle his laugh, but it still slips out. "I'm so proud of you. I should do that too." He fishes his phone out of his pocket, goes to her contact, blocks her number, then goes through all his socials and does the same.

Wow.

"I thought you were here with someone," I admit and cringe a second later. Maybe I shouldn't have brought it up.

He stares at me, confused. "Who would I be here with?"

I twist my ring. "I was at Salty Rims and overheard a conversation about..." Why did I bring this up? I proceed to quickly tell him and attempt to hide my mortification because he knows I was eavesdropping if I heard that much.

Sex doesn't bother me. I have no qualms about it, but it's talking about it to a guy who I've been dreaming about and getting off to that makes this weird.

"I told you I wouldn't bring anyone here and I meant that. I've also just not been in the mood. Even if I was, they're not who —I'm just not in the mood."

I tuck my hair behind my ear. "Do you want to talk about it?"

"About sex?"

"No, but if you want to, we can. I meant about the sand in your eye."

All the humor drains from his face. "Not really. It was just sand."

Sucking in a breath, I wipe my palms on my thighs and stand. "Get up," I demand. "Now."

Daniel doesn't hesitate to do as I say, just stares at me, bemused. "What are we going to do?" The sun is setting behind him, casting a glow around him like a halo.

"You don't like talking about yourself and neither do I, but you need someone and while I'm no therapist, I'm here."

"It's okay. I'm fine. I promise." He smiles.

I shake my head, anxiously fisting my hands at my sides. "I was homeschooled all my life and I think that's why I'm socially awkward and can't make friends. And Mom told me having them would hinder my focus on swimming. Take your hoodie off."

He gapes at me, voicing a disbelieving quiet, "What?"

"I gave a little about me; now you take something off. You give me a little something, I'll take something off. I don't interrupt or ask questions and neither will you. Deal?" My heart careens and my palms sweat. Scary alarms blare in my head, warning me to not share any more, but I want to help him open up.

Hesitantly, he strips off his hoodie and drops it on the grass. "Okay, deal."

35

DANIEL

"I don't think you're socially awkward."

"You met me at my worst, so I don't think you have a clear judgment of who I am." She folds her arms against her chest as if she were self-conscious. "But I'm done sharing; it's your turn."

It threw me off when she shared a tidbit about herself without me having to goad her or beg for a crumb of her life. But that's not what continues to spike my anxiety, rising it to levels it hasn't been in a while.

I don't like talking about myself, especially talking about Adrian. Not because I don't want to talk about my brother and all the good he did in his short life, but I become a mess. I struggle to come back from it, and usually it'll take days before I feel like I'm not drowning.

It's why I had to get out of the house; I felt like I was suffocating and was close to having a panic attack.

Opening Day does that to me. It always happens, but it goes away. Which is why I like to be alone, so no one has to worry about me.

Maybe I should've left the house, gone somewhere else, because I can see the look of concern on Josie's face. I don't want the weight of my problems on her; she already has enough going on. I don't want to be the reason she has more issues added to her plate.

I'm not her problem.

I draw in a long breath, perusing a list of things I could share with her that isn't about my asphyxiating need to...I clear my throat.

"Left and right—I always confuse those two in Spanish. *Derecha* and *izquierda*. Which is which? And don't get me started on sixty and seventy in Spanish too. *Sesenta* and *setenta*? Like who thought of that and why would they make them sound almost the same? Am I right?" I playfully say, hoping I don't give more away than I already have. "Now you take—"

"Daniel," she deadpans. "While I totally get where you're coming from because they used to confuse me too, that's not what I meant."

"I know, I'm sorry. There just isn't much to say."

Her brows quirk.

"What?" I ask.

"I've said that before."

Oh...

For a moment, silence gathers. The sound of seagulls and the ocean lapping in the distance fills the gap between us.

She doesn't speak. She only stares at me patiently as though she has all the time in the world. Her stance and expression feel like they're saying, *there's no rush; I'm here for you*.

I tip my head back, contemplating what I should do. Part of me wants to retreat, but the other part of me is so tired. I can't fake my smiles or act like I'm in control right now because I'm not.

"Growing up was rough. My parents worked in the fields, picking fruit and vegetables. They hardly made anything; it was just enough to put food on the table and pay what we needed to get by. We didn't go on vacations. We didn't get brand-new clothes on the first day of school or really ever; everything was secondhand. Most Christmases we didn't get presents. On birthdays they'd make our cakes. You get the point. Eventually they had saved up enough to start their business, the bakery. They said they missed the bread from Mexico, so if they couldn't get it, they'd make it here, and Dad had experience from when he worked at one in Mexico. Because it was the closest bakery in the area and they lived in the predominantly Hispanic area, it took off. It's doing really well now; they've opened more bakeries and have vans that drive to different areas to sell bread. And they have a food truck for occasions like the bonfire."

Josie's brows lift a bit, surprise and admiration shining in her eyes. She shrugs the dark-green button-down off her shoulders and pulls on the rolled-up sleeves to get it to come off. She tosses it on the ground next to my hoodie.

She hikes the strap of her tank top up her shoulder, lips pursed as if she were thinking. "My mom immigrated here alone. She didn't want to, but her family wasn't supportive and they were hardly getting by in Mexico. When she got here, the only place she could work underage was in the fields. One night she snuck into one of the pools at the high school. The swimming coach found her, and instead of calling the police, she had her swim again. Long story short, as Mom would say, the coach took pity on her, sponsored her, and the rest is history."

I know her mom's story, I found out a lot about her during my research on Josie. I wouldn't say that's stalking—after all, it's all online. Claudia was an insanely talented swimmer. I hardly know anything about swimming, but I understand Olympic gold medals, and she has a lot of them on top of many other awards.

Raising my hand over my head, I grab the neck of my long-sleeve shirt and pull it off, dropping it on top of the other clothes.

Her gaze roams over the tight black Dri-FIT before lifting to meet my eyes.

"Like what you see, Josie?" I brazenly ask.

She rolls her eyes in response, but I don't miss the soft shade of pink that colors her cheeks. "Don't deflect. It's your turn."

I wasn't, but at the same time, I was. I like that she was

checking me out, but I also don't want to continue doing this. Still, I do because sharing what I did with her made me feel a little less anxious.

"My dad wanted Adrian and me to play soccer. He always had us watching soccer games, teaching us, and scrounging up enough money to sign us up to be on a team. We liked it enough and played in middle and high school, but baseball had our hearts. You should've seen the look on his face when we told him we wanted to pursue it and not soccer. You would've thought we had told him we became an *America* fan from the look on his face. He's a *Chivas* fan, by the way," I add because she looks confused. "They compete in Liga MX, the top division of Mexican football. You don't keep up with it, do you?"

She shakes her head. "That or anything else, but I did watch something kind of cool today. It involved a bat and a baseball player who's about six five."

My lips stretch of their own accord. There's nothing fake about this. "You watched me play?"

"I did." She rocks on her heels. "You're kind of good."

I scoff, affronted. "Kind of *good*? Josefine, what game were you watching because that isn't an adjective I'd used to describe how I played today or ever."

Her lips press in a thin line, but they quiver, and her cheek twitches. "Don't make me say it. You're cocky enough as it is. I don't want to over inflate your ego. Your head will get massive until it explodes, and then I'll be toast mateless."

For the first time since I woke up this morning, I feel lighter. I beam at her. "Am I rubbing off on you?"

"Shut up," she mutters, scowling at me like it pained her to say it.

My grumpy girl. "How much did you watch?"

"I only missed the first five, ten minutes of it." She removes the shell clip from her hair, letting the long wavy locks that were held by it fall with the rest. "I removed something," she says as if she could hear the question in my head.

"I thought it was just clothes?" I ask anyway.

She shrugs, her lips curling cunningly before they flatten. "I wasn't lying when I said I don't watch a lot of TV. Mom didn't let me watch it. She said it was a waste of time and I had to focus on swimming. Instead, she'd play the films of my meets and of others, and had me study them for hours. So, I guess I got used to not watching it. I never really picked up a remote."

Dad was like that at times with soccer then with baseball, but Mom would force him to let us watch other things. I'm grateful for that because at times I felt like I was getting burnt out. It makes me wonder if Josie got burnt out? Is that why she stopped swimming? I want to ask but we agreed, no questions. And I can tell that took a toll on her. She looks less like herself, more like the girl I met seven weeks ago.

Quick, think. "You know, now we're going to have to rectify that."

She looks puzzled. "Rectify what?"

"You watching TV. I'm sure you never watched the *Final Destination* series?" She shakes her head at my question. "You haven't been privileged of being traumatized like the rest of us. That's going to change. The log scene will blow your mind."

"Log scene?" She sounds intrigued.

"Yes, it's crazy and traumatizing. There's also this bridge scene and—I'm going to shut up. I don't want to spoil it for you. Matter of fact, tonight, don't make any plans, and if you have them, cancel them."

She lifts a brow in astonishment. "Got any other demands?"

"None as of now, but I'll keep you updated if anything comes to mind," I reply, keeping a straight face. "So, you, me, the couch. It's a date."

I hear the hitch in her breath and catch the way her chest rapidly expands for a second before it falls. "We live together. It doesn't need to be a date."

"It's Valentine's Day. Humor me, Jos," I playfully supply.

I'd prefer it to be real. I want it to be real. I want and need her but...I'm too fucked up. So, playing pretend will probably be the only way I get to have her.

"Will this date include food and drinks?" she questions just as playfully. Although I swear I hear something behind her words, but I'm sure I'm hopelessly and delusionally overthinking it. "Actually, I should probably pay for those. After all, you got me—"

"Josefine, no. As my date, all I want is for you to be happy and to let me treat you. You won't be paying for anything, so don't argue with me. Matter of fact, that's my second demand. Third is that you keep calling me hot."

She rolls her lips then they twist as if she were trying to attempt to stop herself from smiling. "You know, you're very pushy and not so humble from what they've said."

"From what they've said? What do you mean?" I tilt my head, eyeing her suspiciously when her cheeks flame and she darts her gaze away from mine.

"You're supposed to take something off."

"Josefine." I take a step forward, close enough I could grab her. "Where did you get that from? Huh?"

"I'm not going to answer that. You already know the answer to it."

"Tell me."

"Take something off."

"Not until you tell me."

She softly groans, her eyes colliding with mine. "I looked you up. Happy?"

I smirk, playing it cool, but inside, the fireworks are triple what they usually are. "Tell me more. What else did you find?"

"Take something off. I'm done with this conversation. You, me, couch. Date tonight, got it? Let's move on."

I don't prod and kick my shoes off, pushing them to the pile of our stuff. I smile, too smug for my own good, but then it slips, knowing it's my turn to share something. It's always easier when it's not about me.

I shift away from her keen stare, hating that she most likely knows what I'm thinking, what I'm feeling. I wish I wasn't like this; I wish I was as happy on the inside as I look on the outside. But I'm not. My head is dark, barely above the surface, and the water is murky. The gloomy clouds above aren't helping.

She's still staring at me with that same patient look of hers. She doesn't have a lot of that, I've noticed. But for me, her eyes are drowning with all the patience in the world. I don't deserve it.

What should I say? What should I say? What should I say?

I wish it would've been me and not Adrian. If I could, I'd switch places with him in a heartbeat.

I grind the back of my teeth, swallow back those words, and force others out. "When I was in eighth grade and Adrian was in seventh, Dad let us skip school. He didn't tell us why, only said to pack a bag because we were going to be gone for the weekend. We didn't ask questions and did what he said." A boulder lodges itself in the middle of my throat as the memory plays in my head. "A four-hour car drive later and we were in Monterey because MCU was having their Opening Day." The bridge of my nose burns. "Dad got us tickets for the series. Wanted us to see what our futures would look like. Adrian and I were geeking out because it was our first trip away from home. Our first time watching a baseball game that wasn't on TV. Our first time watching our dream school play." My throat tightens. "It was also the first time Dad and Mom had enough money to take us out and not worry about not having enough to pay for the bills. We knew not to take it for granted." I blow out a heavy breath and dryly chuckle. "That day, Adrian and I promised each other that we would..." My teeth chatter and my chest feels too taut; I can barely get any air in. "One day be here, playing together. And now we're..." I get choked up but clear my dry throat. "Not." I swallow back the ball of emotions clogging my throat and finish my story. "Opening Days are weird for me."

Josie's warm hand wraps around my wrist. She squeezes it gently then releases it. She doesn't say she's sorry or fills the silence with words that'll do nothing for me. Instead, she unlaces her Converse, takes them off, and pushes them next to mine.

"Mom and I didn't have a good relationship. Not sure I can even call it that because she didn't treat me like a daughter but *a*..." Her voice wavers and she looks away briefly before glancing back at me. "A person she lived with. I don't know which version of her to miss or even what I miss about her because I didn't really know her."

I want to unpack that and also hug her because she looks and sounds in pain. Guilt fills her voice and her features darken.

"No questions, please," she says a second later as if she could hear my thoughts.

I tug my Dri-FIT off and drop it on the pile.

I don't crack a joke when her eyes roam over my bare chest. I let her look as I consider what I want to say. "Dad and I don't have a good relationship. It's stale at best. Nonexistent at worst."

She grabs the hem of her tank and pulls it off. Leaving her in a cream-colored bra. I swallow as her large breasts softly bounce when she discards her top.

"I'm not really sure what to do with my life," she admits. "I swam because Mom wanted me to. I liked it, I really did, but after she passed, I tried to continue, but then I couldn't. I felt burnt out. Now I'm just here."

I really want to hug her. I really want to say something, but I know she doesn't want to hear it right now.

Hooking my fingers under the waistline of my shorts, I drop them and shove them with everything else. "I haven't opened the Draft Prospect Link email. It's sitting in my inbox unopened, and I'm not sure if I ever will open it."

Josie's brows twitch and lips part slightly. She undoes the button to her denim shorts and slips them off, letting them pool at her feet before adding them to our pile.

A deafening pause stretches between us. Unspoken questions fill the gap. They're too loud, but neither one of us does anything to voice them out loud. There's so much to say, so much to unpack, so much neither one of us wants to admit, but something we both desperately want to get out.

Despite the charged silence, we stay quiet. Standing almost naked, me only in my socks and briefs and her in a bra, a thong—I'm not sure, I'm afraid to look—and socks.

I should ask the questions running manic in my head, but I don't. I step closer, much closer than I know I should. My fingers itch at my sides, but I leave them there.

She cranes her head back, the orange sky illuminating her face. She looks like a goddess. "I shouldn't but I keep wondering why you haven't kissed me yet."

My jaw clenches and I remove my socks. No questions. "I shouldn't but I really want to touch you right now."

Her eyes dilate and breath quickens as she takes her socks off. "I'm not going to stop you."

36
JOSEFINE

"Are you sure?" His voice drops as he inches closer until he's towering over me.

"Yes," I voice, a little breathier than I wanted to sound.

Daniel's eyes darken, and he lifts his hand to my cheek, using his knuckles to caress it. The motion feels far more intimate than I'd like.

Yet, I yearn for more. Crave his fingers to feel me, hold me, squeeze me. The desire for more of him sets alight something in me that rapidly blisters, and I swear if it were possible, I'd be melted in a puddle at his feet.

"Did you see my note?"

"I did…I didn't think…you meant it."

"I did. I've been dreaming of this," he thickly says, his knuckles now trailing down to the curve of my jaw, to the crook of my neck, while his other hand gently grips my waist.

"You've been dreaming of me?" I inhale deeply when I feel his fingers loosen on my waist and brush over the curve of my hip.

He exhales a heavy breath as he nods. "Every night."

"I'm sorry." I wet my dry lips and he tracks the movement. He leans forward, dipping his head until his nose grazes mine.

"Why are you sorry?"

"Those must've been some terrible nightmares."

He loops his arm around my back, the other still caressing my jaw and neck. I softly gasp as he tugs me closer, the callus on his palm scraping my heated skin as he does. If it wasn't for his erection pressing against my stomach, there'd be no space left between us.

"Does that feel like I've been having nightmares, Josefine?" His lips faintly touch mine, and I swear I don't mean to, but I quiver under the touch.

"No." I drop my gaze to our pressed bodies, swallowing hard as I study the thick outline of his large bulge tenting his black briefs. Fuck, he's huge.

I bite the bottom of my lip, contemplating whether this is a line we should cross. He clearly wants this, and I do too, but we just shared things with each other. It's evident he's not okay and I don't want to take advantage of him.

I squeeze my eyes shut before I open them and tip my head to meet his burning stare. "We probably shouldn't do this."

He cups the side of my neck; his fingers brush over my back delicately. "Why not?"

"You're going to regret this and today—"

"I'm not going to regret this. I want you, Josefine, and I'm tired of pretending like I don't." He blows out a heavy breath and skims his fingers down to the band of my thong.

"But today you—"

"Use me," he desperately fills, cutting me off so urgently I almost don't think I heard him right until he repeats it. "Use me. Distract me. I don't care what you do but *use me*."

A heavy weight settles in my throat and sinks down to my stomach. For a moment, just for *one* fucking moment, I thought this was heading in a different direction. I don't know why I expected him to...whatever.

He wants a distraction; I'll be it.

Either way, I want one too.

Standing on my tiptoes, I snake my arms around his neck and

crash my lips to his. I don't go slow or take my time to savor his mouth the way I thought about doing a few seconds ago. He wants a distraction, so I'll give it to him.

He instantly drops his hand from my cheek and slips it around my back. He hoists me up and I lift my legs around his waist, his palms sliding down to my ass.

I vehemently kiss him, thrusting my tongue into his mouth. He meets every harsh stroke of my tongue against his, kissing me just as frenziedly.

I feel like I've stepped on a live wire. Every fiber of my body sparks with hot energy. The pit of my stomach coils, my clit pulsing harder, as I feel his hands roam over my ass, drifting between the crack before he grabs the thin string.

He wraps the fabric around his finger and tugs on it, wedging my thong between my pussy lips.

I whimper into his mouth, tensing and having to pause as waves of pleasure ripple all over my body. "Oh, Dan—"

He swallows the rest of my words as he picks up on the kiss. His tongue, hot in my mouth, massaging, thrusting, plays with mine as he continues to pull on my thong. It grazes my clit but doesn't give me the release I desperately want. Even as I grind onto his stomach, it does nothing but heighten my need to get off.

I tremble, a shiver wracking my body, causing my head to loll. My mouth slips from his.

I raggedly pant, squeezing my eyes tight before I open them and cup his chin, pushing his head back. He draws out the harsh breath, dark hooded eyes impatient and frustrated that I drew back.

Leaning forward, I brush my lips against his and he parts them as if he's getting ready to pick up where we left off. "Eat me or fuck off." I draw his bottom lip between my teeth, nipping it hard before I let go.

He hisses, the muscle on his jaw flexing but he smiles. It's lopsided but smug as fuck. "Is that what you want, Josie?" He lets go of the string and slides his fingers down my ass cheeks, curving them inward until they're gliding over my covered pussy. His finger coasts over the wet material leisurely, painfully slow. "Want me to taste you?" My eyes flutter and I don't realize we're moving until I've opened them again. "Want me to lick it?" He stops in front of one of the lounge chairs. "Want me to defile your soaking wet cunt? Is that what you want, Josie?"

I struggle but somehow still manage to nod. "It's what I need. Do it now."

He gently sits me down on the chair and crouches in front me, tucking my hair behind my ear. "Say *please*."

"Daniel," I warn, feeling immensely dizzy and like I've got a fever. "Don't start. After all, you said I could use you. This isn't about you, it's about me. So make yourself useful." I snap my fingers. It's a bit degrading, but he wanted me to use him.

He darkly chuckles and towers over me. I don't miss the wet stain on his briefs. There's nothing more I'd love than to suck him off, and I contemplate it, but I'm pushed back and my legs are spread before I can decide.

Daniel hovers over me, placing both hands on either side of my head. His chain dangles over my face then the safety pin grazes my nose. I glance at it, but he grabs it and almost as if he were embarrassed about it, drags it around so that it's at his back.

"No questions," he says, reminding me of what I said earlier.

I warily nod, despite wanting to do that. He notices my apprehension and smiles at me, the sheepish look on his face gone, replaced with a smoldering one.

"You're breathtaking." His voice is wanton, dripping with need. I squeeze my thighs, moaning when he drags his lips down to my throat and collarbone, and when he reaches the swell of my breast, I hold my breath. "Goddamn, Josie." He inhales a deep breath as if he were memorizing the scent of me. He drags his tongue over my breast, over my bra, before he bites down on the seam of the cup and pulls it back, exposing my breast.

Daniel tips his head back, staring up at the dark orange almost purple sky and mouths, *Fuck*. His eyes drop to mine, he slowly shakes his head, he licks his lips, and then he says, "You're a fucking godsend."

I sit up on my elbows, smirking. "Praising me doesn't work." Oh, it does, I'm certain I'm wetter than before, but I'm desperate to feel him on me.

"No?" he questions innocently, drawing the stiff peak of my nipple into his mouth. My eyes roll back, head lolling back. "You don't like getting told you're a good girl, Josie? You don't want to hear that you're doing a good job?" He bites my nipple and pays the other the same attention, sucking and biting it but just barely.

"No." My body breaks out in goose bumps, and a whimper clings to the tip of my tongue as he drags his tongue down my stomach, leaving a wet trail until it's at the waistband of my thong. "I don't."

"Okay." He shrugs indifferently, and I almost take it back, but I freeze when he drags his tongue further down. His nose brushes the seam of my pussy over the cotton material, and his tongue flicks ever so gently. "You won't care to hear this, but I love how wet you are. I love how good you're being for me right now. How you've got your legs spread for me, ready to get your pussy eaten. And I know you like—no you *love* this, Josie. You like being told you're being a good girl, don't you?"

I don't bother to bite back my moan, and I do it again when he drops to his knees in front of me, wraps his hands around my thighs, pulls the cotton away from my pussy, and swipes his tongue over my slit.

"Oh." My back bows, my breasts bouncing as I jerk.

"Fine, you don't have to answer. Either way, I'll be hearing you scream all about it." He cockily smirks.

"Righhh—" He lifts his tongue to my clit, circling around it before he flicks his tongue over it repeatedly. My eyes widen and I lose the ability to breathe. "Holy shit," I gasp, jaw dropping when he flicks faster before he comes to an abrupt stop and sucks it. "Fuck!" I moan loud, thankful the neighbors don't live too close. "Oh God..." I whimper, my legs shaking and hips bucking.

He just started. There's no way I'm about to...my eyes roll to the back of my head, body going still before I spasm. I'm shaking against him as he continues to suck my clit despite it pulsing incessantly.

I'm panting, almost on the verge of tears, because I can't stop coming. Jesus, fuck. "Daniel, I need..." He thrusts a finger inside me and eases the hold on my clit. "Slow down. Oh God." I can't breathe.

"Is that what you want, baby?" He laps me, long and slow. "You want me to slow down?" he taunts teasingly, and I swear he's smirking, but I don't know; I can't bring myself to look.

Wait, did he just call me baby? I must be hallucinating.

Slowly and gently, he slips in his finger again then adds another and curls them just a little until I'm seeing stars.

"Jos, baby, you okay?" He thrusts faster, sucking my clit into his mouth.

Incoherent words tumble out of my mouth. I feel delirious, holy...oh God.

He lifts his head, his mouth glistening, his fingers stroking me in a lazy way. I slouch against the lounge chair, my head heavy and dizzy, and I whine.

I can't believe I did that.

"Stop looking at me." I sigh flustered, eyes fluttering.

"I asked you a question," he condescendingly says.

I drag my fingers through his hair—God, it's so silky—and he softly groans before he hisses as I fist it. "You know the answer to that."

"Answer the goddamn question, Josefine. You good?" His voice is gravel, knuckles deep inside me.

I squeeze my eyes tight, grinding my teeth. "Yeah...good."

He drops his head down to where I want him, breath hot against my clit. He drags his tongue around and over it repeatedly, sucking it hard while his tongue strokes it.

My toes curl and my body shakes from the overwhelming need to come.

"You're fucking phenomenal. I love the way you listen. Love how responsive your body is to *me*."

My walls clench around him. I shouldn't have liked how that sounded. Why did I like that, and why do I want him to say it again?

He sucks my clit into his mouth fervently.

"Keep doing that, oh God, yeah, don't stop, Daniel," I cry out, my voice hoarse. "Don't...Don't stop!" I grit, my back arching. I swear my body could levitate right now.

His fingers thrust deeper, getting wet with my arousal. They're so slick, the noises they make shouldn't turn me on, but they do. But when he scissors them inside me, hitting a spot I wasn't sure was possible, my mind goes blank, and everything explodes inside me.

I clench my teeth, my finger scratching his scalp, pulling his hair as he continues to drive into me despite how my pussy clenches around him, pulling them in, refusing to let go.

Moments later, I feel him place a kiss on my pussy before he removes his fingers and covers me back. Through my heavy-lidded eyes, I see him bring them into his mouth, suck them clean, and hum in delight.

I exhale a ragged sigh, feeling spent, but he looks sated as if he's the one who just came.

Once the high wears off, I sit up, feeling shaky and still breathless. Daniel tenderly smiles at me, lips slightly glossy and swollen, staring at me with so much affection it makes my skin itch.

I'm a distraction to him. That's what he needed. This meant nothing.

It's whatever. I needed the distraction too. I got what I wanted.

Sitting up, I draw my eyes below his waist, but he shakes his head. "It's getting late and we still have a date. You, me, and the couch, remember?"

Right, distraction. I don't have the right to let it bother me. I agreed.

His brows draw in, studying me. Concern on his face. "What's wrong?"

"I just came." I play it off, my voice hoarse but for other reasons.

He doesn't look convinced, and I know he's about to push, ask more questions, but I stand and grab my clothes, hating how everything in me shrivels up.

"Tell me about what we're watching tonight again?"

37

JOSEFINE

"I'm not sure if I should be upset or impressed that his ass is bigger than mine." Vi cocks her head to the side, eyes fixed on Angel's butt on the screen.

I wasn't staring before, but now I am. In disbelief, I cock my head, eyes narrowing as I stare at his ass. The white baseball pants he's wearing mold to his legs like a second skin. Showing off his impressive thick thighs and butt, honed from countless hours spent in the weight room.

Angel stands on the mound, shimmying his shoulders when the next batter steps up to the plate. His lip slightly curls at the corner, an almost smile. It feels almost like a taunt before his expression goes stoic.

The sports commentators go silent when he gets in position, waiting patiently and eagerly to see him pitch. It all happens too quick. He slings the ball, but it's too late for the batter because it landed in Noah's mitt with a loud clap after he swung.

"Strike three!" the ump calls.

"Yes, sir! Back-to-back strikeouts!" one of the commentators says.

"That was filthy!" the other adds, just as eager. "Strikes out on 102..." they carry on, but I've already zoned out, my attention drawing to Daniel as he jogs next to Angel back to the dugout with the rest of the guys to switch for the bottom of the fifth inning.

"That's honestly annoying. What the hell?" I scowl.

"Right?" she hums, both annoyed and impressed. "Why is it that guys always have the things they don't care for? I'd kill to have an ass like that."

I nod in agreement, but then I look at her. "You know, you've got a great ass."

There isn't a time we're not together and someone isn't staring at it. And add that she's drop-dead gorgeous, with her long model-like legs—yeah, people are going to stare.

She smiles big, making her cheekbones pop out. "I know but it's nowhere near as bubbly looking as his. Don't get me started on how thick and long Kai's lashes are."

My cheek twitches. "Speaking of Kai, I'd kill for another spam musubi."

She hums in agreement. "You know, they're not that hard to make. The hardest part would probably be making the rice, but if you get a rice cooker, you should be good."

"I don't know how to cook," I admit and don't voice that I'm positive I'd somehow fuck up rice in a rice cooker.

Her head snaps in my direction, brows drawn together, but she stares at me, more amused than judgmental. "Really?" I nod. "Like nothing at all?" I shake my head. "So, what do you do for food?"

"Before Daniel, I'd buy already made meals or grab takeout."

She sits up, her dark brown eyes piqued with curiosity. "Before Daniel? What's that supposed to mean?"

"Don't make it a big deal," I warn her.

"I won't." Still, she sounds too enthusiastic.

"He cooks and meal preps for us. It's really not a big deal." He still does that while I load up the dishwasher.

From the corner of my eye, I see her lips purse then press them together.

"Don't."

"I didn't say anything," she innocently says, raising her hands in surrender. She goes quiet afterward, but I swear she's practically buzzing in her seat next to me.

Vienna wasn't supposed to be here but randomly showed up after I told the girls I was going to be busy and couldn't make the game. It wasn't a complete lie; I had things to do, like homework and cleaning. Still, Vi showed up because she said Pen was going to be with her parents and didn't want to intrude. I wasn't going to say no to her, but I wish she wasn't here because now I can't gawk at Daniel the way I want to.

But I won't deny that I like having her here. This is actually the first time I've had—a person I can genuinely call my friend—someone over besides Daniel. That one time she and Pen were here doesn't count because they didn't stay; they were just helping me finish getting ready for the party.

"Spit it out," I say because she's being weirdly silent.

"It's nothing."

"Vienna."

"No, because you'll not answer my questions and then shut me out."

I blow out a raspberry. "I don't shut you out."

She arches a perfect black brow, giving me this look that says *you're full of shit and you know it.*

"It's just not a big deal." I shrug because he's doing the bare minimum. He's cooking, so what am I supposed to feel? It's not a big deal. Sure he cooks my favorite meals and leaves me little notes in random places like little pick-me-ups. Do I look forward to finding them? Yes, yes, I do, but it's not a big deal because he doesn't make it one, so I won't either.

"Okay." She shrugs just as apathetically.

I stay quiet, mulling over what to say now as we watch Kai step up to the bat. Do I like that she badgers me about Daniel? No. But it doesn't mean I don't like to talk about him, although I shouldn't.

I sink into the sectional, pushing my hair away from the back of my ear to curtain my face. "He ate me out," I whisper.

She bolts up, eyes burning the side of my face. "What did you say?"

"He ate me out," I all too quickly say.

"When? Where? Holy shit! Was he good?" she rapid fires the questions. I can hardly hear them from how quickly they're coming out of her mouth.

I drag my palm to the nape of my heated neck and push my hair away. "Slow down. You're talking too fast." I shakily breathe out, rubbing my thighs together at the memory. "It happened two days ago. Here, outside by the pool. And yeah, he was...*really* good." I close my eyes, swallowing back the moan that tempts to crawl from the back of my throat.

"Aw, you're opening up to me. Did I just unlock another level in our friendship?"

"Yeah, sure, whatever. We leveled up, I guess," I mumble, feeling awkward.

She laughs as if she could sense that. "And then what happened?"

"Nothing. He ate me out while he fingered—" Her eyes go wide, lips stretched so far, all her pearly white teeth are showing. "Me. I came and then we went inside, watched the first *Final Destination* movie, had tacos, and went to bed—not together," I add because I know she'll ask.

We would've stayed up longer but he needed to rest for the second game of the series. Which they won yesterday. I watched it on TV, of course, and gawked the entire time.

"Aw, that's so cute," she coos, her eyes sparkling. "And on Valentine's Day? That's what you call a date."

I don't tell her that he called it that too because it really wasn't. Friends do that sort of thing all the time, minus the whole giving out orgasms.

"We didn't cuddle. It wasn't a date. We just happened to do that stuff on the day that Valentine's Day fell on."

She snickers, sitting back on her butt. "What does this mean for you and Danny? Are you guys friends with benefits? Dating?"

I shake my head and that same shriveling feeling returns. No, fuck that, I'm fine. "No, neither. It was a one-time thing. He needed a distraction; I did too. So...yeah. That's that."

She patronizingly smiles at me. "Josie, my sweet ray of sunshine, be so for real."

"What?" I answer, bemused.

"He bought you flowers." She waves her hand over to the yellow flowers littering my house. Yeah, I still can't get over that and Vi lost it when she saw them and I told her they were from him. "These aren't *just because* flowers. These are *I care about you* flowers. *I think about you* flowers. *I want you* flowers. *You mean a lot to me* flowers. No guy goes out of their way to buy a shit ton of flowers if you don't mean something to them. These are *I like you* flowers."

That makes my skin itch. Daniel liking me? Yeah right.

"He didn't let me return the favor. He hasn't brought it up. And...well, there's nothing else to add to that. Trust me, he needed the distraction badly, and I happened to be there. So yeah..."

The knot in my throat returns, but I clear my throat until it semi dissolves.

Her brows pinch, the corners of her eyes softening, lips pressed together in what looks like sympathy. "What do you mean you happened to be there?"

"I shouldn't have worded it like that. I meant..." I groan, not sure what I really mean, but she's staring at me like she could fight somebody. "I used him; he told me to. It was something we both mutually wanted, but it was never meant to be more. It happened and I'm over it."

Not really. I'm so far from over it, but I knew what I was doing going into it. So I need to find a way to *get* over it.

She stares at me like she's not convinced.

I shrug before she says anything else. "It's really okay. He was great, and gave me what I wanted. We got it out of our systems." For a second time now. "I promise there's nothing between us. We were just horny." And bared parts of our souls to each other.

I can't stop thinking about the things he shared with me. I wish I could do more for him, but I can barely figure out how to help myself.

I *hate* myself.

"Look, Kai got a home run." I point, looking away from her probing eyes.

I hate myself for opening up because now I'm struggling to close that part of me I don't let anyone see. But I hardly shared anything; surely, she can't see that I'm battling with insecurities.

The front door opening and closing makes me stop in my tracks halfway down the stairs.

"Daniel?" I warily call out.

"Josie?" There's a note of levity in my name.

Before I descend the stairs, he's already standing at the bottom. He looks handsome, though he always does. His dark brown hair is damp, making it look darker. The locks at the bottom are slightly dry and winding up in small waves. His golden tan skin is glowing, a little darker than it was almost two months ago, and I've no doubt he'll only get tanner from here on out.

"What are you doing here?" I ask but hate how harsh I sound.

I didn't mean to directly ask that; I just didn't expect him to be here. They won their first series against Cal Poly, and I know all the guys were going to celebrate. At least that's what Pen said in the group chat. She and Vi begged me to go, but I thought a little distance from Daniel would do me good. Plus, Bryson is going to be wherever they're at, so it was a hard pass for me.

A boyish grin grows on his face as he takes me in, not

offended by my blunt question. "Are you going to stand there, or are you going to come down here and congratulate me?"

I lean against the railing, crossing my arms over my chest. "Congratulations, Captain." I smile a little at him from up here.

I'm serious about keeping my distance.

His eyes drop instantly to my lips, and I swear his whole face lights up. I'm not sure why. I look the least bit appealing, and I didn't go to him like he wanted me to.

My heart takes flight as he climbs the steps before he's standing in front of me. "I love working for things. So now that I'm here, can I get a real congratulations?"

It might've sounded a bit snarky, but I meant it. However, this time I tone it down and repeat myself. "Congratulations, Captain. Better?"

"No." He shakes his head.

I drop my gaze, it's quick but still I notice the way his hands twitch, lifting slightly before he settles them by his side.

A hug. He wants a hug.

I shouldn't, but...

I slip my arms around him, pulling him in until he's flush against my body. He doesn't hesitate to wrap his strong arms around me. He inhales deeply, his body going pliant against me.

"Congratulations, Captain," I try again, softer this time.

He nuzzles his face in the crook of neck, another deep inhale, and his arms tighten. I shouldn't have allowed that, but sometimes my body reacts in ways I can't control. It feels second nature, familiar, comforting. It feels good.

So much for distance.

"Did you watch me play?" he asks, voice hopeful and keen, like my answer will determine something for him. I just don't know what.

"There was nothing else to watch, so yeah, I watched the game."

He chuckles, his warm breath fanning my neck, making me shiver. "But did you watch *me*?"

"Do you mean, were my eyes solely on number six the entire two and a half hours? The player everyone calls Sparky? Did I happen to see the multiple double plays, the home run, and hear the commentators get hard-ons from watching him play?"

Daniel draws back. He smiles so bright, it's blinding. He still holds me, and because he's a few steps down, we're at the same eye level. It shouldn't be an issue, but this feels too intimate.

The look on his face tells me he's thinking what I'm thinking, but he doesn't move.

"That number six is something else, huh?"

"Yeah, I guess. A little cocky if you ask me."

"But hot right?"

A laugh tickles my throat. "I guess…"

"You guess?" He looks appalled.

"I mean if you take into account the other guys on the team… he falls somewhere under…"

He holds me tighter; a possessive gleam shines in his now dark eyes. "Don't finish that."

I lean forward, my lips to his ear. "I couldn't focus on anyone else when my attention was *only* on number six."

"Lucky guy," he pridefully states, pulling back so he can look at me.

I should let go. I need to let go. But my brain won't connect with whatever it is that sends the signals to get the rest of my body to work. I stay rooted in my spot, my arms still around his neck, fingers twined through his thick, soft locks.

"So what are you doing here?" I ask.

"Celebrating with you, of course."

"You realize we're standing on the staircase. Pretty positive this doesn't count as celebrating."

"It is as long as you're spending it with the person you want to be with." He stares at me so endearingly, it makes my skin itch again. "How we celebrate doesn't matter, as long as I get to be with you."

My heart manically races. "How do you want to celebrate it then?"

"Can I hold you?"

His question throws me off. "I think you're already doing that."

"No, I mean, can we watch a movie or something and you let me hold you?" he firmly asks, but the question doesn't sound demanding. It sounds like a plea.

"I'm not a cuddler." I get awkward being held for too long or even at all. I know Daniel's held me before, but that was all in the moment and when I wasn't thinking straight. Even now, I'm only okay because he'll let go soon. "I...I get weird and I move and you'll get annoyed and things will get weird. Trust me, I'm doing you a favor."

"Can I be the judge of that?" His face dims like he already knows that I'm going to say no.

I want to say that but maybe being held by him won't be the worst thing in the world. It doesn't have to mean anything.

"Okay."

"Yeah?" he asks, voice bordering on zealous.

I smile at that. "If that's what you really want."

"I really do."

A few minutes later after he's placed a pizza order, he's sitting on the couch and I'm trying to figure out which is the best way to settle next to him. Bryson and I didn't cuddle, and if we *ever did*, we always ended up having sex. It wasn't because I wanted to, but he was insistent, and I just wanted him to shut up.

What the hell was wrong with me? *Hatred and self-loathing*, a self-deprecating voice taunts in my head.

A laugh bursts out of him. "Don't overthink it. Come here."

I scratch the back of my neck and pad over to him. "So how do we do this? Do you want me on my side or on top of you or..."

"I want you however you're comfortable, but we really don't have to do this." He smiles assuringly. "I'm good with you sitting next to me."

"No, I'll cuddle with you. Lie down," I instruct, and on beat, he does. He's on his side, elbow propped up, his temple resting on his closed fist. I sit and stiffly lay on my side, until my back is flush against his front. "Is this okay?"

"As long as it's okay with you." I nod and then he asks, "Can I put my arm over you?"

He literally had his mouth on me and fingers inside me, yet he's still asking for permission to do that? There's no way he's real. I must be dead because guys like him don't exist.

"Yeah," I respond quietly.

He drapes his arm over my stomach, his massive palm resting on top of my hand. Then I feel his mouth hover over my ear. "You're safe, Josefine. I promise."

I twist my head to look up at him. "I know."

My bunched muscles and coiled nerves relieve themselves from the tension they'd been trapped in. Now all I feel is safe and okay.

He stares at me like I'm his most prized possession—something delicate, something important to him. And I hate that because I'm not special, yet he makes me feel like I am.

He smiles at me before his gaze drifts to my lips. I want to look away, but I find myself doing the same, staring at his lips.

I don't let myself think this time as I lift my head and meet his lips halfway. He softly kisses me, not rushing with lust or hungrily like something he needs to get over with. He takes his time as if he were savoring me.

When he pulls back, he smiles down at me, places a chaste kiss to my forehead and holds me like I'm his. It's dangerous I know, but at this moment, I pretend like I am his and not a disintegrating mess.

38

DANIEL

YOU DIDN'T TRY HARD ENOUGH! HE'S NOT DEAD! TRY again or I will! I'll do CPR!

The sharp ring of the doorbell pierces the quiet house, disrupting the memory but not making it go away. It hovers over my head like a dark fog, lingering.

When the doorbell rings again, I realize I zoned out and I'm still sitting on the side of my bed.

Lifting my hat, I comb my fingers through my hair, before I place it back and trudge down the stairs. As I stand in front of the door, I smile but close my eyes because it feels too tight on my face. Blowing out a breath, I attempt it again and this one feels more natural.

Angel, Kai, and Gray stand on the other side. They have grocery bags in their hands and a duffle or a bookbag on their shoulders.

"Took you long enough," Kai huffs. "What are you doing in there?" He smirks, peeking around me as if he hopes to see something scandalous.

"I didn't take that long."

"We rang the bell five minutes ago and we texted you," Angel waves his phone.

All of a sudden, my clothes feel too tight on me, my skull painfully throbs, and my chest flares with anxiety.

Impending doom is what I've been feeling recently. I know why and I wish I could make it go away. I wish I could shut my brain off from the memory, but I can't. Every year close to Adrian's death anniversary, I feel dread, so much of it. And the day of is full of blur-filled panic attacks.

"Sorry, I was finishing up an assignment and—"

Gray barks out a laugh. "Right, sure, *assignment*." He winks at me. "Those assignments..." he says extra loud as I step to the side to let them in. "They make us lose track of time, don't they?"

"She's not here, dumbass." I lead them into the kitchen and watch their gaze coast over it, then the living room, until they finally settle on the flowers.

Josie gave me the green light to let the guys come over a few days ago. I wasn't going to ask, but she said I could bring people over since I live here, so long as it doesn't become a party. Which I'm totally okay with. I invited my old roommates and they came except for Noah. He said he's had enough of us and needs his space.

Which is valid. Since the season started almost two weeks ago, we've had nine games and the last five were back-to-back days. And despite not having a game today, we still had team lift in the morning and practice. It wasn't as heavy as it was during preseason, but it was still exhausting, nonetheless.

"Sure, right." He winks again.

"She went on a run a while ago." That's not a lie, but Kai and Gray are looking at me like they're not buying it.

"What's with the flowers?" Angel asks, amused and shocked.

I couldn't decide which yellow flower to get, so I got one of each. Although I didn't mean to get two dozen of each, but it was the best mistake of my life. Whenever we're in the kitchen or living room, I'll catch Josie smiling as she's looking at them. She's even taken a few to her room. And she's been diligently replacing their water, so they still look good for it being two weeks since I gave them to her.

"Forget the flowers. It feels so...sterile." Kai's eyes roam over every inch of space he can. There's a lot of it, but because there's not a lot in here, it really enhances how white and gray everything is. "It's so cold and—"

"It's not your house, so shut the fuck up." I cut him off sharply.

I noticed that too and when I asked Josie about it—not in the way Kai just spoke about it—she said, her mom liked everything simple. I get simplicity, but this is something else. There are no picture frames, colors, or anything, and because Josie is constantly cleaning it, it doesn't feel like it's been lived in. It actually looks like one of those staged houses.

I wanted to ask Josie more about it, but she looked overwhelmed and annoyed, so I didn't pry. After our conversation two weeks ago though, it makes me wonder how Josie's mom treated her. Now all I want to do is hold her.

"Sorry." He raises his hands in surrender and looks sincerely apologetic. "I didn't mean to offend. The yellow really makes the house look—"

"Kainoa, just shut up." Angel shoves his head after he places the bags on top of the island.

"Yeah, Kai, just shut up," Gray antagonizes, a snarky grin on his face.

He rolls his eyes. "I said I was sorry. Shit, is she in here? Sorry, Josie, I didn't mean that and—"

"I told you she's not here." I take the stuff they bought to make burgers out of the plastic bags. "You're making me regret inviting you."

"Way to go, dumbass." Gray slaps him upside the head.

"Don't—" I only manage to get out before Kai and him are wrestling each other. Now they're on the floor and waiting for one or the other to say, "Tap out."

Angel shakes his head. "Let them sort it out. I'm not getting involved. The last time I did, I got punched and then I punched them and they got mad at me."

I bite back a laugh, remembering how pissed off they both were. Angel has one hell of an arm, so I know how much that punch must've hurt them both.

"So...she's really okay with us being here? Using her pool?" he asks, changing the subject.

"Yeah, she said as long as Bryson was never invited and there were no parties, it was all good."

A lopsided smile curves his mouth. "If that isn't a sign, I don't know what is."

Gray grunts, flustered and breathless, but still he doesn't voice those two words.

"It's not..." I weakly reply because I want it to be something. Hell, it's all I've been thinking about for two weeks now.

Not only because she came on my mouth and fingers... I blink away the memory—that has been living in my mind rent free—and think about Sunday.

The kiss we shared, her letting me hold her as if she were mine, and then falling asleep on me. She hadn't meant to and looked so disconcerted when she woke up. I wanted to beg her to stay, but I knew she felt frazzled about it. So I let her leave.

My mouth or fingers on her hadn't been an issue, but she bolted at affection. I don't know why, but I want to change her mind about it; however, I'm not her boyfriend and she's not mine.

"Don't fight it." He pops the bag of *Churrumais* open and stuffs a handful into his mouth. "If you like her, go for it."

"Weren't you against relationships, and begging me to stay single?"

"What's the point?" he says as he chews. "You're not hooking up with anyone and you're always staring at her."

"I'm not always—"

"You..." Kai grunts and groans before he blows out a heavy breath. "Do."

They're still on the floor. I swear if they break something... The house may not have much, but I know everything is expensive.

I place the plastic bags in the bag holder and change the conversation. "You guys can get in the pool. It's warm."

"Tap out," Gray sputters, slapping Kai's arms. His face is beet red and covered in a sheen of sweat. They're both sophomores, a year younger than me, but I swear they act like they're ten. "I only did that because I want to get in the pool."

"Yeah," Kai says, a little breathless, but doesn't look disheveled the way Gray does. "Sure, okay."

"I don't have it in me to care if you believe me or not." He stands and picks up his duffle. "Which way to the pool?"

I grin, pointing at the glass sliding door that leads to the large backyard.

Kai laughs, following behind him. "Aw, Grayson, come here. Don't be like that. You know I love you, brah."

"Don't start that *mahalo* stuff on..."

We don't hear the rest of what they're saying because Kai shuts the door behind him, leaving Angel and me alone.

He stares at me, extensively like he's trying to figure something out. "What's wrong?"

"Nothing." I play it off, shrugging and lifting my smile.

"I know this time of the year is weird, and April is approaching and—"

"I'm fine." There's a bite to my voice, but I quickly shake it off. "I promise."

"How are the swimming lessons coming along?" he questions, unperturbed by my curt reaction.

"They're...coming along. Not a lot of improvement. I've told Josie she's wasting her time, but she's adamant and won't give up."

We recently had to switch them for Thursdays since most of my games will be Sundays. So today after the guys leave, I'll have another lesson. I still somewhat dread it, but once she's guiding me, her hands touching me, I feel okay.

"You know, I like her."

My back goes rigid at the way he said that.

"Not like that." He snorts and pauses to fish his phone out of his pocket. He reads whatever is on the screen before his gaze lifts to mine. Something feels off about the way he's looking at me, but he smiles and tucks his phone back in his pocket.

"Everything good?"

"Oh yeah, it's—" His eyes dart back to his pocket. "Actually, I'll be back. I gotta answer this."

He drops the bag of chips on the island and walks out to the backyard before I can get a word out. I don't understand why he did that when he's very open with me. I don't muse over it because it must've been someone important, like his mom or siblings.

My focus on Angel is long forgotten as the pretty girl with raven-black hair and rich brown eyes occupies my mind. She shouldn't but I can't help that my body begs for her in the way it never has for anyone else.

Begs, yeans, needs. My body is desperate. No, *I'm desperate*.

She doesn't need you. You're broken. The dark fog, remember it. You're weak, my brain screams.

"Maybe I should start posting more." Kai's eyes narrow on the small screen of Gray's phone. "How much do you think Saint's making?"

Grayson is close with Saint Arlo, a basketball player from North Carolina University. They went to some private middle and high school in Boston and have been friends ever since. At least that's what he told us.

He supports everything he does, like watching Saint's basketball games, Live's on Instagram or TikTok, or whatever stupid shit he gets himself into.

If we have time, we'll watch the games because he's wickedly good. And on occasion the Live's. Though after a while, I stop because the girls are insane and the comments get explicitly thirsty.

"Fuck if I know. I'm sure it's a lot." Gray tsks, his expression not of awe like Kai's but indifference.

I'd be indifferent too if I had the kind of money that would financially set me for life. The kind of money that would set the next six or seven or hell maybe ten generations of my family for life. Not only because his father is the governor of North Carolina and mom is apparently one of the best attorneys there is, but his family comes from old money.

Angel looked him up after we found out he'd been recruited to play here. Then he showed up in an expensive-ass car—which he upgraded to a motorcycle because the car wasn't to his liking—but it wasn't just that or his clothes and shoes that had us doing a double take, but the way he carries himself. With an edge of crisp arrogance that makes you feel like you don't belong near his vicinity.

It was hard getting a read on him at first. At times he's dry, blunt, and conceited, but eventually he warmed his way into our hearts.

"You should go for it. Look at his friend. He doesn't speak and hardly does anything, yet look at the comments on the Live." Angel's chuckle gets muffled by the bite he takes of his burger. "Fucking horny jersey chasers."

"It's the accent and he's...got nice hair or whatever," Gray mutters bitterly.

"Yeah, I gotta admit he's got nice-looking hair," Kai retorts. "But you've got a cute Southern accent and all."

I press my lips together. I can't with them.

"The girls aren't going crazy for it like they are for his," he quips.

"Where's he from?" I ask.

"Apparently, Montana," answers Kai.

"There's no way. He's got a British accent and it's a deep one too. All posh like and shit." Gray stuffs his mouth with chips and speaks with a mouthful. "And don't get me started on how tall that motherfucker is."

"How tall?" I ask, amused.

"Six nine."

We all stare, astonished at his response.

"He's a basketball player," I say after a moment. "They're all tall."

We're all over six feet, with Angel being the tallest at six six, but I've seen some of the basketball players on campus. Despite our heights, most still tower over us; it's kind of insane.

"His girlfriend is hot as fuck," Gray says after he swallows.

"Do you know everything about this man? You sound obsessed." Kai laughs. "But who's his girlfriend?"

"Shut up. We've literally sat next to each other while we've watched NCU play." He swipes his fingers on the screen of his phone then places it in front of Kai. "Julianna Sparks."

Kai's eyes go wide and he picks up the phone, bringing it closer to his face. "This is his girlfriend?"

"I know," Gray softly groans. "Fucking gorgeous."

"Look at her—" Kai goes to place the phone in front of my face, but I push his hand away.

"I'm not going to check out another guy's girlfriend." Or any girl for the matter. Not when Josie's running circles in my head.

"Right, because why should you when you live with someone just as hot. If my roommate looked like Josie, I would—"

"Don't finish that." I cut him off. I try to keep my voice light, but something nasty sparks inside of me. "Just fucking don't."

Kai raises his hands in surrender. "Speaking of your roommate," he murmurs and nods his head in the direction of the glass sliding door.

Josie comes out, body glistening with sweat, wisps of her hair stick to her forehead, her ponytail loose and low.

I drag my tongue across the top of my teeth, inhale a shallow breath, and unintentionally my gaze gravitates to the lounge chair. Since she came on my mouth and fingers, I've been spiraling with fantasies I'm not proud of.

She tastes so good, feels so right, and...I'm zoning out.

"Hey," she says and stands next to me, but she doesn't pull up a chair.

They all greet her, smiles wide on their faces.

"Sit." I stand and pull it back for her. I told the guys to leave it empty because she was going to come eat with us. I wasn't sure if she'd actually show up though because she said she'd think about it. She also said she wasn't a big fan of burgers, but I found out she likes chicken sandwiches and sourdough. "I made you a chicken sandwich with pepperjack cheese and added tomatoes and grilled onions."

Opening the container that's keeping her sandwich warm, I place it on a plate in front of her.

She takes a seat, and it's small but she smiles up at me. "You remembered how I like my sandwich?"

I remember everything about you. "Yeah, and oh..." I open the cooler next to me and pull out a can of Dr. Pepper. "Here."

I think her cheeks burn red but I'm not sure, because her face was already flushed from her run. "Thanks, Garcia."

I take my seat next to her, keeping my gaze on my food now. She's wearing a sports bra and tiny spandex shorts that cling to her in an unholy way.

"So, Josie," Gray starts. "You looking for a new roommate?"

"If you are, don't pick him. Pick me. Choose me," Kai pleads.

"Whatever you do, don't pick either. They're dirty as fuck, loud, annoying, and well...annoying." Angel grimaces, shaking his head.

"Thanks for the heads-up, but I have no desire to live with either of you," she replies, and I smile.

"You know, I have money." Gray flashes her one of those charming, Cheshire-like smiles.

"Congrats. I do too."

His lips instantly fall. "Flirt with me a little, Josie. You're breaking my heart."

"Is he always like this?" she asks at no one in particular, but she does look at me, unaffected by his charm.

"Ignore him." Angel smiles with glee and laughs a little too.

Gray looks offended and gets into it with Kai and Angel.

"How was your run? You going to let me join you next time?" I ask her.

"Not sure you're going to want to do that. I'm fast and I'd hate to—"

"Also, why didn't you answer my email?" Gray interjects. "I wanted swimming lessons too."

She huffs out a breath. "Because I didn't want to."

The guys laugh and I, well, I can't help but fall deeper.

I'm not what she needs.

She crosses her leg over the other and her foot accidentally grazes my calf. She goes to move it, but I place my palm on her knee and keep it where it's at.

We look at each other briefly, discreetly, and that same igniting feeling I felt when we kissed on the couch, burns bright.

I'm not what she needs.

She doesn't move her leg or brush my hand away. Only picks up her sandwich.

I know I should move it, but I don't. Not when she's halfway through eating. Not when we're deep in conversation about random things. Not when the guys ask her questions about stupid shit. She doesn't mind it though; she may look blasé about it, but she's enjoying this. I can tell the way her eyes just shine and radiate happiness, and knowing she's happy makes me happy.

I'm not what she needs.

"The log scene didn't do it for you, but the pool scene did?" Kai looks mortified, mouth agape.

We just finished telling them that we watched all the *Final Destination* movies and now they're all talking about the worst deaths that happened in them.

"I work in a pool." Josie scrunches her nose. "That was more traumatic than the logs."

"Okay, that's fair..."

More mindless conversation and my palm now rests on her thigh.

I'm not what she needs, but she's who I want.

39

JOSEFINE

My fingers hover over the keyboard before I pull them back for the twentieth time, curl them into my palms, and extend them over the keyboard again.

"Hey," Vienna greets, sliding into the booth across from me. She slips her bookbag off her shoulders and settles it next to her.

"Hi," Pen chimes, slipping in the booth next to her.

She asked Vi and me to meet in the Student Union because we haven't seen her much. Not that I've seen Vienna much either. Pen is busy with cheer, Vi with swimming, so it's hard to get our schedules to align. Life of an athlete.

"Hey." I shut my laptop with more force than I intended to.

Pen's brows furrow, eyes darting to it. "Everything okay?"

I stagger, uncertainty gnawing at me.

I've been staring at the email Monica sent me since January; it's already the beginning of March and I still can't bring myself to reply. The only good thing I was able to do was open it and read what it says, but that's as far as I got. Since then, all I've been able to do is stare at it.

Part of me wants to delete it and tell Monica to leave me alone. But the other, very small part of me wants to do it. It's not because I miss swimming competitively, but everything else about it.

I've already shared about Daniel to Vi, and feel like I've opened myself up enough. But this is different and weighing down on me.

"Monica wants me to take the student assistant coach position."

"Monica?" Pen tilts her head to the side.

"My coach, Director of Women's Swimming," Vi answers, a gleam shining in her eyes. "You should do it. That position is so hard to get. If Monica is personally reaching out to you, that means she wants you and only you. Holy shit, that's awesome. Do it."

I know it's a big deal, but anxiety is a bitch, holding a gun to my head. The thought of being back there, a place Mom and I shared, the only thing that kept whatever relationship we had alive, messes with my head.

Shrugging, I brush it off. "I'm thinking about it. What's been up with you guys?"

Maybe they can sense my apprehension, maybe not, but they thankfully change the subject.

Pen talks about the basketball team and how it's uncertain if they'll make it to the NCAA tournament coming up in two weeks. She said they've done decent this season but have lost their recent games, the worst one when they played North Carolina University two weeks ago. She said the only positive to watching that game was watching the NCU players. Apparently, they're hot and she's about to show us their Instagram, until she gets a message and begins acting weird.

"I'll be back." Her lips jerk like she's trying to stop herself from smiling.

We watch as she scurries out of the Student Union, her lips blooming into a grin, until she disappears.

"Did you see her face?" Vi asks, still staring at the part she disappeared from. "It has to be a guy, and I hope to God it is. She needs to move on from her dick ex-boyfriend. I feel rage every time I see him."

I feel the same way, but as much as we want to say something, we don't. Pen doesn't want us to and she's too sweet; she just wants to keep the peace.

An idea comes to mind.

"You know...I have experience slashing tires."

Just as I open my bedroom door, so does Daniel. He's handsome as ever in a white T-shirt with the school's logo, a siren sitting on a baseball and the word BASEBALL underneath it. He's also wearing those dark short blue swim shorts that expose his muscular thighs, and his gold chain that he never takes off.

He hangs his towel around his neck and smiles at me. "I have something for you. I meant to give it to you a while ago, but with the moving and the season starting, I forgot."

"For me?" I take the white, square envelope and when I flip it around, I realize it's a CD sleeve and there's one in it. *Danny's Holy Grail of Happiness*, is scribbled on with a green marker, I can only assume is Sharpie. "You burned me a disc?"

He grabs both ends of the towel, nodding. "Something told me you've never had the privilege of downloading music illegally. I figured I'd bless you with a CD. And if you don't like any of those songs, I don't want to hear it. Matter of fact, you can't dislike them."

"I'm not sure I have anything to put this in." I look at the writing again, my lips only stretching wider.

"I do have a stereo or a portable CD player, but you can also listen to it in your car."

"Those things still exist?" I tease.

"I'm not sure." His smile is tender and his eyes soften. "They're both birthday gifts from years ago. Adrian and I both love music, so our parents gifted them to us. We had to share them of course. I've never been able to part with them."

The pain in his voice strikes my chest, but it's his entire demeanor that has my heart crumbling. The once-vibrant gleam on his face is now dim, almost ashen. He smiles but it doesn't reach his eyes, nor do his words that feel so heavy yet empty.

Grief is funny, he once said.

It is because one moment he's smiling like he's on top of the world and the next, he's remembering a past memory and sheer sadness washes over him.

I step into him, wrapping my arms around his torso. He tenses, no doubt not expecting me to do this. "If you ever want to talk about Adrian, I'm here."

He wraps his arms around my shoulder, his body sagging against mine. He doesn't feel heavy but weightless.

"Besides baseball..." His voice is thick and gruff like he struggled to expel those words. "Music was our thing. We listened to almost everything."

I hold him tighter. "Oh yeah? Is that why you have all those cassettes, vinyls, and CDs in your room?"

"You went into my room?" Daniel chuckles. His question isn't accusatory but elated.

That was three weeks ago, on Valentine's Day. "It's not what you think. I was looking for you because of the flowers and you weren't answering me."

He hums. "Yeah, that's why I have all of them. Some of them were Dad's and others were the ones we bought at pawn shops. We thought they were cool, so we started collecting. I have many more, but the others are back home. I would've brought them, but there's not enough space."

"You can put them in the living room."

"I don't want to—"

"You live here, and I know I'm weird about how things are placed, but I don't mind. I should've told you before. I'm sorry."

"Don't apologize. This is your house."

"And now it's yours."

I feel his heart race against my chest as he holds me. "You're not weird for liking your space clean."

A rock lodges in the middle of my throat. I don't like talking about this, but at this moment, in his embrace, my tongue goes lax.

"Mom hated clutter. She liked to keep things bare and simple; she'd spiral if they weren't. She said in Mexico, in the house that she lived in, things weren't great. She never really went into details, but she also never failed to remind me how good I had it. How she sacrificed herself to have what I have now. And as a reminder, she had me clean. Made sure I'd do it well too." I brittlely chuckle. "No toys, no colors, no nothing. It became a norm I never deviated from." I release a shaky breath. "But now that you live here, you can put things up and have things in the kitchen and living room. I promise I won't stop you."

"I will on one condition."

"What's that?"

"You let me help you clean."

"No, I don't want you to." My brows furrow, feeling irked. I push away, but he still holds me. "I didn't tell you so you'd feel bad for me. I'm telling you because—"

He stares down at me patiently, gently. "I don't feel bad for you. You shared, I listened, and now I want to do something about it. I want to compromise. Don't push me away, Josefine. Please, let me help."

I falter, my lips parting before closing again. "I always clean alone. I like it done a certain way, and if it's not done how I like, it makes me feel...overwhelmed."

"Show me how you like it and I'll do it that way too. Okay?" He tucks my hair behind my ear, then drags his knuckles along my cheek.

"I might get mad."

"That's okay."

"I'm serious."

"I'm serious too."

"I tend to be a control freak. I'm not kidding."

"I like when you tell me what to do." He smiles.

I bite the inside of my cheek, contemplating what I want to do. "I'm—okay, but just know you've been warned. Don't get mad at me when I get mad at you."

He chuckles again. "I could never get mad at you."

When his knuckles descend to the curve of my neck, my body shudders and my eyes flutter. I'm almost tempted to pull him into my room, but it's Thursday, and he has his lesson today, and he needs to rest because he has a game tomorrow.

"I hope you're not trying to distract me because we're still having your lesson." I pull away. Grabbing his wrist, I tug him along with me.

We haven't done anything since we kissed on the couch. He hasn't made a move, so I wasn't going to either.

"Darn, that didn't work?" he sighs disappointedly.

"No, you'd have to do more than just touch my cheek."

"Oh?" he hums but I hear the challenge in his tone.

I ignore it but the rest of my body doesn't. "Thanks for this. If you let me borrow the stereo or CD player, I'll listen to it tonight."

"You can use them anytime you want." He hooks his arm around my shoulder. With anyone else, walking side by side would've been awkward, but it feels nice being tucked under his arm.

The sun is setting just behind the horizon when we finish, painting the sky in pretty hues of pink, purple, and orange.

Daniel sets the foam board and goggles outside the pool, dragging his fingers like a comb through his wet locks. His hair remains slicked back, but droplets drip from the ends, skidding down his tanned skin in rivulets.

I grab my wet ponytail and wring the water from it. "You know, if you believed in yourself as much as you believe in that quirky stance of yours, you'd already know how to swim."

"Quirky stance?" He arches a brow, lips tugging upward in a crooked grin.

"When you're at-bat, you stand..." How do I say it? "Weird. Who does that?"

He chuckles and approaches me. I step back, adding more space between us, but my back hits the pool wall.

"What's wrong with the way I stand?" Mirth glistens in his eyes.

"Aside from the fact that it looks a little uncomfortable and weird, nothing." My eye catches a stray drop and I can't help but track it. It slides past his collarbone, pec, and follows the ridges of his abs until it meets the water again.

"You should come to a game." His gaze flicks to my chest, lingering there before it lifts.

"I'm good." My nipples tighten.

"No, I'm serious. Come to a game." His arms go on either side of me, hands braced on the edge of the pool, caging me in.

"I'm serious too. I'm good." Not only do I not want to go because I know Bryson is there, but I'll be alone. Both the girls are busy and they're the only friends I have. I'll look like a loser alone.

"Let's make a deal." His eyes drift to my chest again, and I'm certain he sees my pebbled nipples sticking out from the thin material of my bikini top.

My body flares with heat and goose bumps. "A deal?"

"Every time I improve, you come to a game. If I learn how to swim, you come to all, or at least the home games." He keeps one hand still perched on the edge, the other dips into the water, until I feel it on my back. His fingers graze my skin only briefly before they're tugging on the string holding my top together.

That stuns me because while we've been going at this for five weeks, he's not made a lot of improvement. I know he's scared and I'm not a specialist, so I don't want to push too hard.

I don't want to go but I do want him to learn how to swim. Hmm...this could be an incentive.

"Okay, deal but you have to make improvements or I don't go," I sternly say.

"And you have to wear my jersey."

I narrow my eyes, shaking my head. "No."

"Please," he softly purrs, leaning forward, his lips hovering over the shell of my ear. "I'll keep begging. You know I will."

I close my eyes as my shoulders tense with anticipation. "Don't care."

"*Por favor.*" He tugs the string harder. He nips the lobe of my ear, lips just barely grazing the skin down to my neck. He inhales sharply as he lets go of the string. I feel disappointed and have to swallow back an aggravated whine.

"Still no..."

"I can beg all night, Jos."

"Don't you have a game tomorrow?"

"What does that have to do with anything?" He pulls back, staring down at me with dark hooded eyes.

"Beg if you want. I still won't care."

"God, you're such a—" His jaw tics, eyes darker than they've ever been.

"I'm a what?" My pussy clenches.

He cups the side of my neck with both hands, his lips just an inch away from mine. "A fucking brat. So stubborn. So frustrating. So hot..." He blows out an exasperated breath. "Can I kiss you? And don't play games with me right now. Yes or no? If I can't, I need to get out."

I'm such an asshole because I prolong my silence, only smirking at him. He looks like he's about to lose his shit, and I'm enjoying it.

"Josie?" he presses, voice brimming with frustration and desperation. "Yes or no?"

"Hmmm...I don't know," I say softly, innocently.

"What don't you know?" he grits.

"If that's where I want you to kiss me." I squeeze my thighs as my clit pulses.

He drops his hand, cupping the back of my neck and rests his forehead against mine, breathing out a string of curse words in Spanish. "Okay," he speaks almost too quietly, and I think he's going to get out of the pool but then he kisses me.

He forces his tongue inside my mouth and it clashes with mine. I have no words to explain the way his mouth vigorously devours mine. It's hot, breathtaking, and clit shattering.

That's how it and the rest of my body feels. On the verge of exploding from how intense every inch of me burns from the way he holds and consumes me.

I moan into his mouth and circle my legs around him in the water. The water sloshes around us, reminding me where we're at and his fear.

He must read my thoughts because he says, "I'm okay, right here. I'm okay as long as you're okay."

"I'm okay." I heave a breath, my chest rising and falling rapidly. "As long as you're okay, Garcia, I'm okay."

His Adam's apples bobs and he nods.

"Whatever you're thinking, just do it," I whisper against him, as if it were a secret he and I are sharing.

That's all it takes for whatever was holding him back to do what he's thinking. He yanks the top of my bikini down, and my breasts bounce out, nipples harder than ever as he takes them in.

"Fuck, Josie," he groans and lifts me a little higher so that my breasts are closer to his face. "I dream of this. I dream of you," he says against my nipple before he sucks one into his mouth.

I tip my head back, moaning as he plays with it. He switches between hard and soft, biting and sucking, rolling and lapping.

"Mmm...Daniel." My eyes roll back, every nerve inside me going off like fireworks. My fingers work their way through his hair, fisting and pulling it, as he continues to assault both nipples.

I gasp when his teeth sink into the soft skin and mouth latches onto the side of my breast, and when I look down, he's looking at me and sucking on it hard. I'm struggling between closing my eyes and keeping them open, but when he pulls back and I spot a dark purple spot, I'm glad I kept them open. He does the same for the other. The pleasure is so intense, so good, I can't help but close my eyes this time.

It's not until I feel him separate our bodies that I open my eyes.

"What are you…" My voice wavers as he sets me on top of the edge of the pool, and I spot two hickeys on my breasts.

"I really want to taste you again," he roughly says and hooks his fingers under my bottoms and tugs at them. I easily comply, lifting my butt to help him take them off. He flippantly tosses the wet material somewhere. "Fuck, Josie, you're dripping, baby."

I can't be hallucinating this time. I know what I heard, and I want him to call me that again. "I was just in the pool."

He grins and spreads my thighs. I bring my arms behind me, bracing my weight on my palms.

"No, you're dripping." He spreads my pussy lips with one hand, and with the other, drags two fingers from my slit down to my entrance. My toes curl and fingernails scrape against the ground.

He lifts his fingers and they glisten. "Come here," he orders.

And I do.

"Open your mouth."

And I do.

He slips his fingers into my mouth and I taste myself. "Close and suck, baby. Taste yourself. That's not water. That's all you."

This shouldn't be erotic, but it is. My clit pulses harder and faster and he notices. He smirks and plops his fingers out of my mouth, dripping specks of saliva on my chest.

"What part did you like?" He stares at my pussy, keeping it parted. "Tasting yourself?" I pulse again. "That I made you do it?" Once again. "Or being called baby?" I shiver, every inch of me yearning to hear it again.

"Josie, baby, is that what you like?" He sounds on edge, his voice a gruff rasp.

I shrug, biting the inside of my cheek. I've never liked pet names, and well, I guess I don't like many things, but I do like that. At least hearing it come from him.

"Yeah," I whisper meekly, feeling weird to admit that out loud.

"I like you like this." He lazily drags his fingers down my slit. They become slicker as I become wetter. "Shy and stubborn..." His gaze is trained on my pussy and legs, they tremble and clench every time his fingers reach my sensitive clit.

I squeeze my eyes, panting like a goddamn dog, feeling overly sensitive. I don't think as I bring one hand between my thighs and rub myself.

"And impatient too." He groans.

My eyes connect with his hungry ones and if I could, I'd flip him off. "Shut up. You were taking too long," I pant, feeling close.

He doesn't say anything; he watches me raptly, eyes never leaving my fingers as I continue to rub over my swollen clit. My stomach contracts, my thighs tense, and everything almost shatters, but then he pulls my hand away.

I whine. No, I'm pretty certain I just sounded like an angry cat because *what the fuck*.

"No. I get to finish you off. You did so good, but now it's my turn." He sinks down but looks up at me. "Wipe your fingers on your tits and make sure you do a good job."

I raise a shaky hand to my breasts and smear my arousal all over my nipples and breasts. He watches me as if he were making sure I did as he instructed. Once he's satisfied, he sucks my clit into his mouth and thrusts two fingers inside me.

"Oh God," I gasp, my body jerking forward.

He thrusts his fingers in and out of me, and sucks my clit as I scream for more. My eyes roll back until all I see is white. I start to sweat and my thighs quiver from how far he parted them. Every time I attempt to clench them, he stops me.

"Danny, I need to come," I plead, on the verge of tears.

"I'm getting you there, baby." He laps my clit, torturously slow, over and over again, until I'm crying out and my entire body is shaking. "I'm getting you there. I promise. You're doing so good, letting me take my time with you. Letting me taste you, fuck your cunt with my fingers. You're doing so good. You taste so good."

I lie on my back, the pressure so intense, I feel dizzy.

I moan loudly, arching my back when he removes his fingers.

"Please," I whisper shakily. "Please..." My voice slips as he drives his tongue into my entrance and his fingers pinch my clit. "Oh..." I grind my clattering teeth, fisting my shaky hands at my sides.

His hot breath fans my pussy as his tongue thrusts as far as it'll go. He's lapping and stroking me while he uses a single finger to flick my clit.

"I can't." I pull away from him, my body thrashing. "I can't take this..." My breath gets caught and I swear I die for a moment. I come so hard, my body shoots up, but that doesn't stop Daniel from eating me or playing with my clit. He carries on and moans, the vibration from his mouth heightening everything.

"Holy shit..." My body slumps and I catch myself briefly before I hit the ground. "Don't stop. Please don't stop," I chant incessantly, desperately, and fist his hair, grinding myself against his face. "Mmmm...yes! Yes!" I squeal out, my body aggressively convulsing.

When he stops, I slouch to the ground. I can't regulate my breathing or get my erratic heartbeat under control. Everything is still spasming and pulsing, and even though his fingers aren't on my clit anymore, it throbs. Like I need more and I think he knows that because he laps his tongue on it and whispers, "I got you," and "I told you you'd be needy," and "You've got a needy pussy, baby."

I don't deny or argue. I moan over and over as he plays with me and praises me and I come three more times.

When he's done and I'm finally able to catch my breath, I push up on shaky arms and look up at him just as he places a kiss on the crook of my thigh. It's bruised and I realized he gave me a hickey there too. I don't know when he did that, but I don't question it.

He smiles up at me. I muster whatever energy my lips have and return it, but he chuckles and I realize I'm not smiling, just staring at him, dazed.

I can't bring myself to care, and drop back on the ground. I close my eyes briefly and hear the water slosh and him quietly grunt. When I take a peek, I see him hoisting himself up and out of the pool. He towers over me, a large tent in his shorts, and I want to return the favor.

He shakes his head, a warm smile still on his face.

"I just wanted you to feel good. I don't need you to do anything."

"But..." I clear my dry throat. "I want you to feel good. You've already done it for me. Let me do it for you." I sit on my knees, my face in front of his erection, and I look up at him. "Let me."

The muscle in his jaw works, dilated hooded eyes strained. "This isn't about me, Josie. This is about you."

"But you deserve it too. I want to make you happy, make you feel good."

"This for me is enough, and you do make me *very* happy." He cups my jaw and my eyes flutter when he brushes the pad of his thumb over my cheek and lip.

I idly sigh. "Promise you'll let me next time? I want to take care of you too." I get why he's doing it, but he deserves this just as much as I do, if not more. "I want to please you."

He swallows and I swear his dick twitches in his shorts. "You do. You let me touch you, taste you, have you the way I did. I was really pleased. I promise."

I'm stunned as he slightly bends and lifts me up, his arms go under my neck and the back of my knees. "What are you—"

"You don't think I'm done, do you? Remember, this is all about you right now. I'm going to help you get cleaned up and then I'm going to feed you and we'll watch a movie."

Despite the voice in my head telling me to stop this right now because, again, this is too intimate, I don't. I wrap my arms around his neck, and I let him take me inside.

My lips stretch sheepishly. "Okay."

40
DANIEL

What started as a dull pinch in my chest has now evolved to prickly flares. With every exhale, my chest bursts with a sharp pain.

"Do you think if we beg enough, they'll give us a tour of the locker room?" Adrian bounces on his heels, eyes trained on the MCU baseball players as they bump fists with the opposing team now that the game has ended.

I laugh. "Yeah, that's not going to happen."

"You wanna bet?"

"Bet what?"

"If they agree, you do my chores for a month."

"Okay, and you'll do mine if they don't."

"Deal." We shake hands and release them when the players giddily start running to the dugout.

"Hey!" Adrian grips the railing, leaning over to get a better view of them.

A tremor shoots through my body, making my hand shake as I attempt to button my jersey.

"I can't believe they agreed," I whisper in disbelief.

My heart squeezes and I swear I feel my lungs collapse. My back breaks out into a sweat and white dots dance in my vision.

I'm not breathing. *Breathe, Daniel. Fucking breathe.*

"*Imagine, this will be our lockers one day.*" Adrian stares at one of the messy lockers in awe.

Picking up my hat from the top cubby of my locker, I drag my drenched, trembling fingers through my hair before I put it on. Wiping my palms down my pants, I grip the safety pin and breathe in and out, slow and steady.

Closing my eyes, I attempt to collect myself, but moments with Adrian play in my head. His smile, his laughs, his dimples. The bridge of my nose burns, the emptiness in my chest far too intense for nothing to be residing in it.

No, something is there.

No, *someone* is in there.

"*So that's how you use the dishwasher.*" Josie pushes the start button and stands back, folding her arms against her chest. "*Did you understand, or do you need me to write it down for you?*"

I attempt to keep a straight face, but my lips deceive me and lift. "*You know, I'm not sure if I got it. You might need to show me again.*"

She pins me with an impatient stare, but her mouth is just as traitorous because it curls into a small smile. "*I don't have the time or energy. Look up a video. Please tell me you're capable of using YouTube?*"

Snarky, I love it.

I manage to suck some semblance of air into my lungs and greedily they absorb oxygen.

"*You're going to have to hold the cord just like this.*" *I show her how to hold the earbuds cord to the portable CD player.* "*Or the music will sound scratchy.*"

"*Daniel...*" *She presses her lips together, amused eyes locked on my fingers twisting the cord.*

"*Don't you dare laugh.*"

Her chin quivers.

"*Josie, don't.*"

Her nose twitches.

"Josefine."

She rubs her nose, but I still hear the snicker she attempts to stifle. It's soft, muffled, but then it snowballs out of her mouth and she's laughing.

"Your CD player privileges have been revoked." I try to keep a serious face but she's laughing and smiling. She sounds so pretty, so free, so her, I bask in the sound of it, forgetting for a moment what we were talking about.

"Don't be like that, Garcia," she says patronizingly, taking the apparatus from my hand and inserting the disc.

Everything stops spinning, my chest doesn't hurt, and the white dots disappear instantly as if they were never there.

I breathe in and out and my world steadies. Memories of last night with Josie play in my head. When my phone lights up with a message, and I see who it's from, I feel so grounded, the tremors stop.

> Josie: Please don't embarrass me out there. I'm not going to waste two and a half hours sitting on the couch to watch you lose

I laugh, catching weird looks from my teammates, but I ignore them, my fingers quickly moving on the screen.

> Me: Keep your eyes on me and ONLY me

> Josie: I don't know. If you play like shit, I might look elsewhere

> Me: Not after yesterday, I know you won't

The three dots appear and disappear, my lips stretching wide as the seconds tick by and the dots come and go until I get a reply.

> Josie: Me coming changes nothing

> Me: Sure, baby, sure
>
> Me: I'm more than happy to show you again

The dots come and go, no doubt because I called her baby. I shouldn't have but I remember how flushed she got yesterday after I did. How she looked shy and that's so unlike her.

I really want to see that side of her again.

> Me: It's okay. Take your time to think of something to say. Squeeze your thighs. I know you'll be thinking of me while you do

I grab my belt, adjusting myself. Fuck, why did I say that? The dots all together stop but a second later I get a message.

> Josie: Put the brightness down

My brows pinch in confusion but I instantly do.

> Josie: Attachment: 1 Image.
>
> Josie: Hold the picture down

My heart thunders in my chest, gaze drifting side to side before I hold the Live picture down. My mouth and throat goes dry, my eyes shoot wide, and my dick throbs.

She sent a picture of her waist down. She's wearing what looks like tiny cotton shorts. I don't know if she rolled them up, but the seam is wedged between her pussy lips, outlining them. She slips her hand between her thighs, pressing her palm down before she clenches her thighs.

> Josie: More like you'll be thinking of me
>
> Josie: Go get 'em, Cap!

I can hear the snark, dry sarcasm in her voice and see the heat in her eyes. I shake my head, wiping a palm over my face to cover my grin.

"What's got you smiling so big?" Angel asks, standing next to me once he's finished getting ready.

"Nothing. Nothing at all," I answer.

"Damn, Sparky." Ryan, our second baseman, slaps my shoulder and ruffles my sweaty hair. "What the hell are you on and can I get some?"

We just finished our game, winning 12-4. While I got three home runs and three RBI, I can't take all the credit. Everyone did their part and got the job done.

"What are you trying to say? I'm Sparky for a reason, aren't I?"

"You were a fucking bolt out there," Lincoln, our right field, chimes in, making a loud whoosh sound. "I don't think I've ever seen you run that fast. And those dives? They were smooth as fuck."

"Forget fast, you were being a cocky little shit out there. Smirking and shit." Angel laughs as he undresses himself. "I don't ever think I've seen you celebrate like that. And why were you pointing at your eyes like that?"

I was sending a message to Josie, *eyes on me*.

"Someone's getting tested," Kai singsongs like a child.

The entire locker room breaks out in a chorus of "oooooo's" and "yeah, he is."

I know they will. I played differently today; my teammates noticed and so did the coaches. Throughout the game, I was asked questions and getting funny looks from them.

I can't explain it; I felt wired, and I guess in a way...I *was* high, not on drugs but on Josie. She just makes me feel alive and on top of the world. It's like she injected herself in my veins and all I feel is euphoria rushing through my body.

"So you live with Josie now?" Bryson's nonchalant question disrupts my thoughts.

The guilty expression on Gray's face gives him away. "Sorry."

I shrug, not bothered. He was going to find out and I genuinely don't care that he knows.

"Good game, Bry," I say instead.

I know behind his indifference, he's mad. I can hear the indignation underneath his tone, feel the anger exude hot from his skin despite him being across the room.

He bitterly laughs, untucking his jersey from his pants. "If you want any tips, want to know what gets her off, what she likes, I'm more than happy to tell you. But she's pretty easy so..."

I inhale a sharp breath, gliding my tongue across the top of my teeth. I fist my hands at my side and Angel notices because he puts his hand on my shoulder, shaking his head.

"It's not worth it. Just let him be."

I loosen my fist, exhaling.

He's not worth it, I chant in my head as I grab my stuff to shower, but when I walk past him, he snickers.

"No hard feelings. I fucked your ex, you're fucking mine. We're even now."

I keep walking but stop at his next words.

"Don't be like that, Danny. Seriously, if you need pointers, I don't mind sharing them with you." He smiles at me, supercilious. "But like I said, Josie's so fucking easy, she'll like anything you—"

My vision tunnels and I black out. I don't remember dropping my stuff or pushing Bryson into the locker until two people are behind me, trying to pull me off him because somehow, we landed on the floor. I don't know who it is and I don't care. I'm on top of Bryson, ramming my fist into his face. I think he tries to hit me and if he does, I don't feel it.

"You don't talk about Josie!" I pummel his face and anywhere I can get my fists. "Run your fucking mouth again! I fucking dare you! Fucking do—"

"Daniel, that's enough!" Coach D shouts, hauling me back. There's another hand on me, but I don't turn around to see who it is. "Daniel, stop!"

I'm forcefully dragged back. Bryson stays on the ground, blood pouring from his face.

My vision only clears when I'm dragged out of the locker room. Coach D and Coach Lewis let go of me, both pinning me with disappointed and angered looks.

"I'm not going to apologize." I clench my jaw, fisting and unfisting my bloody hands.

"What the hell is the matter with you!" Coach D barks, voice booming down the halls, and shoves my shoulder hard. Anyone who's around quickly disperses. "He's your teammate; you're the captain! You should know better!"

"He started it." I breathe out harshly, dragging my fingers through my hair.

"I don't give a damn who started it. He's your goddamn teammate! Is this still about the girl from last year? She's not—"

"No," I clip. "It has nothing to do with her."

"Then?" He crosses his arms against his chest, impatiently tapping his foot, eyes narrowed into murderous slits. "Then what the fuck is it about? What made you so mad, you'd be willing to get suspended, huh?"

I grind my teeth, my jaw aching from how heavy they scrape against each other. "Josefine. I don't need to explain myself anymore. He was already warned not to run his mouth. He knew and still did it anyway. I won't apologize when he already knew what would happen."

Coach D runs his palm down his face, then pinches the bridge of his nose, grunting. "You better not have broken anything." He points at me threateningly. "This is so unlike you."

"Yeah, well, shit happens." I shrug unremorsefully. "He shouldn't have called her easy...called her anything. I wasn't bluffing last time and I won't now or ever."

A string of Italian cuss words leave his lips in a mutter.

"Adam, take him with you. I need to make sure you didn't break anything."

"Am I suspended?" I ask.

"No, we need to test you. You played fucking phenomenal today. I hope to God you didn't break anything or I'll beat the shit out of you." He rubs his eyes. "You just couldn't wait until you were off the goddamn campus. Dammit, Daniel."

If I did, consequences be damned.

41
DANIEL

"Gracias, mama." I shut the engine off, dropping my head on the headrest.

There's a pause on the other line before I hear a tentative breath. *"Tu papa tambien esta muy orgulloso de ti."*

"Sí, claro." I roll my eyes.

"Daniel," she chastises. *"Por favor, no—"*

"I'm sorry, I just got home, I'm tired, and I still have to shower." I climb out of my car, dragging my duffle and backpack out with me.

A poignant sigh leaves her mouth. "Okay, well say hi to Josie for me and let her know I won't forget to bring bread next time."

I halt before inserting the key in the keyhole. "Wait, what?"

"She messaged me on Facebook the other day." I hear the smile in her voice, the tension from a few seconds ago gone. "Told me which breads she liked the best. I promised I'd bring some today but with all the sickness going around over here, I didn't want to be around her and get her sick."

That shocks me. "When did she message you?"

"Just a few days ago." I'm sure she's plotting. "You know... she's single."

My jaw drops. "You asked her? *Mama*." I shake my head, but I feel my cheeks warming. "What did you guys talk about?"

She laughs. "I'm not going to tell you. You'll get annoyed."

Usually, I do because I can't stand that she meddles, but this time, I really want to know. Did Josie say something or anything about me? Is she interested? I shouldn't want that, but I can't deny that I want her so badly.

"I won't, I promise." I attempt to keep my voice level, but interest seeps through.

She laughs again. "I need to let you go. *Estoy muy orgullosa de ti. Síguele echando ganas. Te quiero mucho.*"

Of course she'd do this. The one time I really want to know. "Me too."

As I unlock the door, my gaze draws to my bruised knuckles. Coach D had the athletic trainer look at my hand to make sure I didn't break anything either. I told him I was fine, but he said he needed to make sure.

Bryson's fine too, unfortunately. I didn't see him after I got tested, but I saw the red stain on the floor. I'm not sure how bad his face is, but according to Kai, it's pretty severe. I shouldn't have lost my shit; I don't even remember half of what I did.

I just remember thinking I'd never let anyone hurt Josie again. That meant anyone talking shit or doing whatever it is that would upset her. While she wasn't physically there, I still think about what he put her through. I think about that night on Christmas Day and how defeated she looked with life.

I promised her I'd help her fill the emptiness, and I promised myself she'd never have to go through life alone.

I'm not suspended, but Coach wants to see me tomorrow before the game. I don't know what he's going to do, but I know it's not going to be good.

My phone vibrates in my palm, multiple notifications lighting up the screen. They're all individual ones from most of my teammates and then the group chat with the guys. I ignore them, pocketing my phone as I shut the door behind me because I'm still mad.

I stop in the living room, looking around but there's no sign of Josie anywhere. It's Friday and close to ten p.m. She could be asleep, but that's highly unlikely. Most of the time she stays up late, either doing homework or swimming.

Just as I think that, she slips inside, a towel wrapped around her body and hair in a ponytail soaking wet.

I feel grounded. That's what seeing her makes me feel.

"Hey, Garcia." Those dark eyes soften, and relief washes over her.

I didn't notice it before but after she told me about her mom, I realized how on edge she looks when I'm home later than usual. I know it worries her even though she hasn't voiced it out loud because I feel the same when she's in the water. It's ridiculous considering she knows how to swim, but anything can happen.

Still, to lessen her worries, I update her when I can. I don't give her a specific time when I'll be home, but I let her know I'm on my way.

I don't know what comes over me, but I drop my stuff on the ground, cut the distance between us, and cup her face, closing the space between our lips.

She gasps into my mouth but doesn't push me away. I hear the faint smack of her wet towel hit the floor as her hands circle around my neck and lips part. I slip my tongue inside her waiting mouth, kissing her fiercely and possessively.

I'm kissing her fervently, not allowing her to catch air when she begins to pant and breathe harshly. Still, she doesn't push me away. She lets me deepen the kiss, tasting every inch of her mouth, stroking my tongue with hers.

It's angry, wet, and sloppy but neither one of us breaks it off. I can't get enough of her, I need more, and I know she feels the same way because she's letting me devour her mouth.

When I pull back, she heaves a large intake of air. She looks up at me, her brown eyes dark and intense, lips wet and swollen.

I rest my forehead against hers. All the pent-up frustration I was feeling is now gone. "Hi, Jos."

She huffs, licking her lips. "Hey Garcia."

I lick my own, wanting more, but I restrain myself and pull back because it just dawned on me that I'm still dirty. I didn't shower because I didn't feel like being around the guys.

Bending down, I pick up her towel and wrap it around her.

"Thanks." Her gaze gravitates towards my lips that pulse and burn with the need to latch them back on hers. "Congrats on your win, Cap."

"Let me hear it." I grin.

She cocks a brow. "Hear what?"

"You know exactly what."

Her lips twitch. "If you're talking about me stroking your ego, you're sorely mistaken. The analysts on TV did that enough."

"But they're not who I want to hear it from."

She scoffs a laugh and walks past me. "Good game, Cap," she says condescendingly then scrunches her nose.

"What?" I pick up my duffle and follow behind her as she heads up the stairs.

"Did your sixty-million-dollar showers stop working?"

The baseball facility got remodeled a year ago and apparently that's how much it cost.

My smile widens. "Nah, it was late so I decided to shower here. Can I not do that?"

"You can but at what cost?" She glances over her shoulder as she climbs the steps, scowling. "I think I'm going to throw up."

"I don't smell that..." I smell myself. Jesus. "Don't worry, I'll scrub extra hard."

"Please do. I'm going to have to spray the entire house down," she says when we're at the top and stop in the middle, standing in front of our bedroom doors.

I laugh and she smiles. Neither one of us says a word.

I feel alive. That's what talking to her makes me feel.

She opens her mouth, I open mine, but still no words come out.

I inhale, she softly exhales, but silence still fills the space. It's thick, hot, and suffocating in a way I don't hate. Suffocating in the way I want to feel her thighs squeeze around my head.

Is she thinking what I'm thinking? Does she want what I want?

"Well...I'm gonna go shower." I toss my thumb over my shoulder, slowly walking backward.

"Please do." She takes a step back then spins before she looks over her shoulder at me. Her lips part but then she closes them as well as the door behind her.

I breathe out, tipping my head back before I slip into my own room. I drop my bag, toe my shoes off, and head into the shower.

I'm not sure how long I stand under the hot stream after I've washed my hair and body, debating whether I want to wrap my hand around my dick or get out.

I'm already painfully hard and throbbing. I feel myself leaking precum, desperate for release.

Closing my eyes, I rest my forehead against the marbled tile, still contemplating whether I should or shouldn't jack off to the thought of Josie.

Fuck it.

I slip my hand around my shaft. A groan ripples from the back of my throat as I firmly glide my palm down the length and feel it pulse beneath the rough movement.

"Fuck," I grit under my breath, gliding the pad of my thumb over the crown.

I repeat the motion, slow, firm, and steady, wanting to prolong this for as long as I can as I fantasize about Josie. I think about Valentine's Day, her laying on the lounge chair and yesterday, her outside the pool. I think about all the things I'd still love to do to her and all the things I'd love for her to do to me.

All that comes to a staggering stop as a shadow catches the

corner of my eye. I swiftly look over my shoulder before I look away, but I do a double take, hand freezing mid stroke.

Josie's in my bathroom, a different towel wrapped around her body, hair down and still soaking wet.

There's no way…I'm dreaming…there's no way she's here…is she really here?

"Why'd you stop?" she asks as she approaches the shower, hands clutching her towel.

"Because this isn't real…" I quietly say, not to her but to myself.

She wets her lips, her brown eyes molten and hooded as she drops her towel, letting it pool around her feet. She stands outside the shower. Her wet, naked body glistens under the bright lights.

"Were you thinking of me?" she asks, voice soft, spurring my dick to throb harder. "*Are* you thinking of me and how you kissed me? Because I was."

This isn't a dream because she steps in, standing in front me. Her eyes coast down to my hand around my length and they go round, almost in stupefaction as if she hadn't really paid attention to it until now.

The column of her throat bobs and when her eyes meet mine again, I note how blown her pupils are. Her cheeks are stained a cherry red.

"All the fucking time," I moan and resume gliding my palm up and down. "Every minute of the day."

She licks her lips again, eyes flicking to the motion briefly. "I want to do that."

"Do what?" I grunt, slowing down before I come.

I know this isn't a dream I conjured up, but I'm still afraid to wake up and it being one.

I can't believe she's here, that she was thinking what I was thinking. Could this mean that she might feel what I feel?

I don't ask, but I'll keep wondering it.

Josie steps forward, placing her hand on top of mine, stopping me from moving it. "I want to please you. I want to make you feel good. You deserve it." She swallows again, gaze dropping to my dick. It jerks when I move my hand so hers can take its place. "Wow..." she breathes out.

"Wow what?" I grind my teeth, leaning into her when she squeezes.

She shakes her head and audibly swallows once again. "Nothing."

I grip her chin, tilting her head back. "Say it."

"You're...big," she huffs, dragging her palm down my shaft.

I groan, moving her hand, and wrap mine around her waist. I pick her up and she instantly snakes her legs around my torso. I pin her against the tile, watching her large breasts bounce against me.

I take her mouth in mine, keeping my arm around her and raise the other, weaving my fingers through her hair. She moans into my mouth, grinding her slick pussy against my abdomen. When her ass grazes my dick, I have to pull back.

"Fuck, Josie." I rest my forehead against hers, panting harshly, and attempt to stabilize myself. "I genuinely might come like this."

She shudders under my hold. "Don't. I need you to come in my mouth."

I don't blink. My heart ceases, and my breathing stops. "What?"

"Put me down. I want to make you feel good, Daniel. You deserve it." She untangles her legs, urging me to let her go, but I physically can't.

"No, let me—"

"You've already made me feel good. It's my turn. Let me." She stands on her tiptoes, placing a kiss on my cheek. "I promise you'll love it," she provocatively says against my ear, nipping the lobe, causing me to shudder. "Better than your fantasies."

I breathe in, forcing my hands away from her body and drawing away. I obediently listen as she tells me to sit on the marbled bench and watch intently as she drops to her knees in front of me.

"What did I do to deserve you?" I pinch her pebbled nipple, drifting my fingers to the hickey on the right side of her breast.

"Stopped me from dying," she playfully says but then winces. "Too soon?"

"I'm so happy you're here, Josie." I caress her cheek.

"I'm so happy you're here, Garcia," she echoes, and it does something strange to my chest. "Eyes on me," she slyly says.

I grin, knowing what she's referring to. "Were they on me?"

"The entire time. The way you played today...it was so hot." She grabs the bottom of my shaft and leans forward, tongue lapping over the seam of my crown. She does it repeatedly and quickly as her hand leisurely glides up and down. She hums, and the soft vibration of her mouth makes me shiver.

My body tenses, but I force myself to think of other things and not the girl licking me like I'm the best goddamn thing she's ever had in her life.

"Do you like that on your tongue?" I clench my teeth, fisting her hair to move it away from her face.

Her hooded eyes meet mine, tongue still licking and swirling around the tip. She nods eagerly and purses her lips, only sucking the head into her mouth.

My eyes roll and I pull on her hair, harder than I mean to, but when I loosen my hold, she pulls back, lips slightly swollen. "Don't stop. I'm yours; use me however you want."

I inhale deeply, dropping my head back, tightening my hold on her hair. That's not what I needed to hear right now. I'm going to come quicker than I want to.

"Eyes on me," she sweetly says, cupping my balls.

My eyes flutter, but I somehow manage to keep them open and on her. *"Abre tu boca."* She bites her bottom lip before her plush lips part open. I keep one hand fisted on her hair and wrap the other around my cock, bringing her mouth to it. "Be good for me, Josie, and suck it good."

A tiny moan escapes as she draws me into her mouth. She sucks and replaces my hand with hers. She strokes me long and hard, her hand and mouth finding a rhythm, working in tandem.

"Josie," I moan her name, almost withering from how good her hot mouth feels against me. "That's it, baby, fuck, you're doing so good. Sooo...fucking good."

Her cheeks hollow in, working fast, all while her eyes stay locked on mine.

"You were made for sucking my cock, weren't you?" I breathlessly ask as she slows down and pulls me out of her mouth. She nods and drags her tongue down my length to my balls and sucks them into her mouth. I grunt, spreading my thighs further. "So easy for it," I groan as she works her tongue up my cock. "It fits so good in your mouth."

She whimpers, dragging her tongue underneath the head, following every ridge until my dick is completely soaked in her saliva. *Holy fucking shit, I've never been more turned on in my life.* When she's satisfied, leaving me a fucking breathless mess, she draws me back into her mouth and takes me in deep.

"Keep..." My eyes roll back. "Doing that," I say through clenched teeth, jerking my hips upward when I hit the back of her throat.

She gags, eyes watering and squeezing shut, but I hold her head and meet her mouth with small thrusts.

"You got it. You're doing fine," I encourage, inhaling a shuddering breath, and sit up. "Relax and breathe for me. Don't tense up. I'm not going to get any smaller."

She looks up at me, eyes welled with tears and nostrils flaring. She flips me off and gags again when I push her head down.

"Don't be mean to me. It'll only turn me on more," I taunt, pushing her head once more just for the hell of it.

She gags again, and tears roll down her cheeks, nails digging into my thighs for support. Still, she doesn't pull back completely. She submissively waits for me to tell her what to do and I swear that makes my balls tense.

"I wish you could see yourself. So pretty with your mouth filled like this." I push her head gently, making her draw me in and out of her mouth. "Keep sucking, fuck...just like that. You were made for this. For me. You're so good at this. I might have you do this every day to keep your smart-ass mouth occupied."

She whimpers and I swear I think I see her nod, eyes glittering with hunger.

"You'd do this every day?"

She greedily nods, still sucking, faster now.

I'd revel in her answer if it wasn't for the zap of electricity that shoots down my spine, making my entire body tense. My balls tighten, my dick throbs fast, and every fiber of my body shatters as I come inside her mouth.

Her eyes stay trained on me, but I can't keep mine on her for long. I feel high, dizzy, and dazed, moaning her name as I continue to come. She doesn't stop sucking, relentlessly keeps going, humming and moaning around me as if she were enjoying every second of this, enjoying the taste of my cum in her mouth, sliding down her throat.

I'm spent and speechless by the time she pulls back, still on her knees for me. I may have told her what to do, but in the end, she had all the control and she knows that. That's why she's smirking, staring at me like she just ended my life. In some ways she did, and I'm honestly okay with that.

She licks her lips and I spot a few specks of my cum on her chin. I lean forward, wipe them off, and bring my thumb to her mouth. She happily opens her swollen lips and sucks on it.

My dick jerks, still hard and still very much excited for more.

"How did I do?" She tilts her head to the side after I pop my finger out.

I swallow. "Josie, don't ask me that question. Not when I'm contemplating doing this again."

She blushes and stands, breasts bouncing softly. "Did you mean it?"

"Mean what?" I can't stop feeling ecstasy. My body is buzzing with life. I can still feel her lips, her tongue. God, I want more.

"Every day?"

My dicks pulses. So that wasn't a heat of the moment answer. I wasn't going to bring it up because I didn't want her to feel pressured but now...

"Yeah, I did. Did you?" I grab her wrist and tug her closer.

"Yeah." She nods and places a hand on my shoulder.

"But it doesn't have to be every day. Whenever you want, Josie, I'm yours." She shudders, goose bumps breaking out across her skin. "Let's get out."

The water is still hot, cascading down, but she's not directly underneath it. I go to stand, but she shakes her head.

"Not cold, I'm just...I'm not cold." She glances down between us.

I slip my hands down to her ass, drawing her in until she has no choice but to straddle me.

She looks up at me now as my dick nestles between her dripping pussy. She's so wet, it easily slips between her folds, brushing her clit. "Mmm..." She jolts and slowly rocks her hips against me, tits bouncing, hard nipples grazing my chest.

"We should stop..." I say not finding the strength to actually mean it, lost in the way her breasts move. I need them on my face, in my mouth.

"We should..." Her thighs squeeze around me as she continues to grind herself against my cock, jolting occasionally when my tip hits her clit.

I squeeze her ass, fingers digging into her flesh, and ground her onto me. "But in case we can't...I'm clean...I got tested a few weeks ago."

"And I'm on birth control," she mewls, resting her forehead against mine. "Not that that should mean anything, but just so you know, I'm also clean."

"That's good to know," I huskily breathe, letting her use me to grind against my cock. I slap her ass and feel it jiggle against my palm.

"Oh!" She jerks up, her eyes rolling back. "I'm close." She moans, body trembling against me.

"Use me, Josie." She grinds faster. "Just like that, baby. Rub your needy cunt on me." She wraps her arms around my neck, breathing harshly against my ear as she chases her orgasms. "Just like that. Keep going." I slap her ass harder.

"Oh my gosh," she cries out, leaning forward and pressing herself against me, no doubt adding more pressure to her clit.

Her body convulses then goes tense before she goes slack. "It's okay, Josie. I got you." I grab her hips and rock her, knowing she still wants more but can't keep going. "Just like this, right?"

"Mm-hmm." Her head lolls, letting me use her body to get her off.

She comes again, harder this time, but I don't let up. Not when she's clawing my shoulders because she keeps begging for more despite how her body spasms.

I smirk and lift her off me and she whines.

"Trust me." I switch places with her and sit her on the bench, spreading her shaking thighs apart. Her chest heaves and her face is flushed a crimson red. She leans back, watching me with eyes half closed like she's spaced out. I grab the extra showerhead and spread her pussy lips. Her clit is red and swollen, and every so often it pulses as if it's begging for me. "You're so needy, Josie. How many times have you come?"

She drowsily shrugs. "Three..."

"And you still want more?"

She shyly nods.

"Anything for you." I push a button to switch the water to this showerhead, but I don't immediately put it on her. I lap my tongue across her slit first, tasting her.

She huskily sighs, dragging her fingers through my hair.

I don't stop despite how hard she pulls my hair. I flick my tongue over the swollen nub, feel it flutter against my tongue. It doesn't take long before she's coming again, muttering garbled words.

I lick it a few more times, enjoying how it grows on my tongue and how she bucks her hips, pushing her pussy on my face. When I know she's about to come again, I hold the water over her clit, using the setting with the highest pressure.

Her eyes shoot wide open and she releases a high-pitched squeal. She orgasms hard, her eyes go white from how hard they rolled back.

She's hoarsely crying out, head tipped back as the water continues to spray on her. A moment later, she tenses and shocks me when she squirts. She convulses, back arching, and hips rolling as if she were grinding on something. She gets it on me and I let it be, staring at her, transfixed, as I wrap my palm around my shaft. I masturbate as I watch her squirt on my chest and then I'm chasing my own release again.

I drop the showerhead and stand over her, stroking myself fast and hard. She breathes erratically, chest rising and falling rapidly, body still jerky but she watches. Her lust-filled eyes track every movement. I feel myself tense and then I release all over her body.

I drop my head back, my jaw clenched and breath ragged as I come with her name leaving my mouth. I repeat it over and over, until I've stopped coming. When I force myself to look at her, I see the mess I made on her.

"Shit, Josie." I clear my dry throat. "I shouldn't have—"

She shakes her head. Scooping my cum and bringing her hand between her thighs, she rubs my cum all over her pussy. She whimpers every time she brushes her engorged clit.

My cock throbs at the sight. I don't think as I replace my fingers with hers. Collecting my cum, I slowly push them inside her. She clenches around my fingers, whimpering as I pull out just a little before I shove them back inside.

"You like my cum on you?"

She bites her bottom lip and nods. "And in me."

Fuck me. She quietly gasps as I remove them completely. "I liked you squirting on me."

The darkest shade of red takes over her face. "I...that has never happened."

I can't help how wide my lips stretch. I'm sure it's a megawatt smile.

"Stop looking at me like." She frowns.

"You have to understand—not only did you just stroke my ego, but that's the hottest thing I've ever seen."

"Oh." She tucks her hair behind her ear, lips slightly curling at the corners. "Well...don't expect it to happen again."

"It'll happen again," I say, so self-assured. "I promise." I lean down and kiss her forehead.

42

JOSIE

"Once you eat, you can go to bed."

I'm in a daze, stuck in a cloud of ecstasy. Post-orgasm waves still wrack my body. Every so often my clit softly pulses and my body shudders uncontrollably. It feels like my body is still chasing the high from just a few minutes ago.

"I really would've been okay with just water," I murmur into his neck.

My stomach decided to grumble after we got out of the shower. Personally, I could've skipped food all together and just gone to bed. All I wanted was to put on my pajamas, wrap myself in my blanket, and replay everything that happened in the shower, but Daniel wasn't having it.

He's been taking care of me. More so than usual. It's the bare minimum, but he washed me off after he came on me, wrapped a towel around me, gave me his shirt and a pair of socks so I wouldn't get cold even though my room is just a few feet away from his. Now he's carrying me down the stairs because I told him I didn't feel like walking. I'm holding on to him, my chest to his back, arms wrapped around his neck, legs strapped around his torso.

"No, I want to make this a ten out of ten experience for you.

What kind of man would I be if I didn't feed you after giving you the greatest orgasm of your life?"

I lazily smile. "The greatest orgasm of my life?"

"I'm pretty certain I heard you say it. You probably don't remember. You were too busy screaming my name." I hear the smirk in his voice.

I scoff a laugh. "It's called acting."

Now he scoffs as we enter the kitchen. "Josefine, please. Was it acting when you came the first? Second? Third? Fourth time? Or when you squirted all over me? If you don't remember, I'll gladly give you a play by play with all the details." He sits me on the island, spins, and parts my thighs, settling between them. "I happen to have a pretty damn good memory." He flashes me a crooked grin.

"I'm good," I deadpan.

"You sure, baby?" He lifts a brow. "Did I not leave enough cum inside your pussy? I'm happy to give you more, if that's what your *needy* pussy needs."

I fight against clenching my thighs, but my face might be a dead giveaway because it warms at the stupid pet name. I fucking melt anytime he calls me that. And at the reminder of his cum inside me, my body blisters.

"You look good in red," he conceitedly states, tucking my damp locks behind my ear before he pushes away and opens the fridge.

I roll my eyes, place a cool hand on my searing cheek, but drop it when he turns. He sets the butter, Boursin Garlic & Fine Herb, and cheddar cheese slices next to the stove, but pauses in his spot, eyes raking over me.

"What?" I self-consciously drop my gaze. I'm still in his baseball practice T-shirt. I was going to take it off, but I couldn't bring myself to actually do it. It smells like him and fits me loosely. It's nice considering clothes don't usually fit me like this because I'm tall.

"Keep it." His gaze descends to the hem where it sits on the middle of my thighs. "And don't fight me. While I enjoy arguing with you and begging, it's a little late for the back and forth."

My lips jerk. "It's never too late."

He steps forward into my space, standing between my parted thighs, hands resting on either side of me on the marble. "Don't tempt me. I'll go all night."

I open my mouth, but my stomach grumbles loudly.

He chuckles, pushing away and as he does, from my periphery I note a tinge of red on his knuckle. I look away but do a double take as I notice the rest of his knuckles on his right hand are bright red.

How did I not see that before?

"What happened to your hand?" I grab his arm, spinning him back around before he can get further away. I take a hold of his hand, studying the bruising surrounding the bone. "Did you get hurt during intermission or something?"

I had my eyes on him the entire game. I would've noticed if he would have gotten hurt or looked off. But if something had been wrong, he must have masked it extremely well because the way he played today was different. He was playing with an energy that even the commentators couldn't help but marvel in.

He tries to pull it back, but I keep a firm hold on it. "It's nothing."

"Doesn't seem like not nothing." I gently circle the pad of my finger around the bruising, his stiff hand going lax in my hold.

Daniel studies me tentatively. He looks like he wants to say something, but a wave of uncertainty flares in his eyes. He blinks and it's gone. "It's really nothing. Angel and I were messing around, I went to punch him, but he moved and I punched the wall instead."

I don't know why but I'm not sure I really believe him. I feel like he's hiding something, but he only smiles and draws his hand away.

"I'm okay." He goes to the pantry and takes out the sourdough. "I know it looks bad, but it doesn't hurt."

I want to say something, but I'm not too sure what.

"You're about to have the best grilled cheese." He grabs a pan from the bottom cabinet and sets it on the gas cooktop.

I can't help but feel a pang in my chest knowing he's not being honest with me. I shove the feeling away—whatever happened, it's not my business. He doesn't owe me anything.

"I thought you weren't a fan of garlic?"

"No, but you are."

The ache dulls for a moment as flutters take over. Jesus, I've really gone soft.

I fold a shaky leg over the other, bringing my hand back, bracing my weight on my palms. "You should try it."

A muscle in his jaw works, gaze trained on the way the shirt rides up. "Having you here is going to be a hazard."

I smirk. "Get it together, Garcia."

Daniel grins and while he waits for the pan to heat up, he goes to the living room, and I watch as he flicks through the massive CD booklet.

Yesterday, I helped him bring out the stuff he wanted to put in the living room. Now there's a large bulky stereo, a record player along with CDs, vinyls, and cassettes sitting on the shelf or wherever we could find space.

We agreed to go to the store and buy another bookshelf tomorrow after his game just because he has so much stuff.

"Under Pressure" by Queen and David Bowie blasts from the speakers of the stereo. Daniel bobs his head as he dances his way over to me.

I bite the inside of my cheek, forcing the laugh that threatens to escape as he goofily moves and sings. He sounds horrible, his voice cracks every few notes, and he burns himself twice, but that doesn't deter him from using the spatula as a microphone.

By the time the song ends, small bubbles of laughter slip past my lips and I'm clapping. "Please, I'll pay you to not do that again."

He gasps. "I thought I sounded pretty good."

"Baby goats sound better."

"That's hater behavior."

"No, it's called honesty."

"Hater," he coughs into his hand.

I snort. "You're so lame."

"That's not what you were screaming earlier." He shrugs unapologetically.

My body thrums with need. "Is that going to be your comeback for every argument?"

"Hell yeah, it is." He peers over his shoulder at me and shoots me a wink.

I roll my eyes, but my face burns again.

"Have you listened to your CD yet?" he asks as he flips the grilled cheese over. My mouth waters at how golden it looks in the buttered pan, the cheese oozing out on the sides.

Glad he forced me to come downstairs.

"I have actually. I'm listening to one song each day. Hope you don't mind if I keep the CD player a little longer?"

"You can keep it as long as you want." He looks genuinely happy, his entire mood more vibrant, livelier. "Are you liking what you've listened to so far?"

"Yeah, 'Wobble' is a...masterpiece. It's just what I needed. Really made my day." It's a bit sarcastic, but I mean it.

I was caught off guard when it started playing through the tiny earbuds today. I had expected something soft, maybe even inspirational, but not V.I.C.

"Yeah?" His lips flatten in a line as if were trying to stop himself from smiling or laughing. "I can't wait for you to listen to the rest."

I'm not sure what to expect, but I'm really excited now. It's kind of hard to believe that a few months ago I didn't look forward to anything, and now I look forward to moments with Daniel.

It's really silly though considering he'll be gone in a few months. The thought settles splinters in my stomach.

My chest feels heavy when I breathe in, but I play off the ache when he turns, holding two plates in his hands.

"Bon appétit, mademoiselle." He hands me the plate, smiling from ear to ear.

We talk—well, he mainly does—and listen to music as we eat. I'm partially listening, stuck between reveling in this moment and hating myself for falling for him.

43

DANIEL

When Coach said he wanted to meet with me first thing in the morning, I didn't expect Bryson to join us.

I know he didn't expect it either. He looks deceptively calm, but I don't miss the slight pinch between his brows when he spots me sitting in one of the two chairs in front of Coach's desk.

The left side of his face looks fucked. It's swollen and bruised, and while his eye isn't shut, it's smaller than the other. There's also a small cut on his nose and a gash on his lip.

I wish I could say I feel bad, but I don't. I briskly drop my gaze to my knuckles, flexing my hand. My knuckles aren't as red as yesterday, but they're a little sore. I welcome the pain and only regret I didn't get another punch in.

"Come in." He quickly waves his hand inward.

He swiftly does and takes the chair next to me, knowing right now isn't the time to push Coach's buttons. Not that it ever is, but his expression is grim. Piercing blue eyes sharpen and his mouth sets in a straight line.

"Coach—"

He lifts a hand, cutting Bryson off.

"You don't speak. You listen." He sits up straight, his body visibly rolling with anger. I'm sure like me, Bryson is scared as shit because Coach is a terrifying man. "I'm disgusted with both of your behaviors. So fucking disgusted, I was almost tempted to suspend you—"

"Coach—"

He slams a palm hard on his wooden desk, cutting Bryson off again. "You have lost the privilege to speak! You shut up and listen."

Bryson nods at the fury in his voice and sinks in his chair.

Coach crosses his arms against his chest, veins popping on his face and neck. "I was tempted to suspend you both. Never in the ten years that I've been coaching have I had to deal with this middle school bullshit, but I can guarantee you that it'll never happen again."

My heart races, palms sweat, and I spiral with thoughts of what that could mean.

"As of today, you two will be each other's catching partners, sharing hotel rooms, and sitting on the bus and plane together. Really anything that involves two people. You will learn to get along and treat each other with respect."

Fuck, this is worse than any other punishment. I'd rather be suspended, and I'm sure Bryson feels the same way.

He breathes out a frustrated sigh, every muscle on his face twitching as if he's holding back from going off. "You better be glad you caught me on a good day and that we're on a winning streak. Now get out of here and go get ready. Daniel, stay back for a moment."

Bryson eyes me briefly before he nods and slips out.

"Coach—"

He lifts a hand, then wipes his palm down his face and reclines in his chair. "Daniel, you better be glad the Dean and I like you. Bryson's father is a particular man and let me tell you..." he grunts agitatedly. "Whatever, it's been taken care of. This better not happen again."

"As long as he doesn't speak about Josie again, we'll be okay."

"No girl is worth—"

"I don't mean any disrespect, I really don't. I have nothing but an abundance of respect for you, but Josie is worth it. Consequences be damned."

He pinches the bridge of his nose. "Danny, I understand—"

"Would you kindly disregard it if this was your daughter?" I know I just crossed a line, but I need him to understand how serious this is for me. Josie isn't just *some* girl, she's *my* girl. "If someone was calling her names, talking shit about her that wasn't true?"

Coach removes his hat and drops it on his desk, raking his fingers through his black hair. He breathes in deeply, releasing a brittle chuckle. "I understand, I really do." He pauses, eyes distant as if he were thinking something but he shakes his head. "But don't let this happen again."

I only nod, not sure I can physically voice out loud a promise I might not be able to keep.

"Before I let you go, I wanted to ask about the email."

I wipe my palms on my thighs, anxiety slithering in my chest. "I haven't had the time to—"

"There's no pressure, but you know this is a good way for you to communicate directly with the teams and the MLB. This is an amazing opportunity, and I don't want you to miss out on it." He must sense my hesitation or I might not be hiding it well because he asks a question that makes my chest feel tight. "Regardless, if you decide not to fill out the form, you're still eligible for the draft."

Unlike the NBA and NFL, we don't have to enter the draft. For the MLB you're eligible once you're over twenty-one or have done three years of college. There is also another exception for high school players, but that's beside the point.

I'm eligible and while that's great, I can't help but feel like I don't deserve it.

I just don't know how to tell him or anyone else that.

"How much do you think we'll get once we get drafted?" Adrian asks as we watch the MLB draft. *Every July, he, dad, and I sit on the couch and watch it together.*

"The chances of getting drafted is low—"

"Stop being so negative. It's going to happen and when it does we'll marry models and buy a penthouse."

"Garcia?"

"Sorry, what?" I blink the memory away, look down at Josie who's staring up at me with worry.

"You okay?"

"Yeah," I shift my attention back to the bookshelves on display. I absently let my gaze roam over them, not really looking at one in particular. "I just remembered something."

We came to the store to buy bookshelves and a few more things for the house.

"Do you want to talk about it?"

I muse over her question and walk down the aisle; she follows beside me silently. "It's stupid."

"Hey." She stands in front of me. A touch of irritation mars her face. I know it isn't directed at me; sometimes she looks mad when she's really not. I think it's hot when she looks at me like that, but that's not something I should be focusing on. "Nothing you say is stupid. Unless you're calling yourself hot."

I smile, feeling the constricting pain in my chest dull. I pull my hat off, needing to grab something that isn't her before I situate it on my head.

The need to touch her has been constant. There isn't a day that goes by where I don't want to touch her. We wouldn't need to do anything. I'd be okay with just holding her, listening to her heartbeat and the sound of her voice.

"I was just thinking of Adrian." I clear my throat, but a rock lodges itself in the middle of it, making it hard to swallow.

"Tell me about it." She grabs my wrist and squeezes it, but she doesn't pull away as if she knew this is what I needed to feel grounded.

I'm overanalyzing a touch, but the way she's staring at me steadies me.

"Right here?" I look around. We're in the middle of the aisle, but anyone could walk by.

"Yeah, but no pressure. Just know that I'm here." She smiles and on cue the fireworks go off.

"Every July, Adrian, Dad, and I would watch the draft and we'd imagine ourselves being there. Though sometimes it was hard for me because it seemed impossible, but Adrian was very optimistic. We, uh..." I smother a chuckle at the memories. "We'd talk about all the things we'd do once we started making millions. Like marrying models and buying a penthouse. We'd talk about all the nice furniture we'd buy and many other things." A weight of sadness grips my bones, the words leaving my mouth as rough as sandpaper. She squeezes my wrist again and rubs her thumb in gentle circles on my skin. I drag my trembling teeth along my quivering bottom lip. "I know it sounds stupid, but we were kids and we thought it'd be cool. We knew when we accomplished those things, it'd be our *we made it*. Being here with you made me think about that moment."

Her eyes are soft and understanding. "Really?"

I rub the nape of my neck. "Yeah."

"You realize I'm no model and we don't live in a penthouse?"

My priorities have changed. I don't want any of those things. I want you. I need you, I want to say but my tongue feels heavy, stuck to the roof of my mouth.

"Your house is the nicest place I've ever lived in, so it's pretty much the same thing. And I'm living with the prettiest girl I've ever seen."

Her house doesn't have the typical beach house interior. The furniture, appliances, and everything else is very modern and sleek. It sometimes feels surreal that I get to live in a house like hers. And don't get me started on my bedroom and bathroom.

She drags her teeth along her bottom plush lip as a pink tint colors her cheeks. "Hold on to those memories and make them a reality. Marry two models and buy the penthouse."

"My priorities have changed," I manage to say. "I don't want that."

"What do you want then?" Her gaze holds mine and her hand tightens around me.

You. "Let's make a deal."

Her lips quirk. "Okay?"

"If we're not married by the time we're thirty, we'll get married. And we'll have four babies like we talked about."

Josie blinks, taken aback. "You want to marry me? Why?" she asks like the thought seems unfathomable, something she's not entirely processing.

"Because I see a life with you," I say because I don't want to lie. I don't want to pretend like I haven't thought about it. "Because you make sense. Because you make me happy and I hope I make you happy."

A quiet hum fills the space between us. Her silence feels everlasting, unnerving me.

"You make me happy." She voices shyly, twisting her ring. "And you have a lot of great qualities I'd be dumb to turn down."

I chuckle softly, acting nonchalant about her response and not the way my brain is jumping with happiness. "I do, don't I?"

"But I don't. You might want to rethink your deal."

I quickly shake my head. "There's nothing to think about. Josefine, I like you as you are. You're smart and a smart-ass." She glares but smiles a little bigger at that. "You're resilient. Strong. A fighter. *You.* You have a lot of great qualities. Don't ever let anyone believe you don't because you do." I pause, *really* imagining Josie being my wife. Mine forever. *Whoa.* "And I also like taking care of you. I like doing things for you, so we're good. But just so you know, once we're married, you can't divorce me, Jos. I'm serious."

Her entire face softens and glows. "It's your funeral."

"So do we have a deal?" I pull my hand back and extend it.

Josie places her hand in mine, shaking it. "Are you serious about the babies?"

"As long as you want them, yes." My heart skips a beat.

"Okay, deal."

"Okay, deal," I echo, feeling ten times lighter.

The next two hours, we spend picking out a bookshelf and a few other things. And as I go to check out, Josie goes missing.

I search for her, using a singsong voice as I say her name. I find her in an aisle I wouldn't have ever expected her to be in. The toy section, particularly standing in front of a shelf filled with stuffed animals.

There's a faraway look on her face, like she's lost in thought. I stand next to her, making sure the cart isn't in the way.

"Do you want one?" I ask.

Josie jolts back as if she hadn't realized I was standing next to her. She makes a psh sound. "No, these are for kids. Are you ready to go?"

She briskly walks away before I can answer.

44

JOSEFINE

"I'm so glad you came." A dopey smile curls on Pen's face.

Vi's resembles hers because before we came to The Antisocial Bar, we pregamed. I didn't as hard as the two of them, but I drank enough, so I feel a buzz coursing through my system.

"How could I say no? You guys wouldn't stop blowing up my phone." I'm half serious because it's Monday and half teasing because I hate being home alone.

This past weekend Daniel was in Alabama playing against Auburn. He's been gone since Thursday and should be back today, but it's already past nine p.m. and I still haven't heard from him.

Before then, on Tuesday, he had an away game. He left extremely early that morning but didn't come home until Wednesday evening.

On top of hardly seeing him at home, I rarely see him in class because his practice time changed to the time we hike.

It's been an adjustment, a weird one at that. Before Daniel, I could put up with the loneliness, but now it's odd and I don't like it. I don't like missing him or wondering when he's going to come home. Because in a few months, he'll be gone.

I've physically accepted that, but mentally, I'm struggling.

That's why I agreed to come out with the girls to celebrate St. Patrick's Day. That and they weren't trying to go to a club. I don't mind dressing up, but today I wanted to keep it casual. I'm wearing a cropped green shirt, and maybe I'm making a mistake, but decided to go braless because why the hell not? Paired with a dark denim mini skirt and my all-black Dr. Martens.

"Because you're a horrible replier. If we don't blow it up, you won't respond until the next ten to twenty business days," Vi points out.

"That's not true," I weakly defend. "I just have a lot going on."

She arches a perfectly styled black brow and smiles slyly. "I'm sure you do."

I take a sip of my beer, thankful that Pen doesn't catch that. She's too busy staring at her phone.

"I'll be back. I gotta go to the restroom," she announces, tucking her phone in her tiny purse.

"We'll go with," I say, but she's shaking her head. "No, don't. I won't be gone long, and they'll take our spot if we leave."

We're right next to the bar and because it's packed with possibly every college student, there's hardly any space or seats left.

"I'll stay. You go with her," I tell Vienna. Pen still insists, but I shake my head. "I'll be okay here; I'll save our spots. You shouldn't go alone."

"Okay, you're right. We'll be back," she says and hooks her arm around Vi's and then they're off, the blind leading the blind because they're a little tipsier than I thought.

I snicker at that before drawing my attention away from them to the TVs hung above the bar. One of them plays the highlights from yesterday's game.

My heart thunders when Daniel appears on the screen. He's quickly diving for the ball then jumping to his feet, throwing the ball to the second baseman before he's throwing it to Kai at first, getting both players from Auburn out.

The next highlight that plays is one of him stealing third base. He stands, and my favorite kind of smile curls on his lips as he points to the corner of his eyes. Flutters burst in my stomach the same way they did yesterday when I saw it and every other time, he's on base.

Only on you, I think every single time.

Another highlight plays, but I'm interrupted when someone bumps into me.

"Oh, I'm sorry..." the voice drifts when our eyes lock.

I almost want to laugh at how comical and cliché this is. The girl who slept with my boyfriend and happens to be my roommate-with-benefits ex, bumping into me.

Amanda stares at me knowingly, not surprised or the least bit apologetic.

There's a long stretch of silence. I'm not sure if she's trying to find the words or maybe expects me to lash out, but she stares at me, inquisitive and piercing.

I don't have it in me or care to know if she'll speak so I spin in my seat, darting my attention to the TV.

Unfortunately, I still feel her standing there, watching me.

"Did you lose something?" I ask her.

Her face scrunches with agitation. "What?"

"You're staring at me like you've lost something."

I'd be lying if I said that her standing in front of me didn't bother me just a little. It's not because of confrontation; I don't have an issue with it. It's knowing that Daniel dated her, liked her, and did things with her. It's knowing that she's better than me, at least emotionally. It's knowing that she could give him that and I'm not sure I'd be able to.

I don't believe in love or at least understand what the hell it is, but I'm sure she does. I wonder if they said *I love you* to each other, because couples do that, and they dated for a while. Surely, they did.

She's also drop-dead gorgeous. Naked or not, she's beautiful, there's no denying that. I understand why Bryson and Daniel are both attracted to her. Even I can't help but gawk at her a little.

Amanda flashes me a tight-lipped smile. "Are you sleeping with Danny?"

Wow, she's forward. "That's none of your business."

"It's not and I shouldn't be asking, but I just need to know." Desperation fills her voice. The music is loud, but it audibly pours out of her.

I laugh this time. "If what you really want to ask is if we're dating, the answer is no."

She stands straighter, a wave of relief washing over her. "You know we dated for a while. That's not something you just get over."

"Was that while you were fucking my boyfriend? Because that's also something most people don't get over," I quip.

Her nostrils flare, face glowing red. "It was a mistake. I didn't mean to—"

"You don't have to explain yourself to me. I genuinely don't care. You honestly did me a solid. I should've left Bryson a long time ago." I take another swig and spin around, feeling a little irritated, not for me but for Daniel.

"We're going to work things out," she adds, but her voice wavers like she's not sure if she believes it. "He loves me and he's using you. He's mad at Bryson and wants to get back at him."

I was going to keep my mouth shut, but the sheer audacity. Shame needs to be brought back because what the fuck?

"Do you hear yourself?" I scoff. "You're so pathetic."

"Excuse me?" She jerks back, staring at me as if I had slapped her across the face. Although I want to, I don't.

"You heard me. You're so pathetic." She wasn't holding back, so why should I? "What the hell is wrong with you? It was bad enough you slept with a guy you knew had a girlfriend, but you cheated on a guy who I'm sure treated you like you were his world. You should be embarrassed." I huff out a disbelieving laugh.

"I made a mistake," she grits angrily. "You know nothing about our relationship."

"You clearly didn't know enough about yours," I retort.

Her nostrils flare, jaw clenching. "Fuck you." She goes to walk away but I stop her.

"Have some decency and leave him alone. You know he's done with you. I don't know why you keep showing up and spewing out this bullshit."

She eyes me up and down then aggravatedly blows out a sharp breath. "I really do regret it." She looks dejected but then she perks up and a smug smile splits across her face. "But whatever. I was the best he's ever had, and if it's not with me, it'll be with someone else. I doubt you'll be able to give him what he needs. Why do you think Bryson did what he did? Guys like that only put up with girls like you for so long."

My stomach dips painfully. Of course Bryson did. I shouldn't expect anything less from him, but it still hurts, nonetheless.

I say nothing but flip her off as she walks away because there's no point in arguing or fighting over a guy. Like Vienna, I refuse to do that. That's pathetic even though for a brief moment I wanted to slap her. And I wanted to tell her that that would never happen because I make Daniel happy, he said so. I'd love to rub our deal in her face, but I'm just the girl he made a deal with if he's desperate in ten years.

I'm in over my head to assume he'd actually wait. Happiness doesn't always equate to anything. It's a fickle feeling.

When I know she's gone, I chug the rest of my beer. I set it down and ask the bartender for something stronger.

Dying would've been easier than feeling what I'm feeling.

The girls come back moments later, but they're not the only ones who show up. A few guys circle around us. I think they're lacrosse players, but I'm not sure nor do I care. The girls eat up the attention though. I'm happy for them; they should have fun, but I can't help but think about my feelings for Daniel.

I've never wanted anyone more, but I'm scared of what I feel and not being able to understand it.

"So...what's your name?" one of the guys asks me.

I say nothing, hoping he'll take the hint.

He laughs, his beer-tinted breath fanning the side of my face. "Oh come on. You're here, I'm here—let's get to know one another. I promise not to be weird."

"You already are." I take a sip of my drink and suck in a breath as the tequila burns my throat.

"How so?" He stands a little closer and I shouldn't welcome it but I do. But then I recoil because he doesn't smell like Daniel, doesn't look like him either.

"You're being pushy, you're too close, and you're getting on my nerves," I flatly reply, but he smiles as if I've said a joke.

"Drinks on me. What do you say?" He disregards everything I've said, stepping a little closer, his gaze falling to my chest. "You can get anything you want."

"I can pay for my own drinks."

"Come on. Just give me a few minutes to change your mind."

"You're standing too fucking close." I'm not sure where Daniel came from, but he stands next to me, snaking a protective and secure arm around my waist.

He almost pulls me off the chair. Most of my ass is off the seat. I'd be afraid of falling off if he wasn't holding me as firmly as he is. I shouldn't be okay with him grabbing me like I'm his, warning whatever-his-name is that I'm off-limits, but a needy part of me enjoys this.

The guy raises his hands in surrender, taking a few steps back. "Shit, I'm sorry, Danny. I didn't know she was your girlfriend."

"Just back the fuck away." His voice is thick, almost sounds like gravel as he pins the guy with a dark look.

"Right, yeah." He pivots and huddles around his other friends, not once looking back at us.

"I'm not your girlfriend," I say, keeping my voice even. Hoping I'm hiding how happy I am that he's here.

He's still looking at the guy, protective and annoyed as if he's waiting for him to come back and try something. I'm pretty certain he's not, but Daniel's on alert.

I shouldn't find this hot or like how serious he looks. I've seen various versions of him, but this side is different.

A beat later, he looks down at me and his face softens a fraction. "No, I miss you? No, congratulations? I've been gone for four days, Josie, and that's the first thing you say to me?"

"Congratulations, Cap. You kicked ass out there."

Daniel helps me adjust back on the seat and stands in front of me. He places his hand back on my waist and my skin tingles as his calloused palm softly glides over my back. Then he props his elbow on the bar top and grabs one of my bubble braids.

I crane my head back to look up at him, keeping a straight face at his pout.

"Did you not miss me?" He sounds genuinely disappointed like that wasn't what he was hoping to hear.

"We live together. Why would I miss you?"

His lips twist and he leans in. My eyes flutter as his minty breath and woodsy cologne fill my lungs. I almost collapse in my seat, feeling overwhelmed by having him this close, smelling him, feeling him, hearing him, but I manage to keep myself upright.

"I missed you." There's a longing in his voice that grips my soul.

We're supposed to be casual, so casual that I don't have expectations and didn't make him be exclusive to me. We don't sleep in the same bed after he makes me come and I don't cuddle with him because that's something people in relationships do.

That one time was an exception.

But I'm stupid because I want to be exclusive. I don't want to share him. I don't want to wonder if he's making someone else come and giving them his shirt and socks after. Or if he makes them grilled cheese and plays all kinds of music.

I don't want to keep wondering, but he makes it hard and now he's here, touching me and saying things like that. How the hell am I not supposed to crumble?

"I—" My mouth goes dry. I'm in too deep; this isn't okay. He'll leave soon and I'll be alone again.

I look away and as I do my gaze connects with Kai's. He smirks, his eyes drifting to Daniel then back to me. He curves his fingers making a heart sign and mouths something but I can't make out what it is.

"I need to use the restroom." I quickly finish my drink and push off the seat.

"I'll go with you," he states, his hand still on my back.

"No, you stay here. I won't take long." I start backing away, but he follows closely as if he were my bodyguard. "You didn't have to come."

"It's been four days. Unless you physically tell me you don't want me around, I'm not going anywhere," he shouts, his body flush against mine from how crowded and loud it is.

A zoo breaks loose in my stomach, making my body feel fuzzy and warm inside.

When we get to the restroom, he grabs my hand and spins me around.

"Do you not want me around?" The dim lighting makes it hard to see his face, but I don't have to look at him to know he's hurt. "Do you want me to leave you alone so they can flirt with you?" he grits, breathing out harshly. "Is that what you want?"

My brows hike up, but I bite my tongue before asking something I'll regret.

I don't owe him anything. He doesn't owe me anything, but the tequila is taking a quick effect, the buzz is a little more heightened, making the words easily tumble out of my mouth.

"Are you sleeping with other people?" My cheeks flame at the stupid question. I can't believe I succumbed to this, but I really need to know.

"No." He doesn't miss a beat. "Answer my question."

But I don't. "Why not?"

"Because, Josefine, you've rewired the way I feel touch. Touching anyone that isn't you feels overwhelming and so wrong. It's like my brain can't process that it's not you. I don't know how to make sense of that but I don't want to touch anyone that isn't *you*. You're incomparable. And no, I haven't touched anyone to find that out. I just know. I can't and won't touch anyone that isn't you. Does that answer your question? Can you answer mine now?"

I try to unravel what he said and not twist his words into something they're not.

He made sense; I get what he said. I'm just having a hard time believing I have that effect on him. I've done nothing but bring him stress and test his patience.

"I don't care about the other guys."

Daniel lets go of my wrist and grabs my hips, spinning and guiding me until my back touches the wall. He leans in as I tip my head back. "Tell me. Do you not want me around?"

"I always want you around."

"Why did you let him get so close to you?" he questions, his voice dropping an octave.

"You were watching me?"

"I'm always watching you."

Oh. "Because I wanted to stop thinking about you."

I don't know if it's the tequila or my brain's unwillingness to cooperate, but I can't get it to stop formulating words that I swore I'd never say out loud.

"You were thinking about me?" His fingers lift up to curve around my waist, idly brushing my skin.

"I'm always thinking about you."

"Did you miss me?" I hear the smile in his voice.

That shuts every loud thought in my head, focusing on three words.

"All the time," I awkwardly admit. "But I don't want you to think I'm going to start being clingy. I promise I'm not. You were gone for a while, and it was weird not having you around, so don't think too much into it. I missed you, but it's not a big deal, so don't make it one."

I look away, hating how my entire body burns at my admittance.

He hooks a finger underneath my chin and tilts my head back, forcing me to look up at him. "You're a big deal to me, so I'm going to make it one. And I want you to be clingy, just for once, *be clingy* for me, Jos."

I grimace, hoping that hides the blush on my face. "That's embarrassing. No thank you."

"Can I be clingy?"

"Aren't you already?"

He chuckles, cups the side of my neck, and leans down. God, how I missed the sound of that. "Not really but I'll show you clingy."

"Oh yay. Just what I wanted," I reply sarcastically.

"Don't pretend. Be honest with me. Admit you like me needy," he gruffly says against my lips. "And while you're at it, tell me whatever's happening between us is staying strictly *between us*."

Blood roars in my ears, and my body is floating as if I were on cloud nine.

"Isn't it obvious?"

"Say it," he demands, not content with my answer.

Everything I say to him, what I do, how I feel, it's a lot. That's why I didn't want to open up, to talk about what we're doing because it scares me. But what's the point in denying what we both know is true?

There's no point in holding back.

"Yes, I like you needy and whatever is happening between us is staying strictly between us. That shouldn't have been a question. You already take up most of my time; I don't have it for someone else." And I don't want to give it to anyone else.

"Even when I'm not around?" His lips graze mine.

"Even when you're not around," I reiterate, pecking his lips because I can't help myself anymore. "Happy?"

"Always with you." He eliminates the tiny space between our lips and kisses me hard.

45

JOSEFINE

"You have glitter on your lips." I lift my finger to the corner of his mouth, rubbing the shimmer away, but it only spreads up to his cheek.

"I don't care." He tips his head just slightly to the side and kisses my wrist.

We're still in the dimly lit hall. There are a few people passing by, couples like us leaning against the walls, making out or talking. I only noticed them once we pulled back to catch our breaths.

We said we were going to head back to where everyone is at, but every time we move, his lips find mine. I'd stop him but I haven't found the will to let that happen.

"It doesn't bother you? You have it all over you." Remnants of my lip gloss are smeared outside the line of his lips. It's not much but enough that when the light hits him just right, it glimmers.

"Nah, it's probably not enough." His fingers teasingly glide up my back and into my shirt but falter. He lays his palm flat on my back and drags it side to side. "No bra?" His voice deepens. "Hmm..."

Daniel sucks in a breath, slipping his fingers around my rib cage and they rise beneath the curve of my breast.

Maybe I should stop him, considering there's other people around, but I don't. I let him touch me. His thumb caresses the underside of my breast and my breath hitches when his thumb flicks my hard nipple.

He keeps his eyes on me, still softly stroking me. "You look beautiful."

My lips quirk. "Say what you really want to say."

"I'm trying to be respectful."

I silently laugh, squeezing my thighs. "Your hand is on my boob. I don't think there's anything respectful about that."

His Adam's apple bobs and I feel his free hand linger at the back of the waistband of my skirt. "I mean it, you look beautiful."

"But?" I provoke, pushing my chest into him.

"But you also look really fucking hot. You'd drown me in holy water if you saw what's inside my head right now." Daniel clamps my nipple hard and twirls it between his fingers.

I squirm, biting my bottom lip to stop myself from moaning.

"Your body is so accessible to me. I could easily push you into that restroom. Lift your skirt and pull your shirt up, bend you over, and eat you out or fuck you. Or do both."

I close my eyes as a faint moan claws out.

"Eyes on me, baby," he roughly orders and pinches my nipple hard again, his blunt fingernails digging into the tender skin.

I gasp, forcing them open and shiver when he shoves his hand inside the back of my skirt. His fingers graze the top of my ass cheeks and hook under the waistband thong.

"What color is it?" he asks.

"Green," I answer breathlessly. He doesn't ask but I'm certain he knows I wore it for him. I wasn't sure if he'd show, but despite today's holiday, I put them on thinking of him.

"I bet it's pretty." I get caught up with the feel of his fingers on my nipple and throaty words that I don't realize what he's doing until I'm tensing and gasping loudly.

He pulls my thong up, the wet material wedging between my

pussy lips, grazing my throbbing clit. I shudder at the euphoric sensation and bite my trembling lip, discreetly rocking my hips as he continues to pull.

"Can you come like this?" he asks, his voice a rough husk.

I attempt to shrug but my shoulders are so stiff with tension, I can hardly move them.

"I think you can." He kisses the corner of my mouth, whispering, "No, I know you can." He stops tugging but keeps a firm hold on my thong, leaving it lodged between my folds. "You keep your eyes on me and keep rocking your hips," he encourages, rubbing my nipple between his fingers. "Yeah, just like that. You're doing so good. You're almost there, aren't you?"

I break out into a sweat, feeling embarrassed and aroused as I grind myself into practically nothing. He's hardly playing with my nipple, hardly doing anything really, but it's enough that I feel my body tighten with anticipation.

"Y-yeah," I sputter.

He smirks and leans down until I feel his breath on my ear. "Hurry up and come."

"Why?" I stupidly ask, feeling dazed.

"Because I said so." It's so fucking arrogant and slightly demeaning, but it causes my entire body to seize and the orgasm to burst.

I drop my head to his chest, swallowing back the moan that threatens to spill out as my body spasms against him. He holds me close to him, arms wrapped around my back in a hot embrace.

I'm not sure how long we stand here but the spasms don't stop, only become faint over time. "Oh my gosh."

"I told you before and I'll tell you again, you have a really needy pussy, Jos. What would you do without me?"

I weakly hum. "I'd be fine. I have my fingers and toys." Although they wouldn't do anything as amazing as he does.

He pulls back to stare down at me. "You have them?"

"Yeah, not many, but I do."

He groans, dropping his forehead to mine. "I'm not going to make it all night."

I stupidly smile and try to pry away from him, but he doesn't let me. "Let go. I need to clean myself up."

"Fuck that, you're going to feel what I did to you." He grips my hip with one hand and adjusts himself with the other. God, he's so huge, it did nothing for him. "If another guy comes up to you, I want you to remember this and feel what I do to you. Because only I can do this to you. Only me."

I clench my thighs from the roughness of his words, feeling how wet and sticky they are. God, he sounds so hot and possessive. "Okay, at least let me fix my thong."

"No. You're going to stay just like that and once we get home, I'll help you clean up."

I wonder how much Pen and Vi will hate me if I leave now?

"Interesting how the same color lip gloss you were wearing is now on Daniel's face." Vienna's gaze darts to his face and back to me.

When we returned to the bar area, he got pulled away to play pool by a couple of guys on the team. He must feel us staring because he turns and his heated eyes collide with mine. He winks at me and turns but not before I catch the glitter on his cheeks and the glimmer on the seam of his lips.

"Yeah, interesting." I lift my shoulder in a half shrug, shifting on my feet only to feel the lace graze my clit.

I take a sip of my drink and relish the cool liquid and how it helps me sort of mellow out. The thong is buried deep in my pussy, and every time I move, it rubs against my clit. It's also drenched, making my thighs slick with my arousal.

It should feel uncomfortable, but I'm more turned on than I've ever been. I'm also restless, frustrated, and ready to come again.

"So, I'm going to pretend I didn't see Danny's tongue shoved down your throat." Penelope stands between us. She scrunches her nose but grins. "I thought clothes were going to come off."

I choke on my saliva. I knew someone was going to see us, but I didn't expect his sister of all people.

"Look at his face. He's practically wearing her lip gloss and he looks proud of it too." Vi snorts. "Please, so much for getting it out of your system."

"What?" Pen blanches. "This isn't the first time?"

Their eyes zero on me, but I draw mine to my Irish mule. I think that's what it's called; I'm not too sure, but it's a St. Patrick's Day drink. I take a long drink, but I can't savor the whiskey because they're scrutinizing me.

"Don't ask questions you don't want the answer to," I reply nonchalantly but my body reacts differently, thinking of all the times he's made me come and the one time he made me squirt. I still can't believe that happened.

"Oh my gosh, how many times are we talking?" Vienna grips my arms and shakes it. "Do tell all your filthy dirty secrets."

Pen grimaces but doesn't beg me to stop talking.

"Are we talking about kissing or coming?"

Both their eyes go round, but their expressions are so different, it's comical. Vi looks like she's on the brink of losing her shit, ready to hear every detail. Pen looks disturbed but something else lurks in her eyes. I don't know how to explain it, but she looks almost happy...I think?

"Why are you—" I abruptly stop mid-sentence, locking in on a familiar face.

I normally wouldn't look or care, but his face looks different. There's a nasty slight yellowish-green bruise on the left side of his face.

The last time he looked busted up was when Daniel punched him because of Amanda. Did he do it again? Is Amanda right? Will he eventually end up back with her?

I drink, hoping it'll numb the sinking feeling in my stomach.

I shouldn't care. Right from the get-go I knew he might still be stuck on her. I let him use me to distract himself because in some way I'm doing the same. Distracting myself from the emptiness...*though* it's been a while since I felt the aching void that felt endless, on a loop.

Who am I kidding though? I was never using him to distract myself. I did it because I liked what he did to me. I *like* him.

"What are you—oh." Pen tracks my field of vision and looks a little too smug when she grins. "He deserved that."

Does she want them back together? I'm going to throw up.

"Who are you talking about?" Vi scans the bar with a puzzled expression.

"Bryson," she says with disdain. "Danny warned him."

"Wait, Josie's ex? What happened?" Vi asks a little too eagerly while I hope that I get drunk fast enough, I don't hear. "Why did Danny warn him? What did he warn him about?"

Her curious eyes bounce between Pen and me, but I shrug indifferently, at least I hope I do.

"You don't know?" Pen asks me.

"About Daniel punching Bryson over Amanda? Yeah, I—"

She scoffs but her brows arc in surprise, then flit to the pool tables before she looks at me. "No, he didn't punch Bryson over Amanda. This was over you. I can't believe Danny didn't tell you."

I'm taken aback, my cup suspended in the air. "Over me?"

"The first time was a warning. The second time was Bryson fucking around and finding out."

I reel back in astonishment, shaking my head in disbelief. "But Bryson said—I thought—are you sure?"

Her eyes narrow. "What did Bryson say?"

"That it was over Amanda. I figured it was true because they dated for a while and well, I don't know. I figured Daniel got jealous or something."

She rolls her eyes. "If that was the case, Danny would've done something a long time ago. The worst he did when he found out she cheated was yell at Bryson, but he hasn't done anything since then. That's until you. A month or so ago, he was talking shit about you in the locker room. Daniel punched and warned him not to do it again. The second time was on the first Friday of this month, I think. I don't know what was said after their game but all I know is that Danny didn't hold back."

My jaw falls open. I close my mouth, but it goes slack again. "He said he accidentally punched the wall because Angel moved and—"

"Oh, shit." She winces. "I guess you weren't supposed to know. Ugh, I don't know why he didn't tell you, but I promise he meant well. Don't be mad."

It must be the expression that I'm making because she studies me with caution, but Vienna has a megawatt grin on her face.

"I need to go talk to him." I march over to him, not sure how to feel about what she just told me.

"Wait, Josie!" Pen calls behind me. "Don't be mad!"

I ignore her and as I get closer, Daniel spots me. His lips cast downward at my face, and he stares at me with concern.

"Jos, what's wrong?" he asks once I'm standing in front of him.

"Why did you punch Bryson?"

46

DANIEL

Josefine looks furious.

I've seen her mad but never like this, and it pains me to think she's angry because I hurt him.

"What were you thinking?" she asks once we're outside and away from the bar.

I lift my hat, dragging my fingers through my hair before I place it back but backwards. Her eyes flick to it for a moment before darting back to me.

"He was talking shit."

"He's always talking shit. That doesn't mean you should punch him." Her face scrunches with displeasure. "Why didn't you tell me the truth?"

I exhale harshly through my nose. "Because I didn't want you to know what he said because it's shit. I don't want you to think you are those things, and I didn't want to hurt you."

"I don't need you to protect me." She repeatedly points at her chest with her index finger. She does it so hard, I hear each thump.

I grab her hand, making her stop. "Not too hard." Her stiff hand softens in mine, and she looks at me like she hadn't realized she was doing that. "I still think about that night on the cliff. I sometimes dream about it. Sometimes I think of the what-ifs, Josefine, and when I do, I get really fucking sad. I don't want you to hurt yourself. I don't want anyone to hurt you. So yeah, I punched Bryson and I don't regret it. I'd do it again and again."

"I'm sorry you had to witness that." She scowls, yanking her hand back. "I'm sorry I've put you through that, but I'm not going to kill myself. Take your pity and obligation elsewhere because I don't need it. And next time, let him run his mouth but don't punch him."

She turns but I stand in front of her, not letting her walk away. "Are you upset I hurt him?"

The question both hurts and pisses me off. She's made it abundantly clear she doesn't like him, but what if I misread the signs.

She incredulously stares up at me but then brings her palms to her face. She drops them and a devastated expression mars her face. "No! I'm not upset you hurt him. I'm upset, I'm annoyed, I'm frustrated that *you* could've gotten hurt. That *you* could've gotten in trouble."

Oh. "You're worried about me?"

"Yes! I worry about you because I care about you! You could've broken your hand or gotten suspended, or hell if I know but don't do something stupid like that for me ever again."

My lips uncontrollably rise.

"Stop smiling." She frowns. "I'm not worth it and I wish you'd understand that. I'm sorry you had to witness that. I'm sorry you dream and think about it, but I haven't thought about ending my life since that night. You don't have to worry about me. Bryson's words aren't going to set me off. It's not the first time he's talked shit about me, and I know it won't be the last. So whatever he says, just ignore him."

"Josie." I take a step forward, and she takes three back.

"No, I'm mad at you right now."

"Josie." Another step forward, but this time she only takes two back.

"I can't believe you did that and lied to me," she huffs out.

Grabbing her hips, I tug her, closing the space between us. "You're worth it. I need you to understand that I don't like the thought of anyone fucking with you. I'm not doing this out of pity or because I feel obligated, but I do think about that night because..." I swallow. "Because I just do. I can't help it, and I can stand here and lie but there's no point." Raising my hands, I cup the side of her neck. "I care so deeply for you and it's not because of how we met. I care for you more than I care about anything or anyone. I need you to understand that I'd do anything for you. I need you to understand that I don't regret what I did and wouldn't change anything about it."

She's not frowning but she has a cute little pout. "You say I'm stubborn, but you should look in the mirror. You're worse."

I'm smiling again. "For you, I'll be whatever."

"I thought you had punched him because of Amanda," she says in a quiet voice like she's embarrassed to have admitted that.

My brows furrow, dropping my hands to her waist. "Why?"

"Because I saw him the first time you punched him. He lied about it at first but then said it was because of her. I figured you snapped because you got jealous."

I peer over my shoulder at the bar, contemplating going back to punch him again.

"Daniel." She cups my jaw, urging me to look at her. "Don't think about it."

"I'm not going to, I promise." I let the thought go. "I don't care about her. I stopped a long time ago. I neither like nor love her."

"Why are you telling me that?" She drops her hand, letting it hang limply at her side.

"Because I want you to know you're all I care about. All I think about. All I want."

My ongoing issues with my asphyxiating thoughts stopped me from saying it out loud. I don't want to be her problem, something she needs to worry about. But I want to be selfish, just this once. I want to make her mine, and I want her to want me just as much.

I'm not going to push because I don't know where she truly stands with me. She doesn't believe in love, I know that much, but I'd love to be the difference. I'd love to win her over, but I don't want to rush it either.

Her eyes narrow and search mine. They don't soften or look happy; she looks at me with an unreadable expression that both unnerves and flusters me.

"You've developed Stockholm syndrome. I'm sorry," she says seriously, and I can't help but laugh.

"Jos—"

"No, you're not saying what I think you're saying." She shakes her head in disbelief.

"I am. I like you, Josie, and I really want to stop pretending like I don't."

She pulls away and paces, bringing her hands behind her head. Is she…freaking out? Fuck, what did I do?

"Josie, stop. Look at me." I grab her by the shoulders, steadying her gaze with mine. "Talk to me. Tell me what's wrong."

"I'm severely and mentally fucked up. You don't need that. I'm giving you an out now. Run, seriously, while you can because I am not someone you should like."

I wrap my arms around her shoulders, holding her firmly against me. If only she saw how dark it can get in my head, she'd be the one running.

"My heart begs for you."

"Maybe it's heartburn?" she mumbles into my shoulder.

I smile. "It's not. I promise. Lately and for a while my heart and mind have been in a complicated relationship. They can't agree so things don't make sense or align, but you have somehow made them work together."

Her breath catches and body goes taut, but she doesn't say anything.

"Josie." I hook my finger under her chin, making her look up at me. God, she's so beautiful. I swallow hard, knowing I'm about to ask something that might ruin our relationship. That's if my confession didn't already. "Do you like me?"

I hold my breath and feel my heart plummet because she doesn't answer and looks away.

Oh.

Oh.

"That's okay. I didn't expect you to feel the same way. I just thought you should know." A rock roots deep in my throat, making it hard to get any other words.

"No, uh," she mumbles and looks up at me. "I," she sighs and her lips twitch into a small, awkward smile. "I do like you."

The rock instantly disappears. "You're not messing with me, are you?"

"No, I'm serious. I'm sorry it took me a second to admit that. It's just that I...I don't know." She shrugs. "This freaks me out a little. I've been thinking a lot about my feelings and you recently. I want you. I like you."

"But?" I know there's one. I can feel the discomfort radiating off her body.

"If I tell you something, you won't laugh at me, will you?" Josie tears her gaze away from mine and pulls away from my hold. She twirls her ring around her finger and puffs out a quivering breath.

"No, I promise I won't." I give her space, tucking my hands in my pockets to stop from reaching out to her.

She closes her eyes before lowering her head. "I don't want to lose you as a friend. I don't know if I want to take a chance on my feelings, knowing there's a possibility of losing you if things don't work out."

I know it took her a lot to gather those words and say them out loud. I'm so proud of her.

Screw the space, I take her into my arms. "That's not going to happen. We'll take things slow, we don't have to label this, share beds, or change anything. We'll take it day by day."

She wraps tentative arms around me. "Okay but...sharing beds wouldn't be the worst thing in the world."

I draw back, looking down at her. "I want that as long as you want it."

"I do," she abashedly admits.

I smile at her. "I'm strictly yours like I hope you're strictly mine." My heart thrashes, liking the sound of that.

Her lips stretch into a small smile. "Strictly mine. Strictly yours."

"We might have traumatized your sister." Josie pants against my lips as we stumble into the house.

I slam the door shut behind me, she drops her purse on the floor, and the keys follow suit, jangling loud on the hardwood floor.

"How so?" I lift her and she wraps her legs around my waist, causing her skirt to roll up her thighs. I pin her against the wall as she weaves her fingers through my hair at the nape.

I slip my hand down and under her skirt, cupping her ass hard. She moans, angling her head to the side to give me access to her neck.

"She said she saw your tongue shoved down my—" She gasps when I bite hard on the erratic pulse beneath her jaw, then I lick it to soothe the sting. She moans, knocking my hat off as she rakes her fingers up my hair. "Throat."

"She'll be all right." I grunt, gently sucking, careful not to leave a mark even though it's all I want to do. "I have something for you," I whisper against her neck.

She shudders and stops pulling my hair, but still keeps her fingers knotted between the locks. "What is it?"

"It's upstairs." I peck her lips, feeling a little nervous about giving it to her.

She tries to climb off me, but I don't let her. I keep a firm grip on her ass as I make my way through the house and up the stairs until we're in my bedroom.

"You're surreal." I kiss her again because I can't get enough of her and I know I never will. And now, even though there's no label to what we are, she's my girl, mine, and I intend to keep it that way forever.

"I hope that's a good thing," she says, bemused and a little bashful too.

"I'm sorry." I sit on the edge of my bed with Josefine straddling me.

"What are you sorry about?" Her brows pinch together and her lips purse like she wants to say more but doesn't know how.

"About everything. Before you say it's not my fault, I'm still sorry. I know it changes nothing, but I hate those who made you think…who made you feel…who…I hate them so much."

"Don't hate. It's not worth it." She cups my cheek, offering me the faintest smile. "Please stay you. I like your soft heart."

I smile, the anger fading away. "My soft heart?"

Her face flushes and she casts her gaze down. "Yeah, you have this thing where you see the good in things. I don't want that to change about you."

I dip my head to meet her stare. "Okay, I promise it won't."

We hug. I'm not sure how long we do this for, but I lock up and enjoy every single second of it. It's not until I open my eyes and spot the bag that I remember why I brought her up here.

"I hope you like what I got you." I stand and sit her on my bed.

"You really shouldn't have." Her tone is aloof, but I note the curiosity burning in her eyes.

"You know me; I love a good holiday." My cheeks warm as I hand her the bag and the card I made her.

She grins, opening the card first. It's not as thoughtful as the others. I've been busy with baseball and classes, and now that Bryson and I have to share a hotel room at away games, it made it hard to work on it.

But she reads it and stares at it like I've gifted her something expensive. "It's not as great as the others but—"

She shakes her head, cutting me off. "No, shut up. I love it. I'm so happy you're here, baby."

My heart painfully squeezes. It shouldn't, but hearing her say that makes me feel glad I stuck with my promise.

Shaking off the thought, I lift a brow, smirking. "Did you just call me baby?"

"I was testing it. Not sure how I feel about it though." It's cute when she blushes and she's doing that now. "What do you think?"

"You can call me whatever you want." I perch on the bed next to her. Truthfully, I want to hear it again, but I don't want her to feel pressured. I kiss her shoulder and snake my arms around her waist.

"I don't like cuddling," she says, and I tense, drawing my hands away but she stops me. "Sorry, I didn't mean to sound so dry, and I didn't mean I wanted you to move." She pauses and exhales a shuddering breathing. "I don't like cuddling with anyone, but I really like it with you. I like doing things with you. So, uh, if you want to, you know, hold my hand, or hug me or even kiss me, you can. Whenever you want. If you want."

I'm stupidly smiling and holding her so close to me. I'm sure at any point she'll beg me to let go, but she nuzzles into me. "I'll do whatever you want. Anything you want. Whatever you say, I'll do it."

"Okay." She nods and looks away, but I know she's smiling and probably feeling shy about it.

"I'm yours, Josie. You can also do those things and more. Whatever you want."

Hopefully this means coming to my games and wearing my

jersey. I don't say that out loud, but I know she knows what I'm referring to.

She nods and focuses on the bag. My heart hammers as she pulls the white tissue out then gingerly grabs the yellow Care Bear. Her brows shoot up and she sucks in a sharp breath.

"I saw this in Alabama and thought of you." I study her expression but it's stoic.

Josie stares at it for a long moment, fingers rubbing over the yellow faux fur. Silence eats up the seconds and maybe even minutes, but then she stands, looking a little spaced out.

"I-I need a minute." She sets everything down and walks out of my room, not sparing me a glance.

I don't know what that's about but I'm up and following behind her into her room. "Josie, hey, talk to me, baby. What's wrong?"

She shakes her head, and her back is to me, but I see her wipe her face with her arm. "It's nothing, I'm fine. I just needed a minute." She sniffles.

"Hey." I'm standing in front of her and embracing her in a hug. "Talk to me. I'm your person, remember?"

"It's stupid. It's nothing." But she defeatedly drops her head on my chest and sniffles louder.

"I'm here," I softly offer and rub her back.

At first, she doesn't say anything and then I think she won't until she shrugs. "It's honestly really stupid. You're going to laugh, but I didn't have toys growing up. Mom thought they were a waste of time. She didn't have them as a kid and thought I didn't need them either. Like I said, it's really stupid. I don't even know why I'm crying." Her voice cracks. "I just need a minute. I'll be over there in a moment."

I hold her tighter, kissing the crown of her head. "It's not stupid. Let it out. Your feelings are valid."

"She wasn't a horrible person. She was strict, but I had everything I needed. I don't even know why I'm crying," she grumbles and pushes away from me. "I'm okay, I promise. You can leave.

I'm not going to be mad. Like I said, I just need a minute. I'll be all right."

"Here's the thing, and listen to me closely..." I cup her jaw with both hands, staring at her red, tear-filled eyes. "When I said I like you, I didn't say that for the hell of it. When I said I like you, I meant I like *every* version of you. That includes all the moments whether they're good or bad. That means all your little expressions, all your dry snarky comments, all your smiles, laughs, and everything that comes from you. I like it all, Josefine. I know it's hard for you to open up. I know it's scary and I know this is probably a lot for you, but *I am here* and as long as you want me in your life, I'm not going anywhere. So..." I bring my lips to her forehead and kiss it but let them linger there. "I'll give you a moment. Take your time. I have forever."

I kiss her forehead and let her go, but I don't make it far before she's clutching onto my hand.

"Please don't go," she quietly pleads, clutching onto my hand hard.

I wrap her up in a tight embrace, and she does the same. "I'm right here. I'm not going anywhere."

47

DANIEL

"You know, I'm starting to think you lied to me." I lift my goggles and wipe the water off my face with my palm.

Josie's brows scrunch in. "Lied about what?"

"I don't think you really like me."

She rolls her eyes, sputtering an incredulous laugh. "Okay, break is over."

I grab her waist before she can move. "I just got back. I thought we'd watch a movie and cuddle, not be here. It's not that I don't appreciate you doing this. I do. I just really want to hold you." I circle my arms around her waist, tugging her close to my chest.

Her lips curl up just a little. "You're so needy."

"I am for you." I kiss the crown of her head.

It's been ten days since St. Patrick's Day and since things sort of changed between us. It's nothing drastic, but enough change that my feelings for Josefine have evolved into something more fierce.

Our relationship doesn't have a label, but we're doing enough that Josie doesn't feel overwhelmed or suffocated. And it's enough for me. I'm not second-guessing what we are because I know she likes me. She's allowing me in and that's all I want.

"That sounds enticing."

"Yeah?" I slip my hands under the water and cup her ass. She lifts her legs and wraps them around me.

"Yeah." She tips her head back, lips brushing against mine ever so slightly. "But we're not going anywhere until we're done."

I groan but peck her lips. "Tease."

"And if you want me to go to the game tomorrow, you gotta show me that you've improved."

I softly groan. "Really, Jos? I thought you'd come now because I'm yours and you're mine. I'll beg."

I'll never get over the tint of pink on her cheeks anytime I say that.

"That changes nothing, Garcia. I know you don't care about this, but I really do." She cups my cheeks, softly smiling at me. "I want you to learn. It's important to me, and it should be to you too."

Dropping my gaze, I say nothing because I don't know what to say. She's been teaching me for two months now and while I've slightly improved, I don't believe I'll ever learn. I keep begging that she give up, but she's stubborn and won't.

"Come here." She unhooks her legs from me and grabs my hand, pulling me with her. We stop at the wall. She lifts up, sits on the edge of the pool, and motions for me to do the same. I don't question and do as she says.

For a while neither one of us says anything. I think I know what she's going to say and while I could work a way around the conversation, I decide to let it be. Usually anxiety spikes, sending my mind and heart to go manic, attempting to abort and run, hide, do something other than talk about what I usually would rather bury, but she somehow makes that not happen.

I can't say my anxiety and dark consuming thoughts have disappeared, but she makes me feel really good. She's therapy and medicine all in one. I feel anchored and high all at once with her.

I don't think she knows the control, the grip, she has over me.

I don't think she understands what I'd do for her, how strongly I feel for her.

She grabs my hand and laces her fingers through mine. "Do you want to talk about what happened?"

A knot forms in my throat and my chest tightens. "Uh...I..."

"You don't have to tell me anything, but I want you to know that I'm here." She delicately traces figure eights on top of my hand, over my knuckles, along my fingers.

I kiss the top of her head, and stare over the horizon, absorbing my surroundings. It's a pretty peaceful Thursday. The air smells saltier than ever and the seagulls are loud but not obnoxious. In the distance, I hear the ocean's wave lap, and the sky is painted in pretty streaks of pink, purple, and orange.

I hardly see her. I don't want to ruin today with the depressing memories, but I also do want to talk. It's getting harder and harder not to speak about it. I stopped a long time ago because I didn't want to sound like a broken record.

Puffing out a fatigued breath, I rake my fingers through my wet hair. I shift uncomfortably, feeling on edge, my gaze flitting to the deep part of the pool.

"I..." I sullenly laugh. "I'm sorry, I thought I could do this, but I can't." My throat constricts and my body feels painfully stiff.

"That's okay. You don't have to say anything," she softly supplies, still dragging her finger along my skin. "I'm here either way."

I look down at her and she looks up at me. "I had to be sedated," I somehow manage to say.

She doesn't look shocked or confused; she just nods, and her gaze darts to our hands.

"They said he was dead, but I..." I clear my hoarse throat. "I couldn't believe that. I was there. I saw it happen. I saw them do CPR. I saw his body and how his eyes..." My teeth clatter and I grind them to make it stop. I breathe out heavily and slowly. "Just an hour ago, he was laughing, and then he was not. They said he was dead, and my brain—they said I was in shock." I don't blink as tears fill my vision, blurring everything around me. "I had to be sedated and when I woke up, I had to hear it again and again because Mom couldn't stop repeating it. It was like if she said it enough times, it wouldn't be real. And then my dad, he..." I shake my head. "Leaving the hospital without him should've made it real, but it didn't. Leaving the hospital was..." My voice cracks and I drop my head because the tears are coming and I can't make them stop. "I'm sorry."

"Don't be," she whispers despondently like she understands, and I know she does. "Let yourself feel. Making yourself numb will only make you want to stop breathing. So, talk to me. Let yourself feel. It hurts and that'll probably never go away, but you can share your pain with me. I can't promise I'll make it go away, but I'll do my best to lessen it."

She raises her hands, wipes my tears away from my cheeks, and continues tracing her finger over my hand.

"I don't want to give you my pain."

"I have pain; you have pain. I'm pretty sure they'll somehow cancel each other out."

That's nowhere near being true, but I find myself laughing. She peers up at me, a tender smile on her face as her eyes search mine.

"I know I didn't make sense, and I know I should tell you the whole story. And it's not that I don't want to tell you how he—"

"It made sense, and you don't need to tell me anything," she reassures me. "Grief is funny," she repeats my words from a while ago and squeezes my hand. "And really weird."

"Do you...do you want to talk about your mom?" I ask, remembering what she said not too long ago about which version of her to miss or what she should miss about her.

She shrugs and her nail digs a little deeper into my skin, but I don't mind it.

"I feel guilty," she starts and kicks her feet under the water. "For not missing the version of her I had. Guilty for wishing I could've gotten a different version of her. Guilty because she worked hard to make me be her, and now I can't step foot in a place that's named after her. I feel guilty because I want to hate her, but I can't. I feel guilty because I'm mad she left everything under my name. Now I have it all and I don't know what to do with it. I don't know what to do with my life, and I feel guilty because how dare she fucking die." Her voice breaks and a guttural groan rips from the back of her throat. "I know that sounds so messed up. I know I'm a shitty daughter for feeling this way. It's not like she planned to die." She slouches, releasing a dejected and empty sigh. "I'm sorry. This is why I don't like talking."

"Don't be sorry." I pull her into a hug and she lets me. "Share your pain with me. Let yourself feel."

"I haven't been numb in a while. I look forward to things..."

"Yeah?" I breathe easily. "What kind of things?"

She nods. "Things like...waking up with you in the mornings. Sharing coffee with you. Talking to you. Being with you. You," she shyly says, and I smile.

"I feel the same way. I look forward to all things consisting of you."

She bites her lip as if she were trying to conceal her smile, but it's so big, I see it.

"Pen told me about Monica's offer. You should think about it. I'll go with you if you need me to go."

"Your sister really doesn't know how to keep her mouth shut," she humorously says.

"In her defense, I was asking her about you."

She quietly laughs. "You think I should take it?"

"I think you should do what makes you happy. You already do swimming lessons, and I know you enjoy those." But I can tell this isn't enough for her. She craves more; she just doesn't want to put herself back in a place that'll remind her of her mom. "Do this because you want to, not because you have to fulfill something that your mom would've wanted."

She takes in my words but stays quiet. I seize up, wondering if I messed up by saying that, but she wraps her arms around my neck and breathes out like she's relieved.

"Do you want to talk about the email you've been putting off?"

I don't mean to squeeze her a little tighter, but she doesn't complain or push me away. "Knowing he's not here to watch me do it. Knowing he won't get to do it." I admit, "I don't feel like I deserve it."

"I get that, but you do deserve it. Don't let your mind trick you into feeling you're not worthy of it because I know no one deserves it more than you."

I want to disagree, but she speaks up.

"You deserve good things, Daniel. All and every good thing, you deserve." She breathes out a poignant sigh. "I hate I'm sorrys wholeheartedly. Anytime I hear them, my skin itches. It's all I heard when Mom passed," she whispers in my ear with a gripping pain, I feel every tremor in her voice choke my soul. "So I shouldn't say this because maybe you'll hate it too, but I'm so sorry." She shakily breathes, voice catching in her throat. "I'm sorry you're hurting. I'm sorry I can't take your pain away. If I could, I would."

I squeeze my eyes shut and hold her. If she knew about the dark fog, it'd make her feel worse.

I need to be happy for her. I can do that. I can be happy.

"It's okay." I cup her jaw and tip her head back. I hate myself as I see her red-rimmed eyes and the tears that cascade down her cheeks. "I'll be fine." I smile, hoping it's big enough, bright enough, just enough she doesn't worry. "I promise." I wipe away the tears and kiss her lips. "Don't be sad. I'm okay. I promise. Come on, let's keep the lesson going. I really want you to come tomorrow." I kiss her one last time and pull her for another hug. "I'm fine."

48

JOSEFINE

I FEEL HAPPY.

It's hard to believe that I'm actually thinking that, but I am. Granted, there's this gnawing feeling. I'm not trying to be pessimistic, but I can't help but feel like I'm overlooking something. I just don't know what it is.

"It's about time you came," Pen says as we make our way down the steps to take our seats in the stadium.

"I kind of gave Daniel an ultimatum. Otherwise, I wouldn't be here." That's a lie. I would have definitely been here. Before, I didn't have a reason, but now I do. He's mine.

"What was that?" she asks, elated.

"That if I didn't see any improvements during our lessons, I wouldn't come." I follow behind her as she steers us into the row we'll be sitting in. The row right next to the home dugout.

We take our seats and then she turns to look at me. Her eyes soften in admiration and her smile equally matches it. "Thanks for not giving up on him."

"You don't need to thank me. I'm just—"

"I do. He trusts you and has made more progress with you than he ever has with anyone."

"Did he tell you about it?"

"Not willingly. I had to pry it out of him. He doesn't sound anxious talking about it like he used to. And he raves about you, so you must be doing something right." She grins.

"He does?" I twist my ring, hating how easily my cheeks warm. I've no doubt she's clocked it because she's giddy now.

"Yeah, it's 'Josie said I'm doing a good job' or 'Josie said she believes in me' and 'Josie this, Josie that.'" She leans in like she's going to tell me a secret. "I know this is going to sound biased because he's my brother, but please give him a chance. He's—and don't tell him I said this—a pretty great guy. He cooks, he's sweet, his love language is acts of service, he's loyal. That's not even one fourth of all his great qualities. Put him out of his misery and give him a chance. I promise he'll be good to you."

My face is on fire and my lips are stretched so wide, my cheeks are starting to ache. I'm telling myself to cool it, but I can't. Daniel told me he wouldn't say anything about us until I gave him the green light.

I've been holding off because I'm afraid to make it real and then for everything to fall apart. I don't want to be scared, but Daniel isn't someone I'm messing around with for the hell of it. This is real and he's special to me. I don't want to mess things up.

"I can't..." I nervously tinker with the button on my jersey.

"Oh wait. You don't like him?" She backs away, face full of regret. "Don't listen to me, and don't feel bad about it. I'm sorry. I didn't mean to be pushy, but Danny likes you and I thought maybe you liked him because of the kiss at the bar. I completely misread the signs." She gives me a tight-lipped smile. "So...are you guys in a...friends-with-benefits kind of situation?" She scowls at her question, like she's disgusted to know that about her brother.

I can't relate but I guess I get it. If I had a sibling, I wouldn't want to know either.

"No, in a *relationship* type of situation."

She stares at me, perplexed. "Wait, what?"

I shouldn't say anything. This is something I should probably talk to Daniel about, but this is his sister. Maybe he won't mind.

"We're together. We're just taking it slow."

Her jaw falls slack, but slowly her lips curl into a radiant smile. She sits up, crossing a leg over the other, hand gripping the armrest. "So technically you guys are dating?"

I guess it's time to call it what it is. "Yeah, we're dating. Daniel's my boyfriend."

That sounds crazy to say but so nice. I really like the sound of that.

"I knew it!" an eager voice says behind me.

My body goes rigid, my neck too stiff to turn, but I don't have to because I recognize that voice.

"*Hola.*" Pen stands and greets her parents. When she sits, they stay standing, staring down at me. His mom, Esmeralda, is wearing the same smile Pen is, but her dad, Julio, he's just staring at me.

This isn't how I wanted to introduce myself to them again. I've spoken to his mom before but never his dad, except that one time we said hello at the bonfire.

When I don't stand, Esmeralda bends down to hug me, catching me by surprise. I know I should probably return it, but I don't. She doesn't look offended when she draws back.

"I'm so happy you came. I brought you the bread you told me you like so much. *Conchas*, *mantecadas*, and *orejas* but we left it in the hotel room. I would've brought it if I knew you'd be here. I'm sorry."

She thought of me. She remembered.

"Thank you, but it's okay. This was kind of last minute." I twist my ring again and tell them about the ultimatum.

They don't say anything at first, their gaze faraway. I side-eye Pen, wondering what I could've said wrong.

"Danny didn't tell them about the lessons," she answers my unspoken question.

My brows arc high, shocked that he didn't tell them and worried he probably didn't want them to know that.

"He's really letting you?" Julio asks me as something flashes across his eyes.

"He didn't want to at first, but we talked." I fiddle with the other rings. "And now we do this once a week. It's been a little hard with his schedule, but we're making it work."

"And he's making progress?" he questions with a strain in his voice.

"Yeah, slowly but surely, he's learning. He's a lot more confident than he was two months ago."

They both look shocked.

"Two months?" Esmeralda's voice is thick with emotion.

I nod, offering a small smile. "And I'll take as long as he needs. This isn't something that should be rushed."

"No, no, it's not." She places her palm on my shoulder. "Thank you for helping him."

"You don't need to thank me. I'm just doing my job."

Julio shakes his head. "We do. Danny would've never told us. He doesn't like—"

"*Papa*," Pen warns, sighing wearily. "Wonder why he doesn't?"

He rubs the nape of his neck. "Can you...keep us updated?"

"If Daniel wants that, I will," I answer.

His forehead wrinkles, eyes narrowing like he didn't like the answer, but he chuckles. "Thank you for being patient with him."

I sheepishly shrug.

He smiles like he understands how I feel. He's nice but stoic, it's weird and I kind of don't mind it. "You should come to the bakery sometime."

"Uh, yeah, one day."

"Anytime you want." Esmeralda grins, and they both take a seat next to Pen.

"Sorry about that," she whispers and digs in her clear vinyl bag, pulling out a baseball.

"That's okay. What'd you bring that for?"

"For you." She places it on my palm, and looks to the kids by the railing, getting their baseballs and jerseys signed by the players.

Daniel's taking pictures with a few kids and when they're done, his eyes instantly find mine. Sparks, flutters, butterflies—I'm not sure if those are the words or if there's one to describe the rush that spreads through my body at seeing him.

Whatever that word may be, I'm so happy, I can't remember ever genuinely feeling this. I place my palm to my chest, rubbing it because my heart is going crazy.

"Go." She gently shoves my shoulder, snapping me out of it. "The game will start soon."

I'm up and heading toward him. He tracks my movements, eyes set ablaze as they coast down my body then linger on the jersey with his number.

Mine do the same, trailing over every inch of him and the turquoise uniform with the white pinstripes he's wearing. He's so tall, broad, and muscular, I can't believe he's mine.

Which reminds me.

I stand in front of him and because of where I'm standing, he has to look up at me. This isn't the time or place for unholy thoughts, but he looks devastatingly handsome staring up at me from this angle.

I brace my hands on the thick railing, and he rests his on either side of me.

"I messed up."

He cocks his head, brows cinched with worry. "Why do you say that?"

"I know we said we'd take it slow, but I slipped up and told your sister we're dating. I also said you were my boyfriend and had no idea your parents were behind me, so now they know about us."

"Jos…" His brown eyes sparkle, and a megawatt smile splits across his face. His arms now dangle on either side of me. "I'm really trying to play it cool right now and not look like a dork, but you're standing here wearing my jersey and then you tell me that."

"You're not annoyed? I'm the one who said slow and now I'm telling the world you're my boyfriend." It was just his sister and parents, but I'm sure they're his world.

"Annoyed? Baby, I want the whole universe to know you're mine."

Now I'm cheesing. "Oh, so you and me, we're official now?"

"This has always been official to me," he gravely says but still smiles. "A label isn't going to determine what we are. I'm yours, strictly."

My heart is going crazy again and I'm feeling weirdly shy now. "Okay."

"You're so cute." His gaze sweeps over my face. I'm sure he's noticed how red I am and he knows it has nothing to do with how bright the sun is.

"Can you sign this?" I ask to take the attention away from my face because it's hot and I'm smiling more than I ever have in my life.

Daniel chuckles huskily, grabs the Sharpie from his pocket, and takes the ball. As he's writing, he says, "You look beautiful."

"Is that what you're really thinking?"

He briefly closes his eyes and smirks when they open. "Keeping it G, Jos. Don't do this to me now."

"I'm wearing green," I tease him.

His brows furrow before they set in a straight line with realization. He clicks his tongue and laughs under his breath. "The jersey and the green when we get home."

I roll my lips together and shrug. "Win first."

His dark eyes lock with mine, and challenge and heat swirls in them. "Here. I'll see you later, baby."

I'm grinning all the way back to my seat. I don't want to, but I can't help it; I feel so damn giddy. Pen looks the way I feel when I take my seat next to her, but she doesn't make a comment. Nor do her parents, but I feel them every so often look my way with smiles on their faces.

When I finally look at what he wrote on the ball, I laugh, garnering looks from Pen and her parents, but I don't look at them. I look up at my boyfriend, who's already looking at me.

Eyes on me

We're at the bottom of the sixth inning and Daniel's walkup song, "Pursuit of Happiness" blasts through the speaker as he walks up to bat.

"I don't know if Danny told you, but this was Adrian's favorite song and the last song he listened to before he passed," Pen solemnly says.

I glance at her, but she stares straight ahead. "He actually didn't, but he's shared things with me about Adrian."

"Yeah?" She stares at me, surprised.

"It's not a lot but he has. I know it's hard and I'm sure it must be hard for you too."

Her lips twist to the side. "It is but it's harder for him. Especially around this time of the year. The anniversary of Adrian's... death is coming up. So just a heads-up, if Danny looks off or acts a little different, that's why."

"No, he didn't tell me, but I'll keep that in mind."

Now that I think about it, I've noticed a shift in him. Sometimes I catch him zoning out or forcing his smiles. He thinks I don't notice, but I do. I've asked what's wrong, but he says he's tired or thinking about the draft or homework.

I know it's not personal, but I wish he'd let me in. Maybe it's my fault, and I shouldn't have let it go. I should've kept asking. Maybe I don't look approachable enough? Or maybe it's me and my constant whining about my dead mother who I hardly had a relationship with.

Florida's pitcher throws the ball, a fastball Pen says it's called. I still don't know the names of all the pitches—I'm not sure I'll ever know them—but I can kind of tell the difference between them.

He gets a strike on Daniel, but at the second pitch, Daniel makes contact with the ball. It's a fly ball, landing center field, but it bounces off the center fielder's glove and onto the grass. He quickly scoops it up, throws it to their shortstop, but Daniel makes it to second base and Noah has already come home.

Pen stands and smiles down at me, but it's off. The same way Daniel's has been. "I'll be back. I'm going to the restroom and then heading to the concession stand. Do you want anything?"

"I'll go with you." Esmeralda stands.

I'd offer to go but something tells me they need a moment alone. "I'm okay."

My eyes stay on Daniel, but my mind drifts to everything we've talked about. I want to be enough to be able to help him, but what if I'm not? Maybe that's why he didn't tell me; I'm so emotionally fucked, and he knows that.

I squeeze my eyes shut, hating how my thoughts start to spiral out of control.

"You know..." Julio takes the seat next to me. "I've seen Danny smile but never like that. Well, I have, but it's been a while."

"Really?" I find myself saying.

"Yeah..." He trails off. "I also never thought I'd see the day he'd willingly want to learn how to swim."

"I kind of coerced him."

He huffs a chuckle. "No, I can guarantee you didn't. He willingly allowed that because he trusts you. So thank you for taking the time and being patient."

I twist my ring. "You shouldn't thank me. I'm just doing my job."

"It's more than that for Esme and me. You have no idea how much this means to me. I know Danny might not think that; I've made mistakes I can't take back, but I mean what I said. I'll forever be grateful to you."

My throat constricts at his despondent, grief-stricken words. I stop twisting my ring and look at him. "It's not my place to tell you this, but maybe you should talk to him."

I don't know what that'll do between Daniel and his dad. It's not like I really know what happened. Daniel's been reluctant to share with me, but I understand complicated relationships.

Despite my strange relationship with my mother, I regret not talking to her when I had the chance. I don't want the same to happen between Daniel and Julio.

49
JOSEFINE

"Bidi Bidi Bom Bom" is the song of the day.

My lips curl up so high, the same way they did earlier at the stadium as I turn the volume dial to max. Surprisingly for how old the stereo is, it doesn't sound too bad.

I'm on day twenty-two since Daniel gifted me the CD and I've heard just about everything both in English and Spanish. There's no telling what'll play next, and I'm both intrigued and excited for the day to end just so I can hear a song.

I know I could listen to everything in one go, but it makes it more thrilling like this. And I'm certain Daniel also looks forward to this. He'll ask me about the song of the day and what I thought about it.

The front door opening and closing has me turning around. I'm nervous and happy. My thoughts feel like marbles, scattering and bouncing all over the place in no particular direction.

My heart is going haywire, my brain isn't functioning properly, and my skin is covered in goose bumps from my neck down to my legs.

When Daniel steps into the living room, my first instinct is to run to him, but I stay rooted in my place. My gaze bounces to his suntanned face, the backwards hat, the crooked grin that drops when his gaze darts to my outfit. Then to the stuff he's holding in both hands.

He's holding a bouquet of a variety of yellow flowers and assorted throughout are tiny white flowers. They're beautifully wrapped in a cream-colored paper, with a pastel yellow bow holding it together. In the other, he's holding a large brown paper gift bag.

"Hi, pretty girl." There's a rough edge to his voice, and his smile looks strained, like he's forcing it to stay up.

Heat spreads throughout my body, and I'm smiling uncontrollably as he walks to me.

"Hi." I push the word out of my mouth, feeling unsteadily happy. My legs wobble and my stomach somersaults when he stands in front of me. There are so many things my mind is screaming at me to do—jump on him, hug him, kiss him—but I can't do anything because I feel stuck.

I'm never like this and I'd be lying if I said I wasn't a little overwhelmed by how much happiness I feel right now. I can't even find a way to sabotage this moment because my brain is obliterating any negative thoughts.

I'm actually enjoying this. I'm really happy. I think I might cry.

Don't be weird.

"You make me so happy," I stupidly blurt out.

The tension on his face melts, and his smile is as blinding as the sparkle in his eyes. With everything still in his hands, he envelops me in a hug. It's different from any other hug we've given each other.

It's all-consuming, and my heart, mind, and soul feel entwined to his. I'm so deeply absorbed in him, I don't know what else to feel other than pathetically and ardently—no, that feeling is too soon. We just began dating. There's no way I actually feel that. I can't feel that; I don't even know what that feeling actually is.

I pull away, realizing the song is about to end and rush over to the stereo to turn it off.

He grins, eyes sweeping over me again. "You make me so happy."

I'm crushing so hard for him, it's insane. I'm blushing and smiling so much, I think I'm actually crashing out. This can't be healthy, can it?

"What are those for?" I eye the gorgeous flowers in his hand.

"You know I love a good holiday." He sets the gift bag on the sectional, drops his duffle on the floor, and stands in front of me.

"Holiday? I don't think there's a holiday today."

"It's Josie said I'm Her Boyfriend Day. This is one the biggest holidays of them all. So naturally I had to get *my girlfriend* these."

The backs of my eyes burn. "But you got me flowers last month—a lot of them..."

Don't cry!

"That was last month, and they're dead now. This is this month, and next month will be next month."

I laugh. "Don't you dare get me flowers next month."

"If it means I get to see you smile like this, expect them every month." He kisses the crown of my head then retrieves the gift bag. "I also got you this."

Daniel takes the flowers from me and hands me the bag. "You understand you don't have to get me anything to like you, right? I really don't—"

He places his finger on my lips, keeping it there to shush me. "Whatever I buy or do for you is nonnegotiable. Don't make this difficult. Accept the gifts, Josie. They're going to keep coming whether you want them to or not."

I softly swat his hand away. "Okay."

"Now if you could kindly hurry up because I'm really struggling here." He clears his throat, gaze drifting to my chest where the first few buttons are undone, exposing my cleavage. "I didn't know you owned two of my jerseys?"

I only had one but after sitting out in the sun for almost three hours, I had started to sweat. I bought another, showered when I got home, and put on a matching green bra and thong.

"It was hard to pick one. You guys have so many."

"I will get you the rest if you promise to wear them all the time."

I smirk. "You improve in the pool and I will."

"Deal," he rapidly says, eyes darkening with need. "Now open."

"You're so..." The rest of my words get caught when I open the bag and find a bunch of picture frames. They're all different sizes and colors. Some look vintage, while others look retro or rustic. "What's this?"

"I wasn't sure which style you'd like the best so I got a little bit of everything. I was thinking we could put them around the house, fill them up with pictures of us, but it doesn't have to be us; it can be anything you want. You've let me put my things around and I think it's time you start doing that too."

I attempt to speak, but I'm struggling to find the words. I never rearranged the house because I felt like I shouldn't. It never felt like my house despite it being in my name, and I never had the desire to want to mess with anything.

It was in denial at first, thinking Mom would burst through the doors and she'd be angry that the house didn't look the way she left it. Then I accepted she wasn't ever coming home. Still, I couldn't bring myself to make any changes.

But things are different now. The house has drastically changed since Daniel moved in. It's still clean, but the daunting echo that used to follow me around isn't anywhere to be heard. He's filled every inch of this place with him, and I don't mean that physically. Him just being here, making this place his home, *our* home.

Don't cry!

"Do you like it?" he asks hesitantly.

"I'm having a moment here, and I'm trying to remain calm," I honestly say. I'm doing my best to regulate my emotions and not go off anytime I feel overwhelmed by how much he cares about me. I look up at him, and my world steadies. "I l...like you. I like you a lot."

He cups my face and brushes his lips over mine. "You don't have to remain calm. You can let yourself feel whatever you want as long as you let me hold you." I nod, drowning in an ocean of emotions. "I really like you a lot." He pecks my lips a few times before he pulls back. "There's one more thing."

My brows furrow and I dig through the bag until I find a light brown envelope. I get giddy because I love his cards.

"I didn't have time to make one this time. I'm sorry." He sounds genuinely disappointed in himself.

I don't deserve him.

"That's okay." I pull the card out and grin at the cartoon squirrel on the front. Above it reads, *I have something special for you*, and when I open it, I burst out laughing because the squirrel is holding two nuts and underneath it reads, *I want to share my nuts with you*. And underneath that it reads, *I'm so happy you're here, Jos.*

He laughs too and stares at me with pride, like hearing me laugh is something he just ticked off his goals list.

"I can't with you." I suppress my laugh, taking the flowers from his hands and setting them and the bag on the coffee table. Wrapping my arms around him, I circle my legs around his waist as he instantly snakes his arms around me and lifts me up.

"I want to do something for you," I say into his ear, playing with the hair at the nape of his neck.

"What's that?" He looks at me hungrily.

Instead of telling him, I connect my lips with his. I kiss him deep, savoring him, slipping my tongue inside his mouth and stroking it against his. He reciprocates the kiss with as much vigor, but it's softer this time, knowing we don't have to rush to get it out of our systems.

Daniel doesn't break the kiss as he moves backwards until the back of his legs hit the sectional. He plops down, and I moan into his mouth as I settle right underneath his erection. His cock and the denim push into my clit, grazing it, and I shudder from the sensation.

It feels so good, I grind myself a little into him just to feel it again. Daniel groans against my mouth but doesn't stop kissing me. Instead, he deepens it. Our tongues become frantic and sloppy as if that'll fulfill the need for both of us to get off.

His tongue is thrusted so far down my mouth, I feel the vibrations of his grunts against the side of my throat every time I grind upward against him. I'm moaning with every rock, sucking his tongue, swallowing his saliva, tugging his hair.

Dry humping shouldn't be this hot, but it is. I'm squirming, loving how hard he is, reveling at how the denim of his jeans and the lace of my thong dig into my pussy and rub against me.

His hands slip under the oversized jersey and he palms my ass, squeezing it hard before smacking it. I shoot forward, squeezing my eyes at the sting, but then I tremble with pleasure. He smacks the other and the same feeling of pain and pleasure returns.

I'm panting into his mouth the second time around, breathing heavily, aroused and sopping wet. My nails dig into his back, and he faintly hisses before he slaps my ass a third time.

I scratch and hold on to his back, bucking my hips into him, holding on as the orgasm ripples throughout my body.

"Mmm..." I moan repeatedly, body going limp but quivering as he forces my hips to roll against him. "Daniel, fuck...fuc..." My clit pulses hard with each rub, and because I'm already sensitive, it doesn't take long before I'm coming again.

I shoot up, throwing my head back as euphoria takes over my body. I feel numb and high all at once. I don't have control. I feel like I'm getting carried away and all I can do is watch while my body drowns in ecstasy.

"You look so pretty riding me like this," he says huskily, squeezing my hips punishingly as he peppers kisses down my throat. "I wish you could see yourself from this angle." His lips brush my collarbone and descend to my cleavage.

I'm still in a state of bliss. Disoriented, I do nothing but watch as he brings his fingers to my jersey and undoes the buttons—one by one until the jersey is parted in the middle, exposing the transparent lace to him.

"I can't believe you're mine." His jaw hardens, voice dropping so low it makes my pussy clench.

"I think the same thing." I follow his line of vision and fingers as they pinch my pebbled nipples through the lace. Then he pulls both cups down, and goose bumps scatter around my breasts. My nipples become extremely sensitive when he flicks one.

"Yeah?" He flicks the other one.

"Mm-hmm." I feebly nod, squeeze my thighs around him, and slowly rock into him.

When his gaze drops down, he hums. "You made a mess on me. Look. Soaked right through, baby."

Sure enough, there's a dark wet stain on his jeans, right where I was grinding against him. Even the lace is darker where it's drenched from me.

My heart thunders as I climb off him. He grabs my hand to stop me, but I pull it back and kneel in front of him.

"Come back," he pleads and tries to adjust himself. He's so hard, it almost looks uncomfortable how his dick pushes against the denim, begging to be let free.

"I want to do something for you," I repeat what I said earlier. I lean forward, keeping my eyes on him, and lick the wet spot on his jeans. I lap my tongue over the denim, tasting myself and feeling him twitch against me.

His hooded eyes flutter shut momentarily before he pries them open to keep them on me. "Take it out, Josie." It's a painful, desperate plea and when I gently graze my teeth along his length, he whimpers, "Please, baby. Please take it out. Please..." he whimpers again. I thought hearing him moan was hot, but hearing that aching sound leaving his lips makes me wetter.

I unhook the button from his jeans and pull his zipper down. He doesn't wait for me to ask and lifts his hips so I can pull them down along with his boxer briefs. It doesn't take long before he's kicking his shoes and clothes off to the side.

I blink once then twice, still in awe at and a little nervous about how thick and long he is. A shiver works its way straight to my core. I'm both excited and embarrassingly overwhelmed to taste and choke on him. I don't know what this says about me, but I liked having his cock shoved down my throat. I liked gagging on it and feeling my saliva running down the side of my mouth.

"You did so good last time." He cups my cheek and drags his thumb down to my lips, pushing my bottom lip down to part my mouth open. "And you're going to do just as good, right? Remember, your mouth was made for my cock. Just look at yourself; it's already open and ready to taste. Lean in, baby, and suck."

He fists my hair as I tilt forward and draw him into my mouth. As his precum coats my tongue, I catch a brief glimpse of him smirking before my eyes roll back. I like how he tastes, like how he fits in my mouth, and like how I gag every time the tip of his cock hits the back of my throat.

"Eyes on me," he groans, pulling my hair hard.

I open them, wincing from the pain, but still continue working him in my mouth. With every suction, my cheeks hollow, my jaw aches, and tears fill my eyes.

I don't blink or close my eyes despite how my mind is screaming at me to do that. I keep them trained on his as I suck and lick every inch of him. The tears eventually trickle down my face, but I don't stop. It only encourages me to keep going. I feel gratified, seeing him like this—pupils blown, body taut with tension, long legs lazily sprawled out—and despite how he holds my hair and whispers rough words of encouragement, I have all the control. I decide how much, how fast, how deep, and he greedily, easily, and happily accepts.

"Jos," he half whines, half whimpers when I pull him out of

my mouth. A long string of saliva clings from the tip of his dick to the bottom of my lip before it snaps.

"Spit right here." I point to the middle of my breasts.

His brows raise to his hairline. A savage look takes over him and a second later he's spitting on my breasts. Daniel is grinning in a way I've never seen before. He looks like he just won the lottery, and I can't help but smirk.

I grab my breasts and push them together to smear the saliva. "It wasn't enough. Do it again."

I sit up, pushing and spreading them for him. He happily obliges and spits on them twice, then reclines back and fists his cock. He lazily drags his palm down his shaft, stroking himself as I smear the saliva, and when I'm done, I push his hand away.

"You're so hot," he grunts, jaw clenching and voice deep and throaty. It doesn't sound like him. "I'm so fucking obsssessed with you."

"Yeah?" I lick my dry lips and lean forward, placing his cock between my breasts, pressing them on him until I know I have a firm grip on it. I've never done this, but I do what feels right and glide up and down him, occasionally licking the precum off the tip. "Does this feel good?"

His eyes roll back and he sinks deep into the sectional. "Yeah... yeah..." he absently and breathlessly replies. "Sooo...fucccking good. Jesus, Josie, keep doing that. Your tits are fucking phenomenal."

"I really want to do a good job," I sheepishly admit.

As much as I like control, I want to know I'm doing well. No, I *need* to know. I need to hear those words come out of his mouth.

Daniel places his hands on my hands, stopping me from moving. "Everything you do is beyond good. I don't just mean this; I mean in everything. You are good, you are enough—as you are, and what you do—as you do it. It's all good." He pulls me up to stand, hooks his fingers on the waistband of my thong, and drags it down. "You've done so good, really, *really* good, but I don't want to come on your face today. I really want you to ride me, but only if you want."

I'm both emotional and horny. I'm between wanting to smile and cry, but I do neither. I just squeeze my thighs and hold my breath and make myself chill out because the last thing I need right now is to tear up.

"Yeah, I want that." I go to take off the jersey, but he stops me.

"Keep that on." He swallows hard, gaze slowly sweeping over me.

"Okay, but can you take your shirt off?" I really want to see and feel him.

He reaches over his head and pulls it off, throwing it somewhere on the floor.

I blatantly check him out as I straddle him but stay hovering over his cock.

Daniel grabs my hips and when he glances down, any trace of humor dissolves. "I should get a condom..."

"You should..." I trail off and wait for him to make a move, but he doesn't lift a finger. "We shouldn't be irresponsible."

"No, we shouldn't..." He drags his teeth along his bottom lip and tugs me down a little.

I grab his cock and align it at my entrance. "You really shouldn't fuck me like this."

"I really shouldn't." He squeezes my hips and urges me to lower myself.

The crown nudges my pussy and slips past my lips, and I squeeze around him. I suck in a breath and he hisses. "I'll get off in a bit. I promise..."

I sink a little more and close my eyes as he stretches me.

He moans and glides his rough, calloused palms under the jersey and cups my ass. "Yeah, take your time, baby. Take...your time..."

A little more and I'm panting and feeling dizzy. Fuck, he's so huge.

I grip his shoulders, holding my breath again, as I lower myself some more. Inch by inch, he stretches me. You'd think I'm losing my virginity from how tight I am.

"Your pussy feels...I'm going to come. You're so tight and wet. Holy shit, you feel so goddamn good. Fucking hell, Josie," he says as his eyes stay on my wet tits as they bounce with every movement.

I don't know what takes over me, maybe it's the way he's staring at me, how he feels inside me, or his words, but I force myself all the way.

My jaw drops, but no air comes out. It stays lodged in my lungs as my pussy grips and pulses around him. A cry is the closest thing I make to a sound, and I think I hear Daniel groan my name, but I'm not sure. I can't focus on anything but how insanely stretched I feel, how deep he's hitting inside of me, and how amazing I feel.

"Josie, I don't think I'm going to last," he says like he's pleading with every inch of his life. "Don't move."

"I have to. I *need* to," I impatiently whine.

I'm in a state of euphoria. My body is so aware, I can physically feel him throb inside me, feel how I'm drenching his cock with my arousal, feel how deeply connected we are.

"Josie," he breathes against my chest, biting my collarbone as I grind just a little. "I'm serious. I'm not going to las..."

I roll my hips, pushing my ass out and bucking forward, pressing down hard against his pubic bone to feel pressure on my clit. He holds me down, but I grab the back of the sectional, bouncing on him because I know my breasts will too. He stares at them and has this dazed look in his eyes, lost in his perverted fantasy to stop me from moving.

I know I've screwed myself over because I've never not used a condom, and now I don't know how I'll ever want to use one again. This feels too good. He slips in and out so easily, so quickly. I feel his soft, sweaty skin against me, feel the ridge of his crown, feel every inch of his skin slapping mine, his balls against my ass. And the noises—they're so erotic and hot, I can't stop bouncing.

The built-up pressure in my core explodes and I come a second later. I slowly stop moving, jerking every so often as the orgasm wracks my body.

I stop moving all together, at least for a second, because Daniel rocks his hips and grabs mine and makes me grind on him.

I cry out, shaking my head for him to stop because I'm sensitive but the words leaving my mouth are the opposite because I'm screaming, "Yes! More! Don't stop! Don't fucking stop!"

He doesn't. He fucks me relentlessly until I come again and he follows shortly after. He groans, his head tipping back, his veins popping in his neck, and his jaw clenching hard as he releases inside me.

I slump against his sweaty chest, breathing harshly. He wraps his arms around my back and holds me until our breaths even out.

"I can feel your cum coming out," I murmur tiredly.

He lifts me up and pulls out of me. I shudder at how empty I feel and hate that he's not back in me. I almost ask him to fuck me again, but my thoughts freeze as he sits me on the couch, drops to his knees on the floor, and spreads my thighs.

He stares at my pussy, and as his cum seeps out of me, he spreads it all over, paying special attention to my clit.

"Daniel," I whine, spreading my thighs further for him. "I'm really sensitive."

"I know, baby." He kisses the inside of my thigh but doesn't stop rubbing his cum on my clit. "You're going to come for me one more time."

"I don't think—" I gasp, fisting the cushion as I feel the pressure build up. My eyes widen and lips part open as he continues to play with my swollen nub. But I lose it when he spreads my lips and laps it, long leisure licks that feel like fucking torture. It's too much. I'm sitting up, pulling his hair, attempting to stop him, but I'm also grinding into his mouth.

And like that time in the shower, pressure grows until I can't hold back. I know it's not just an orgasm because it feels so different. What I'm feeling right now is an out-of-body experience. I drift into a different universe as I squirt.

It gets all over him, and I'd be embarrassed if he didn't look like he's reveling in how it lands on him.

I'm physically shaking when I come down from my high. "I can't believe you made that happen again."

I know there's a mess, but I don't dare look. I'm still very turned on but tired.

I don't fight him when he lifts me up and carries me up the stairs. "I told you it would happen again. I love watching it."

I nuzzle into his chest and say nothing more as he brings us into his shower.

50
JOSEFINE

"Do you want to talk about it?" I twist on my side, resting my chin on Daniel's bare chest.

He raises his arm behind his head, smiling down at me. "I'm fine, I promise."

It's the last day of March. A few months ago, that meant nothing to me—just another month passing by, but this time around, it's different.

April is the month that Adrian passed away, and from what Penelope has told me, it's a very hard time of year for her family, especially for Daniel. I don't one hundred percent understand grief. It's always weirdly evolving, never consistent but it's there. This past December was rough for me. I almost ended my life over it. I wasn't even close with Mom, but I struggled.

But unlike me, Daniel was close to his brother, so I know if my mom's death anniversary was hard for me, this time of this month is difficult for him.

"Are you sure?" I don't want to push, but I want to be a good girlfriend. I want him to know that I'm here for him, that I'm not emotionally stunted. That I can be someone he can feel comfortable sharing things with.

"I'm sure." His voice is gentle and sweet, easy to get lost in, but something about it feels off. "We shouldn't go. Let's just stay here. I'll grab takeout and we'll go for round three afterwards."

I force my lips to raise, not wanting to look like I'm disappointed. He's not expected to share how he feels. He'll talk when he's ready.

Usually halfway through the season, the baseball team meets up at one of their teammates' houses for a small get together. And as of now, they've won all twenty-eight games since the season began, so they really want to meet up. They're also all kind of superstitious, or at least most of the team is. Daniel isn't, which is why he doesn't care to be there.

"You're the captain. You need to be there." I grab the safety pin, twirling it around my finger. "And I'm pretty sure we're past round three."

It's been four days since we had sex in the living room, and since then, any chance we get, we're naked—in all the areas of the house and in all the positions we can think of.

That's how we found ourselves in his room. Our hiking class was canceled and he didn't have practice today, so we came straight home.

"I'm talking about today." He grabs me and slips me over his body so I'm straddling him.

The sheets pool around his waist, leaving me naked on top of him. He raises his hand, brushing the hickey on the side of my breast.

"The next round can happen later tonight, I promise." I drag my finger along his abs, feeling goose bumps grow beneath the pads of my thumbs. "We need to go. I don't doubt Angel will drag your ass out of here. He seemed pretty serious."

He blows a raspberry. "I know he will. You know, I won't be upset if you don't want to come. I have to put up with Bryson, but it doesn't mean you have to."

I thought about that and couldn't bring myself to care. "I know but I'm not going there for him. I'm going there for you.

He's pretty forgettable. I probably won't notice he's there anyway."

He chuckles, tracing designs with his finger on my thigh. "He said a lot of shitty things, Josie. If he says something to you, I won't—"

"You won't do anything," I warn. "I promise it'll be okay. There isn't a thing he hasn't said about me that can hurt me. So don't let him antagonize you. I promise it'll be okay. Plus, he hasn't said anything to you since the talk with your coach, right?"

Daniel told me about having to share hotel rooms with him and the other things. I hate that for him, but he said it was worth it.

He sits up, resting against the headboard. "Right. He hasn't said or done anything since then, but I wouldn't put it past him to do something petty today."

"No matter what happens, it'll be okay. I'll be okay. We'll be okay, okay?"

He hauls me in for a hug, kissing the crown of my head. "Okay."

Sometimes I don't understand what Daniel sees in me.

He's a social butterfly, a ray of sunshine. I'm not. I know it's easy for him to socialize with the people in this house because they're his teammates, some of whom he's been playing with for three years. The others are either freshmen or transfers, but he treats them all the same. But it's not just them I'm referring to but everyone in general. He has a way about him that makes people easily gravitate toward him.

It's not just his talent that people are drawn to but just him in general.

So why he's with me when I'm the complete opposite is beyond me.

I keep thinking that as he holds my hand, stays by my side,

refuses to leave me alone even when I tell him I'll be okay. I understand part of the reason is because I don't really know anyone here except his closest friends, and the other part is because of Bryson.

He's been around, but he's kept his distance. Though I've caught him rolling his eyes and scoffing when he walks by us.

I'm not sure what he thinks that'll accomplish, but it does nothing for me. I hate that Daniel feels so deeply about it when I couldn't care less.

"Hey." Gray drops on the couch next to Daniel, sipping whatever's in his cup. "We just need to know."

Kai sits on the armrest, Noah stands next to him, and Angel is in front of us.

"Shut up," Daniel deadpans, the smile on his face slipping as his arm tightens around me protectively.

I look up at them then down at Daniel since I'm sitting on his lap. "Need to know what?"

"They're stupid. Don't listen to them." He shakes his head, shooting murderous glares at his friends.

"I promise it's not that bad." Kai smirks, winking at me playfully.

"When did this"—Gray waves his index finger between Daniel and me—"become official? Exact date would be great."

I stare at them, amused. "Why?"

"We're big fans. We've been shipping Janny since day one." Angel grins.

"Janny?" I smile a little at that but cringe too. "Don't ever call us that."

"I kind of like it," Daniel says happily and slips his hand under my shirt, stroking my back. "Janny...Janny...Janny..." he says over and over again in different tones as if that'll somehow make it sound better.

I shake my head and he chuckles. "It's a no for me. So why do you need to know the exact date?"

"Because we placed bets," Noah bluntly states, leaving me

stunned because he usually doesn't speak. "We knew this was going to happen. If you can tell us the date, that'd be great."

Daniel's hand freezes on my back. "I tried to stop them. I promise." He aggravatedly sighs. "I swear I had nothing to do with this."

I stoically stare at them. I don't say anything. Just watch as their humored expressions slip.

"It wasn't done maliciously," Kai quickly supplies. "We were just giving Danny a hard time."

I hum, letting the silence stretch out. They look uncomfortable, almost awkward. Except for Noah and Angel, I can't tell what they're feeling, but I do think they feel a little bad about it. At least Angel does; Noah looks unapologetic, apathetic.

My lips lift upward a tad. "So did you guys choose a date, or was there a time frame?"

They look relieved and laugh knowing I'm not mad about it. I actually feel a little jittery inside, knowing they were talking about me, about us. How long ago was this? Why did they think we'd become a thing? What made them believe we'd get together? I have so many questions, but I won't ask them.

"You got a killer poker face. I genuinely thought you were mad," Kai says.

I shrug indifferently. "I don't care. Date, or time frame?"

Daniel's face softens and continues caressing my back.

"It started as a time frame, but we all had the same time, so we set a date," Gray answers. "I said March 16th."

"March 21st," Kai says.

"March 22nd," Noah adds.

"March 28th," Angel says.

"All in March? You all really believed we would—"

"Yeah, Danny went batshit on Bryson over you," Gray whispers because he's a few feet away from us. He's playing beer pong, but I swear he keeps glancing in our direction every so often. "And apparently, he has a little gem thing in his wallet that you wore? Yeah, we knew it was going to happen."

My head swivels down at him. "The rhinestone? You still have it? I thought you threw it away?"

He looks a little bashful, his cheeks tinting pink. "I couldn't get rid of it."

"You guys can do that couple shit later. Tell us who got it right." Noah interrupts the moment, looking disturbed by our interaction.

"Gray. He was the closest," Daniel states. "It was March 17th," he proudly and happily announces.

I thought he was going to say the 28th, but the moment I took a chance on us, it was official for him. Even though we weren't labeling our relationship yet.

"Fuck yeah, pay up, bitches." He stands, lifts his palm upward, and curls his fingers in and out.

I watch in disbelief as they all pull their wallets out and each hand him a hundred dollars.

"They're ridiculous. You see why I needed to move out?" He kisses my shoulder.

I stifle my chuckle as Gray makes a show of counting his money and smelling it too.

"What a glorious day. We need drinks. We need to celebrate." He chugs the rest of his drink and waltzes off merrily into the kitchen.

My phone vibrates in my pocket. "I need to answer this." I hold it up, showing Daniel it's Vi. She's on a date and said if things weren't going well, she'd call me. "I'm going to go outside."

The baseball players aren't the only ones here. Their closest friends and girlfriends are here, along with their friends. So much for a small get together.

"I'm going to use the restroom and then I'll be out there," he says, kissing my temple before I get up.

Not too long ago, this open public display of affection would've made my skin crawl, but now I want to drown in whatever he's willing to give me.

"Okay." I flash him a smile and quickly make my way to the backyard. There are people littering the yard and pool, and it's loud but not as loud as inside.

I answer, pressing my phone to my ear as I walk away from everyone. "How shitty is the date? One through ten? Ten being *get me the fuck out of here.*"

She quietly laughs. "As good as dating a frat boy will be. It's a five-ish."

"Do you want me to pick you up?"

"No, no. You're with Danny, *your* boyfriend." I hear her muted squeal followed by a giggle.

"Shut up." I smile into the phone. "I don't mind leaving."

"No, it's okay. I'm calling to update you and ask how low you'd think my standards were if I went home with him?"

Now I laugh. "Nothing you do will make me think your standards are low. And if you compare yourself to me, you're like soaring up in the clouds."

"We'll call it a lapse of judgement because look at you now. Dating Daniel Garcia."

My heart skips a beat. "Yeah, he's pretty great."

She hums in agreement. "I love it when hot and nice people date each other." I wouldn't say I'm nice, but I keep that to myself. "Anyway, I'm going to let you go. I'm going home with him. I can't say what I will and won't do, but I'll call you tomorrow."

"Okay, but if you need anything, call me. Be safe."

"Yes, Mom. Will do."

My lips twitch as I hang up and make my way back. I'm busy staring at my phone, replying to Pen's message, when I bump into someone.

"Sor—oh." It's Bryson. He's standing right in front of me, and something tells me I didn't bump into him by accident. He put himself in front of me. For fuck's sake.

I walk around him and ignore him as he calls my name.

"Josie, wait. Please, I just want to talk."

"What?" I turn, sucking in a large breath for patience, and hope to God, I don't push him in the pool. "What do you want? You've already called me a bitch. A whore. A slut. Easy. I'm too much. Not enough. I'm this and I'm that. So what now? What do you want to say that you haven't already?" I ask, smothering my frustration and anger down.

"You couldn't have gotten with anyone else? It had to be him of all people?"

"What's your problem with Daniel?"

"He thinks he's better. He—"

"This is about jealousy? You're so pathetic."

I should've known it was always about jealousy. I wouldn't doubt he slept with Amanada to spite Daniel. He was always talking about him and keeping up with whatever anyone was saying about him. How lame.

"I know what I said. I know what I did. I'm sorry. I want you back. I need you back."

I pivot, not caring what he has to say, but he grabs my arm and jerks me back. Daniel squeezes himself between us, pushing Bryson's chest hard.

"Don't fucking touch her," he warns, circling an arm behind me and around my back.

"I'm fine. Let's just go," I urge him, gripping his arm, and thankfully he relaxes and turns to look at me. I smile up at him. "I'm okay."

He exhales a sigh. "Okay."

I take his hand in mine and pull him away, but Bryson pushes him. I see Angel and Noah from my periphery approach us, but everything happens too quickly. Bryson pushes him again and Daniel loses his balance and falls into the deep end of the pool.

"What the fuck did you do!" I yell at him, ready to jump in, but Angel dives in before I get the chance.

"It's just water. He'll be all right."

"You stupid—" I lose it, and knee him in the balls hard.

He shrieks, falling to the ground, cupping himself. "What was that for?" he wheezes. "It's just water," he cries out.

I ignore him, running to the other end where Angel and Noah help Daniel out of the pool. He's coughing out water, trembling and breathing raggedly, but then his breaths quicken, his eyes bug out, and he fists his soaked shirt, pulling it away from his chest. He's hyperventilating.

"Daniel." I drop to my knees. "You're okay, baby. Breathe. You're okay. Breathe with me." I take his shaking hands in mine and motion for him to follow me. "Breathe in and out. Yeah, just like that. Breathe. You're okay. In and out. Just like that. You're doing good. Keep doing that."

I continue to talk him through it until his breathing evens out. Once it does, I search for any bumps or scratches, making sure he didn't hit his head or scratch himself, but he's fine. At least for a second I think he is, until I notice the faraway look in his eyes and how empty they look.

"Hey."

"I'm okay." He blinks, then looks at me, swallowing hard. "I need a moment."

He pushes up to stand, but I follow behind him. "Hey, I'm right here, remember? I'm not going anywhere. I'm here, Daniel."

"I need a moment, Josefine. So please, not right now." He picks up the pace and walks back inside, leaving me outside.

51

DANIEL MARCH 31st

"What happened? Why are you—"

"Is that for me?" I glance at the cup in Gray's hand.

"Yeah." Dubiously, he hands it to me, eyeing me like he can feel the dread I'm absorbed in, see the black cloud above my head. "Why are you wet? What happened?"

Shards of glass stab every inch of me, puncturing my skin, taking hold of everything inside me and slicing right through. Everything inside me hurts, the agonizing screaming voice in my head only growing louder.

"Nothing." My heart violently hammers and a voice screams in my head, begging me to hide, to run, but I stay put and chug the entire thing in one go.

"Damn, hold up. There's tequila in there. A lot of it." He gawks at me dumbfoundedly.

I shrug, indifferent, and toss the empty cup into the table and take the other from his hand, chugging that one too.

The alcohol settles hard and fast enough in my body, it somewhat ebbs the vicious need to hide. It dulls the pain and brings my heart to a steady beat.

"Thanks. You should make more." I plaster on a smile just as I hear the back door opening and closing.

"I thought you were only drinking one tonight?" Gray asks, studying the empty cup in my hand.

"It's a good thing we don't have a game tomorrow," I reply, picking up the other cup from the table and strolling out of the kitchen into the living room.

"Danny!" I hear Angel shout over the loud music, but I keep walking, taking sips of my drink as I make my way upstairs. "Hold up."

"Hey, what's up?" I inattentively ask, scowling at how my feet feel in my wet socks and shoes.

"What's up?" He sounds incredulous. "What's wrong?"

"Can I borrow some clothes?" I disregard his question, asking my own, and take another drink.

"Daniel, hey, look at me." He grabs my arm once we're at the top of the stairs and spins me around. He searches and studies me, worry washing over his face, making me only lift my lips higher and drink some more. "What the hell was that?"

"What? Bryson pushed me in the pool. It's nothing. Can I borrow some clothes?"

He looks taken aback. "What about Josie? You left her outside."

My smile almost crumbles. I never wanted anyone to see me that way, especially her of all people. I won't let it happen again. I just need to change out of my clothes and drink. Drink until I can find some semblance of stability before I lose it.

"I told her I needed a moment." I grind my teeth, remembering her scrutinizing gaze, hating how scared she looked for me. She shouldn't have witnessed that.

He tips his head back, drawing in a breath. "What's wrong? Talk to me."

"Nothing. Can I get some clothes?"

"Daniel—"

"I'll just ask Gray."

He grumbles under his breath and opens his door, allowing me to go inside.

Angel leans against the closed door. "Talk to me and stop acting like you're okay. I know you're not."

I clench my teeth, fighting against the black fog in my head and the urge to disappear. "It was the water. You know how I feel about it, but I'm fine, I promise." I smile wider. "Can you give me the clothes now?"

"I know, but you've been swimming with Josie. I thought—"

"It made her happy, so I did it. I told you and everyone else that the lessons weren't going to help, but you guys don't listen." A chill shoots down my spine and the stabbing returns. So I drain half my cup and stop myself from finishing the rest because Angel's looking at me weird. "Listen, it's not a big deal. Thanks for getting me out of there."

He gives me a brittle nod and grabs a change of clothes and a towel for us. "Are you leaving now?"

"No, why?" I kick off my shoes, dry off, and change into his clothes.

"You want me to kick everyone out? I don't mind. I know Noah's ready for everyone to leave." He lightheartedly chuckles, but it sounds stilted as he changes.

"No, don't do that. I'm seriously fine." I wave it off and run a hand through my damp, disheveled hair. "My hair look okay?"

Angel goes quiet, the silence drawing out before he nods. "Yeah, it looks good. It always does." Another pause. "Oh, let me get you some shoes."

"Right, thanks." I grab my cup, finish the drink, and wallow in the numbness that comes with it. "I need to hurry up. Josie's waiting for me."

He takes my wet clothes and hands me the shoes. "I know something is wrong. Whatever it is, you can talk to me. I'm your best friend."

"The water freaked me out a little, but I'm good. Stop worrying. I swear, I'm great."

I open the door before he can get another word out and find Josie standing outside. She lifts her head, and there's a doleful look in her eyes as they sweep over me like they did outside.

"Hey, I was just going to you." I cut the space and wrap my arms around her, inhaling her lavender vanilla scent. She smells so good, feels good too.

I'm thankful for the alcohol that courses through my system because I feel nothing but numb and painfully happy. She doesn't need to see me in any other way but happy.

"Hey." There's a brokenness in her voice that stabs my heart. "Do you want to get out of here?"

"No, why?" I cup her jaw and tip her head back to look up at me.

Her brows knit, confusion and concern flickering over her face. "Daniel, don't..." She circles her arms around my waist. "Don't pretend to be okay. Let yourself feel," she whispers. "It's okay to feel whatever you're feeling. I'm right here. I won't go anywhere."

I kiss her but she draws away.

"Have you been drinking?"

"Just a little." I kiss her forehead and smile down at her. "There's nothing to feel. I promise I'm okay, so please stop staring at me like something is wrong. I promise there's not."

She isn't buying it. She stares at me long and hard. Long enough, I can feel her infiltrate my mind and read every pulsing, detrimental fear running manically in my head.

"Everything's fine," I evenly voice, raising a crafty smile that I've perfected over the years. The kind that no one ever asks questions about. "I promise. I'm sorry I left you out there. I just needed a minute, but I'm good."

Her expression doesn't waver; it hardens for a fraction before it slightly softens. "Do you want to go home?"

"No, I want to stay a little. Stay with me?" Sweat beads my back and heat flares inside, making me hot.

"I..." she falters, eyes bouncing over with hesitation. "Yeah, I'll stay with you."

Despite the wave of relief that washes over me, dark clouds loom in the distance.

It's fine. I just need to drink a little, then I'll sleep it off, and be as good as new tomorrow.

Josefine March 31st

Daniel's drunk.

"Just one more," he slurs.

"You said that two hours ago," I softly say, surveying his face.

His face is flushed, eyes are glazed, and he has this dopey smile pasted on.

"I know, but..." he laughs to himself and cups my face, his heavy-lidded eyes pinned on me. "You're so beautiful. Like really, really beautiful, do you know that?"

I smile and attempt to guide him away from the kitchen table filled with all the drinks, but he doesn't budge. He's rotated everywhere, from the keg stand, to the beer pong table—anywhere alcohol is at.

"And I really, really, like, really like you." He kisses my forehead and inhales. "You smell so good. I love the way you smell. I have to tell you a secret."

"Yeah? What's that?" I grab his hand and usher him to the corner of the kitchen, doing my best to keep him steady as he stumbles over his feet.

Once we're in the corner, he leans down until his lips graze my ear. "I'm obsessed with you."

My body warms. "Yeah?"

"Mm-hmm, sooo obsessed...I just want to make you happy. You deserve to be happy. I'm sorry." There's melancholy in his voice and when I peer up at him, sadness dims his eyes.

"You don't need to be sorry. I am happy. I promise." My heart lurches in my chest.

"I do. I am. I'm sorry," he whispers the words fragilely.

"No, it's okay. Let's go home, okay?" I grab his hand, once again trying to get him out, but he pulls me back to the table.

"Just one more, just one more." He spins us around and walks backwards to the table, but in the process, he crashes against someone and their drink spills all over him.

"Sorry, Danny." Ryan, one of his teammates, winces. "I didn't see you."

"It's all right," he flippantly remarks and gives him an okay sign.

Angel's next to him in an instant and levels me with a look of apprehension. I think I'm mirroring the same expression because he nods.

"You mind cleaning this up?" he asks Ryan.

"Yeah, I got it." He smiles at them, unaware that Daniel isn't acting like himself.

I get it. They've always seen him happy, and he looks that right now, but I know something is wrong. I wish I knew—other than being here physically for him—what to do to make him feel better.

"Come on, you need to change." He places Daniel's arm around his shoulder and snakes his arm around his back.

"You got him?" Noah eyes the guys, but stares at Daniel's wobbly body the longest.

"Maybe come with, just in case," Angel supplies and leads him through the house until all four of us are up in his bedroom.

"You guys are doing way too much. I'm fine." He stumbles over his words and feet as he attempts to take his shirt off. "I'm fine. F. I. N. E."

"Here let me—" Angel says, but Daniel swats his hand away. "Danny, don't—"

"It's okay. I got it." I take his place.

"There you are. I missed you." He pouts and pulls me in for a hug.

"I'm right here." I let him hold me and walk him backwards until he's in front of Angel's bed and force him to sit. "Here, let me help you take this off."

He easily lets me, but when his shirt comes off, he looks down at his chest and he shoots up. "My chain. I need my chain." He pats his chest repeatedly, as if that'll make it appear.

"It's okay. I'll go look for it," I quickly offer. "Let me help you put this shirt on and then I'll go get it, okay?"

"I need my chain." He tries to walk, but then his eyes glaze over and he falls back on the bed. "I need…" he sluggishly chuckles, bracing his elbows on his legs and covers his face with his palms. "Really need my chain. That's the only thing keeping me alive."

I look at Angel and Noah, but they look as confused as I feel.

"Hey." I kneel in between his parted legs, peering up at him.

He drops one hand and uses the other to hold his head. His eyes are half open, and a dazed smile blooms on his face.

"I have to tell you another secret," he whispers.

"Yeah, tell me," I whisper back.

"Sometimes…I wish I was dead." My heart drops and I rear back, looking up at the guys because he said that loud enough, I know they heard.

A knot grows in my throat, making it hard to speak, but before I get the chance, he's mumbling and slurring words that make my throat and heart constrict.

"I thought I could distract myself. I thought I could be happy. But I'm not." He laughs, shaking his head. "I'm not happy, Josefine." He looks directly at me, eyes red and rimmed with unshed tears. "This distraction isn't working."

"Wh-what distraction?" I hold my breath and his hand. No matter what he says, I can take it. He's hurting; I can be here for him. I know he needs to talk. I know he needs to feel. I can be strong enough for us. I can.

"Us." He shrugs, removing his hand from mine and points between us. "I knew I didn't deserve you, but I wanted you anyway." He cups my cheek. "But it's all pointless. I should just die, like Adrian did. He won't get to experience this, so why should I? I lied to you and to me. This was never going to work."

My bottom lip quivers. "No, I don't want you to die. You have so many people who love you. So many people who want you here. None of this is pointless and you deserve all good things. You do."

"You say that, but you're no different. Your mom died and you don't think you deserve anything even though I know you do. Maybe we're the same. We both want to die—"

"Okay, Daniel, that's enough." Angel talks over him and from my periphery I see him approach, but I raise my hand, stopping him.

"It's okay," I say, directing my attention back to him. "No, I don't want to die, and I don't want you to die either."

"I don't know. Sometimes I can't read you. Sometimes I don't know what you're feeling," he mumbles, some of his words heavily slurred, but I feel each one like a knife to my chest. "Sometimes I don't know if I'm doing enough to make you happy. I know you'll never love me so what's the point?" He flicks his attention to the floor, lips curling up a bit. "This distraction isn't working anymore. I can't anymore. This, us, isn't enough. I don't know how to be enough. I don't know...I don't know, Josefine...I miss Adrian. I want to die. I tried...a lot of times before, but I never could. I wish I could be like you—easy to stop caring. Maybe it would've made things easier. I'm sorry."

He tried? My stomach plummets, making me feel nauseous and dizzy.

"What are you sorry for?" My thick voice quavers.

"I thought I could hide what I felt to make you happy."

I know he's drunk, but I can't do this.

It's not his fault. I'm so emotionally fucked, he made himself miserable to make me happy.

Rising to my feet, I shove all my feelings away. "I'm going to help you get ready for bed, okay?"

"Not right now. I—"

"Please." My voice breaks and fingers tremble. "Please let me help you get ready for bed."

He yawns loudly, rubbing his eyes. He looks like he's in a trance. I'm sure the alcohol is taking more effect now. "Okay, I should go to bed."

The guys remain by the door watching me help him get ready. Daniel's still mumbling words under his breath, but not what he was saying a few minutes ago. It's all random and jumbled, but he's calm and that's all I want, all I need before I leave.

As soon as I lift the comforter to his shoulder, he's turning on his side and falling fast asleep.

I lean over and whisper against his temple, "You deserve good things, Daniel. You deserve to be happy. I'm sorry it couldn't be with me." Then I kiss the top of his head and walk away.

"Josie." Angel stands in front of me, blocking my path. "I had no idea he felt this way, but I swear this doesn't have anything to do with you. He likes you; he really does. I've never seen Danny so—"

"Don't." I get choked up but clear my throat because I'm not going to break in front of him. I don't need his pity. "It was never going to work out. Can you tell him—"

"Let him sleep it off and then you guys can talk it out and—"

"When he wakes up, tell him to come pick up his stuff and that I'm not going to kill myself."

I dip under his arm and run down the stairs and out the door, but freeze in my tracks because I came with Daniel.

I look up at the night sky to stop myself from spiraling, but a tear still spills when I see the stars. The sky hasn't looked like this since that night Daniel stopped me from ending it all.

"Come on. I'll take you home."

I startle, jumping back, and swiftly brush the tear away. "I don't need a ride."

"I will throw you in my car," Noah threatens. "Don't test me because I will."

I give in because I can't bring myself to fight him.

The ride back home is silent, and I expect it to stay that way when I get out, but he speaks up.

"Alcohol's a bitch, but he didn't mean it. At least about you. I'll see you around." He watches me go inside and then he drives off.

He made himself miserable to make me happy.

Once I shut the door behind me, I'm suffocated with the realization that I had forgotten what *silence* was until now. Drowning with the reality that no one could ever truly want me. It was only a matter of time before Daniel acknowledged that he couldn't continue putting up with me. If he said that drunk, I don't want to imagine what he'd say sober.

52

DANIEL

April 1st

My incessantly throbbing head wakes me. I pry my bleary eyes open and flinch a second later at the light that probes through the curtains.

I turn on my side, gently patting the bed next to me, wanting to pull Josie into me.

I force my eyes open because I don't feel her, and this bed doesn't smell like her. I instantly realize why when I scan the familiar room.

Tossing the covers off me, I jump out of bed but regret it a second later as everything spins. I perch on the side of the bed, holding my pounding head.

"Josie?" My voice is hoarse and my throat is dry. I have to swallow to wet it and call out again. "Josefine?"

The door opens a moment later, but she's not the one who comes in. It's Angel. He holds a steaming mug, a bottle of ibuprofen, and a water bottle.

"Morning," he greets, his lips pulling into a pinched smile.

"Hey, do you know where Josie's at?"

"Here, you're going to need this." He sets the mug on the

nightstand and hands me the water bottle and ibuprofen. "We need to talk."

"Where's Josie?" I stand, setting the stuff down, and notice I'm wearing a different shirt than the one he let me borrow yesterday.

A look of apprehension crosses his face. "You're going to need to sit down."

"Where's Josie? Why are you being weird?" I go to walk out, but he stands in front of the door, blocking me.

"Sit down," he firmly instructs. "She's not here."

"What do you mean she's not here?" Panic grips me. "Get out of my way." But he doesn't move. "Get the fuck—"

He drags his hand over his hair, behind his head. "I'm sorry. She...she broke up with you."

Everything inside me crashes hard. I reel back, shaking my head in disbelief. "Stop messing around. Where is she?"

I pat my pockets for my phone, but I don't feel it.

"Danny..." His face pinches with pain and discomfort, and a strangled groan rips from the back of his throat. "You said some things last night. A lot of things that I wasn't even—fuck." He rubs his eyes hard. He looks at me with a confliction of emotions, but the one that overrides them all is devastation. "I'm sorry. I'm so sorry. I didn't even know. I didn't think—I'm so sorry. I should've been there for you more. I'm sorry."

My stomach roils, the alcohol threatening to rise. "What are you talking about? Why are you sorry?"

"You told Josie..." His shoulders sink as he expels a demoralizing breath and tells me in detail everything that happened last light, everything I said and what she did, as well as what she said. "She wants you to get your things from her house and said she wasn't going to kill herself."

I break into a cold sweat, bringing my hands behind my head, pacing, trying to remember last night, but only blurry, two second clips flash in my head. All of them, a cloudy picture of her face.

"What did I do? What did I do? What did I do?" I murmur

under my breath. "I didn't mean to—she's not a distraction. She's —" The weight of my words sink to the pit of my stomach, making it churn until I feel bile rise up. I gag and almost trip over my feet as I run to his bathroom and double over onto the toilet.

My throat burns as the acidic liquid spills out, and my stomach constricts excruciatingly as the vomit continues to pour out of my mouth. I'm convulsing violently, gasping for air until my stomach empties.

I'm not sure how long I stay crouched over the toilet, but when I'm done, I fall on my ass, my back smacking hard against the tub.

"Here." Angel hands me a small wet washcloth and flushes the toilet.

I wipe my mouth and drop it on the ground, burying my face in my clammy hands. My breath grows shallow, and my chest becomes tight with every inhale. I can't breathe. Fuck, I can't breathe.

"I can't..." I'm gasping for air or choking on it, I don't know, but I'm suffocating; everything's going black. "I c-can't breathe. Angel...I can't—"

"Hey, you're okay." He's in front of me in an instant, hands on my shoulders, but he feels so far away. "You're okay, Danny. Breathe in and out," he instructs, and I think, *he sounds distant. Why does he look blurry? I can't breathe.* "You're okay. I'm right here. Breathe in and out. Danny, look at me. I'm right here. I'm not going anywhere. You're okay."

I think I nod and faintly hear him until his voice grows louder.

"Danny, look at me," he urges, squeezing my shoulders, and when I finally do, his trembling lips lift. "Breathe...yeah, just like that. Breathe."

My throat, my chest—everything hurts, everything burns. I want to speak, but I can't. Everything feels tight, swollen, like I'm on the brink of death. I'm shaking. I can't stop shaking.

"What's wrong with me?" I gasp sharply, my voice breaking.

I'm not sure if I actually even said those words or if I thought them.

"Nothing is wrong with you. You're just hurting." His breath catches, but he clears it. "There's nothing wrong with that, but you need to talk to someone."

I shake my head. "I-I'm fine. I'm fine. I'm—"

"You're not. You told Josie you attempted...many times. That's not—" He blinks several times, pausing as he sucks in a harrowing breath. "fine. That's not fine. I can't lose you. Dammit, Daniel." His words are a mere choked whisper as he blankets his arms around me, holding me tightly until it slaps me back to reality. "I'm here for you."

It's as eye-opening as it is scary as fuck because I realize he knows and she knows. What will they think of me? What have I done?

My gaze flickers aimlessly as my mind sinks into the dark void I was trying so hard to stay out of.

I want to talk, to move, to hug him because he needs it, but I can't do anything but sink further into a lifeless pit.

Dropping my head on his shoulder, I close my eyes and feel nothing.

It hurts and that'll probably never go away, but you can share your pain with me.

Josie.

"I need to talk to Josie. I need to make things right. I need her." I sit back, forcing myself to snap out of it.

He tugs back, staring at me emphatically. "You need to rest. Maybe you can see her later and—"

"No, fuck that. I need to see her now. I need to make things right. I need her to know that I didn't mean what I said because I didn't. I swear I didn't."

"I know you didn't. I know you really care about her."

"I need to see her." I push up on my feet and he follows suit.

"Why don't you drink the water, swallow an ibuprofen, take a shower, and then I'll bring you to her, okay?"

"You don't need to come. I'm going to talk to her. I'm going to make things right. I don't want to lose her."

Something flashes on his face that makes me think he doesn't believe it'll happen. But then he nods. "I'm coming with. You shouldn't be driving after last night and right now."

Reluctantly, I agree. "How did she get home last night?" I hate myself.

"Noah took her. He made sure she got home safe. I promise."

I really hate myself.

I find her outside, sitting on the grass with a towel wrapped around her body, staring straight ahead. She doesn't turn or make a sound when I approach her.

"Josie, I'm sorry. I'm so sorry."

She rises, turning around before I get to stand in front of her, and takes a few steps back, adding distance between us.

"Josie." I stretch my hands out, but she takes another step back. "Josie, please. I'm so sorry. I didn't mean to hurt you. I didn't mean what I said. I shouldn't—I wish I could take it all back. I'm sorry. Please forgive me. Please," I plead desperately, with every inch of me.

Her eyes level with mine and my heart squeezes. I try to reach out for her again, but she steps back.

"Josie, baby. Please, please, please," I beg and drop to my knees, staring up at her desperately. "I'm so sorry. I'm so sorry."

Her bottom lip quivers and she bites it. Shaking her head, she stands in front of me and sinks to her knees. She circles her arms around my neck, and presses me to her wet body.

I bury my face in the crook of her neck and pull her as close to me as I possibly can. My world steadies and I breathe easier.

"I'm sorry," she delivers in an agonizing tone.

"You have nothing to be sorry about. It's me. I'm sorry. I shouldn't have said what I said last night. I shouldn't have—"

"Daniel," she achingly whimpers and pulls back just enough to cup my cheeks and tilt my head back so I can look at her. There's a sorrowful look on her face, like she's the one who's sorry, who's struggling with words. "You deserve good things. You deserve to be happy."

My brows pinch in. "I am happy. You make me happy."

"No, no, I don't. You are *not* happy with me. You've made yourself miserable. You've put your needs, your feelings, yourself last for the sake of making me happy. I think you lied to yourself enough that you believed it, but you're not. I can't make you happy. I can't give you the emotional stability you need. I wanted to..." She gets choked up on a sob. "So badly give it to you, but I can't. I don't know how."

I vigorously shake my head, tightening my hold on her. "You can. You have. I *am* happy with you. I want you. I need you, Josie. Believe me. Please."

She sadly smiles at me. "You deserve good things."

"*Please* don't give up on us."

"I missed the signs." She laughs with remorse. "I should've seen them because *I've* been there, but *I* overlooked them. I didn't do enough. I'm sorry you had to hide yourself. I'm sorry you—"

"It's not your fault. I'm fine."

"Stop saying that!" She drops her hands and jerks away from me. "You are not fine. I'm not enough for you."

"You are! You are enough for me! So enough, I can't stop drowning in you. I crave you. I want you. I need you. I lo—"

She wraps her arms around. "Don't. Don't say that. You'll regret it."

I kiss her temple over and over. "I'm not. I do, Josie. You need to believe me. I—"

"You need to put yourself first. I need you to love yourself first. I need you to take care of yourself first. You can't be with me and not do that. You just can't."

"I can do both. I can, I will, I promise."

"I know you will but not with me. I need you to let me go."

"No, Josefine, I can't." My heart accelerates, and my brain fights to figure out what to do, what to say, but she withdraws from me.

"You can and you will." She smiles at me and those fireworks still fucking blast. "Please take care of yourself." She kisses my forehead and stands, but I anxiously grab her wrist, drawing her back to me.

"Don't do this to me. I need you. Please don't go." I grind my teeth, wishing the tears would stop, but they won't, and hers don't either.

"You deserve good things." She wipes my tears away. "You deserve to be happy. I'm sorry I couldn't show you how, but you'll find it. I know you will."

She looks away as she slips her hand from mine and walks away from me, not once turning back while all I do is stare at her.

53

DANIEL

April 2nd

"Stop looking at me like that," I grumble.

Angel grabs my arm, jerking me away before we enter the weight room, and shoves me further down the hall until we're far away from everyone.

"So we're not going to talk about it? You're just going to act like everything's fine?" The hurt expression on his face makes me look away.

"I don't know what you expect me to say."

He grips my shoulder. "I'm here for you. Talk to me."

"I'm fine." I shrug his hand away and turn, but he grabs my arm.

"Fine is *not*..." He peeks over again, making sure no one is listening. "Drinking to forget. Fine is not someone admitting they've *attempted* multiple times. That's not okay and after yesterday, you can be upset. Be mad. Be anything instead of fucking fine."

Since yesterday there's this never-ending sinking feeling. Like an aftershock inside my body, every nerve clenches with dread.

I'm so overstimulated. I don't know if I really feel something or nothing at all.

I don't know what to do. I don't know how to feel. I don't know how to be without *her*.

Regardless of what's going on, I need to keep moving. I need to do something other than nothing or I'm going to crash. There's this weight in my chest, almost like a ticking time bomb, waiting to go off.

I need her so badly.

"I'm fine." I plaster on a smile and nod for him to follow me. He doesn't at first, but a moment later, he's behind me and we're walking into the weight room.

My roommates say nothing to me, but I feel their stares. They helped me move out because I physically couldn't touch anything without breaking down or knocking on her bedroom door to give me another chance.

Angel had to force me out of the house while the guys grabbed my stuff. He had a feeling that was going to happen and called them. They didn't say anything to me and still didn't this morning. I can tell they want to, but I'm hoping they'll stick to keeping their mouths shut.

They do. They say nothing and act no different than they do on any other day. But that doesn't change how I feel. I can't hide or shove the dark cloud looming over my head away. But I try hard, I smile, I play along, I laugh, I do it all. It still does nothing for me because once I'm in the locker room after weight lift, I notice how little I feel.

Closing my eyes, I rub my temples and breathe in and out.

"I bet you're happy, huh?" I hear Bryson's condescending voice behind me.

"Not right now." I grab my stuff to shower, but it seems like he's set on pissing me off because when I turn, he steps closer.

"You think you're better. You just—"

I clench my teeth, fisting my hands, but I don't punch him. I promised Coach I wouldn't. "I don't know what you're going on about, but get out of my way."

"Any girl. You could've had any girl, but you picked Josie? Of all the girls, you just had to pick her?" His nostrils flare and a flash of glooms strikes his face.

"For fuck's sake." I pinch the bridge of my nose. *Breathe in and out.* "Get over it."

"Get over it," he mocks dryly. "I bet you're happy, huh? You bring her around me. You live with her. You get to parade her around. Get to—"

"We broke up!" The pressure in my chest expands through my body. My fingers stiffly curve in, making them hard to move. "We're not together!" I inhale a shallow breath. "I don't live with her!" Why is it so hot in here? "I don't know what you fucking want from me!" My ears are ringing, and my hands shake. "I don't —" Why is everything so blurry? I squeeze my eyes shut for a second, but when I open them everything tunnels. "I don't—" Why can't I breathe?

My chest is pounding. God, it hurts. It really fucking hurts.

I walk away, or at least I think I do? I'm walking, I'm moving.

No.

Stop!

Everything hurts.

I can't breathe.

My chest—my lungs, they violently expand but I absorb no air. Did they stop working? Why aren't they working?

My face. I can't feel it. Why can't I feel my face? My face. My chest. Why is nothing working? Am I dying?

My legs sway with every step despite how heavy they feel.

I need to sit. I need air.

I can't breathe.

You make me so happy.

I drop to the ground. I don't want to, but I do. I don't know what I'm doing.

I tuck my legs to my chest, raising my palms to cover my ears, but the piercing ringing doesn't stop.

Where is that noise coming from?

Why can't I breathe?

"Get...everyone..."

Yelling. Who's yelling?

"Out!"

I can't see. Am I sweating? Stop sweating!

I'm always thinking about you.

Everything's spinning. My thoughts aren't mine. I can't control anything. I'm so lost. I'm so hot. Am I dying?

"I can't..." It feels like someone is choking me, it hurts so bad. I don't know if I got the words out.

I rock back and forth, squeezing my ears, but noise persists incessantly.

"...hurts," I sputter out and manage to inhale a tiny breath, but it only makes me dizzy.

"Hey, Sparky. You're okay." Coach? When did he get here? I can't see him. Everything's so dark. Why can't I see him? "You're okay, Danny."

"I...I'm...dying..."

"You're not dying." He moves my hands away from my ears and holds them. "You're okay. Just breathe for me, okay? In like this," he softly instructs. "Then out like this. Breathe for me."

I do but it hurts worse. Everything inside me swells and feels like it's getting stabbed with a million knives.

"Danny, you've got it. Breathe for me."

"I-I can't..."

I know you will but not with me. I need you to let me go.

"You can. You're doing it right now."

His face comes into view. It's blurry, but I see him.

"You're having a panic attack. You're okay, Sparky. I need you to breathe for me, okay? You can do it, just breathe," he instructs again just as gently as the first time.

"I'm...not dying?" Am I crying? I feel the hot tears streaking down my face. I'm drenched in them and sweat, so much sweat.

"No, no. You're not. You're okay. You had a panic attack." His face is a little clearer now, and now that I see him better, I see that he's crouched on the floor in front of me, still holding my hands. "But I've got you, okay? I've got you. Keep breathing for me, okay? You're doing good."

I attempt to nod but my neck is so tense. "I'm sorry." I raggedly pant, feeling so embarrassed.

"Don't ever apologize, Sparky. Things happen and sometimes those things are out of our control." He sits next to me, brings his arm around my shoulder, and hugs me.

"I don't know what I'm doing." I choke on a sob, the void in my chest burns. I don't understand why when there's nothing there.

There is so much effort put into existing. What the fuck even is the point? Why do I keep trying?

"That's okay not to know. We're going to figure it out together, okay?" There is so much hope in his voice, I believe it for a second until it slips from my fingers. "We need to have the doctor check you out and then we'll go from there, okay? But you're going to be okay, Danny. I promise you will be."

"Danny?" Penelope whispers, stepping into my room.

I clutch my comforter, burrowing myself deeper into my bed.

"I'm fine, Pen." I close my eyes, my head sharply pounding. "You don't have to be here."

She rushes to my side. I don't open my eyes, but I know she's sitting there, probably watching me with concern.

"Don't say you're fine. You had two panic attacks. That's not fine." She leans over me, wrapping her arms around me, and envelops me in a tight hug. "It's okay not to be okay. Don't be embarrassed."

"Did Gray tell you?" He has a thing for not keeping his mouth shut.

"It doesn't matter who told me. You're not okay. Do you want me to call Mom and Dad? We can drive back home and—"

"No. I don't want you to call them. I don't want them to know about this."

"But they should know. Especially with—"

"Adrian's anniversary, I know! But I don't want them to know. I don't need them to worry over nothing."

I shrug her off me and sit up, frustratedly dragging my fingers through my hair. Anguish floods her face as she scans mine. I know I look like shit. I got looks from my teammates outside the locker room after I finally got the strength to stand.

Coach D'Angelo and I sat on the ground for almost thirty minutes. I would've stayed there longer but Dr. Emerson, our team doctor, wanted to do a further assessment, and I needed to shower.

There were a series of things he said. Panic attack, dehydration, depression, stress, anxiety, medication, and so much more, but I kept coming and going.

At times, I was watching myself drift away. I wanted to pull myself back, force my body back in my own, but I couldn't. I just watched it go. And at others, I was hearing what he was saying, but I couldn't connect to anything.

A part of me felt untethered from my body, while the other was watching that disconnected part teeter over the edge. So close yet I couldn't feel a thing.

I was just there.

I was told to sit out of today's game and this coming weekend. Not too long ago, I would've fought against doing so. While baseball sometimes made me feel guilty, it was one of the two things I had that gave me purpose.

Now that I don't have her, they could kick me off the team and I couldn't bring myself to care.

"This isn't nothing." She grabs my hand. "This is your health.

You matter, Danny, and I'm tired of you pretending like everything is fine. I know since Adrian—"

"Dad doesn't care. He pretends to care but he doesn't. You know that. He blames me for what happened to Adrian. You were there! You heard him say it. So why would he care now? When he hasn't since then."

We were in high school. He was a freshman, and I was a sophomore. It was spring break. One of our friend's parents on our baseball travel team invited Adrian and me to go to the beach with them. Dad and Mom wouldn't let us go at first. They'd never been fans of us spending the night at other people's houses, so going away for an entire week was definitely a no. But eventually we wore them down after begging and having our friend's parents ask them. They were hesitant, but they had rules, rules we swore we'd follow. They made me promise as the older sibling, to take care of him, make sure he didn't do anything stupid or act out.

I did everything until they went jet skiing. I was supposed to go, but I'd gotten a cramp and needed to sit it out. I didn't want Adrian to go because he'd be in the ocean, but he promised to keep his life jacket on, and our friend and his older brothers said he'd be all right.

The life jacket was faulty; the straps came off, and somehow he fell off. He panicked and they tried to grab him, but he was flailing his arms and freaking out. The waves just happened to be stronger that day and it kept pulling him back.

Everyone acted quickly; the lifeguard got to him and took him out of the water. My friend's parents held me back while I screamed at the lifeguard to save him, to not stop doing CPR.

Mom and Dad got the call and the moment they showed up, Dad said, "It's your fault," "I should've gone with him," and "I shouldn't have let him go." He repeated that over and over.

A lot happened that day, but I remember everything. Dad's words, most of all.

"I know." Her eyes glisten. "But I know he didn't mean it.

He's sorry. I know he is. You have to talk to him and Mom. You have to tell them how you feel. You have to—"

"This just isn't about Adrian. *She* broke up with me."

She reels back, eyes triple in size. "What? But I thought—what happened? Oh Danny, I'm so sorry. I had no idea. Angel didn't tell me that."

It was Angel?

"It's not her fault. I said things I regret, things I didn't mean. I'm so stupid. She was already going through it, and I just had to —" My eyes burn. "I need to be alone. I don't need them here. I don't need anyone here. I need you leave me alone, Penelope, because I'm fucking losing my mind and I can't—I need to be alone," I beg and drop back in the bed, lifting the comforter over my head. "For once, just listen to me. I just want to be alone."

There's a loud silence, the kind I hadn't heard since Adrian, and although I shouldn't, I drown in it. I let myself fall deeper in the void and ignore what she's saying, if she's saying anything at all.

I just let myself drift away.

54

DANIEL

April 3rd

There's a muted knock on my door and an indistinct voice; I think it's Coach D'Angelo, but I'm not sure because my back is facing the door, and my foggy gaze is pinned to the wall.

I blink but otherwise I don't move. I stay still, gripping my comforter close to my body, letting it shield me from everything.

"Danny...you..." His voice comes and goes. It sounds distant and there's an echo to it. "Danny, how are you?" I think he asks again.

Why is he here? I just want to be alone. Is that too much to ask?

Closing my eyes, I murmur words, hoping they're enough so he'll leave me alone. "I'm fine. Just resting like Dr. Emerson suggested."

There's a heavy dip in my bed. I think he's sitting, but I don't turn to look. He heaves a heavy sigh, but he doesn't speak. At least I think he doesn't. I'm not sure, and my mind is floating again. Everything feels distorted, and the connection between my brain and body isn't there.

"—leave of absence."

"Hmm?" I blink again.

"After talking to Dr. Emerson, I think it's best if you take a leave of absence. But I don't want you to worry about a thing or the media. We want you to see Dr. Jarvis; she's the psychologist for—"

"I don't need to talk to anyone. I'm fine. I just need to sleep."

"This isn't negotiable." He places his hand on my shoulder. "It's okay to ask for help and..."

I tune him out, knowing it won't do me any good to argue.

I only hear half of what he says and mumble an, "okay," knowing it's what I need to say.

"We're all here for you, Daniel."

April 6th

"Hey," Angel quietly says.

I hum, keeping my back to him.

"I didn't wake you, did I?" I hear the soft pad of his footsteps get closer.

"No."

"We missed you out there." The dull ache in his voice squeezes my chest. I want to say something to fix that, but I physically can't get out of the void. I close my eyes, burrowing deeper in the comforter. "We were close, but we lost again. It pains me to say this, but Cal Central is good. God, I fucking hate them and Miles's stupid face."

My mouth opens, but as hard as I try, I can't force the words out. They stay clinging to the back of my throat, refusing to let go.

"It's okay though. We can't win all the series." He fills the silence. "Are you hungry? Noah is cooking, although I'd be careful because Gray is trying to help. I think he's making one of the sides. I don't know, but chew carefully. If something tastes off, spit it out. The last thing I need is for you to get food poisoning." I hear the smile in his voice. "I want you to be on top of it when you come back."

"I don't know if I'll go back."

"You will. Don't say that. Everything's going to be okay, Danny. Just take it easy. We're here for you, okay?"

April 9th

"We're back. We went into overtime, but we won." Kai enters my room. I feel him sit on the side of my bed, and for a while, he's quiet. "How are you feeling?"

I shrug even though I know he can't see my shoulders under the comforter.

"Coach is making us all do one-on-one meetings with him. I'm not a fan; I don't like talking about that kind of stuff either, but I'm doing it. Although it's stupid because the worst I feel is homesick... I shouldn't be upset about—I'm sorry, I shouldn't have said that. Talking about this is weird, but I want you to know that as much as I hate it, it's good to open up. I know it's hard and I know you're hurting, Danny, but you should do it."

My thoughts spiral, making my head pound.

"Don't apologize." My voice doesn't sound like my own when I speak.

"We're all here for you. The guys have been asking about you. Even Bryson. I know that sounds hard to believe..." He trails off. "We all love you. Don't forget that. If you need anything, anything at all, we've got you. We can't wait for you to come back whenever you're ready. We're here for you."

April 11th

I'm sorry it couldn't have been me, Adrian, I'm so fucking sorry.

"Hi, Danny." Pen pads into my room and lies next to me. "I —" Her voice quivers, but she quickly clears her throat and lays her arm over my covered body. "I miss him."

Today's the anniversary of Adrian's death. There would've been no anniversary if I had just been with him. Why didn't I go? Why didn't I check his life jacket? Why did I let him go?

"And I miss you. I don't know what's going on in your head, but I want to know. Talk to me. Tell me what's wrong. I'm all ears. Please don't keep shutting yourself out. Please," she desolately begs and sniffles. "I love you, and I don't want to lose you too."

I clench my teeth, fighting back the tears. The hole in my chest has grown, but it still burns despite nothing being there. I don't understand what the hell is going on with me.

"I'm going to be fine. I just need to be alone."

"You keep saying that. You don't need to be alone. You need—"

"I need Adrian, but he's dead. I need *her*, but she left me. That's all I fucking need, and I can't have either. So just leave me alone, that's all I'm asking. Just fucking listen! I want to be alone! I *need* to be alone!"

I hear her cry behind me, but she doesn't move her arm. "Whatever. I'm not going anywhere. I'm here for whenever you're ready to talk."

I want to ask about *her*, but I don't want to find out what she thinks about me and how fucked up my head is.

"I'm here for you."

April 14th

"I think I made a mistake. I should've gone to NCU." Gray stumbles into my room. "Let me tell you, the girls there are hella fine, all of them. Oh, guess what," he animatedly says as he plops down on my bed. "I met Julianna and, unfortunately, Landon. I swear he could be a serial killer. He has this vibe—anyway, she's just as hot as the pictures, and her friends?" He hums in approval. "Yeah, I definitely came to the wrong school. If it hadn't been for my parents, I'd be there, but you know...I'm glad I didn't go there. I'm happy I came here. I'm glad there was a mix-up and I moved in here with you guys."

I draw out a fatigued breath, wishing he'd stop talking, wishing he and everyone else would leave me alone. But as much as I want to yell that, I don't, I can't. I stay hidden underneath my comforter, masking it all with a, "hmm," to let him know I'm still breathing, that I'm hearing what he's saying although I physically can't grasp anything.

"I know you're lost in your head right now. I know it feels like a fucking maze and it's dark too, but you'll get out. You'll find the exit. I promise you will. You just need to keep going. Follow the damn light, Daniel. We'll be at the end waiting for you. Love you, man. We're here for you."

April 16th

"I don't have words or really anything to make you feel better. I just want you to know that I'm here. We all are." Noah's voice and his words continue to drone into my head until I close my eyes and fall asleep again.

April 17th

"Daniel?"

My eyes pop open but I go stock-still at the familiar voice. I want to move, to do something other than lie here, but I can't. I'm afraid to hear the disappointment in his voice, to see it on his face too.

I wish he wasn't here. I hope Mom isn't either. I didn't want them to worry. They texted and asked why I haven't played. I told them I strained something; that's what Coach told everyone else too.

"*Daniel, mijo.*"

I stay hidden inside the dark corner in my head, hoping this is all a dream or a figment of my imagination. But it's not. I feel the weight of his body on my bed and the heat of his tentative palm on my back over the blanket.

"I'm sorry." His voice sounds frail and cracked. "Penelope called and..." He releases a broken breath. "I'm sorry. I'm so sorry."

My body painfully seizes at his agonizing words. "It's not your fault. I just want to be alone."

"No, you don't need to be alone. I'm sorry if you..." He clears his throat. "You couldn't talk to me or your mom. I had no idea. I didn't know how to talk to you and—"

"*No te preocupes.* I'm fine. I'm seeing a therapist and—"

"You are not—"

I shove everything off me and sit up, shoving his hand away. The sorrow on his face makes everything inside me crumble. I hate that even though it's been five years since Adrian, I'm still causing him pain, that *I'm* the reason for it. The burden of knowing I'm hurting him burns me alive. I don't know how not to do that.

"You shouldn't have come! I'm fine! I'm fine! I'm—" My breath catches and tears blur my vision. "I'm sorry. I didn't want to worry you. I didn't want to—" I suffocate on a breath and try to fight back the sob that rips out of my throat.

He wraps his arms around me in a crushing hold, shaking his head, repeating, "Don't apologize. You didn't do anything wrong. I'm sorry. I should've talked to you sooner. I'm sorry I failed you. *Perdoname, Daniel*."

"It was my fault." I bury my face against his chest, hating that the tears won't stop falling out. "I shouldn't have let him go. I'm sorry." I let him hold me instead of pushing away, knowing I don't have the strength in me to fight anymore.

Sobs wrack my body, making it shake uncontrollably against his, but he doesn't pull away. He holds me like he did when I was a kid, when I'd get hurt or he hugged me just because, and for some reason, that makes me cry more.

I don't know how long he holds me for, but it's not until I'm hiccupping and breathing out harshly that I genuinely feel a tiny morsel of myself again.

He rubs my back, his chin resting on my head, as he whispers words that I don't make out until my breathing evens out.

"It was never your fault. I shouldn't have ever said what I did. I shouldn't have acted the way I did. I was so mad, so sad, and you were there. I'm so sorry this had to happen for me to talk to you. I wanted to so many times, but I never knew how. I never knew how to pull you back to me, to fix what I broke. I'm sorry. I should've listened to your mom, to Penelope, to Josie. I should've talked to you. *Perdoname*."

Fresh tears fill my eyes. "J-Josie told you to talk to me?"

"At the game. I should've done something. I was just afraid, upset, angry—not at you, but I ended up taking it out on you because I was stupid. I know it's not enough, but I am sorry. I don't want you to hate me. Please let me in; don't shut me out."

"I never hated you. I thought you hated me, so I just stayed out of your way," I admit, biting the inside of my cheek until a metallic taste coats my tongue. "You never looked at me the same after Adrian's funeral. You didn't look at me at all. I felt like I wasn't doing enough for you. I want to be enough. I want to make you and Mom proud and happy."

He pulls back, keeping his hands on my shoulder, and looks down at me. His face is just as puffy and red as mine feels. A small smile curls on his lips. "*Nosotros siempre hemos estado orgullosos de ti.* I know I didn't show it like your mom did, but I've always been proud. I've recorded all of your games on TV and have taken so many pictures, I had to get more storage on my phone. I'm sorry I didn't show it enough or at all, but I promise I've always been proud of you. You could stop playing now, and I'd still be proud of you."

My brows raise in surprise. "But you would always say I did 'just good' or I could always improve."

His face flushes. "It's not an excuse, but you know I've never been good with words. Anytime we were around each other, I felt you draw away, like you couldn't wait to get away from me. I didn't know what to say. I'm sorry."

He embraces me again and I let the silence draw out. The emotions and light swirling in my head overwhelm me.

"I thought if I left, it'd be easier for you. Sometimes…I thought it'd be easier for everyone if I was…*gone.*" He hugs me tighter. "I-I tried a few times over the years, but I never could go through with it. I don't know why. But I do know I hated myself every time because it wasn't fair that I got to enjoy my life and Adrian didn't. I wish it had been me. I'm sorry it wasn't me."

I feel guilty. He stayed fifteen and I'm twenty-one. It's not fair. It's just not.

"Do not apologize." His breath catches and a deafening silence washes over us at my admittance.

Until the moment I got drunk and made an ass out of myself, I never admitted this, but he needs to know; I can't hold on to it anymore. The guilt keeps dragging me down. I don't know how to not feel it.

"You, Penelope, and your mom give me purpose. I don't know what I'd do without all three of you. I'm so sorry for making you feel this way. I'm so sorry you felt that was the way out. We need you in our lives. We need you. We love you."

His words are both liberating and overwhelming.

"I'm not fine. I haven't been for a while. Well..." I clear my throat, the large lump making it hard to speak. "I was okay when I was with...Josie." Angry tears rush down my face. "She made me feel like *me* again, but I felt guilty for feeling okay. I felt guilty that Adrian would never get to experience *a Josie* in his life. I hated myself because she—" Memories of her play in my head. "Was it for me and she made me happy. She made me feel so good, I looked forward to a future with her. I wasn't thinking about Adrian and the future he wouldn't get to have. How selfish is that? He died because of me, and I was happy planning my future with her?" I close my eyes, focusing on the rapid beat of his heart. "I'm not okay, and I'm tired of pretending like I am. I don't want to feel like this anymore, but I don't know how to not feel... empty."

"He didn't die because of you. I need you to understand that. It wasn't your fault. It never was. You have the right to be happy with Josie, so let yourself be happy with her. I saw the way you looked at her, how she looked at you. Your mom saw it too. And it's all Penelope talks about."

"We're not together anymore," I say through clenched teeth. "So can we not talk about her right now because if I'm being honest, it's making me feel really anxious." I fist my trembling hands. "I just wanted you to know I'm not fine, but I want to be."

He nods. "We're going to work through it together, okay? Things are going to get better. I promise." He pulls back a little to stare down at me. "Thank you for talking to me. I'm so sorry it took this for me to be here, but I promise I'm not going anywhere. I'm here for you always, Daniel. I love you."

I don't force a smile like I usually would just for the sake of looking okay. He doesn't look disappointed when I don't and that makes me breathe easier.

"I love you too," I say, realizing I'm not stuck in the void. I don't feel happy, but I don't feel empty either.

55

JOSEFINE

April 3rd

WHAT ARE YOU SORRY FOR?
I thought I could hide what I felt to make you happy.

I skim the empty living room, stalling on the areas where his stuff used to be. I struggle to breathe when I glance at something else. My head spins and my lungs compress painfully the more I look, absorbing the reality of what my life is again.

Dark. Empty. Alone.

My bottom lip wobbles, but I press my lips together to make it stop. That only makes them cast downward and quiver harder.

His friends came and grabbed his stuff. I didn't want them to. I didn't want to hide in my bathroom while they took his stuff. I wanted him to stay. I wanted to tell him I was capable of loving him. That I was capable of being enough to help him, but I couldn't because I knew I wasn't enough to be what he needed emotionally. But who am I kidding? I was never going to be what he needed in general.

I inhale a breath, but it gets stuck in the middle of my throat when I spot the gift bag, the one I know holds the picture frames *we* were supposed to fill. The flowers he got me are still in the vase in the middle of the island. The words we shared right here, where I'm standing, stay confined in this space, choking me with the reminders of us.

Letting me know all they'll be are memories.

Just that.

Suppressing what I feel, I head back up to my room and spend the rest of the week in bed.

April 7th

I stall inside the restroom, not wanting to go to the class he and I have together. I skipped last week because I couldn't bring myself to see him, but I couldn't today.

I want to say it's because I'm so close to being done with classes, but I'd be lying. I just want to see him. Something is wrong with me because I know seeing him will hurt, but I need to anyway. Just one more time. That's all I want.

I don't know what I'll do once I do. I want to believe I'll keep it cool and not succumb to the emotions I keep suppressing. My brain keeps sending these signals to let it all out, but I don't need to do that. The last time I did, I almost ended it all.

I don't want to die, but I don't want to be sad. I can't let myself spiral. I just can't.

Pushing all my thoughts away, I head to the classroom. When I step inside, my chest clenches when I look at the table we sit at. He's not there yet, but the memories are.

"Josefine." Professor Carleson waves me over the podium where he stands.

"Hey."

"Hey, I just wanted to let you know Daniel won't be joining us anymore due to his baseball commitments." Everything in me sinks. "But don't fret. You can join Maddy and Annie."

He points to the girls sitting in the second row, and they're looking at me with friendly smiles on their faces. Mine resembles something like it, I think. I'm not sure. I can't make myself care what's on my face when the inside of my body is shattering.

April 9th

The endless loop has returned. I don't know how to get out of it, and it's driving me crazy. I'm stuck between screaming, crying, or doing nothing. I don't know how to snap out of it. I don't know how to be without him.

I can't even be in my own house anymore because it all smells like him—my room, the living room, the kitchen. There are little reminders of him every-fucking-where. From the gift bag still sitting in the living room, the flowers that are now dead, the bear he gave me, the ball he wrote on, the stupid jerseys, the goggles and board, the portable CD player with the disc. I never finished listening to the songs and I know I never will. The Post-it notes... I have so many, and I know there's more in the house, but I won't look for them.

I need to sell the house. Have someone move everything for me. I can't be there anymore.

That's why I'm here on campus. There's a possibility I could run into him but it's slim. I'm staying away from all the buildings he has classes in, away from the areas his teammates usually are. His friends probably hate me, the same way Bryson's friend hated me after I broke up with him.

Unlike Bryson's friend who I didn't care for, Daniel's were different and knowing that's gone too, fuck, why do I even care? I'm used to being alone.

I'm fine alone.

I repeat that over and over, but when I set foot in the library, the thought dies when I spot Penelope. I haven't heard from her since the night Daniel got drunk.

I don't have to wonder how things will be like between us because she turns, stares directly at me, rolls her eyes, and focuses back on her friends.

Right. I saw that coming. After all, they're siblings. I know how much she cares for him.

I thought I could hide what I felt to make you happy.

I...I'm fine...alone.

April 10th

Sometimes...I wish I was dead.

His resigned words ring in my ears, repeatedly and scarily, until they've seeped in the crevices of my brain, branding themselves with a burn so deep, I feel them sear into my veins.

How did I miss the signs?

I swim faster, overexerting myself. My body begs for me to stop but I keep going. I ignore my lungs and how they pump excessively to keep up.

I'm not happy, Josefine.

Why didn't I ask more questions? Why didn't I pick up on the signs? Why couldn't I see them? He saved me, but who was saving him?

We both want to die.

My body gives out, sucking air it's desperately seeking despite me still being in the water. In the process I swallow a lot of it, so much, my throat and nose burns as I cough it back up. I lift myself up and climb out. I crawl on my hands and knees away from the pool, sputtering the water out but as I do, my shaky arms give out and I collapse.

"Fuck," I groan, smothering every pent-up emotion wanting to burst.

I missed the signs because I'm an unfeeling piece of shit.

I deserve to be alone.

April 15th

My phone buzzes on my nightstand. It's probably Vienna; I haven't answered her messages. I don't know what she wants or what she knows, but I know I don't want to talk to her. I don't want to take out what I feel on her.

I'll get angry if she tries to get me to talk, and I don't want to do that. I don't want to do anything. I can't get out of bed, and I hate it because it's not my room; it's one of the spares. I couldn't sleep in my bedroom because some of his things are in there.

I feel everything in me slowly detaching and losing control. I don't want to, but I just don't know how to make it stop.

Make yourself feel, I told Daniel, but it was a bunch of bullshit because I did and now, I'm alone. I let myself be happy, but he wasn't. He was faking it, and I didn't see it.

I close my eyes, but I catch something as I do. Something yellow.

It's a Post-it he randomly placed, one I was hoping I'd never find.

I want to pretend it's not there, but my body is moving robotically in a way that's not mine, going towards it. When I grab it, the tiny string that was keeping me tethered to sanity snaps.

I'm so happy you're here, Josefine!
With love, Garcia

Tears are running down my face before I can stop them. I don't know when they had the chance to build in my ducts, but they're furiously pouring down. I crumble the paper, drop it on the ground, and stalk to the kitchen. I grab the vase with the flowers still in them and throw them across the living room.

The glass shatters against the wall, the water spills everywhere, and the dry wilted petals and leaves unhurriedly fly everywhere.

Absently, I grab something else, slinging it across the wall, not caring if it breaks or where it lands. But it's not enough. I'm still vehemently raging, and there's not enough of anything in the living room to destroy.

I head to the only place I've never touched, her goddamn office. The one place that I always steered away from. I push the door open, grabbing her medals, trophies, picture frames, papers —anything that meant everything to her—and throw it against the wall as hard as I can.

It all rips, breaks, or falls to the ground. When I'm done, when I'm slumped against the wall staring at it all, I realize how empty I am because this changes nothing.

She's not coming back. *He's* not coming back.

Feeling did nothing but make me realize how alone I am.

I exhale harshly, raising my knees to my chest but stop when I see a streak of red running down my forearm. I somehow cut the side of my hand and didn't feel it. It bleeds a lot, not enough I could die, but it's bad enough it drips on the floor and my clothes.

I let it be and slump down on the floor in a fetal position. I'm too tired to care and move.

I really wanted to make him happy, is the last thought I have before I close my eyes and fall asleep.

"Josie!"

I peel my eyes open, but close them when I see the mess in front of me. I can't deal with this right now.

"Josie!"

My brows furrow at the distant voice. It's feminine and familiar.

"Call 9-1-1!"

"No, don't do that." The words are barely audible, but I think they heard me.

"You're bleeding and your house—"

Vienna's frantic, shrill voice has me sitting up. "Wait, what are you doing here?" But it's Angel standing next to her, his phone in his hand, that has my eyes almost popping out of the sockets. "Why are you guys in my house?"

"I don't know what he's doing here, but you weren't answering your phone! What the hell, Josie? You had me sick and worried and then I find you like this? Who did this? I'll call the police and—"

She was worried? "No, don't. I'm okay. I did this, but I'm okay. It's really not that bad. Wait, how did you guys get in?"

"I broke a window. It was the only way I could get inside," Angel answers.

"You broke my window?" I feel so disoriented and anxious. "What are you doing here?" *Is Daniel here?* I want to ask, but I don't. Still, he must hear the question in my head.

"It's just me. I, uh, I came to check up on you."

"Why?" Vienna and I simultaneously ask.

He side-eyes Vi and then looks down at me. "I know about Christmas Eve. I just wanted to make sure you were okay."

"Isn't that something Danny should be doing?" She stares at him quizzically and skeptically.

"We broke up," I mumble. Saying it out loud makes everything shatter inside me again.

She gasps, staring at me with disbelief. "What? How? I'm sorry, I don't think I heard that correctly. You guys broke up, but Josie, he looks at you like—"

I shake my head, rubbing my eyes as they sting. "I really don't want to talk about it. I'm sorry I worried you, and I still don't understand what you're doing here, but I'm fine. I just..." I'm embarrassed now. They weren't supposed to see me like this. "Had a moment."

"He says he's fine too, but he's not. So don't lie."

"What happened on Christmas Eve?" She's not being pushy, but she looks and sounds concerned.

I lower my gaze, hiding my face behind my hands. I'd lie but maybe she'll leave me alone if she hears how fucked up I am. "I was going to kill myself, but Daniel stopped me. Is that what he told you?"

"He went back every day after that until I followed him on New Year's Eve," he confesses.

"Josie." Vienna sits on the ground in front of me, her face distraught. "I—" She clears her throat and blinks repeatedly as if she were trying to stop herself from crying. She sits up and hugs me.

That takes me by surprise. I don't know what to do, so I do nothing but sit here.

"I'm fine," I whisper but my voice breaks. "I'm fine."

"Don't say that. You're not fine. You don't have to pretend. We're here for you."

I feel so awkward and don't mean to but accidentally make eye contact with Angel and see him nod. He doesn't know me like that, so why does he even care?

"You guys don't have to be here." I'm pleading more than telling them. I told Daniel the same thing and he stayed and now he's not here. I can't afford to let myself care for anyone else.

"I'm not going anywhere. I'm right here and I'll be here as long as you need."

I'm crying again. I didn't want to, but the tears just keep coming down, and Angel is looking at me.

"I'm here too," he says but then he walks out.

"You're not alone. As long as I'm breathing, I'm going to have your back, Josie. You're stuck with me for as long as we're alive."

"Stop, don't say that." I'm full-on sobbing now into her shoulder, but she holds me. To make matters worse, Angel comes back with wet and dry paper towels.

"I'm just going to clean this up." He kneels down, grabs my hand, and wipes the blood off.

What's going on?

Vienna sits next to me, hooking her arm around my shoulder as he cleans my wound. "You're going to be okay. We got you, okay?"

I manage to stop crying, only hiccuping every so often. It's the only noise that drowns out the silence.

When he's done, he walks back out again.

"You're not alone," she softly says and looks at me, a watery smile on her face.

"But—"

"No buts. There's no backing out of this friendship. We're going to figure things out, and you're going to let me. Okay?"

That freaks me out, but I nod anyway.

"Where do you keep your cleaning supplies?" Angel asks.

56
JOSEFINE

April 15th

I ANXIOUSLY FIDGET WITH MY RING, STARING AT MY spotless living room. "Seriously, why are you here?"

Vi had to step outside to answer a phone call, leaving Angel and me alone. We're both standing in my living room that he cleaned up all by himself. I still can't fathom that he did it or why.

He levels me with a stare as if he were assessing me. It's the same look he wears when he's going to pitch. It's a bit unnerving and I hate it.

I think he senses what I'm feeling because his gaze softens as if he didn't realize he was looking at me like that.

"To see how you were doing."

"Why?" I sound defensive but other than when Daniel's been around and the occasional seeing him on campus, we've never spoken to each other. "If you're here to call me a bitch or whatever, go ahead. Get it out and leave."

He smiles, amused. "Why would I clean your living room and then call you names?"

I shrug. My question sounds ridiculous to me too, but there's no telling what could happen. After all, he's Daniel's best friend and I broke up with him. When I broke up with Bryson, despite his friends knowing what he did to me, they all called me names.

"I broke up with him. I kicked him out. He probably hates me. I figured all of you do too." The words leave my mouth, tasting like bile.

He shakes his head, staring at me, puzzled. "Danny's not like that. He's too kind for his own good. I don't think he could hate somebody even if he tried, especially you of all people. He cares about you a lot, more than he's probably ever cared about anyone. Which is really fucking rude because I'm his best friend."

My lips twitch but his other words settle like a hot iron to my chest. "You heard what he said. Let's not pretend like that didn't happen. Drunk or not, you know there's some truth behind it." I pause to gather my thoughts because they're starting to scatter. I feel myself tipping over the abysmal edge at the reminder of his words.

"Yeah, he was drunk but despite what he said, I know it wasn't directed at you. You just happened to be there." He winces. "This time of year is hard for him, for all his family, and then Bryson pushed him in the pool and it triggered him." He pauses. "And I know that's why you're not upset at what he said. You're mad you missed the signs because I'm mad. Do you have any idea how much of my life I've spent with him? We practically grew up together. I know—well, I thought I knew everything about him, but I didn't. I didn't know he was struggling. He was always smiling, always laughing, always trying to make someone feel good. Even Bryson, who didn't deserve it—Danny was there for him when he had bad games." He rolls his eyes. "I should've seen the signs, and I'll always hate myself for missing them."

I scrunch my nose, hating how it stings. *I'm not going to cry in front of him*, is what I tell myself, but a stubborn tear spills because he's not wrong.

I furiously wipe it away. "I didn't want to break up with him, but I needed to do it. I don't know how to emotionally help him. I'm so—"

"You're kidding, right?"

"What?"

"I may have missed the signs, but he was different with you. Call it love or whatever people in relationships feel, but he just looked lighter with you."

I scoff incredulously. "Lighter?"

"Yeah, you had him giggling in the locker room. You don't strike me as a funny person."

"Hey." I'm taken aback.

"Did I lie?"

"Well, no, but I could be funny."

"Right," he sardonically muses.

"Is this your way of making me feel better? Because you're doing a really shitty job at it."

"My bad. Let me tell you, Danny was...*is* Feral. Obsessed. A little unhinged when it comes to you. Never seen him like that." He flashes me a haughty grin.

My stomach flutters. "What's your point with all of this?"

"I just want you to know that I get it. You struggle with your emotions or whatever, but if you think about it, we're all a little fucked up."

"Is this your way of making me feel better?" I ask again.

"Yes, no. I knew I should've brought Kai with me. He's good at this stuff." He ponders over it, like he's regretting not having brought him. "I'm trying to be inspiring."

"Inspiring?"

"That's probably not the word." He scratches the back of his head. "Oh, fuck it. Look, I'm not good with these kinds of things. I'm so out of my depth here if I'm being honest with you. I don't know anything about relationships, but I do know my best friend. I know Daniel enough to know that whatever he feels for you isn't fake or something he felt he needed to feel to make you happy or better. I get what he said was shitty, but he was drunk, and you were there. I can't make sense of it, and I'm not going to try either because it's a little confusing for me. I just know Danny would do anything for you. You could kill someone and he wouldn't question it; he'd probably grab a shovel. That's the kind of bullshit he'd do for you."

My lips slightly curl upward as I think about the night he came with me to slash Bryson's tires.

He pushes off the wall and grips the sectional. "I get why you're put off by me. I mean, I randomly showed up and broke your window, which I intend to fix, by the way. I know before this, we didn't really speak. I should've made an effort, but I never knew how. What the hell would we even talk about? But then I thought about Danny, how he's so extroverted and somehow finds a way to make conversation. I bet he could somehow make the wall talk. I don't know how, but he would find a way."

A laugh tickles my throat, but I swallow it back. "Yeah, he would."

"What I'm trying to say with all of this is that I get it. You're emotionally fucked, but aren't we all? I know you feel guilty and think that you could've done more for him, but you did what you could, and I can guarantee it was enough for him." He pins me with a look of empathy. "Don't take this out on yourself or him. You don't need that, and neither does he. Maybe sleep on it, think about it, I don't know. Do what you gotta do, but don't give up on him."

The desperation in his voice chokes me, making it hard to speak.

"And also, I'm here too. As you can see, I'm not good with motivational speeches or heartwarming words of affirmation, but if you need to talk, I'm here. I'm good at listening. Or if you want to break shit, there's a rage room not too far from here. I could take you to it if you want. I can swim, but I don't think I'll be able to keep up with you. I'm not opposed to painting my nails if you're into that kind of thing. Or getting piercings, I don't mind those. But I won't wax my body, so don't even think about it. And I draw the line at watching rom-coms. I've tried but I just can't."

I try to stop it but a laugh bubbles out of me. He smiles at that. "Why are you being so nice to me?"

He stares at me for a beat. "Because someone has to be. You won't; you're too hard on yourself."

"You sound like him." The words leave my mouth in a hushed whisper.

"I learned a lot from him."

"How's he doing?" My heart races and my palms sweat.

There's a distant look in his eyes. "Uh, not good, but I don't want you to think I'm here because I want you to go see him. Don't show up because you feel like you need to. Don't do that to him. Show up because you really want to. Show up only if you know you're not going to walk away."

"What if I show up and you're wrong? What if he realizes I'm not what he wants?" My insecurities eat me alive, and voicing this out loud paralyzes me with fear.

"I guess the only way to find out is to show up."

April 17th

My muscles are frozen. I struggle to lift my hand to knock on the door. But once I do, my body uncomfortably prickles and I break out into a sweat.

It took me two days to build up the courage to come to Daniel's house. It shouldn't have been hard to make that decision, but there was an infestation of trepidation swarming my body.

The overconsuming negative questions took over my brain, preventing me from thinking straight. It wasn't until Vienna forced me out the house and into her car, that I had no choice but to come see him.

Since she found me in Mom's office, she's been staying over. I didn't want her to, but she didn't really give me a choice. She hasn't been overbearing; she's just been there, and I appreciate that more than she'll ever understand.

I look over my shoulder, peering through the window of her car. She gives me a thumbs-up and flashes me an encouraging smile.

The team will be gone for an away series this weekend. Angel said if I wanted to come, it should be now because they leave in a few hours and won't be back until Monday.

I'm both dreading and excited to see Daniel. I keep trying to think of what I should and shouldn't say, but every thought in my head is a jumbled, anxious mess.

Everything comes to an abrupt stop when the door swings open. My heart feels like it's in my throat, and my stomach tangles into nervous knots.

"Josie, hey?" Kai's brows shoot up but then they furrow. "You're not here to see Danny, are you?"

I stand straighter, fighting the urge to walk away. "Yeah, I am."

He winces. "He's not here. He actually just left."

"Oh...where is he? I really need to talk to him."

Angel stands next to him, smiling at me apologetically. "Hey, did you not see my message?"

"No, my phone died. I didn't have time to charge it." I hadn't planned to come now. Vienna literally pushed me out the house. I barely got my shoes on.

"Is that Vi?" Kai looks over my head.

"Yeah."

"I'll give you two a moment." He walks around and past me. "It's good to see you, Josie."

The sincerity in his voice shocks me, although it shouldn't; Kai's always been nice.

"I, uh, I know I should've come sooner, but...I'm here now and I really need to talk to him. I promise I'm not going to walk away."

A pained sigh leaves his lips. "He went back home."

"Back home?"

"His parents showed up a few hours ago. He wasn't doing good—"

"What do you mean he wasn't doing good?"

"Come in." He opens the door wider and motions for me to come inside.

I stand in the middle of the living room, staring at the full duffles laying on the couch. He goes to move them, but I stop him. "Don't worry about it. What did you mean he wasn't doing good?"

"I didn't tell you because I didn't want you to feel obligated and I didn't want to guilt trip you into coming. But he had two panic attacks and didn't want to get out of bed. Since the beginning of this month, he's been on a leave of absence."

My lungs shrivel up, and I stare at him, unblinking. "What?" I shake my head thinking back to what Professor Carleson said: *baseball commitments*. "But he's not been in class because of baseball."

"They're not disclosing what's going on to give him privacy. He's going through a lot, and the media is shit. People will use what he's going through to taunt him. I'm sure you know as an athlete how brutal people are."

"He wouldn't get out of bed?" My eyes water, and I struggle to breathe.

I should've done more. I should've been here for him like he was for me.

"No, but he's okay now. I promise, he's where he needs to be. Whatever you do, don't blame yourself. This isn't just about the two of you. This is more than that. When he's ready, he'll be back."

I want to nod, but I can't move. "Will you let me know when he's back?"

His eyes go taut around the corners, lips pinched in a tight line. "That's why I had also texted you."

"What is it?" I dig my nails into the heel of my palms.

He shifts his grief-stricken gaze away from mine, like he can't find the strength to say it while looking at me. "Before he left, he told me...it was for the best that you guys didn't see each other." He pauses and steadies his pitying eyes on me. "I don't know why he said it, but just give him some time and space to get everything sorted out, okay? He's not in the right headspace. I'm sure it has nothing to do with you."

My body hollows out, and the last bit of hope I was hanging onto dies. I mean, what did I expect to happen?

"Right. I'll see you around," I reply listlessly.

57

JOSEFINE

April 18th

"That's everything." Vi slumps down on the sectional next to me.

"I could've done that, but thanks." I don't look up at her out of fear I'll cry. We're only four months into the year and I've cried more this year than I ever have in my life.

"Don't thank me. I would've wanted someone to do it for me."

I couldn't touch the things Daniel has given me without feeling like I was going to spiral. Every time I attempted to grab something, I was on the verge of losing it. So, Vienna put everything away in the room he had been staying in while I sat it out.

"You really don't need to be here. I promise I'll be okay. If you're here out of fear I'm going to kill myself, I'm not." My ring easily slips around my clammy finger as I twist it.

"There were a few times in my life when I contemplated it too." Her words are hushed and reluctant as if she were afraid to admit that.

We look at each other simultaneously. My mouth parts, but

I'm afraid of saying the wrong thing, afraid of pushing her away like I did Daniel. So I stay quiet and nervous.

A solemn smile tips her face, and her eyes grow distant. "It was after Mom passed. I couldn't cope with her being gone because she wasn't just my mom but my best friend. Everything I ever did, being the person that I am is...*was* because of her." She sighs heavily and I don't think when I grab her hand and squeeze it. She glances at it and her face softens. "I couldn't be happy. I tried but I felt stuck and empty. Every time I tried to fill the hole, I kept digging it deeper. I hadn't even realized I was doing that. Until one day, I just thought what's the point? So I'd think about ending it all, but then something would happen. Like my sister would ask if I could braid her hair because Dad was shit at it, or my brother would ask if I could cook because my cooking tasted like Mom's. They were constantly asking me to do things, and eventually I realized that they needed me. The sadness is still there—that's not something I think will ever leave—but I've learned to grow with it."

I'm crying and don't realize it until a tear slips to my lips and I taste salt on my tongue.

"I'm not here because I fear it'll happen. I'm here because I get it. I'm here because whether you want to admit it or not, you don't want to be alone and you're shit at communicating your feelings."

"Hey!" I defensively say, but huff a laugh when her face brightens and she gives me a knowing stare. I remove my hand from hers and wipe my cheeks, and she does the same.

"You know I'm right. Communication and feelings aren't your forte, but you can't ignore them forever. They're pesky little bitches; they'll follow you everywhere you go, and eventually they'll catch up."

"I wasn't trying to ignore them. I just didn't understand what I felt. That was until Daniel. It was all confusing at first, but slowly everything started making sense." I stare at the spot where he gave me the flowers. "The emptiness, the dread, the endless loop—it all evaporated like it was never there. He made me feel seen. He made me feel safe. But now that he's not here..." A black hole takes residence in my chest, sucking the life out of me. "I feel like I'm back from a funeral I can't remember. I feel stuck again, grieving something we could've been. It's like grieving Mom all over again. Except the difference is that he's alive. I barely started making sense of what I felt for her and now I have to make sense of what I feel for him. I don't want to be stuck, but I don't know how to climb out."

She embraces me in a hug. "Tell me what you feel."

"Nothing," I numbly say.

"No, you do feel something. Tell me what it is. Don't be afraid. The worst I'll do is hug you tighter."

My shaky lips lift a bit before they fall. "I-I feel..."

"Say it," she softly goads.

"I feel sad. I feel mad."

"Why?"

"Mad because Mom died. Mad because she never once said she loved me, hugged me, did anything but what she thought was necessary. Mad because despite it all, I hate how much I miss her. Sad because I keep thinking about what we could've been. Sad because she's not here and I feel like a failure. Sad because Daniel came into my life, showed me how fucking beautiful it is, and now he's not here. Sad because he's hurting. Sad because he needed someone and I didn't do enough. Sad because I miss him. I'm—" My voice breaks. "I'm sorry."

"Don't be. I'm here for you. Remember, we're a part of the dead's mom club. So that means we're stuck with each other. We grieve together. We help each other. We'll figure it out." She clears her throat, but I know she's crying.

"You're being way too nice to me." I cringe, knowing her shirt is covered in my tears and probably snot.

"Trust me, I could be mean, but I have a therapist, Jarvis. She's a real pain in the ass, but she's also pretty great. You should talk to her. She works with the athletes here."

I remember someone telling me I should speak to her when Mom passed.

"Yeah, I'll think about it."

April 20th

I could burn this entire house down and I'd still be able to point at exactly where Daniel and I stood when he gave me the flowers. It's almost been a month since that moment, but I can still remember it like it happened just a few seconds ago.

The only thing I can't remember is the actual feeling of being happy. I know I was; I was on the verge of tears because of his gesture. But now I don't know what that physical emotion feels like. I keep trying to chase it, hoping I'll move fast enough to catch it, but it's like trying to catch the wind.

I dart my attention back to my screen, staring at the message thread between Daniel and me. I bite the inside of my cheek, hating the way my throat constricts over the stupid name. I'm not sure when he grabbed my phone, but he changed his contact name to: **MY VERY HOT BF**.

The last thing he said was that he was on his way outside, right before Bryson showed up.

I close my eyes briefly before I open them and type out a message. But a second later I delete it and type another. And I repeat the action ten more times before I decide against sending the message and toss my phone on the coffee table.

I hunch over, burying my face in my palms, and groan loudly but stop when I hear the doorbell ring. I ignore it but then it rings again.

I can't even self-loathe in peace.

Marching over to the door, I jerk it open, feeling immensely agitated, but it vanishes because Penelope is standing on the other side.

I expect her to cuss me out or maybe even slap me but not apologize.

"I'm sorry."

I flinch back, stunned. "What are you sorry for?"

"For being a bitch. Ignoring you. For being angry. I shouldn't have, but he's my brother an-and I-I..." She exhales a sorrowful sigh and a tear creeps down her cheek.

A voice in my head screams to stay in my spot, but my hands are moving of their own accord, wrapping around her until our bodies are flush against each other.

"I thought you hated hugs?" Her voice quivers.

"I'm trying out this new thing. Don't get used to it," I reply, feeling awkward when a second later, tense silence surrounds us. "You're not a bitch. You were doing what you thought you needed to do. He's your brother, after all."

"I know, but I didn't know what really happened. I just assumed, and I shouldn't have. I'm sorry, Josie. I just know how much he cares about you, and seeing him hurt like that...it wasn't your fault. I'm sorry."

I rub her back as she cries into my chest. "Please stop crying. I genuinely might evaporate because my body is not used to me crying this much."

She hoarsely laughs. "This is weird for you, isn't it?"

"Very, but it's okay."

She draws back, wiping the tears away. "I really am sorry for not being here for you too."

"You weren't obligated. We're not family and you haven't known me long. It's okay. I promise I don't hold grudges." I offer a small empathetic smile, hoping it doesn't look strained.

She returns one of her own, making her dimples pop out. "We may not be family, but you're still my friend—and my closest one at that. I really am sorry."

My heart thunders and I cross my arms against my chest as if that'll do something to stop it from racing. "Please stop. I should be the one apologizing."

Her brows cinch. "For what?"

"Not doing enough for him. He did so much for me, and I wasn't there for him."

"You were enough. I promise."

"So enough he thinks it's best if we don't see each other? I guess in hindsight, I deserve it. I told him to let me go. He was just doing what I asked."

She sighs deeply. "It has nothing to do with you. He'll come around. He just needs time to figure himself out."

I nod only because I don't want to cry.

"I missed you,"

"Me? It's only been a few weeks."

She chuckles. "Yes, you, and it's been a few weeks too long."

The tightness in my chest eases. "Missed you too."

Her face gleams and her eyes sparkle. "Are we okay?"

"We never stopped being okay." I peer over my shoulder. "Do you want to come inside? Vienna will be here in a bit."

"You don't have to ask me twice." She squeezes past me. "Wait, so does this mean I get to hug you now?"

"Let's take it easy."

She laughs, and as she kicks her shoes off by the door, a thought comes to me.

"So, who's the guy you soft launched on Instagram?" I didn't know anything about it until Vi told me. I've been staying away from social media because I know if I don't, it'll lead me to looking up Daniel. "I thought Angel was helping you find—"

She purses her lips, tucking her hair behind her ear. "He's not and it's ah, not real. I'm just using this guy to move on, and he agreed so yeah. Anyway, have you eaten?" She quickly shifts the conversation, not meeting my stare.

That piques my interest, but I don't get to ask anything because she asks me if I've eaten again.

Hmm...interesting.

It's not long before Vienna is waltzing in my house with food, and once we're done eating, they sit on either side of me on the sectional, staring at me like they're contemplating something.

"What?" I take a drink of my water.

"We know," Vi starts, a warm smile on both their faces. "We don't tell you we love you or hug you because we know it makes you uncomfortable and that's the last thing we ever want to do."

"But," Pen chimes in. "We love you and we want you to know that no matter what happens, we'll always be here for you. We'll always be in your life, and you can't get rid of us, so don't even try."

That catches me off guard. It's unexpected, making my skitch itch and anxiety whirl in my stomach. It's not because I don't believe them or don't know they care about me, but it's also for that exact reason.

"Oh." The bridge of my nose stings. "I-I don't know what to say."

"You don't have to say anything," Vi supplies, clutching my hand. "We just want you to know that we love you."

"We really do," Pen says. "And that no matter what happens, it's us against it all. You got us for life."

From my periphery I see her scoot closer and then Vienna does too. I know what they're doing. A part of me wants to retreat, push them away and believe that these girls, who I haven't known for long, care about me. But I'd be lying to myself if I really made myself believe that. I know they care, otherwise they wouldn't be here.

"Fuck." My voice quivers and the tears that gather spill once they wrap their arms around me. "Dammit. Why are you guys like this?"

"Because we love you, Josefine." Now Vi is crying.

Pen sniffles and I don't have to look at her to know she is too. I can't look anyway because my vision is blurred by the onslaught of tears that won't stop spilling.

"We wanted you to hear it from us. We wanted you to know how much we care about you."

"I-I love you too." That was so weird to get out but also...kind of nice. "Now if you don't mind..." I get choked up. "Get off me. I genuinely feel like I'm evaporating as I speak."

They both laugh and squeeze me once more before letting go of me.

"Thanks for being here. It means a lot." I smile at them, wiping the tears away.

Vienna saw me physically at my worst, and Penelope, despite what happened between her brother and me, is still here. She also knows about my crash out, and even knowing that, they're both still here. Like it doesn't matter how unstable my emotions are, how awkward I am, how I'm not as bubbly as they are—they're still here.

They still want me for me.

I'm enough for them.

They're going to stay.

April 21st

"Josefine," Monica warmly greets me, motioning for me to come into her office.

She emailed me this morning, asking if I could meet her. I assume it's because I still haven't gotten back to her and she probably wants to let me know they've offered it to someone else.

"Thanks for meeting me on such short notice." She sits, her posture laid-back.

"Yeah, no problem." I take a seat across from her and wipe my palms on my thighs.

She smiles. "I'm going to cut to the chase. I'm sure you're busy and probably don't have a lot of time."

I shrug but I don't nod. Other than hiking and a few assignments, I don't have anything going on in my life. There's meditating. Pen says it's good for the soul or whatever. So I'm trying it.

"I don't mean to be persistent about this, but I just wanted to know if you've thought about the offer?"

I can't hide my shock fast enough. "Oh."

"You seem surprised."

"Yeah, I figured you would've already offered it to someone else."

"No. I still want you to take it."

"Why me? There are a lot of qualified candidates who I'm sure would kill for this."

She sits forward, I think crossing one of her legs over the other. "I'm going to be frank with you. You are brilliantly talented and I'd hate for that to go to waste. You have an eye for this and are the most qualified, if not overqualified, for this position, but I know you're uncertain about what you want to do career wise and maybe this could help you figure it out. I know you teach swim lessons, so you're obviously not done with being in the water."

I stare at her, stupefied. "How do you know this?"

"You made a comment to Ross."

Right, her. She's the Associate Head Coach for the Women's Swim team. When I decided to quit swimming, I spoke to her because I refused to talk to Christian. She tried to convince me to stay, but I was overwhelmed with Mom's death and I wanted nothing to do with swimming. But in doing so, I think I crashed out and told her about my uncertain future.

"Oh." I drop my gaze to the sleek floor.

"If you really don't want this, you can tell me no. I promise there will be no hard feelings." I'm sure she means it. Her voice is soft and understanding.

Discomfort twists in my stomach as I go back and forth, debating whether I want to tell her it's hard for me to make up my mind.

But the words vomit out before I can stop them. "Maybe I do want to do it but the thought of stepping back in that natatorium makes me anxious. Since Mom passed, I've been struggling, and I'm afraid to freak out or do something really stupid. That's why I don't think I'm suited for the position. I appreciate you thinking of me, believing in me, wanting me to help, but I'm not mentally ready."

I breathe out a shaky breath, my legs bounce, and my eyes flicker away from hers.

"Josie..." Her voice wavers. "I'm sorry. I had no idea."

"It's fine. I'm trying to be open about how I feel." But what I really want to do is hide. My skin prickles because there's more than one person who knows I'm a mess. That I don't have my life together and I'm in shambles.

Monica stands and circles her desk, taking the seat next to me. I look at her, feeling perplexed. "I hate that you've been going through this, and that I might have made you uncomfortable by pushing this onto you. That's the last thing I ever wanted to do."

"It's fine, really. I just thought you should know."

A tinge of sadness flares on her face. "I appreciate you opening up to me and letting me know. But you know, it's not okay to think that's okay. Don't be afraid to open up because you're worried about how people will perceive you. Your mental health is your priority; don't let anyone else make you think otherwise. What can I do to help you?"

I stay quiet, unsure how to reply. I've never had this many people want to help me and be genuine about it. It's both unnerving and a relief. I kind of feel like throwing up.

"There's a therapist on campus, Jarvis," she starts. "I know therapy sounds like a lot and may be overwhelming, but I promise she's amazing. I understand how difficult it is to express yourself when maybe you're unsure how, but if there's anyone you'll want to speak to, it'll be her."

"I looked. She's pretty booked," I admit.

"Do you want to talk to her?" There's a look of determination in her eyes.

My heart rattles anxiously. "Yeah, I'd like to."

"Okay, don't worry about anything. I will get you an appointment with her."

"No, you really don't have to do that."

"I want to." She smiles at me, placing her hand over mine. "It's no problem at all."

It's okay to accept help. Stop being so stubborn. "Okay, thank you."

April 28th

"I don't like Jarvis. I don't like therapy. I don't want to do it anymore."

Pen's lips twitch. "Don't be like that. It's good for you."

"I know. It's just…"

"I get it," she says to fill the void of silence as we stand in front of the jellyfish. "It's exhausting."

It's been a week since I spoke to Monica. She didn't waste a second to get in contact with the therapist because that very same day, I spoke with Jarvis. She said she wanted to see me twice a week. Today's the third time I've spoken to her, and just like last week, I've left feeling drained but also like a tiny rock—one of the millions—on my chest, has been taken off.

I don't like her because she's horrible but she asks questions, the kind that provokes me to feel so deeply. She's all about identifying the cause, and to do that, we have to find the root. Meaning, I have to dig so fucking deep, it makes me want to rip my hair out. Not only do I have to talk about Mom and our relationship, but I also have to talk about Daniel, and just the mere thought of him makes me want to cry.

Then she pointed out what I didn't understand or wanted to acknowledge. I'm depressed, struggling with depersonalization, understanding grief, have self-sabotaging tendencies, and what love means and is.

Needless to say, therapy is going…okay. I just don't like the aftermath of it because I'm left thinking, feeling, wondering, and then I spiral a little. Which is why I'm at the aquarium.

I didn't want to come. All I wanted to do was lay around and sleep off the exhaustion and not be with Pen. I appreciate her company, but being around her makes me think of Daniel. It's not her fault she's related to him, but it makes my chest ache.

I'm sure she knows how I feel, but she never addresses the elephant in the room and I'm thankful for that.

Despite my feelings, I needed to decompress and she knew that. That's why she forced me out of my house and brought me to the aquarium to have dinner with Vienna. She's working, not as a mermaid, but she's doing something else. Her break won't be for another hour, but we came now because I really needed it.

"Hey, I forgot my ChapStick in the car. I'll be back. I won't be long."

"Okay. I'll be here."

I watch the jellyfish rhythmically and gracefully drift back and forth. I stare hard and long enough until my vision clouds and the colors inside the tank mesh together. But my brain doesn't feel as muddled as my vision because my thoughts of Daniel come alive.

"I miss you," I murmur.

"I missed you too."

I cease in my spot, but my heart takes off at the familiar voice.

"Hi, Jos."

58

DANIEL

April 28th

"I'M READY TO GO BACK."

"You're ready to tell me what you've been afraid to say?"

I nod, more sure of myself than I felt at the beginning of the month.

I've been talking to Jarvis, the university's therapist, twice a week for almost a month now. She's a sweet, fifty-something-year-old that makes you want to share all your deepest and darkest secrets, but also doesn't fuck around. She's patient and nice but immediately clocks my bullshit, which she calls masking.

Since we started our sessions, she's asked me what I'm afraid of. At first, I said "nothing" but then I stayed quiet, scared to actually say it out loud. She never made me feel pressured to say it, but she said I couldn't play until I gave her an answer. That was her and Coach D'Angelo's ultimatum.

"I'm afraid of what will happen if I move on. Afraid to let myself be happy."

I want to but then I feel guilty.

Jarvis has time and time again talked me through my guilt, reminding me it's not my fault. She has helped me find coping mechanisms for the panic attacks, my depression, and my anxiety. But even though she helped me find ways to control what I'm going through, it was only doing so much to help me. So she also prescribed medication because I'm struggling with post-traumatic stress disorder from witnessing Adrian drown. I have a lot of issues that have been festering for years, and meditating and breathing alone weren't going to help regulate them.

I didn't want to at first, not because I thought there was anything wrong with it, but taking the medication was accepting what I've been trying to ignore. I knew I couldn't do that anymore and I really want to get better.

It's only been a month, and things haven't magically changed. The weight of what I feel is still there, but it isn't heavily weighing down on me like it did before.

We've also talked about my relationship with my dad and how we can work to establish a healthy connection.

Which has helped because I've been staying with my parents for a week and a few days, and while Dad and I aren't best friends, things aren't uncomfortable.

Jarvis tenderly smiles at me from the screen. "That's understandable but I want you to remember something, Danny. You can move on, but that doesn't mean you'll forget Adrian or that you're not deserving of what you've accomplished and achieved. You deserve to be happy, so let yourself be happy. Step outside the box, you're allowed to do that. It's okay to let go of it."

I hadn't realized I put myself in a box until I spoke with Jarvis. I was unconsciously caging myself in, allowing that box to get smaller and smaller. That's until Josie happened. I unintentionally let her in, sharing and doing things with her that made me feel alive. And in doing so, I subconsciously outgrew the box and needed to get out, because I not only liked the space, but I needed and wanted to make it for Josie. But anytime I tried to get out of the box, the overwhelming guilt forced me back in.

And that led to everything crashing and me blacking out when I punched Bryson both times.

My lips lift slightly.

"Oh, you're smiling? You want to share?"

That only makes them stretch wider. "You remember Josie?"

"The girl you're constantly talking about? Yes, I remember her."

Jarvis also happens to be a smart-ass.

"She said that to me too." I press my lips together to stop them from trembling. "She made me happy. I don't feel like I deserve her, but she's someone good. Actually, she's better than good. She's amazing. She's dry and a little mean but..." I chuckle but Jarvis cracks a smile that makes it sound louder. "I love it. I..." I quiet down. "I couldn't remember what feeling alive was like until she came into my life."

"It's never too late."

"I don't know if I can fix what I broke. I hurt her, Jarvis. I don't know how she'll want me back."

"Why are you already setting yourself up for failure?"

"I-I'm not. I just—"

"Unless you can predict the future, there is no reason why you can't talk to her and communicate what you feel. You aren't the same person you were a month ago."

"You think so?"

"I know so. I believe in you, Danny. It's time you start believing in yourself."

"*Cómo te fue?*" Mom asks when I step into the kitchen after my session.

I stretch my arms over my head until I hear the muscles pop on my shoulders. I never knew talking about my feelings could be this exhausting.

"It was good. I told Jarvis I was ready to go back."

Mom and Dad already knew about my plans to return. I talked to them about it yesterday after we had another lengthy chat about Adrian, baseball, and life. I never knew how badly I needed this—them—until I came home. But they're not the only things I need.

She stops stirring what I think is *caldo de pollo* in a pot. "I'm going to miss you. You know we're here for you. Anything you need, you call us and we'll be over there."

Dad steps into the kitchen, smiling at me. I'm still getting used to that, but I don't feel as weird about it anymore. "You know, you can stay as long as you want and need. This will always be your home."

"I know but I'm ready to go back. I miss the guys and playing. And since I've filled out the MLB link, I have meetings and many other things to do." I submitted it a while ago, but after everything that happened, I never looked at my email until a few days ago. "I also have a lot of homework to make up."

"*Estamos bien orgullosos de ti.*" Dad's lips widen.

"Thank you for everything you've done and continue doing. I wouldn't be here without you." I keep it short because Mom's eyes are shining, and I just know she's going to cry and then Dad might cry, and then I'll stall and never leave.

"We're your parents. You don't need to thank us. Just keep doing your best." Mom is standing in front of me. "Oh, and whenever you can, bring Josie to see the bakery."

"We're not...together."

"Yet Daniel, *yet*. I didn't raise you to be so negative." She slaps my shoulder but then pulls me into a hug. "You want to eat before you leave?"

I glance at Dad who shakes his head, telling me it's best if I shut up. He lives with her, so he has to put up with it, but I don't.

"It's seventy degrees, Mom. It's too hot to eat that."

She rolls her eyes. "One day you're going to want my food, but you'll be hours away."

I laugh, hugging her tighter. "Yeah, just not *caldo*."

The house goes dead silent when I step in. Shocked eyes land on me but in a flash, they're radiating pure joy. Kai and Gray jump up from the couch, barreling toward me, but Angel stands in front of me, keeps his back to me, lifting his hand up to stop them.

"He just got back. Give him some space," he orders but then turns and hugs me. "Did you drive by yourself? Why didn't you tell me you were coming? We could've driven to—"

"I thought you said to give him space? You're literally suffocating him. Move." Gray jerks him off me and hugs me next, but a moment later, Kai is doing the same thing.

"Give him some fucking space." Noah jerks them all back. He doesn't hug or touch me but gives me a head nod. "Everyone's been miserable without you."

"You included?" I grin.

He grimaces. "No."

"Oh, he missed you. He's just, you know, being Noah." Kai snorts.

Noah rolls his eyes. "Are you back for good, or are you still taking a break?"

"Yeah, I'm back for good. Uh..." I comb my fingers through my hair, hating the nervous tumble in my stomach. "I'm sorry you guys had to witness that. I'm sorry for putting you all through that. I didn't mean—"

"Apologize one more time and I'll really fuck you up, Daniel. Then you'll really be out for the rest of the season." Gray punches my shoulder, but then draws me into another hug. "You don't apologize. We all go through it, okay? I missed you, baby."

"I missed you too," I say before he lets go.

"You don't need to apologize, but how are you feeling?" Angel asks. His warm, steady brown eyes hold mine with understanding.

"I'm okay, not fine, just okay." I shift the weight of one foot from the other. I've never openly talked about my feelings to them. They saw me at my worst a few weeks ago, but I never told them how I was feeling. "I'm working through it."

"If you need anything, anything at all, we're here for you." Kai gently squeezes my shoulder. "We're seriously glad you're back. Oh! You know who's going to be happy you're—"

Angel cuts him off with a curt shake of his head. "Shut up."

"What?" I ask, gaze bouncing between the two. "If you say Amanda, I swear I'm moving out."

Because I have her blocked, I haven't heard from her, and I hope it stays that way.

"No, it's Jo—"

"Shut up," Angel says again.

My heart races and I restlessly drum my fingers against my thigh. "Let him talk. Who?"

Kai glances at Angel who shrugs and eventually nods. "Josie. She came the day you left. She wanted to see you."

"She did?" My mind races with a million thoughts.

"Yeah, but you said it was best if you guys didn't talk. I told her, oh fuck—did you not mean that?"

I wasn't thinking. I was upset and I thought saying that out loud would help me, but it did the opposite.

"It's okay. It's not your fault." I sigh. "I need to go up to my room and set this down." They part, giving me space to head up the stairs. The only one who follows me is Angel.

"I promise it's okay. I'm not mad at you," I tell him when we're in my room. Boxes filled with my stuff are still scattered around. I don't bother with them. I drop my duffle on the floor and sit on my bed. "I'm mad at myself. I wasn't thinking. I was—"

"It's okay. She knows that." He leans on the edge of my desk. "I talked to her."

"You did?"

"Yeah. I won't say she's doing one hundred percent okay. She kind of crashed out and I had to break into her house."

"What?"

He proceeds to tell me everything and why he did what he did. "I just wanted her to know you'd be back and things would be okay. Though I'm not great at this stuff like you are. I kind of told her we're all mentally fucked up. I can't tell whether she found that insulting or helpful, but she didn't punch me, and I think she smiled. She's really hard to read, but I think we're cool."

I don't know whether to laugh, hug him, or cry a little. "You did that for me?"

"For you. For her. Loneliness is a bitch. I thought about the cliff and...I really don't know if I helped, but I wanted her to know she wasn't alone."

I shoot up. "Thank you for—"

"Don't thank me. I'm here for you—and for her, if she wants. She's little Miss I'll Fuck You Up If You Try To Help Me."

I kind of smile. "Do you know what she was here for?"

"I don't, but I did tell her to only show up if she isn't going to walk away." He pushes off the desk and pauses at the doorway. "She's at the aquarium with Pen."

"How do you know that?"

"Stop asking questions and go see her."

I check my reflection on the window, making sure my hair isn't out of place and I don't have anything on my face. I had already checked in the mirror, but I'm a little anxious and need to do something with my hands.

My nerves are shot, my heart feels like it's in my throat, and my stomach is fluttering incessantly.

"Danny..." Relief coats my sister's voice. As I turn, she wraps her arms around me, squeezing the life out of me. "I'm so happy you're back. How are you feeling?"

I texted her before coming to the aquarium to make sure they're actually here. She asked if I wanted to wait until they left and Josie got home, but I can't wait anymore. I need to see her.

I return it, making sure I don't mess up the tulips I got for Josie. "I'm okay. I'm sorry about how short I was with you. I didn't mean—"

"It's okay. I'm not mad. You did piss me off, but I guess I'll give you a pass this time,"

"So I can keep letting you *borrow* money?" I teasingly say.

"Exactly. You know me so well." I hear the smile in her voice.

I let go, eyeing the large building with trepidation.

"Don't be nervous. The worst that'll happen is that she'll tell you she doesn't like you."

"Jesus Christ, Pen, you're not helping." I glare at her.

She laughs. "Relax. It's going to be okay, I promise. She's where the jellyfish are at."

I nod, not answering because my tongue feels heavy. So I wave goodbye and make my way inside. It doesn't take long for me to find the jellyfish exhibit. I blow out the breath I didn't know I was holding when I spot her.

I don't stagger or stall because I need to be close to her. There's a deep, aching yearning in my bones and my cells, and every molecule inside my body that pulses, prays and craves to be next to her.

My vision tunnels, my brain shutting out everything around me except for the only person who matters.

She doesn't notice or feel me standing behind her; she stays rooted in her spot like she's zoned out.

"I miss you," she quietly says to herself.

I resist the urge to pull her to me and stand next to her. "I missed you too."

She goes unnaturally still, not turning to look at me.

"Hi, Jos."

When she lifts her head and her eyes collide with mine, hot adrenaline shoots throughout my body. Everything in me is racing, but my mind is steadily in place. I'm not floating or barely holding on, I'm grounded and I'm not touching her.

Her lips part and eyebrows pull in, creating a deep crease between them. She takes two steps back and my heart drops.

I—

Josie throws herself against me, circling her arms around my shoulders. She clutches onto me like she's afraid I'll let go of her, but she's sorely mistaken if she believes I'll ever let that happen.

59

JOSEFINE

"I'M SORRY," WE SYNCHRONICALLY SAY.

"Don't—" we say in unison. "I—" And again before we go quiet and continue to hold one another.

"I swear if I'm dreaming..." My voice quivers.

"You're not. I'm right here. I'm right here, Josie," he whispers against my hair. "I'm not going anywhere. I promise."

I breathe him in, sink my fingers through his hair at the base, and drown in the sound of his heartbeat sporadically dancing with mine.

Neither one of us speaks or moves for a while until we both know it's time we pull back and talk.

I hesitantly retract my arms, but it's not until I hear the crinkle of paper and catch yellow from my periphery that I pull all the way back. I was too stunned that he's here, so I didn't focus on anything else but his face.

"I'm sorry I was almost late. I hope you like them." He holds out a bouquet of yellow tulips and his cheeks flush. "And this is for you too." He reaches into his back pocket and hands me a mini notebook.

"I love them. Thank you." I take them both and my eyes

water, but I don't blink, afraid I'll break down in front of him. "What's the special occasion?"

He flashes me a small, boyish grin that makes my heart stutter. "You're the special occasion. That didn't sound too corny, did it?"

I smile, holding my thumb and forefinger up, leaving a small gap between the two. "Just a little." He chuckles, making my lips stretch wider. "What's the notebook for?"

"For all the things I wanted to say to you but couldn't while I was gone." His eyes glaze with sadness. "I—" He clears his throat and scans the room. It's just us; I doubt anyone else will show up. It's a little late and it's a Monday. There's not usually a lot of people around this time of the day and week. "I'm sorry."

"You don't need to apologize."

"I do because I hurt you and that's the last thing I ever wanted to do. I want—*need* you to believe me. What I said to you that night, it had nothing to do with you. I was upset, angry, and embarrassed." He squeezes his eyes shut as if the memory is playing in his head.

I grab his hand, brushing my thumb over his knuckles. His eyes open and shift to our joined hands. "It's okay."

"It's not, because I made you think you don't make me happy, but you do. Being with you has been the happiest I've ever been, but because of that, I felt guilty." He expels a shuddering breath. "I want to be honest with you. I don't want to lie or pretend."

I inhale, not wanting to let myself get carried away with his words despite how loud the voice in my head screams that it believes him.

"Okay, talk to me." I swipe my thumb over one of his knuckles repeatedly, soothing the tension residing on his face.

"This..." He pinches the safety pin hanging from his chain. "Was my promise not to kill myself. I wanted to so many times, thought about it so many times, tried but I couldn't go through with it. I knew it would devastate Mom, Pen, Angel, maybe even

Dad, although now I know it would have. The safety pin is a reminder that my hurt would be someone else's if I did it. I didn't do it, but my thoughts of it never stopped. They were there...just biding their time. Until you."

I breathe, wanting to say something, but I stay quiet knowing he's not done.

"My thoughts were still dark, but being with you, talking to you, things were different. I was living and dreaming of a future with you. And that overwhelmed me and made me feel guilty because it meant I wasn't sad or had thoughts of ending it all. Being happy with you meant I was *really* okay. Being happy with you meant that I was leaving Adrian behind. And I didn't think I deserved that; I didn't think it was fair that I could be happy and he couldn't. I felt so ashamed that I couldn't feel anything but happy because I had you," he wistfully admits. "Being with you has made me the happiest and most peaceful person I've ever been in my life. Being with you felt like getting a restart in life. Being with you made me feel like me again."

My eyes water, and my throat tenses.

"Peace? I didn't test your patience? Stress you out? Take a few years off your life? Your blood pressure must've been insane anytime you were around me."

His lips quirk up, and his muted eyes light up. "No. You electrified my soul. This is the most awake I've ever mentally felt."

"Oh," I say in a hushed tone, my tears falling before I can stop them.

He cups my face and wipes them away from my cheeks.

I sniffle. "I'm sorry. I'm so sorry."

"Don't be. I'm okay, not fine, but I'm okay." He pauses then adds, "I'm seeing a therapist. I'm working on myself, Josie. I want you to know that I want to get better. I want to be better for you, for me. So no lies or pretending. This is me, how I feel. I'm okay, not fine, but I'm okay."

"I'm sorry," I say after I manage to stop the tears.

"Please don't be."

"I am because I feel like I made it about myself when you needed help."

"It wasn't your job to fix what you didn't know. Even if you did know, it still wouldn't have been something you needed to make yourself responsible for," he softly says.

"I still would've wanted to help you, and I still do. I just didn't know how and that made me mad because *you are* the one thing I care most about, and knowing I couldn't help fucked with my head."

"Can I hug you again?"

"Please," I whisper. He doesn't hesitate to wrap me in his arms.

"I want you back, Josie," he desperately voices. "Tell me what I need to do, what you need, and you've got it. Just think about us. Take as long as you need, as long as you want. I'll wait, but think about us. Please."

"There's nothing I need to think about." I cling to him, and I'm just as desperate as he sounds. "I want us, this, everything, all of it. I need you. I'm not perfect and I have issues, a lot of them—that I'm working on—but I want to be here for you, Daniel. I want you to let me in and share your pain with me. Share what you feel on the good, bad, and in-between days. I told you once and I'll tell you again: Don't hide from me, please. Let me in."

"Even on the dark days?" His trembling voice drops an octave.

I tug back, leveling my gaze with his amber eyes that fuel my soul on fire. "I'll love you even on the dark days."

He gapes at me in disbelief, but his hands tighten around me. "I'm going to need you to say that again."

My heart careens, and my lips crack into a shy smile. "I'll love you even on the dark days. I-I know that's hard to believe. I know I've never been the most uh, sentimental, sappy, or even loving person. I know I haven't shown you enough how much I care about you. I know I'm shit at expressing myself and maybe you'll find it hard to believe that I care this deeply for you..." I pause, wanting to gather my thoughts because I'm rambling, but the words continue to spill out like a broken dam. "That I feel this intense fire, consuming burn in my body for you. I know you don't get that, maybe that didn't make sense, fuck, I'm so nervous right now—" His lips stretch wide. The corners of his lips could practically be touching the corners of his eyes. "Stop looking at me like that."

"Okay." He flattens his lips, but they roll back up.

"I sound like an idiot, don't I?"

"No, God, no." He tucks my hair behind my ear. "You sound like the girl I love."

My heart stops working. I almost heard him say it before, but I thought that was out of desperation to make up for what he said when he was drunk. At least that's what I kept telling myself. My brain was stuck on sabotaging his words and any moment we had together.

But right now, I can't find any reason to doubt he means it.

"Do you believe me?" He caresses my cheek.

"I do." My eyes flutter. "Do you believe me?"

"I do, baby."

I drop my head on his chest. "I missed hearing you say that."

"I missed you." He rubs my back and kisses the top of my head. "You know, you are loving. Don't ever feel like you're not. I don't need you to be loud about loving me or do big gestures to show me that you do. I know that you do, in the way you hold me, how you see me, how you let me in, how you accept me for me. You *are* loving, Josefine, and I'm privileged to be the one you choose to love."

"Oh." I exhale a quivering breath and then look down because I don't want to cry again. How did I get so lucky?

He cups my jaw, tilting my head back to look at me. "I love you, Josefine."

I melt into his hold, but he holds me steady and firmly. "I love you, Daniel."

"Can I kiss you?" he achingly asks.

"Why are you asking? Please just do it."

"Thank fucking God. Come here." He crashes his lips to mine, and the entire world becomes clear and so fucking beautiful.

60

JOSEFINE

"You kept them." Daniel peruses the box filled with every single Post-it note he's given me, along with his cards.

Even though I was put off about his intentions at first, I never could get rid of that first one he gave me with his phone number and every other one after that.

They were papers with words on them, I thought at first, but then they became more. They weren't just words he was saying for the hell of it or to placate me. They were little reminders every day that Daniel was—*is* happy that I'm here. But saying *little* is a huge understatement because those words saved my life.

"I sometimes thought about getting rid of them, but I could never bring myself to," I mournfully admit, not looking up at him. "It was hard to believe that you cared about me and genuinely meant it. You didn't know me and I thought—"

"Hey." Daniel turns, cupping my face to make me look at him. He sweetly smiles at me, warmth and love shining in his eyes. "You don't have to explain yourself to me. I get it. You didn't know me, and I was very insistent."

"You were, but your insistence…" I breathe out shakily. "Saved me."

Shortly after we talked at the aquarium, we came back to my

house. While we decided to get back together and expressed how much we love each other, there is more we need to talk about.

We're currently in what used to be his room, looking at the stuff Vienna had stored for me here. It was the things Daniel gifted me and I couldn't bear to look at when he was gone.

He drops his hands and snakes them around my shoulders, hugging me.

Flashbacks of that night play in my head. I'm scared thinking that I almost ended it all, but I'm also relieved that he was there.

"Do you want to talk about that night?" he cautiously asks.

"I don't know how to get the words out," I quietly say.

"You don't have to talk about it now, but if you ever want to, I'm here."

"No, I want to now," I answer a little more confidently.

I pull back and tug him down to sit next to me on the bed. He laces his fingers through mine and with the other, uses his index finger to draw patterns on the top of my hand. I roll my shoulders back, closing my eyes as that night plays in my head. I rest my head on his shoulder and exhale an anxious breath.

He stays quiet and circles an arm around my back. "Take your time. I'm not going anywhere."

I nod, looking down at our joined hands as more flashbacks flood my brain. "After Mom's death, I tried to live normally or at least find my new normal. I thought, how hard could it be?" I pause because I know how bad this is going to sound, but I say it anyway. "You're going to think I'm a shitty person for thinking this, but I thought, we weren't close, we lived together but we hardly saw each other unless it involved swimming and even then, we didn't know each other well enough. So why should I have cared that she was gone? She died, so what? It's not like she gave a damn for me physically or even emotionally."

"I don't think you're a shitty person," he softly says, kissing the top of my head.

I smile because of course he'd say that. He somehow always finds the good in me that I struggle to find. "Well, I felt like a shitty person because for days I felt that way. I thought, it is what it is, she's dead, her not existing wasn't any different than when she was alive. It wasn't until I was told to take bereavement..." My chest grows heavy and I bite my bottom lip to stop it from quivering. "That I started feeling her absence in a way I hadn't when I first received the news she had passed. And then there was a culmination of things that felt so insignificant in the moment they were happening. But they felt that way because I kept brushing them off until I couldn't any longer. Like accepting that she had a will in my name. She had left everything to me and I couldn't understand why, when she never once uttered she loved me or said she was proud of me." My knee bounces anxiously. "It all suddenly came crashing down. I didn't know how to navigate my feelings or begin to understand what I was feeling towards her. It was so overwhelming. And then I started drowning in my emotions, suffocating with the realization that my life's purpose was to fulfill whatever she demanded.

"I tried to keep going, thinking of what I had at the moment: school, swim, and Bryson. But then I thought, 'then what?' Those two words were constantly revolving around my head. I couldn't shut them down, no matter how hard I tried. And the people around me didn't make it easier. They didn't see me. No one did. They saw my Mom and everything she did. No one ever saw me. They just saw her in me. I was so lonely.

"And then he cheated, but even then, despite the hurt, I also didn't care. Then I stopped caring about school, about swimming, about everything. I tried hard to come back from not caring, but those two words were so persistent. And then it was Christmas Eve, the anniversary of her death. That day the 'then what' was quiet, everything was. It was weird but so peaceful because it had been the first time in...ever that my head was quiet. Everything was, and then I just...*knew* I was done trying to make sense of those two words, my complicated feelings towards my mom, and being alone."

He pulls me up and I straddle his thighs. I bury my face in the crook of his neck, and he embraces me in a firm, protective hug.

"The silence was nice," I plainly admit. "It was the nicest thing I had ever experienced and I never wanted it to stop. So I didn't think. I walked and walked until I ended up at the cliff and was ready to die. I was ready to welcome silence forever, but then you showed up, pulled me back, and begged for me not to go. God, I was so mad at you for doing that..."

"I know," he says in a hushed voice, rubbing my back. "But I'd do it again."

I smile into his neck. "You won't have to. I promise. I hadn't ever thought about ending it all until that night but after then, I could never bring myself to do it. I was scared because your 'please don't go' words wouldn't stop echoing in my head. They were annoying at first, but it was because I felt like I was your pity project. I didn't think you actually cared, at least that's what I kept telling myself. Jarvis says I was self-sabotaging because deep down I knew you weren't, but I couldn't let myself believe someone actually cared. I also didn't want someone to care for me. Because who would be stupid enough to want me? I wasn't worth it, but you made me feel like I was."

"Because you are worth it." He draws back a little and hooks a finger under my chin, making me look up at him. "You are worth it, Josefine."

"I feel that now, but in the moment, I didn't and then that night when you got drunk and you said those things..." I don't want him to feel bad or blame himself, but he nods at me, looking at me thoughtfully, letting me know he wants to hear it. "I started to believe that maybe I really wasn't. Because I thought you were making yourself miserable to make me happy. You are so precious to me and the thought that you were so unhappy made me hate myself."

He sighs, eyes flickering with regret. "I'm so sorry. I hate that I made you feel that way. I wish I could take it all back."

"It's okay."

"It's really not, especially because of what I'm going to tell you."

I nod, letting him know it's okay for him to proceed.

"This is going to sound bad, but there is no other way to say it. Jarvis says, I was using you as a crutch after I opened up to her and told her being with you has been the safest I've ever felt. And because it was only with you, I was seeking grounded security. With you, I felt free of judgment, and in my drunken state, I thought because you'd been through it too, I could tell you what I was feeling. So I bared my heart to you because you were my safety net, but in doing so, I let it all out and I hurt you. I didn't mean to; that's not how I wanted to tell you then or ever, really. I also didn't mean to use you to ground myself, but being around you, I couldn't hide who I was because unknowingly *you* saw me and I felt good, but I despised myself for it. I didn't want anyone else to suffer because of me, but I still managed to fuck it all up because you did. I'm sorry, Josie. I really am."

"Don't be." I cup his cheek and softly rub the pad of my thumb along the bone. "I'm not mad. You were hurting—we both were—and that made us do and say things."

"Things I regret but I'm...I'm working on them, Josie. I really am. Like I told you at the aquarium, I'm trying to get better; it's just going to take some time because my head, it's really dark in there."

"Do you want to talk about it?" He doesn't meet my stare like he's embarrassed or struggling to accept he said that out loud. Either way, it doesn't matter because I'm not going anywhere.

He swallows hard. "It's really fucked up in there, Josie. It's dark enough, I'm consumed in thoughts of also wishing for silence. I haven't in a while though, but that's as dark as it's gotten. There's this pitch-black fog that sometimes comes when I think about my future. And sometimes, it just comes because I don't feel like I deserve good things. Like I don't deserve you."

I don't stop stroking his cheek. "If you let me in, I'll hold a flashlight, and we'll find a way out together."

His eyes light up. "You'll do that for me?"

"I'll do it for the rest of our lives." I smile at him, and he feebly smiles back. "As I continue to remind you that you deserve all the good things."

He squeezes his eyes tight as they mist over, and he shakes his head as if he were trying to stop himself from crying.

"Let yourself feel." I brush my lips against his and softly peck them.

Daniel smiles against mine, gently kissing me. After a moment, I climb off him and we lie back. I lay my head on top of his chest, hearing his heart beat a little wildly.

"The guilt has always been there, but it felt heavier when I did certain things that revolved around Adrian. Those days that felt too much, I'd think about the most painful way I could die because I felt that was what I deserved. But then someone would need me for whatever reason and I couldn't go through with it." He grows quiet, drumming his fingers on his thigh. "And then I'd hate myself because I felt guilty for not being able to go through with it, but I'd also be mad because my family and friends needed me and I was thinking of dying. It was a dark cycle I couldn't get out of. So I smiled because it was the only thing I thought I could do, the only thing I felt I was good at, the only thing I knew I couldn't fuck up. You can't hurt anyone if you're smiling." He releases a pained sigh. "And then you happened…"

The drumming stops, and his erratic heartbeats become steady.

"The guilt was there; it never left, but I felt it less. One moment, I was reliving a memory with Adrian and a second later, I was thinking of you. A dark cloud would loom as I thought about him—the desire to suffocate was so fucking real some days…" His voice is hoarse, but he clears his throat and I weave my fingers through his, squeezing his hand. "But then it faded away when I thought about your smile and your brown eyes. Some days I just wanted to…" He inhales sharply. "Shoot myself because I felt so much and I didn't know how to make it stop. I didn't know how to not feel the hole in my chest. I didn't know how to continue existing when he didn't but then..." He swallows. "I'd think about all the things we've done."

We haven't done much, I want to say, because we really haven't. There are moments we've shared, and they're special to me, extraordinary even, but I'm not sure they'd be considered *the* moments that make life special.

I'm mad at myself. Why didn't I do more?

"You did more than enough," he says as if he could hear my internal turmoil. "Because those moments we shared are the essence of my existence." He shifts on his side and cups my cheek, staring down at me. "Those moments made me feel me again and are the reason why I looked forward to every day as long as it meant I got to make more with you."

My heart expands, and my eyes well with tears. "I look forward to every day with you too."

Agony floods his face. "Don't cry, please. I don't like seeing you sad."

"I'm okay. I promise I'm not sad; I just feel so much for you. I don't think I'll ever be able to express it the way that you do. But I'll try to do my best to show you, to be here, to make sure you know that *I see you*. I want every version of you and nothing, and I mean literally nothing, will ever change how I feel about you. I'm not going anywhere. I promise you I'm not."

"I'm so in love with you." He tips his head up and kisses my forehead.

"I love you." I smile.

"Do you think we can pause for a little? This is a lot, and I just need a break from it."

I nod because I feel that way too.

"You don't have to ask. We can do whatever you want." I get up, grabbing the portable CD player and the little box from one of the boxes and lie next to him, snuggling into the crook of his arm.

"No, you didn't!" He laughs disbelievingly at the brand-new

earbuds I bought. I meant to give them to him, but I never got the chance.

"I never finished listening to the CD you gave me and your earbuds are shit. No offense."

"A lot taken." He pinches my side.

My cheek twitches. "Don't worry, the old earbuds are tucked safely away."

I hand him one and I place the other in my ear. Then I turn on the CD player. The beat of the song playing filters through the little buds, but once I hear the lyrics of "Hot Stuff" by Donna Summer, I lose it.

"I love this song, don't you?" Daniel keeps a straight face, but I know he's trying not to laugh. "The lyrics are just so...exhilarating, huh?"

I laugh. "Exhilarating?"

"And..." He presses his lips together. "Stimulating."

We both laugh, and while he sings, I hum along because I don't know the words.

61

DANIEL

"If you guys pull this bullshit again, I'm fucking someone up and it won't be Josie," Noah threatens, striding into the kitchen.

"Fuck anyone up. Just don't touch Daniel and we'll be okay." Josie's voice is just as leveled and equally threatening.

Noah is nowhere near being scared of Josie, but I see the admiration and respect he has for her. It reflects in his eyes the same way it does when Coach D'Angelo is talking to him.

He stares at Josie, and she stares right back. Never thought I'd see the day that someone could rival his scarily blank expression, but she mirrors it so well. On him, it's whatever, but on Josie, it's both unnerving and hot.

If it wasn't because we promised everyone food, I would've kicked them out. The guys didn't have to, but they helped me move back in her house. The decision might be rash considering we just got back together yesterday, but we both want—*need* this.

We're still not done talking. Last night, we talked about our fears, insecurities, the desire to stay hidden, and everything we tried so hard to bury away. It was stupid because we were trying to keep the wounds that never healed behind a tiny Band-Aid. It did nothing for us but eventually infect the wound until we had no choice but to tear the Band-Aid off and accept what we'd been denying.

We only stopped because we knew we needed it, and we were both emotionally drained. It'd been a long day, so we got ready for bed and listened to the CD I burned for her while she hugged the Care Bear I gave her.

"And us too, right?" Gray butts in.

"Is your name Daniel?" She doesn't break eye contact when she replies.

I smirk and snake an arm around her front, and with ease, she lets me tug her back to my chest. She's slightly stiff, but once our bodies are pressed against each other, she goes lax.

"What the hell, Josie?" he scoffs, offended.

"Yeah, what the hell?" Kai defensively chimes in.

"Don't take it personally. I like you both, I do, but I love him. So do the math..." She points her thumb over her shoulder at me then rests her hands on top of mine that lay on her stomach.

The guys glare at me, but I shrug unapologetically and shoot them a wink, grinning like a damn fool.

"Mmm, forget my offer. I don't want to paint my nails with you," Angel tsks, pinning her with a faux disdainful look.

"He doesn't mean that," I whisper in her ear.

"You both disgust me," Noah mutters and the guys seem to share the same sentiment because they're scowling at us.

"You might want to close your eyes then. This will make you vomit." She turns and circles her arms around my shoulders and stands on her tiptoes, brushing her lips against mine.

Someone grunts, gags, or mutters something, I don't know, nor do I care. I'm lost on how soft and plush her lips feel against mine.

"We got food!" Pen and Vienna shout from the front door before we can really get the kiss started.

"Dammit, I guess—"

"You should know by now that I don't live to care what others think," Josie sultrily whispers against my mouth. "Kiss me. We need to make up for all—"

I close the tiny gap between our lips and kiss her hard, shutting out the loud protests and whistles.

"I'm happy you're back." Kai hugs me then pulls back. "I know we've all been fucking around with you but we're all here for you. Even Noah. I know he looks like he doesn't care, but he was worried about you."

I smile. "Thanks, man. That really means a lot. If you ever want to talk about home or anything, you know I'm here for you too."

I might've not been in a good headspace to tell him that the day he told me about feeling homesick, but I remember. I do hate it took me this long to let him know I am here for him too.

"Thanks." He tucks his hands in his pockets, a lopsided grin curling on his face. "I should get going before Noah and Gray start bitching."

"Yeah, I'll see you tomorrow."

"I'm so glad you're back," he spins and heads on over to Noah's car.

"Wait, where's Angel?"

He turns, walking backward. "Left with your sister and Vi. Something about—actually, I can't remember, but the girls will drop him off."

I nod, although I'm unsure what that's about, but whatever. "Night, Kai."

He shoots me a wink and hops into Noah's car.

I shut the door behind me and head up the stairs, knowing Josie's up there.

"Josie." I enter her room but go still. She's sitting on the side of the bed, holding the tiny notebook I gave her yesterday. "Jarvis suggested I do that. I'm no poet, so everything I wrote is probably really sappy and corny. Maybe even sad and desperate, so beware."

She quietly chuckles and pats the spot next to her. I happily take my seat and circle my arms around her, resting my chin on her shoulder.

"Hi, Josie. It's April 19th."

She starts reading and I close my eyes, prepared to cringe.

"Another day without you and it REALLY sucks. I hope you know, if you decide to take me back (and I'm going to work my ass to make that happen), I'll never let go of you. I shouldn't have lost you in the first place. Really hate myself for that and I hate what I said. I didn't mean it. I swear, I didn't. But I don't regret begging and getting on my knees for you. I'll do it again (you know I've never been opposed to begging). I miss your face. I really miss holding you. I miss your voice. I miss your smile. I never told you this, but these tiny fireworks always go off in my chest when I see you smile. I can visualize them being shot up, making that little whistle-like noise all while getting really excited about it happening. And when I lock in on your lips, they go off. That's just what your smile does. I'll leave what your brown eyes do to me for another day.
I'm so happy you're here!
With A LOT of LOVE, Garcia

Okay, that day I wasn't too bad. I was home with my parents and mentally doing a bit better.

She sets the notebook down on the nightstand. "I hope you know I'm getting asked to get buried with this. Fireworks? I do that to you?"

I nod and she looks over her shoulder up at me, eyes flooding with a range of emotions. "You do. All the time. You okay?"

Her cheeks flame. I swear, she's so cute. "Oh yeah, I'm... processing and trying to remain calm. You sometimes—*all* the time—overwhelm me, but in a really good way, I promise," she quickly adds, making me smile hard. "I didn't understand it, but Jarvis said I have an avoidant attachment and that my fight-or-flight is very trigger happy. All of this—you—spikes this need to either fight you because my brain is trying to sabotage that this isn't real, or run and hide because I don't want to hear that it wasn't."

"Your feelings are valid, but I want you to know this is very real." I tip my head down and kiss her shoulder. "But on the days that it doesn't feel like it is, I'll be here to remind you. I promise."

She sinks into my hold before she bolts up. "Oh, I almost forgot."

I laugh, amused, as she hurries to her desk, opens one of the drawers, and pulls out what looks like a Post-it. "What's that?"

She stands between my parted thighs and hands it to me. "I never got back to you about names and what we'd do."

My brows furrow in confusion until I read the paper.

Sage(D)
Taryn(J)
Professional baseball player
Swim coach

I burst out laughing. "You remembered?"

I hear the smile in her voice. "You said we needed names and secret identities. The names are still TBD, but they're starting to grow on me."

Wrapping my hands around her, I pull her back with me. I land on my back, and she lands on top, straddling me. "Wait, swim coach?"

"I think I'm going to take Monica's offer. I'll be a student assistant, but who knows, maybe one day a coach. I know it might mean that we'll have to do long distance. Which is something we really haven't talked about, but I want to if you do?"

"Jos, I'll do whatever you wanna do. As long as I get to be yours. We'll make it work, I promise." And that's a promise I intend to keep. "I'm so proud of you."

Her face softens and her eyes glisten. "Really?"

"Yeah, I've always been proud of you."

"I'm really proud of you too."

We stare at each other, not filling in what we both know that means. It's not because we don't want to, but because we just need the silence for a moment.

She leans forward and hugs me. "I should thank your parents."

"For what?" I nuzzle my face into the crook of her neck, inhaling her.

"For making you. They did a great job."

I grimace. "Ew, no, Josie, that's not the visual—" I stop mid-sentence as giggles burst out of her mouth.

"I could've said for not pul—"

I shut her up with my lips on hers, kissing her deeply until she's panting for air. "You can thank them by coming to the bakery. They won't stop asking about you coming to see it, and I know they won't until you go."

"That's right. I remember your dad asking me to come see it."

That stuns me because while he's immensely proud of it, he's never gone out of his way to ask my friends or girlfriends to come. "This is official."

"What do you mean by that?"

"You're pretty much part of the family. You really can't leave me now. If my Dad asked you personally, that means we're married. Sorry, I don't make the rules."

She laughs, chest shaking against mine. "That makes no sense."

"Humor me, baby," I say against her cheek before I kiss it.

"I didn't see you kneel or give me a ring. So, no."

I sit us up and stand, heading for the bathroom. "I don't have a ring with me, but I'll kneel for you right now."

"I guess I'll take it," she aloofly says, but I hear the glee in her voice she's trying to hold back.

"And you'll be a good girl while you do."

I hear the hitch in her breath when I set her down.

62

DANIEL

"Morning." Josie pads into the kitchen wearing nothing but my T-shirt.

I lean a hip against the counter, soaking in every inch of her. From her disheveled wavy hair, down to the rumpled shirt, and every bit of her skin that's visible.

"Stop looking at me like that," she bashfully says but still manages to fit a little frown on her face.

"You know I can't." I grin, stretching my arms and parting my legs for her to stand between them. She quickly does, snuggling against me. I wrap my arms around her and kiss the top of her head. "You're wearing my shirt and you're mine. I'm going to stare at you. Plus, you weren't complaining last night when I was looking at you. So don't start now."

She scoffs. "I'm pretty sure eighty percent of the time, you were staring at my boobs."

I gasp. "That's not true. That was like fifty percent. I was also staring at your ass, your pussy, your face. I wish you could see yourself when you're coming. I swear it's an experience I'll never get over."

Josie muffles her laugh against my chest. "Maybe we can record it happening and then watch it together. I really hope I look as good as you're always raving about." I hear the mischievous tone in her voice.

She could very well be playing around, but my thoughts derail off track as I picture it happening. I stop breathing and my pulse picks up. "Are you being serious?"

"Mm-hmm. We have cameras, don't we?" I nod hastily. "So why not? Let's do it. You'll be gone soon, and I'll need something to get off to."

My cock throbs. "Then we need to make several videos. I want to make sure you have plenty of things to watch while I'm gone."

She cups my semi-hard dick through my shorts. "What are we talking...bedroom, shower..."

"Pool...kitchen...living room..." I groan, closing my eyes only to open them back up because I forgot about the oatmeal in the pot. I glance at it, thankful I put it on low heat, but still I part from Josie to turn the burner off. "I'm going to call Coach and tell him I won't be able to make it to practice today."

I turn, pinning her against my body and the counter before I lift her up and sit her on it. She circles her legs around my waist, slips her arms around my shoulders, and shakes her head.

"You can't do that. Today's your first day back and you have a game later today."

"I'm not playing though." I peck her lips.

Because I haven't really trained in a month, Coach and Jarvis thought it'd be best if I sat this one out. They also don't want to throw me back out there after everything that's happened.

She draws back, and a small smile curls on her face. "How are you feeling?"

I play with the hem of her shirt as I consider how I feel before I say it out loud. It's not that I don't want to tell her. I trust her more than I've ever trusted anyone, but my first instinct is to plaster on the biggest smile I can muster and lie. It's always been easier to pretend that I'm fine than to admit that I'm not out loud so I don't worry anyone. But I know it's not what I need to do. I need to say exactly what's going on in my head instead of bottling it up inside. The last thing I want is another panic attack.

"I'm ready to go back and do what I love. But I'm a little anxious to actually be there physically. The guys saw me have a panic attack in the locker room, Coach D'Angelo talked me through it, and then I left. They don't know what I've been going through, only that I'm not okay. I hate that I abandoned them and hate how long I was gone. I know it needed to be done, but I can't help but feel like I disappointed them."

She brushes my hair on the side soothingly. "You didn't abandon them. You needed to take care of yourself, to put yourself first because you never do. I'm sure they know that, and I'm sure they're not going to be upset because you left. If anything, they'll be happy because you're back and you're okay. I know I am."

I meet her stare then hug her. "I'm sorry about everything."

"You really need to stop apologizing. I get it. I didn't at first because of my own issues, but look at us. You're not hiding. I'm not running. We're here, together, and I'm not overthinking your hug and you're not faking your smile for the sake of pretending to be happy. We're far from perfect and we'll never be and that's okay. We'll keep working things out, finding out what works and what doesn't. And we'll do it together."

"God..." I clear my throat. "You're amazing."

"Thank Jarvis for that. She's all about embracing my emotions. It still makes me want to throw up, but it's easy to do with you."

I chuckle, kissing her cheek. "Everything is easy to do with you."

Pink colors her cheeks. "Even swimming?" She pauses, studying my face. "There's no pressure whatsoever. If you don't want to, that's okay, but I'd really love for you to learn. Even if it's not with me. I found someone who—"

"I'll do it with you. I can maybe squeeze thirty minutes to an hour a day or something, but we'll make it work." I smile and when her gaze drops to it, her eyes light up.

"Really?"

"Yeah, we never got to play Marco Polo and you know how much I love games," I playfully say but then I get serious. "And you're right; it's important and I should learn how to do it. I really want to learn."

She twirls a lock of my hair around her finger. "We'll take it slow, but I promise you'll be swimming in the deep end before you know it. You're going to do great, and I'm going to be there every step of the way, okay?"

"Thank you." I rest my forehead against hers.

"No, thank you for helping me fill the emptiness and for being patient with me."

"You deserve to be happy. You deserve good things, Jos," I repeat what she said to me.

We hug each other and bask in the silence that follows after until we have to part to get ready for the day.

I'm bombarded by all my teammates the moment I step into the locker room. Hugs and questions get thrown my way. Thankfully, no one asks about the panic attack or sounds disappointed in my leave of absence. They're just happy I'm back like Josie said they would be.

"Give Sparky room!" Kai yells. "Let him breathe. He just got back."

"Stop making him feel so important." Noah rolls his eyes at me. "He's just a guy. Who was the reason we weren't so shit. I hope you all get your shit together now that he's back."

"Love you, Noah." I grin at him, glad he's being his grumpy self, deflecting the attention from me to him.

They all throw quick excited words at me, pats on my shoulder and back, and disperse to their lockers to get ready for our pre-game workout and something new Coach has implemented.

I go to mine and pull my phone out, finding a message from Josie.

> My Josie♡: Check the outside of your bag's pocket

I search one pocket and then the other until I feel a thin piece of paper. When I pull it out and read the Post-it note, the tornado of anxiety twisting in my stomach dies.

You make the world brighter and better!
I'm so happy you're here!
With love, Jos<3

I fold the paper in half and tuck it in the sleeve of my wallet where the rhinestone is.

> Me: I know fate is real. I know because you exist

> My Josie♡: You know I've never been a believer, but you make it so easy to believe. I love you and your hot face

> Me: I love you!! Just my hot face?

> My Josie♡: 😊 And your hot everything. Go warm up or whatever it is you guys are supposed to do! I'll see you at the game

My cheeks ache from how big I'm smiling, but it falters at the person who says my name behind me.

Bryson stands there, hands tucked in his pockets, staring at me like a child who's just been scolded. "Hey, Danny."

"I don't want to—"

"I'm sorry," he cuts in quietly.

"What was that?"

His eyes dart around then he dejectedly sighs because everyone is staring—discreetly, but they're still staring. "I'm sorry about the shit I said and for pushing you in the pool. I didn't think—I didn't know about your fear and if I would've known, I would've pushed you on the ground or something. I'm also...sorry about everything else. I'm...glad you're back."

I narrow my eyes, staring at him dubiously. "How much were you paid to say this?"

He gives me a tight-lipped smile. "Not paid. I-I mean it. I'm trying to do the right thing here for fuck's sake. I'm sorry for being a dick."

"A piece of shit, but I'll let 'dick' slide." I flash him my friendliest smile when he glares at me.

"Are we good?" He cocks a brow, sticking his hand out for me to take.

I want to say fuck no, but the ACC tournament is a few weeks away then soon after is the NCAA Regionals. We all need to be getting along and working as a team, and as the captain, I need to set an example.

I clutch his hand. "We're good. Just stay away from Josie."

His brows arc in surprise, despite how tense his face looks. "I thought you guys broke up?"

"We're good. *Really* good. And you and I will be good as long as you stay away from her."

He tugs his hand away, and his jaw tics. "Whatever."

"I mean it. Stay the fuck away from Josie."

His eyes harden, jaw clenching again. "She was my girlfriend first. We have history."

I don't smile like I naturally would to keep the peace, but I don't make a show of looking angry or annoyed either. I just blankly look at him, and funnily enough, he squirms a little. Is he nervous?

"Well, now she's your ex and one day she'll be my wife. She moved on; it's time you do too."

His eyes widen and I swear he looks defeated, but then he rolls his eyes. "Whatever. She downgraded anyway."

Bryson stalks off, his face blistering red.

Gray stands next to me, but he doesn't say anything, too enthralled in whatever's on his phone. No, I think he looks annoyed. That's new.

"What's up with you?" I ask him.

"I hate group projects. Hope whoever created them is burning in hell." He furiously types on his phone. "Fucking Christ, I'm an athlete and I still get my shit done. What's everyone else's excuse? Now my grade is going to be shit because she—I swear she's been a pain in my ass all semester. Thank God it's almost over."

Kai and I lock eyes, wondering what that's about. Grayson is everything but ever actually mad. An arrogant little shit by default but never angry and never because of a grade. But what he's feeling is valid because I'd be mad too.

My gaze snaps to the door when Angel steps in. He looks a little disheveled and out of it.

"You good?" I quizzically stare at him.

A crooked grin grows on his face. "Yeah, I'm good. I'm really fucking good."

I realize now he looks sated, not zoned out. Right, he's all about superstitions. "Please don't tell me who the girl was. I really don't want or need the details."

"I wasn't planning on sharing." He winks at me. "It's good to have you back, *papi*."

It's good to be back.

Being out in the field is still weird, but the lump in my throat doesn't feel heavy. Even the weight on my chest feels fairly light. Jarvis said it's normal but also said the only way it wasn't going to get worse or spiral into a panic attack, was to accept out loud what I feel.

It felt ridiculous at the time, but now that I started talking about it, I feel better. The guilt still lingers, but every day does feel lighter. And now that Josie's back in my life, I'm happy. I'm okay, not fine, but I'm okay.

I finish signing a couple of jerseys then slide down the line.

"Hi," the girl says, wearing an oversized jersey with my number on it. "I'm a really big fan." She twirls a wisp of her hair around her finger. "Can you sign my jersey?" She gives her back to me.

"Hey, yeah, no problem." I sign the inside of the number.

She rubs her glossy lips together, and a cunning gleam shines in her eyes. "You want to write your number while you're at it?"

"I'm very taken."

"That's a bummer." She clicks her tongue, leaning over the padded railing, showing me her cleavage. "You want my number in case things don't work out?"

I bite the inside of my cheek. "I'm very in love with her."

"I'm very in love with my vibrator. Doesn't mean I can't use a different one," she whispers. "I also have this baseball. If you'd rather write your number here."

I wet my lips, puffing out a breath. "Okay." I take the ball from her hand and scribble something on it. "But this stays between us."

"I promise." She raises her right hand then takes the ball. She reads what I wrote and huskily laughs.

"Hey!" Pen shouts, holding her phone up. "Let me take a picture before you have to go."

"What do you say, number six?" Josie sits on the padded railing. "We can put them in one of the picture frames you bought."

I slip my arm around her waist and stand taller. Pen takes a multitude of pictures then waves me off before she goes to take her seat next to Vienna.

"I'm so glad you're here, even though I'm not playing." I take her hand in mine.

I'm still warming up with the team and doing this new thing Coach implemented. He has us lay flat on the ground and look up at the clouds and call out whatever we see. We did that for thirty minutes and I, along with the other guys, really enjoyed it.

"I'll be wherever you are. Playing or not." She smiles at me.

"You're obsessed with me."

She shrugs bashfully, twisting a ring. "Yeah? And?"

"Good because I'm very obsessed with you." I slide a ring off her finger and unhook my chain and add the small gold band to it. "Now I'll get to have a little piece of you everywhere I go."

She toys with my chain then drops it, letting it softly hit my chest. "I'm going to go sit down because you're making it hard for me. You're in your uniform and then you stand there, look at me like that, and say that to me."

"Josie?" I grab her wrist before she walks away.

"Yeah?"

"My last name looks really good on you. Really hate that I can't see you wearing it all the time."

A breathtaking smile lifts on her face. "What's that saying? Take a picture, it'll last longer? Something like that, right?"

My eyes widen and my throat dries because I know what she's insinuating.

"Good luck, Cap."

63

JOSEFINE

Three Months Later

"Marco," Daniel calls out, eyes closed, hands stretched out, floating above the surface.

"Polo," I quietly say, tacitly wading through the water to get around him.

He stealthy moves with a confidence he didn't have a few months ago. He's come a long way and knows how to do almost everything but float in the deep end for a long period of time by himself. But I'm hoping that changes today.

I press my lips together to stop myself from laughing when he lunges at absolutely nothing. I'm certain he knows I'm not there, but he's trying to get me to laugh. And it's working because he does it again and I slip up. A tiny noise expels from my mouth.

"Josie, baby, I hear you. You know I'm going to catch you, so just give up already."

I roll my eyes at the arrogance in his voice. We were playing best two out of three, and unfortunately, he has already caught me twice in a short amount of time. My pride is too big, so I demanded we play again, and he accepted because he wants to beat his record.

The media is full of shit because they don't know how not so humble Daniel is.

"Marco." Like a shark, he prowls through the water on a mission. It's both hot and frustrating.

It doesn't help that the hot July sun is making him glow in a way that's hard to look away from. Damp dark brown hair slicked back, sharp jaw, sun-tanned skin, rock-hard body dripping wet.

I look away before my libido gives me away.

"Polo," I whisper and use the ledge of the pool to move around until I'm in the deep end. I silently push off and tread to the middle.

"I'm going to get you; you might as well come to me now."

"You're really starting to piss me off."

"Save your anger for later. You're going to need it." My favorite kind of smile blooms on his face. "Marco."

"You're not going to get me this time." I smile, still treading in the deep end. "Polo."

"It's going to happen." He moves around, but after a bit, he stops and I laugh because he's nowhere close to me. "Wait..." He's processing. "Are you in the deep end?"

"I'll give you a five-second peek."

Daniel opens his right eye and scans the pool quickly before he does a double take and lands on me. His eyes close again and he blows out a breath.

"I believe in you. I really do," I spur him on.

He gingerly moves through the water and once he's where it dips off, he takes a step forward. I watch him with caution, ready to swim to him if I need to, but I know I won't have to. I know he'll swim to me.

"You got it," I say under my breath. "Come to me."

"Marco." He breathes, slowly treading through the water like I've shown him how to do before. His head stays above the water, arms loose and relaxed at his side, legs kicking a calm and steady motion.

"Polo." I try to maintain my composure the closer and more

confident he gets as he treads to me. But when he's in front of me, I can't help but exhale a laugh. "You did it. Open your eyes. You're doing it!"

He pries them open and for a second, he tenses up, but he doesn't stop moving.

"I got you," I say, only grabbing one of his arms, although I'm not really holding him afloat; he's doing that all on his own. When I know he's okay, I draw my hand away.

"Oh! I'm doing it, holy shit! I'm floating on my own." He laughs disbelievingly, dropping his gaze down to his body under the water. "Josie, you did it. You—"

"I did nothing. You came here on your own. *You* did it," I proudly state, but my façade almost crumbles as my eyes burn.

"I've got a great teacher." He clears his throat, blinking repeatedly.

"I'm proud of you."

He nods, growing quiet as he soaks it all in. I do too.

These past seven months have been nothing more than awakening, invigorating, and really emotional. I didn't only learn how to live again, I learned how to love, and opened myself to being loved.

I've also learned how to accept that I won't have the answers to or control over everything. Especially regarding Mom. I've talked to Jarvis a lot and still do. She helps me understand and to a certain extent I do. I know it's not my fault for how Mom treated me. I couldn't have done anything differently.

But I know the tiny hole in my head won't ever be filled because despite our relationship, she was still my mom. She died and that grief will never go away.

Understanding and accepting that part is hard because it's closure that I know I'll never get. But I'm learning to adapt and learning to live without allowing my guilt for what I feel for her eat me alive.

Which is why I finally let myself enter the aquatic center at the university and told Monica I wanted the position. I don't know what'll happen when the season starts—if I'll make a career out of coaching, but I'm hopeful everything will be okay.

"What are you thinking about?" I ask him, breaking the silence and tip my head so that he'll follow me back to the shallow end.

"Adrian. Fate. The cliff." He follows close by me and when we're standing side by side, he circles his arms around me. He releases a shuddering breath and pulls back, cradling my face in his large hands. "This might sound silly, but I think he sent me to find you that night. I hate that's how it happened, but I'm really happy I found you, Josie."

"I wasn't scared, but I contemplated it before jumping. Like I was waiting for something to happen," I confess. "And then it did. You showed up."

He kisses my forehead. "I'm never going to stop showing up. Even when I'm all gray and wrinkly, I'm going to be there. I promise. So get used to my hot face and hot everything because you're never getting rid of me."

I tip my head back and laugh, but it gets drowned out as he captures my lips with his. "So clingy."

"You love me clingy." He rests his forehead against mine.

I comb my fingers through his hair, smiling hard. "I do. I really do."

EPILOGUE
DANIEL

Seven Years Later

"Are you going to be here tomorrow?"

"A little after noon, but we'll be there, I promise."

My friend looks over his shoulder. "They'll be here. He promised."

His daughter pops up on the screen, grinning from ear to ear. "It's Christmas tomorrow!"

I smile at her. She's a little version of her father—hair, face, and all. "I know. Did you send your letter to Santa?"

She enthusiastically nods. "Mm-hmm, I did."

My friend shakes his head at me, a warning to not engage because his daughter is a talker. But I only see her so often, so I don't mind. She spends the next ten minutes going over her list in detail until her mom tells her to get ready for bed.

"I tried to warn you." He chuckles, taking a drink of whatever's in his mug.

"I know but I don't mind." I shrug.

He stares at me for a beat. "So have you talked to Josie about *your* Christmas list?"

I glance at the bathroom door. I don't know where we're

going or what we're doing. All she said was that we needed to come down to Carmel-by-the-Sea and that she had booked a hotel room. She's currently getting ready, though I'm not sure why because it's close to midnight, but I didn't question her. I got ready and now I'm waiting for her.

I sit up against the bed's headboard. "I threw hints, but I don't want her to feel—" I glance at the door again. "Pressured. She's got a lot going on."

Josie and I have always been on the same wavelength regarding kids. We both want them, but we've been too busy with our careers to start having them.

Seven years ago, I was the first round second pick in the MLB draft to the Seattle Thunder. My life drastically changed, but so did Josie's. On top of that, we had to do long distance for almost three years. She needed to finish school, had been working for the women's swim team at MCU, and wanted to sell her house. She felt guilty letting go, but she knew it's what she needed to do. When the house sold, I saw the last bit of hold her mom had on her being released.

Everything aligned not too long after that in Seattle. Now she's the Assistant Coach for Seattle State University. Though Josie might move up to Associate Head Coach, but I'm not too sure. She doesn't seem interested in it. Especially as of recently; she almost seems indifferent about it. I can't understand why and when I ask, she brushes it off.

I know she'll do what's best for her, and I'll support what she decides to do, but a while ago, she seemed excited about it. I don't know what changed, but I'm trying not to worry. We've been very big about communicating, so I know whatever's going on, she'll tell me eventually.

"You know, you can always babysit our kids whenever you want. Hell, if you want to keep them for a year or two, they're all yours. You won't hear me complaining. I know their mom won't either." He takes another drink. "Having them might make you not want to have them. Let me tell you, they fight, they're messy

—forget having a clean home. That's nonexistent. Don't get me started on how boundaries don't exist to them. They follow me every-fucking-where. I can't eat or do anything in peace." He rolls his eyes, groaning like it's such an inconvenience to him, but I know he loves being a dad.

There are people who are parents and then there are people who are *made* to be parents. My friend is the latter.

"But they're cute as shit." I think of all the pictures and videos he's sent me of his kids.

"Yeah, they really are, aren't they?" He beams with pride.

The bathroom door swings open and Josie steps out. "Ready, Garcia?"

A burst of adrenaline rushes through my body at seeing my wife.

As soon as she moved to Seattle, I proposed and a year later, we got married. I would've proposed a lot sooner, but I knew I needed to take things slow. She was still figuring herself out, and while I was too, I knew she was it for me. But for the sake of not rushing or overwhelming her, I took it slow, and the wait was honestly worth it.

"Ready, Jos." I turn the screen, letting the two greet each other and then promise to call him when we're on our way before I hang up. "So where are we going?"

"You'll know very soon." She flashes me a small, tentative smile and intertwines my fingers with hers. She tugs me out of the room and down to our car.

Josie doesn't let me drive, and on the drive to wherever we're going, she's oddly quiet.

"Everything okay?" I play with the ring on her fingers that are slightly clammy.

"Yeah, everything's okay." She drums her fingers on the steering wheel, almost like she's nervous, which is so unlike her.

Something doesn't feel right, but I don't prod. I know this time of the year is as strange for her as it is for me. Her mom passing and this being Adrian's favorite holiday never fails to make us both feel sad. Though over the years, it's become easier to enjoy. And that's better than dreading, feeling empty, and wanting to hide in the bleak darkness.

It also helps that I'm married to my best friend; being with her has made today and every other day worth living.

Then there was the copious amount of therapy. It helped me build a relationship with my dad. The first few months were strange and at times awkward. But then we slowly figured things out. He apologized, and I forgave him.

"I'm here," I remind her, lifting her hand and kissing every knuckle.

She smiles and those fireworks go off. "I know. I'm here too."

I do most of the talking, and she replies with a single word or soft hums. But I stop when she parks in a familiar parking lot.

"Come on." She climbs out, and I follow behind her.

"You're not here to murder me, are you?" I scan the empty dark lot. "I knew those shows were going to give you ideas. Damn, I should've signed the prenup. This was your plan all along, huh? To take all the money?"

Lately, she's been obsessing over true crimes. It's all she watches or listens to.

She laces our fingers. "Our relationship has run its course. It's time I start—"

"No. I refuse. You can kill me, but you're not allowed to be with anyone else or remarry. That's my only demand," I say as we make our way up the trail.

She laughs, squeezing my hand. "You're okay with me killing you but not me being with someone else?"

"Baby, I gotta draw the line somewhere," I severely state.

She laughs harder. "And that's where you want to draw the line?"

"Yes." I don't miss a beat.

Josie guides us off the course. I follow her blindly, not only because I know where we're going, but I'll go wherever she goes.

"Lucky for you, I don't plan to kill you, and I definitely have no desire to be with anyone that isn't you."

I kiss the crown of her head. "Yeah, I'm really lucky."

She grows quiet once we're at the cliff that led us to be where we are now. We go nowhere near the edge, but we're still so close, we feel the cool breeze that comes from the water crashing against the side of the cliff. The roar of the waves is deafening, but it's no match for the silence between us.

I revel in it because before it'd unnerve me. Now I feel nothing but happiness being with her.

"I used to tell myself that this was the only cliff I never wanted to come back to," she begins. "The memories still lingered here and I hated that. But after talking to Jarvis, I told myself I'd one day be back. She said it'd be good to replace the bad memory with a good one. I just never knew what. But I finally know what I can replace it with..." She trails off, puffing out a jittery breath.

She reaches inside her pocket and draws out something. I can't make out what it is but then she hands it to me and turns on the flashlight to her phone. She points the light to the thing wrapped in red tissue paper in my palm. It's not too big, but it's not small either. When she nods, I carefully remove the paper.

My breath gets lodged in my throat and my eyes go incredulously wide. I don't blink, breathe, or move as I stare at the pregnancy test in my hand. "You're pregnant?"

"I am. I found out—"

I'm hugging her before the words are out of her mouth. Josie giggles and squeals. When I lift her up, she wraps her legs around my waist, but then I realize what I'm doing and I put her down.

"I'm sorry. I didn't hurt you, did I?" I warily say, palming her flat stomach. "I wasn't too rough, was—"

Her face lights up in amusement, but her eyes flood with tears as do mine. "No, it's okay, I'm okay. I promise." She lays her hand on top of mine.

"I'm going to be a dad," I breathlessly say. "You're going to be a mom. We're going to be parents. I love you." I cup her cheek, kissing her softly and pull back to say it again. "I love you. When did you find out? I thought you had the IUD?"

"I love you too." A watery smile pulls on her lips. "I found out a few days ago, and I took it out a month ago."

I gape. "A month ago?"

"Yeah, I was ready, and I knew you were too. You weren't so subtle."

"I didn't pressure you, did I?"

"No, not all. I've been ready and have been for a while. I was just a little nervous and afraid that maybe I won't be a good mom."

I hug her carefully, cradling the side of her head. "You're going to be the best mom. Our baby is so lucky. Just like I am."

She sniffles. "You think so?"

"I know so."

"You can squeeze me a little tighter. I'm pregnant, not paper. The baby is going to be okay."

I chuckle but stop because hearing those words does something to me. I hold her just a little firmer, protectively, but I'm still cautious. "Is this why you don't want to take the position?"

"Yeah, I thought about it, but I want this baby more, and remember, you promised me four."

"I remember. I'll give you all the babies you want. Hell, I'll give you anything you want."

"You already do that," she counters happily.

I cup her neck, looking down at her. "We're going to be parents."

"Yeah, we are." She breathes, her smile bigger than before, and I know mine is mirroring it. "Daniel?"

"Yeah?"

"I'm so happy *we're* here." She seals the space between our lips.

The End.

988 LIFELINE

About 988
The 988 Suicide & Crisis Lifeline provides free and confidential emotional support to people in suicidal crisis or emotional distress 24 hours a day, 7 days a week, across the United States and its territories. The 988 Lifeline is comprised of a national network of over 200 local crisis centers, combining local care and resources with national standards and best practices.

988 LifelineIf you need emotional support, reach out to the national mental health hotline: 988.

WHAT'S NEXT?

Excited to find out who will be the next Monterey Coastal baseball player getting a book? Follow me on Instagram @e.salvadorauthor and sign up for my newsletter to get all the updates!

Book 2 coming 2026

ALSO BY E. SALVADOR

The Knights Series:
A college basketball romance series

Book 1: All I Need

Lola & TJ's story

A secret baby, he's the basketball captain, she's a live painter, slow burn romance

Book 2: Only With You

Julianna & Landon's story

An enemies to lovers with lots of banter, he tutors her, forced proximity romance

ACKNOWLEDGMENTS

I wrote another book?! It shouldn't be shocking, considering I had already written two but I'm (this might be shocking) not very good with words. I know, I know, how? Words and I, we have a complicated relationship. Sometimes I'm afraid I'll say too much, not enough, the wrong thing, and yeah...I'm sure you catch my drift. But here we are, three books down!

There are so many people I'd love to thank for helping, listening, and/or just being there for me:

My Husband, my rock, my soulmate, my coffee maker. Thank you! THANK YOU SO MUCH!!! No seriously, he's the real MVP. Always listening to my rants, ideas, being there when I'm crashing out over my characters and imposter syndrome. I seriously couldn't have gotten the book finished without him. I can't wait to write many more books with him by my side!

Madison, my best friend/wife/person, despite romance books not being your cup of tea, thanks for letting me yap your ear off about my books and all the romance stuff. I don't want to over inflate your ego because it's already massive, but you truly are the best, one of a kind(slightly being sarcastic because I can already feel you being really smug about this).

My sweet baby angel, Savanna Rose. What would I do without you? Thanks for listening to my many, and I mean my many long voice memos. Thanks for keeping me sane, all your words of encouragement, and your positivity. I'm so thankful to have a friend like you!

Millie, I love your chaos! Thanks for holding my hand across the sea, for laughing with me when I say stupid stuff, and for being a ray of sunshine!! Thanks for putting up with my hot mess of words and emotions. I adore you forever!!!

Emily, you just got here and I annoyingly squeezed my way into your life, but thanks for staying and now being a victim of receiving millions of voice memos from me. So happy for our friendship and you're forever stuck with me!

A BIG BIG special thanks to my beta readers Kristie, Catherine, and Isabella!! I can't thank you enough for reading this massive book and for all your feedback. You guys seriously rock! The in-depth feedback, your honest thoughts, your reactions, everything helped me so much! I'm so thankful to have all three of you help me! I'll never stop being thankful for all you did! And thank you for constantly cheering me on, you guys are so wonderful, I'm so happy to have gotten to know you all!

My editor, Erica, thank you (x's a million) for reading over this very thick manuscript! This book wouldn't be where it is without your help. Your feedback was/is so helpful and I'm so grateful to have been able to work with you! I can't wait to work on the others with you!

Summer Grover, the magical creative genius that you are! I still haven't been able to lift my jaw off the floor after showing me the cover! I'm still obsessed and will NEVER be able to get over how gorgeous it turned out!

Special thanks to you, my readers. Thank you from the bottom of my heart and soul for sticking around, supporting, and loving my characters. You're all the reason I'm so motivated and excited to share this and many other stories. Thank you once again for being so wonderful!

Thank you for being here!

With Love,
E

ABOUT THE AUTHOR

E. is a Mexican-American romance author who loves a good happily ever after and iced coffee with light ice.

When E. is not overthinking or creating multiple Pinterest boards for the hundred book ideas she has, she's writing or reading. And when she's not doing any of those things, she's spending time with her two sons and husband.

Instagram/TikTok: e.salvadorauthor
Goodreads: e. salvador

Made in the USA
Monee, IL
16 August 2025